Praise for *Beyond the Flames*

"Great characters and one heck of a thrill ride. The author, a veteran first responder, brings the heat!" **— Lesley Kagen, NYT bestselling author of *Whistling in the Dark* and *Every Now and Then***

"Greg writes with such intimacy and immediacy all while painting a vivid and exciting story that leaps off the page. A real page turner with heart." **—Michael Graf, Emmy Award-winning filmmaker, screenwriter**

"Gregory Lee Renz's masterful writing and ingenious storytelling make this narrative unique and utterly captivating. The setting is finely drawn, allowing readers a vivid sense of place and time. From the escalating conflict to the unforgettable characters, this story offers entertainment that fans of thrillers will relish." **—Readers' Favorite Reviews**

"Two seasoned firefighters and a police captain try to save young girls from a dangerous gang. Behind the hard-boiled, tough-talking cop and firefighter stereotypes, there are numerous layers of complexities that touch on real psychological and social issues. Complex, fast-talking characters add intensity to this action-laced thriller... readers will be glad to be along for the ride." **—Kirkus Reviews**

"*Beyond the Flames* is a gripping story of heroism, heartbreak, and healing. Greg Renz writes from personal experience about fighting flames and saving lives in a way that sizzles with authenticity."

—John DeDakis, writing coach, award-winning novelist, and former editor on CNN's "The Situation Room with Wolf Blitzer." www.johndedakis.com

"Few novelists are in a position of capturing the drama, decisions, and danger of firefighting as Retired Milwaukee Fire Captain Gregory Lee Renz. His background blended perfectly with a flare for vivid reporting in his prior novel *Beneath the Flames*, and here continues in *Beyond the Flames*, which explores the psychological and physical challenges of fighting fires in buildings and hearts alike." **—Midwest Book Review**

"Greg Renz knows how to tell a story. From the first paragraph of *BEYOND THE FLAMES* to the last, I kept wondering what was going to happen next. Here are strong characters, emotion, suspense, humor and an interesting love story."**—Jerry Apps, author of *SETTERS VALLEY* and several other novels and nonfiction books.**

"In this crackling follow-up to *Beneath the Flames*, his award-winning debut, Greg Renz delivers a novel that succeeds on multiple levels: as a thriller, a character study, and slice of life on mean big city streets." **—Doug Moe, journalist and author of *Moments of Happiness: A Wisconsin Band Story* (with Mike Leckrone)**

"*Beneath the Flames* was an undisputed Homerun; well, hold on to your seats; author Renz did it again. *Beyond the Flames* is a Grand Slam."—**Dr. Nicholas L. Chiarkas, Ed.D., J.D., Author of the award-winning novels *Weepers* and *Nunzio's Way***

"Suspenseful and heartfelt, *Beyond the Flames* is a page-turning story with an intensely satisfying plot, on par with the best crime-thrillers on the market. Great character development in a tightly-woven plot that leads to a satisfying conclusion with just the right amount of nerve-wracking scenes that keep you rooting for characters you've grown to love."—**Valerie Biel, award-winning author**

Fresh from the success of his prize-winning novel *Beneath the Flames* retired Fire Captain Greg Renz, turned author, is out with another behind-the-scenes thriller *Beyond the Flames*, in which he takes readers on wild rides through mean big city streets. There are kids and old people, weirdos, wackos, porn victims, corrupt officials and lots of good and decent people of all races in *Beyond the Flames*. Greg Renz has produced another "hot" novel.—**Bill Stokes, Award-winning journalist and author of twenty books.**

"In the heart-pounding pages of *Beyond the Flames*, Gregory Lee Renz orchestrates a symphony of raw emotion, searing action, and unwavering courage. Rich in detail, action, and emotion. This stunning release will break you apart and remind you that we can all be put back together again, stronger and wiser than before."—**Laurie Buchanan, author of the Sean McPherson crime thriller series**

"A riveting read all the way! Excellent suspense and fast-paced action combine with tender moments and characters we come to care about deeply." —**Christine DeSmet, author**

"A truly splendid sequel to Gregory Lee.Renz's award-winning debut, *Beneath the Flames*. Renz has become a masterful storyteller, basing his tales on his 28-year, real-life experiences as an inner-city firefighter. He serves up an action-packed mystery with characters who will linger in readers' thoughts long after they finish the book."— **Joanna Elm, author, *Fool Her Once* and bestseller *Scandal***

"*Beyond the Flames* does not disappoint. This is an action-filled story that provides a real-life portrait of a hero who comes to terms with the life he has been dealt. You'll be astonished at the hero's accomplishments - both large and small - and understand how one man can overcome his adversities. Read this book NOW."—**Laurie Scheer, writing mentor, developmental editor, Mediagoddess**

Beyond the Flames

(a novel)

Other books by Gregory Lee Renz

Beneath the Flames

Beyond the Flames

(a novel)

Gregory Lee Renz

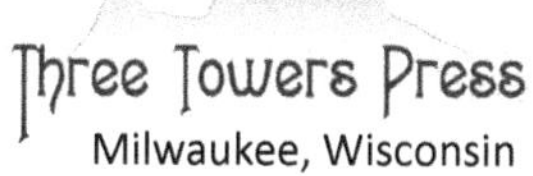

Three Towers Press
Milwaukee, Wisconsin

Published by Three Towers Press
An imprint of HenschelHAUS Publishing, Inc.
Milwaukee, Wisconsin
www.henschelHAUSbooks.com

ISBN (hardcover): 978159598-998-7
ISBN (paperback): 978159598-999-4
LCCN: 2024941755

Cover design: Elaine Meszaros, www.EMGraphics.net

Printed in the United States.

For Paula

Without your love and support

This story would never have come to life

Foreword

Retired Milwaukee Fire Captain Gregory Lee Renz is uniquely qualified to tell this story. He was part of a dramatic rescue of two little boys from their burning basement bedroom. He received a series of awards for this rescue, including induction into the Wisconsin Fire and Police Hall of Fame in 2006.

The strength of this novel lies not only in its action sequences but also in its emotional depth. The author's exploration of firefighters' psychological and emotional challenges is enlightening and moving. Readers are given a rare window into the mental fortitude required to cope with the stresses of the job, the impact of traumatic events, and the constant balancing act between duty and personal life.

Each page transports the reader into the heart of infernos, feeling the searing heat and the deafening crackling of flames. Also, you will enter the quiet moments of reflection and doubt, the camaraderie forged in the firehouse, and the personal battles fought long after the fire has been extinguished. Renz's extraordinary talent as a storyteller vividly describes instinctive decisions that mean the difference between life and death and the mental and emotional toll that comes with the territory.

As a former NYPD police officer, I assure you that the author's deep understanding of the subject matter shines through in every detail, making the characters' experiences feel real and relatable. This novel is more than just a story about firefighters; it is a heartfelt tribute to those who dedicate their lives to protecting others.

Without giving the ending away, I promise it will be both satisfying and leave you wanting to read more from this brilliant author and extraordinary storyteller.

– Nick Chiarkas, former NYPD police officer and author of the award-winning novels *Weepers* and *Nunzio's Way*

Chapter 1

September 1956

Saturday finally arrived. Lee Garrison's best friend Ben, a second grader, waved and trotted across the street carrying a brown paper grocery bag. "How you like first grade so far?"

"Hate it."

"You only been goin' a week. Gets better."

Ben pulled a book of matches from his back pocket and shoved it in front of Lee's face. Ben grinned as Lee gawked at the naked lady on the cover. They both giggled and crawled through a narrow opening under the massive front porch of Lee's three-story house.

"I think my mom was real sick last night," Lee said.

"Was she puking?"

"Nah. Heard her groaning real loud. Woke me up. Scared me."

"She in the bedroom with your dad?"

Lee nodded.

Ben laughed. "Don't you know? Grownups make all kinda sounds when they play in bed."

Mom and Dad never play, Lee thought.

Ben rubbed his hands over his upper arms. "Kinda cold." He turned the grocery bag upside down and shook out a pile of old newspapers. "Let's make a fire. Then we can play marbles."

Ben was smart. Lee trusted him to know things. They wadded the newspapers and tossed them in a pile. The flimsy red-tipped cardboard matches kept bending as Ben tried to light them. Lee took the book of matches and struck a match to the strip of emery just like his dad did when he lit his cigarettes. The match tip flared orange, releasing a gray puff of pungent smoke. He tossed it on the pile of newspapers. The boys clapped their hands as the fire flickered to life, consuming the pile of newspapers. Within seconds, the crackling flames mushroomed across the underside of the porch planking.

Ben cried out, "Oh, no," and fled for home. Lee knew he should do something, but what? He scooped handfuls of dirt and tossed them on the burning pile. Flames rolled over his head, moving toward the opening they had crawled through. He scooped faster. The caustic smoke caught in his throat. He gagged. Flames licked over the opening. He remembered from school how they were told by a visiting firefighter to crawl on the floor if they were ever in a fire. He squirmed toward the narrow opening on his belly, the only way out. The intensifying heat stung his back. Lee gritted his teeth, clawing and kicking his way to the opening—and out into daylight. Flaming talons shot out of the opening as if reaching for him. Lee backed away, breathless. He should tell his mom or dad but was transfixed by the flames billowing from under the porch.

Ben's dad came running from across the street. "What the hell?" He bounded up the porch steps and banged on the front door. "Hey, Merle. Grab your garden hose. You got a fire under your porch."

The door slammed open. Merle's jaw dropped. "Holy shit. Call the fire department. I'll grab the hose." He shouted into the house, "Betty, get the hell out. The house is on fire."

Betty bolted from the house and went to Lee. "Did you see how it started?"

He wanted to tell her Ben made him do it, but no words came out.

Betty hugged the boy's shoulders. "It'll be okay, Honey. Don't worry."

Merle sprayed the fire with the garden hose. The weak stream did little to slow the flames engulfing the porch. Sirens wailed in the distance. Lee's face stung from the radiant heat of the fire. He and his mother backed across the street. Merle shielded his eyes with his arm while spraying the feeble stream of water. The sirens grew louder as flames climbed the weathered brown clapboard siding of the house, sending a cloud of dark gray smoke into the clear blue sky. Merle tossed the hose and trudged across the street with his hands behind his head.

Lee's entire body prickled with electricity. Was this really happening?

A scarlet-colored fire engine roared up the street. It stopped one house past the burning home. Two firefighters loaded hoses on their shoulders and followed another one to the rear of the house. One firefighter, wearing a light blue helmet, stayed behind, connecting a large hose to the hydrant next to the engine. A fire truck pulling a long trailer with a huge aerial ladder on top turned onto their street. A firefighter steering the back end of the trailer swung it wide as it rounded the corner. The whine of the siren became deafening as the fire truck rumbled down the street. Lee covered his ears. The truck pulled to a stop in front of the burning home. The siren trailed off as if it were running out of air. Six firefighters jumped off the rig. Three of them pulled ladders from the rear of the trailer.

Merle shouted to the other three who were heading to the back of the house, "The fire's on the goddamn porch. Why the hell you idiots going back there?"

A firefighter wearing a red helmet shouted, "Stay back!"

Merle pointed at the burning house and hollered to the gathering crowd, "What the hell's wrong with them? Fire's right there."

The three firefighters who carried ladders to the house placed one against the house and climbed to the roof, carrying two ladders with hooks on the ends. They slid these ladders up the roof, hooking the ends over the ridge, then all three climbed to the peak.

Lee's mom pulled him close. The chaotic scene unfolding in front of him filled Lee with a strange mix of awe and dread.

"Goddamn those idiots," Merle shouted. "No fire on the roof."

Two firefighters burst through the front door of the house carrying a hose. They hit the burning porch with a torrent of water, then sprayed the outside wall of the house. Within seconds, the fire was out. As they continued wetting down the front of the home, Merle charged across the street and up to the firefighter wearing a red helmet with a frontpiece that read "Captain." Merle shouted, "You in charge?"

"Get back."

"What kind of shit show was that? The fire was right in front of you."

The captain smiled at Merle with the look of someone about to lecture a child. "All right then. Let's talk. Come over here."

"I pay taxes. I expect firefighters to know what the hell they're doing. Jesus."

"Cool it, Jocko. If we attacked the fire from the front of the house and it had started inside, we'd lose the whole damn place. So we attack from the inside out."

Merle stuck his index finger under the captain's chin. "What the hell were those idiots doing on the roof?"

"These old houses don't have firestops in the walls. A fire anywhere in the house can spread to the attic in seconds." The captain slapped Merle's hand away. "Those idiots were up there to open a hole in the roof to ventilate the smoke and flames in that event."

"I didn't know."

"Not surprised."

Merle dropped his arms to his side and slumped. "How bad is it?"

"You're damned lucky we got here when we did. We kept the fire to the exterior. You should be thanking those idiots instead of bitching."

Lee heard all of this. He no longer wanted to be a pilot when he grew up.

The captain asked Merle, "Any idea how it started?"

Before Merle could answer, Ben said, "Lee started it."

Merle grabbed Ben's shoulders. "How do you know that?"

"I saw him. Told him not to."

Ben's father pushed Merle away. "Best talk to your own boy."

Merle clutched Lee's arm. His face pinched into a fierce scowl. "That right, boy?"

Lee swallowed back the sour vomit rising from his stomach. He'd seen that look before. He wanted to say it was all Ben's idea, but the words froze in his throat.

The captain said, "You want me to talk to the boy?"

"I'll take care of this. Won't happen again. Guarantee it." He dragged Lee to the back of the house. Betty followed. Merle opened the back door and threw Lee onto the kitchen floor. "You stay right there. I got something for you."

Betty stood at the open door with her hands over her mouth. Lee couldn't bear seeing the disappointment in her sad, bleary eyes. He had to turn away.

Merle came back with a pack of Marlboros. He yanked Lee off the floor and sat him on the kitchen chair's plastic lime-colored cushion. "Stick out your arm, boy."

Lee did as he was told, his heart racing, while Merle lit two of the cigarettes. He put one in the glass ashtray while puffing hard on the other one until the end glowed orange. "You like fire? Let's see how you like this." Merle pushed the end of the glowing cigarette onto the top of Lee's hand.

Lee cried out, "Mom!"

Merle pushed harder as the burning end sunk deeper into Lee's hand. Betty went to Lee's side and yanked Merle's hand away. Merle balled his hand into a fist and punched her hard in the stomach, knocking her to the floor. She gasped and clutched her stomach with both hands.

Merle picked up the other cigarette and sucked on it until the end glowed orange. Glaring at Lee, he said, "See what you made me do to your mom?"

Lee refused to cry out. He couldn't let his dad hurt his mom anymore. Merle continued working up Lee's forearm with the burning cigarettes, pushing the ends deeper and deeper into the flesh. Tears stung Lee's eyes. The smell of burning flesh and tobacco smoke blended into a sickening stench he would never forget.

The deep burns left permanent scars scattered over the top of his hand and up his forearm. In school, the other kids would call him Lee the Leper.

Betty lost the baby boy she was carrying.

Lee Garrison blamed himself.

Chapter 2

November 2006

The fire alarm chimed five times over the PA system of Milwaukee Firehouse Twenty-Four at 1:30 a.m. Fire Captain Lee Garrison rolled out of bed, pulled on his boots, yanked up his bunker pants, and snapped the red suspenders over his shoulders.

The dispatcher called out the responding companies, "Battalion 5 and Battalion 2, Engines 24, 22, and 34, Ladders 13 and 3, and Med 13 respond to a report of a house fire at 4050 North 62nd Street. Repeat..."

Lee rushed to the rig, stopping at the computer to grab the response printout. The driver was already at the wheel. The diesel engine rattled to life, spewing black smoke. Lee slipped into his smoke-stained yellow turnout coat and climbed into the tall cab of Engine 24. Two firefighters in the rear jump seats pulled the straps of their mask harnesses over their shoulders. The veteran crew was geared up and out of the firehouse in under thirty seconds, racing over city streets, the siren wailing. The red and white strobes sparkled off shimmering crystals of sleet.

En route to the incident, the rig radio came alive. "All units responding to 4050 North 62nd Street be advised of two children trapped in the burning basement."

Lee turned to his two firefighters in the jump seats. "Basement fire. Got two kids trapped. Chief's coming from another fire. We'll be first in."

The two firefighters nodded. The driver hunched over the steering wheel, pushing the rig faster, slipping and sliding over the slick roadway. Sleet pelted the windshield like a swarm of angry bees.

They fishtailed onto North 62nd Street, coming within inches of sideswiping a parked car. Smoke hung over the entire neighborhood, making it nearly impossible to know which house was on fire. They inched down the street, straining to see through the smoke. If they passed the house and had to circle back there was no chance those children would survive.

Fighting the adrenaline fogging his brain, Lee focused on how they were going to attack the fire and rescue the children. He hated basement fires. No ventilation. The stairwell would be like a chimney and they would have to crawl down through searing heat and blinding smoke to get to the children.

Halfway down the block, a ghost-like figure of a heavy woman in a white soot-stained nightgown emerged from the smoke, her arms flailing. Lee jumped from the cab of the fire engine as it rolled to a stop. The lady clutched his arm and tugged him toward the burning home while pleading, "Two girls in the basement. Please, please hurry." He followed her to the rear of the burning ranch home while his crew loaded hose on their shoulders.

Swirling black and gray smoke gushed from the basement stairwell. Lee's stomach tightened into a nauseating ball. No way could those girls still be alive down there. He'd have to wait for his crew before going in to search for their bodies. Department protocol.

The lady dropped to her knees, clasping her hands in prayer, looking up at Lee, her eyes bulging. Her piercing cries sent a shiver up his spine. "Those girls was calling for help right before you got here. Please don't let them die. Please, please, please, get them out. They all I got, sir."

If the girls had any chance, Lee had to get them out. Now. Screw protocols. In one motion, he removed his helmet and slid the facepiece of his breathing apparatus over his head and onto his face. Cool air hissed into the facepiece. He pulled on his heavy leather fire helmet, took a deep breath, and crawled down the stairwell, trying to stay below the searing heat. At the bottom of the stairs, he swept the floor on all fours, praying the girls were there. Nothing. He called out for them, hoping for the slightest sound of life. The only answer was the crackle of fire off to his left.

Staying low, he went right, colliding with nameless objects in the ink-black basement. He slammed small objects out of the way and crawled around larger ones, desperate to find the girls before their time ran out. While sweeping the floor in front of him as he moved over the basement floor, he struck the wooden leg of what he thought to be a table. He ran his hand up the leg and came to the bottom of a bed frame, giving him a flash of hope that the panicked girls were hiding under the covers. He checked the top of the bed and then flipped the mattress over. Nothing.

At the foot of the bed was what felt like a pile of bedding. Lee rifled through the pile and found a large rag doll. He pulled the ragdoll to his facepiece and peered into the serene face of a little girl, maybe around five years old. Her long braids hung to the shoulders of her limp, lifeless body. Lee's two firefighters called out from the stairway. He followed their voices through the darkness and handed the child off to them. The heat of the fire bled through his turnout, prickling his back. He crouched low, made his way to the bed, and dug through the bedding. He found another little girl. This one much smaller, maybe around two years old, also limp and lifeless.

Lee shielded the child from the intense heat and crawled back to the stairwell where he handed her off to another firefighter who was calling out in the darkness. Two more innocent children losing their lives so senselessly gut-punched Lee.

Fire crews swarmed the basement, blasting the fire with their hose lines while ripping the walls and ceiling apart with axes and pike poles. Lee directed operations while reporting to the battalion chief on their progress. The fire was out in under fifteen minutes, but the Red Devil had taken its deadly toll. The crews spent another thirty minutes pulling apart the rest of the walls and ceiling to ensure there was no hidden fire.

On the way up the stairs, Lee clenched his teeth, knowing what he would see when he got outside. Two tiny bundles lying side by side in the yard covered by bright yellow plastic sheets. The ME taking notes. Police taking statements from neighbors. And family members howling in primal agony over the loss of their little ones. Lee had seen this play out too many times. These were the responses that never left him. Something as simple as a child crying out in a grocery store could trigger sweating and heart-pounding visions that were never far from his thoughts.

Lee and his two firefighters stepped outside and saw—nothing. The yard was empty. Where were the bodies? Where had they taken them? As he tried to make sense of what he was seeing, Battalion Chief Johnson trotted over, waving his arms, and announced, "Nice job, Engine 24. Both girls were resuscitated on scene. MED units are transporting."

The other companies crowded around and broke into applause.

Lee should have been able to enjoy this.

* * *

The next morning, Lee dragged himself up the back steps of the aging, brown three-story house he had grown up in and nearly burned down when he was six. Gunshots and sirens had been rare in this area of the Washington Park neighborhood back then. Now they were background noise. In those days, neighbors all knew each other. Now everyone kept to themselves. All the old neighbors were long gone, some dead, others moved to the suburbs.

The kitchen was quiet. A hint of stale urine hung in the air. "Hey, Dad, where you at?"

"In here," croaked Merle from the front room.

The room was dark. Lee opened the shades and spotted Merle crumpled at the foot of his black leather recliner.

"Who the hell are you?" Merle asked, wiping at his red-rimmed watery eyes.

"You fall again?"

"Can't get nothing by you, hey?"

"Jesus, you pissed yourself. How long you been down?"

"Stop yacking and get me up."

"Where's your walker?"

"Walker?"

Lee gritted his teeth. "Let's get you to the tub."

Merle's eyes cleared. "It's you."

After bathing Merle and helping him dress, Lee ordered him to walk back and forth five times from the front of the house to the kitchen with his walker before he'd make him breakfast. Merle did as he was told, cussing nonstop. This was their morning ritual. If Merle wanted to eat, he'd have to get in his walking first. When he finished, Merle lowered himself onto the kitchen chair from his walker, glaring at Lee. "It ain't right, the way you treat your old man."

"Now you know me?" Lee shoved a bowl of oatmeal across the gray Formica table at Merle. "Better than the way you treated Mom."

Merle dipped his spoon in the oatmeal. "At least she didn't have to eat this swill."

"Don't eat it."

"How was your shift?"

"Brutal. We ran all night. I'm exhausted. And now I gotta take care of your sorry ass since you won't take care of yourself. That's what ain't right. It's not like you were father-of-the-year."

They ate their oatmeal in silence. When they finished, Merle struggled to his feet and took two shaky steps toward the front room.

Lee said, "Get back here and use your walker. See, that's what I mean. Goddamnit. I gotta get some sleep. Try to stay off the floor till I get up."

Lee went to his bedroom and paused at the dresser, glancing at the drawer that held the 9mm Glock he had purchased two years ago after reports of increasing burglaries in the area. He fell into his twin bed and slipped into a fitful sleep.

Chapter 3

Two weeks later

Lee woke, shivering again. His sheets were soaked with sweat. He stared at the dresser drawer. It was the first thing he looked at every morning. He got up and pulled the Glock from the drawer. He gripped the cold handle, examining the metallic black barrel.

Was today the day?

Two weeks ago, he had saved the lives of two children. Why couldn't that be enough?

Merle called out from the kitchen, "When you gettin' up, for Christ's sake."

Lee put the gun back into the drawer and slammed it shut. *It's only five,* Lee thought. *What's he doing up so damned early?*

Merle shouted, "Stop slamming the drawers in there."

"Pipe down, Old Man."

Merle was at the kitchen table hunched over a bowl of chocolate ice cream. "About time you got your ass up. Had to make my own breakfast." He scooped a heaping spoonful of dripping ice cream, waved it at Lee, and shoved it into his mouth, his bloodshot watery eyes trained on Lee.

Lee grimaced, then said, "Keep it up and you'll eat yourself into a nursing home."

"A man should be able to eat what he wants."

"Not if he needs a nursemaid."

"I can take care of myself."

"Great. I'll move out."

Merle shoveled another spoonful of ice cream into his mouth, watching Lee for a reaction.

Lee had to walk away before he let the old man draw him into another senseless argument. He went to the basement, where he had a carpeted workout area with a full rack of weights along with an elliptical trainer and training bench. Firefighting was brutal enough without letting himself go flabby. Today was a workday so he went light, pumping out one hundred pushups, two hundred crunches, fifteen curls with fifty-pound dumbbells, and finishing with thirty minutes on the elliptical trainer. Outside of his nagging back, he was in damned fine shape for fifty-six.

When he finished his workout, he headed upstairs and showered, put on his work clothes, and headed to the back door. "I'm going to work," Lee said to Merle on the way out. "Use your damn walker."

* * *

Lee pulled his ten-year-old blue Taurus into the back lot of Firehouse Fifteen to report for his first day at his newly assigned quarters. The early-morning December sun cast an orange hue over the cream-colored firehouse. Much had changed from when he pulled into this same parking lot for his first day on the job in 1974. It was hard to believe that was thirty-two years ago. The lot was now laced with potholes and surrounded by a razor-wire fence. Homes that had been across the street and on each side of the firehouse were gone, the lots overgrown with tall dried-out weeds that swayed in the frigid December breeze.

Retirement was 350 days away. Reassignment to an inner-city fire company of outlaws led by that dickhead Ralph was not the way Lee had hoped to finish his career. This was going to be a long year.

He had to stick it out to get his full captain's pay, which would dramatically increase his pension. He was already struggling to pay the bills with the cost of his mom's assisted living facility. If he stopped paying, she could end up in one of the run-down inner-city nursing homes the fire department responded to all too often. So many people waiting to die in those overcrowded and understaffed facilities that smelled of death and decay. There was no way he could ever commit his mother to living out her remaining years in such a miserable environment.

Lee was well past his firefighting prime. He carried the weight of thirty-two years of service in his thoughts and body. He lugged his turnout gear into the busiest firehouse in the city that was permeated with the fumes of thousands of responses: smoke, diesel exhaust, tires. The twenty-four-hour shifts would be brutal. This firehouse responded to over 6,000 alarms a year, making it the fourth busiest in the entire nation. Yes, this was going to be a long, long tour. He placed his gear next to the rig and took the off-going lieutenant's gear to the basement storage area. After taking a walk around the firehouse to inspect his new home, he headed to the kitchen to meet his crew.

The black and chrome commercial-grade Bunn coffee maker dripped coffee into a nearly full pot. Cigar smoke mingled with the aroma of fresh-brewed coffee. All these years later, tobacco smoke of any kind gagged Lee. Seated on the wooden benches at the long oak table were five off-going blueshift crew members and four on-coming redshift crew members, Lee's crew. He lowered his gaze to a burly bear of a man with a pockmarked face and bulging thyroid eyes who grinned and said in a gravelly voice, "Morning … Captain."

"Put that goddamn cigar out, Ralph."

Ralph blew his last puff of smoke to the ceiling, "You must have really screwed up to end up at this hell hole."

The others chuckled.

Lee crossed his arms and cocked his head. The chuckles stopped. Lee locked eyes with Ralph, neither of them looking away until Ralph ground out his cigar. "That better ... Captain?"

"This is my firehouse," Lee said. "You slack-jawed morons will follow department rules. Break them, I'll be on your ass." He looked around the table, waiting for a reaction, then barked, "Everyone got that?"

They all nodded except Ralph, who examined his crushed-out cigar.

"Now, everyone to the apparatus floor."

The blueshift lieutenant said, "But Boss, it's 7:30. Why do we...?"

Lee swung around, scowling at the lieutenant, who jumped up from the table and headed to the apparatus floor. The others followed, congregating at the rear of the fire engine.

"This firehouse is an embarrassment," Lee said, sweeping his open palm at the soot-darkened walls.

The beet-faced lieutenant raised his hand, "Sir, with all the runs, we can't..."

"Save it. I don't care if you're washing walls at midnight. It'll get done." He paused, daring anyone to question his orders. "I want all that crap off the tops of the lockers." He scanned the group, stopping at Ralph. "Ralph, you're out of uniform. I don't want to see you wearing white socks again. Got it? And shave. You look like a sleaze."

Ralph saluted Lee with his middle finger.

Lee narrowed his eyes at Ralph. "Okay, then," he said, drawing the words out. To the rest of the crew, he said, "That's it for now."

The off-going crew hurried out the door. Lee ambled to the kitchen. His crew didn't follow.

* * *

Once the captain had gone into his office, the crew hustled back to the kitchen to finish their morning routine of BS and coffee before morning duties. Ralph snatched his half-crushed cigar from the ashtray and relit it. Crusher, the portly driver, said, "Sure you wanna do that?"

"He's pissed because the chief's got a hard-on for him," Ralph said, examining the lit cigar, grinning.

Kenny, the lanky red-headed firefighter, said to Crusher, "The captain was put on charges and suspended for rescuing two kids. Today's his first day back."

Crusher frowned. "What the hell you talking about?"

"Went in by himself without backup."

"On charges for making a rescue? What kind of department is this coming to?"

Ralph took a deep drag off the cigar and blew a stream of smoke across the kitchen. "Chief's trying to run him off the job. That's why we're stuck with the jag. His mother should have done the world a favor and drowned him at birth."

Rick Anderson, a skinny, young Black firefighter who sported a tuft of hair below his lower lip, asked Ralph, "I heard he isn't liked, but why's the chief want to run him off the job?"

"Not liked? Ha. More like despised. He'll be able to hold his retirement party in a phone booth. Sooner the better."

Ralph blew out another cloud of tobacco smoke, flicked the ashes of the cigar in the ashtray, and said, "The captain and the chief were buddies during training. They got into it pretty bad about a year out of the academy. Now that the chief runs the department, I'm thinking he's looking for payback."

"Firefighter Anderson to the office," blared over the kitchen loudspeaker.

"Captain's calling," Ralph said. "Better hustle your ass in there, cub."

Anderson looked like he was about to face a firing squad. He groaned and headed down the hallway.

Ralph rose. "Let's get that hose work done before Captain Prick has another fit."

Crusher and Ralph went to work scrubbing dirty hose from the previous night's fire while Kenny went to the grocery store. When Anderson came out to the apparatus floor, Ralph asked, "So what did our fearless leader have to say?"

"I'm not supposed to say."

"Spill your guts, kid."

"Said you guys are a bunch of outlaws. If I was smart, I'd be careful about joining in on any cocklockery, whatever that is. And if he catches me breaking any rules, I'll be turning my badge into him."

"What else?"

Anderson winced.

"What?"

"He said if anyone makes any racial comments about me or any of the residents in our area, he wants to know about it."

"More of that diversity bullshit." Ralph waved his left hand. "Sorry, kid. Didn't mean you."

"He sure doesn't like you."

"Screw him."

* * *

The aroma of roasting beef and melted butter welcomed the crew when they entered the kitchen at noon. Kenny had meatloaf, buttered roasted potatoes, and candied carrots set out on the counter. The captain strolled into the kitchen and peered at Kenny. "Better be good."

"Cub, get the captain a coffee cup," Kenny said to Anderson.

"I can get my own," the captain said as he reached for the cabinet door.

"Boss, you might not want to..."

The captain opened the door. A large red plastic cup tumbled out. Water showered down on him, soaking his shirt. He stiffened and stood motionless, water dripping from his chin.

Ralph mouthed, "Nice job, Kenny."

Crusher whispered, "Oh, shit."

Anderson jumped up from the table, grabbed a dry white dishtowel, and wiped the counter down. The captain ripped it from his hand, wiped off his face, and shoved it back at him. The captain sliced off a thick hunk of meatloaf and slammed it on his plate with a metal spatula. All of them jumped. He piled potatoes and carrots onto his plate with the same ferocity. He took his place at the head of the table without saying a word. The others lined up at the counter and silently served themselves. As they ate, the only sound was silverware clanking on the oversized platters they used for dinner plates.

The captain said to Kenny, "Nice try on lunch. Hope supper's better." He rose from the table and scrutinized his crew. "Since you ladies have time to screw around, you can strip and wax the kitchen floor after lunch. All I want to see are asses and elbows." He headed to the office.

Ralph threw his hands up and said to Kenny, "A water trap? What the hell is wrong with you?"

Kenny turned to Anderson, "Damn, kid. You gotta be quicker."

Crusher chuckled. "See the look on the captain's face. That might have been worth doing floors."

"You did get to him good," Ralph said to Kenny.

They broke into laughter.

Chapter 4

The next morning before Lee opened the back door to his house, he smelled it—feces. *Now what?* he thought, gritting his teeth. The foul odor caught in the back of his throat when he opened the door. "Dad?" No answer. "Dad, where you at?" He rushed toward the sound of groaning. He pushed on Merle's bedroom door.

"Oww. Stop!"

Lee was able to push the door open a crack. "Dad, move away from the door."

"Can't."

"Hang in there."

Lee bolted out the back door and stomped through knee-high snow at the side of the house. He tried opening the window to Merle's room. It was locked. Lee trudged through the snow to the garage and got a putty knife. He was able to wedge it into the crack between the window and the frame and jimmy the lock. The window had not been opened in decades and wouldn't budge.

"What the hell you doin' out there?" Merle hollered.

Lee ignored him and went back to the garage for a hammer. He forced the putty knife around the window frame, pounding it with the hammer. When he finally worked the window loose, Lee slid it up and crawled into Merle's room.

"About goddamn time," Merle said. "Thought you firefighters were supposed to be good at breaking in."

"You okay? How the hell…?" The overturned dresser had Merle pinned against the door.

"Don't need a goddamn lecture. Just get me up."

Lee hoisted the heavy dresser off Merle and pushed it back against the wall. Merle's white boxers were stained brown with feces and drenched in urine.

"Where's your walker?" Lee asked.

"Just get me up."

Lee lifted Merle from behind, smearing his blue Dickie work pants with excrement. "Let's get you to the tub. Can you walk if I help?"

"Don't think so."

Lee heaved Merle to his feet and wrestled him to the bathroom. Sparks of pain shot down his left leg from his lower back as he guided Merle into the bathtub. "Jesus, Dad, you're turning into a tub of guts. You need to push away from the kitchen table once in a while."

"Yeah, yeah, yeah. Only pleasure I got left is eating."

"Seriously, I don't know how much longer I can take care of you."

"Why? 'Cause I went down? Why'd you put that damn dresser in my room? Lucky I wasn't killed because of you."

"I'm dead tired. Had twenty-five runs yesterday … I can't do this anymore. I got nothing left. Plus my back's giving me hell. Where's your walker?"

Merle pursed his lips.

"We need to find someplace that can take care of you."

Merle stared at the water filling the tub. "Nope."

Lee was too exhausted to argue.

After they finished in the bathroom, Lee brought Merle his walker from the front room. "Can you please start using this?"

After Merle headed to the front room, Lee went to his bedroom and glanced at the dresser drawer containing the Glock. He collapsed into the small bed.

Later that afternoon when Lee got up, he found Merle staring at the blank television screen.

"You need something to eat?" Lee asked, trying to sound pleasant.

Merle continued staring at the blank screen. "I don't want to be put away."

"Why don't you come visit Mom with me today? You can check the place out."

"She don't want to see me. You know that."

"Can you blame her?"

"Just leave me be."

There was no way Lee could pay for both his mom and dad to stay at Pleasant Manor. Why did he even bring it up? But what were the options? Merle wasn't in bad enough shape for a nursing home yet. And why should this be his responsibility? It's not like he felt any love for his father. The only attention he got from him growing up was the back of his hand or worse. But he couldn't escape the obligation prison. The only way his mom agreed to let Lee put her in Pleasant Manor three years ago was if he agreed to take care of Merle. Her mind was fading and Lee couldn't refuse. She was dealing with the terror of losing herself.

"I should let the bastard be," Lee said to himself as he left the house. Snowplows had gone through the neighborhood while he had been sleeping. His car was snowed in.

"Why the hell not?" Lee shouted. It took an hour to shovel his car out. When he finished, he headed to the memory-care wing of Pleasant Manor in the quiet suburb of Wauwatosa. On occasion, not often, she'd be herself, her eyes clear and alert. Those days, they spent the day reminiscing about fond memories of his childhood. It wasn't like every day growing up was filled with pain. Most days, Merle was simply distant. As Lee got older, he learned to steer clear of Merle when he had that far-away look. If Merle had ever hugged Lee, he couldn't remember.

His mother loved talking about Lee's high school wrestling days. She never missed a meet. Merle even came to some. Lee was the star of the Washington High School team, taking second place in the state tournament. She was so proud of him. Those memories still brought her joy when she was lucid. Merle never told Lee he was proud of him. Instead, he called him a loser when he took second place at state.

Lee stopped at the desk to ask how she was. The receptionist smiled and said, "She's excited about you coming today."

"Me or…?"

"Sorry."

His mother met him at the door to her room. "Albert, honey. I knew you'd come see me. I missed you so. Where you been?"

"I missed you too. Christmas is coming. What would you like me to get you?"

"Anything you get me will be perfect, my love."

She smiled and buried her head in his chest. He led her to the couch and together they watched *The Price is Right*. He had been told that it was best to go along with her and enter her world. Reminding her about who he was would only confuse and frustrate her. Giving her brief joy was the best he could hope for, despite the awkwardness.

Chapter 5

Raucous laughter echoed down the hallway as Lee approached the firehouse kitchen the next shift. He strode through the entryway. The room went quiet. He ignored the leaden silence and went to the cabinet containing the coffee mugs. He paused and peered over his shoulder at the crew, raising an eyebrow.

Ralph, who was chewing on an unlit cigar, said, "We're not that stupid."

"Who the hell is that?" Lee said, pointing to a scraggly-bearded hulk of a man with shoulder-length red hair sitting next to Ralph. On his brawny upper right arm was a tattoo in blood-red letters that read "Momma Failed."

"That's my kid," Ralph said. "Brought me some black socks so I wouldn't be out of uniform. That OK with you … Captain?

"Tell him he can leave. No visitors until housework is done."

"I'm sitting right here, asshole," Ralph's son said. "Tell me yourself." He rose and approached Lee. Every head at the table jerked in their direction. Lee squared his shoulders. He was not about to back down from this punk.

Ralph sprang to his feet, got between them, and said, "Ace. Stop. Take it easy. Go."

Although it was the middle of winter, Ace was wearing only a black T-shirt under a faded denim vest. The back of the vest had white rockers with Hells Disciples MC at the top and Milwaukee at the bottom all inscribed in black. In the middle of the vest was a white sneering skull engulfed in flames with crimson eyeballs set deep in the sockets.

Ace looked Lee up and down, flashed his middle finger at him, then brushed by him out the back door.

Lee said to Ralph, "You must be very proud."

Ralph turned away and whispered, "Pound sand."

"What?"

"Nothing … Captain."

"Good."

Lee went back to the cabinet and grabbed one of the thick cream-colored firehouse coffee mugs. He held the stained coffee pot well above the cup and poured, leaving a layer of foam on the steaming black coffee. He went to the table and stopped. The blueshift lieutenant got up from the seat at the head of the table and said, "Sorry, Boss. I'll move."

Lee took his seat and sipped his coffee, thinking about the visit with his mother. In some ways, he envied her. The only things she remembered were things that brought her joy.

One by one, the off-going blueshift crew members filtered out of the kitchen, leaving their lieutenant at the table with Lee and his redshift crew. The lieutenant said to Lee, "Had a house fire yesterday. Outside of that nothing major to report. We got started on the walls like you ordered but kept getting interrupted by runs. Over twenty runs again."

"Your crew did a sloppy job repacking the hose. Don't let that happen again."

"Yes, sir. If that's all, I'll…"

Lee raised his hand. "Go."

Lee drummed his fingers on the warm mug, wondering what to do about his dad. Maybe he could get someone to come in and help.

But how would he pay for it? He should have sold their house in Washington Park years ago before the value tanked in their blighted neighborhood, but both his mom and dad pleaded with him to keep it. While he stewed, the crew made small talk about Christmas plans with their families.

At nine o'clock, Lee rose and said, "Break's over. I'm not responding with sloppy hose lays. I want them repacked this morning."

"That's bullshit," said Ralph. "Bluesers should have to do that."

"Can't wait for them to do it. I want it done today. That's an order, not a request."

* * *

Later that night, an alarm came in for an auto accident at Eighteenth and Walnut. When they arrived on the scene, a late-model black Honda Civic was turned on its roof with a rusting white Chevy pickup wedged against the passenger door. Gasoline ran onto the asphalt from the overturned auto.

Lee shouted to Crusher, "Get the foam set up."

The rest of the crew ran to the car. A young man was hanging upside down in the driver's seat. In the passenger seat, a young woman hung upside down, blood dripping from her head. The stench of gasoline burned Lee's nostrils.

"Anderson, get a line laid out," Lee ordered. "Kenny and Ralph, we can't wait for the Jaws. We gotta get them out now." He keyed his portable radio. "Dispatch, Engine 15 requesting two Med units and a Jaws unit."

A heavyset man with a gash on his head leaned against the pickup truck. Lee called to him, "We'll get to you as soon as we get these people out. Go over by that tree."

Kenny supported the unconscious young man while Ralph cut his seat belt. When he was free, Lee helped them slide him out of the overturned car. Lee and Kenny carried the young man well away from the leaking gasoline. The neighborhood lawns were snow-covered. They had to lay him on a dry area of the sidewalk in the event a defibrillator was needed No time to grab an emergency blanket. Kenny stayed with the young man to assess him. Lee returned to the car.

The passenger door was crushed in. Ralph had crawled through the driver's door. He was able to drape his hand around the young woman's back and support her while he cut her loose from the seat belt. He carefully lowered her and guided her out. When Lee could reach them, he supported her neck as they removed her from the car. Bile crawled up his throat when he saw gray matter oozing from the gaping wound on her forehead. They carried her over to Kenny and the young man.

Kenny performed chest compressions on the young man. "Anderson, forget the line," he shouted. "Grab the defib machine and set up the O-two. Quick."

Ralph checked the young woman's carotid artery. "No pulse."

Lee knew these two young people were gone but they had to go through resuscitation protocols with the defibrillator and perform CPR until a Med unit called it.

Lee waved Crusher over. "Give Ralph a hand with her. I'll check the other driver."

The man was leaning against a tree on the other side of the road. When Lee approached him, he slurred, "Wasn't my fault." His breath reeked of alcohol.

"Why don't you sit and I'll check you out."

The man staggered toward Lee, waving his fist. "Wasn't my damn fault."

"You okay?"

"What do you care? More worried about them scumbags than me. Look at my truck."

"I asked—are you okay?"

"Kiss my ass."

Lee clutched the man's coat collar. "You killed those people, you miserable piece of shit."

"Screw them."

A red mist of rage blurred Lee's vision. He threw the man to the ground and pressed his knee to his chest. He clutched the man's windpipe and drove his fist into his face. Blood streamed from the man's broken nose.

Crusher ran to them and pulled Lee off the man. "Jesus, Boss. What the hell? I'll stay with this guy. Go help Ralph."

The red mist cleared and Lee stared at the man on the ground, who was hacking up a crimson pool of blood. *Not again,* he thought. Lee's chin dropped to his chest.

Both young people were pronounced dead by the Med units when they arrived. The intoxicated driver of the truck was transported to Froedtert Hospital.

Chapter 6

The crew was dead quiet on the ride back to quarters. The captain went to his office as soon as the fire engine came to a stop. Crusher, Ralph, Kenny, and Anderson went to the kitchen.

"What the hell was that?" Kenny asked the group.

"Anderson, make some coffee," Ralph ordered. "We got some talking to do."

The aroma of brewing coffee spread through the kitchen while the crew sat in silence at the table waiting for the pot to fill. After the last drips, Anderson filled three coffee mugs and set one in front of each of the crew members, then filled one for himself. "What are all those round scars on the captain's hand?"

Ralph cleared his throat. "We all know what we saw. If we report this to the chief, we're rid of Captain Prick for good."

Anderson asked, "Won't it be in the police report, how the guy's face got bashed in?"

"They'll think he hit the steering wheel. They'll be more interested in nailing the drunken bastard with homicide. They won't believe anything he says."

Crusher bit his lower lip. "I don't like the boss either. But, damn. He could get fired if it comes out he assaulted the guy."

"If he's smart, he'd retire before he's canned."

"That drunk had it coming," Kenny said, eyeing Ralph. "I'm surprised you didn't jump on the guy. You're usually the one who loses it."

Ralph waved his chewed-up cigar in the air. "Yeah, but I never went that psycho. He wanted to kill the bastard. If it comes out that we covered this up, we'll all be on charges."

The captain shuffled into the kitchen, his shoulders sagging. He glanced at them, splashed coffee in his cup, and headed back to his office.

Crusher shook his head. "Can't do it. Can't jam him up. Not for that. That drunk killed those kids."

"Me either," said Kenny.

"What about you?" Ralph asked Anderson. "You're still a cub. You'll be terminated if this comes out."

"I'm with them."

"Then I'll do it myself. You can all say you didn't see anything. Oh, and Anderson, I wouldn't ask the captain about those scars on his hand. I asked him about those once. If looks could kill, I'd be on the wrong side of the sod."

* * *

Lee sat alone in his office, devastated. Why had he let that guy get to him? Losing it like that sickened him. This wasn't the first time he lost it at a fatal car crash. They triggered wrenching emotions from early in his career when he was the cub on Engine 15. They had responded to an auto accident on Fond du Lac Avenue in the early morning hours. As they approached the scene, Lee's stomach jumped. The smashed-in red Toyota Corolla looked like the car of his best friend and classmate from the academy, Brian Peters. The car had been broadsided on the passenger side by a massive white Cadillac with rusted door panels. When they pulled to a stop, Lee ran to the car. He yanked the driver's door open and gasped. Brian was bent over the steering wheel. He gawked at Lee and gripped the top of his head with both hands.

"You okay?" Lee asked.

"Sorry, Lee. We…"

"Sorry. Sorry for what? Are you okay?"

Brian glanced at his passenger, lowered his head, and sobbed.

Lee ducked his head into the car. Blood oozed from a gash on the forehead of the young woman. It was Sheri, Lee's fiancée. He looked from Sheri to Brian and back to Sheri. "What are you two...?" Lee didn't have to finish the question. The looks on their faces said it all. He yanked Brian out of the car and crawled in. "You okay?"

Through shallow breaths, Sheri whispered, "Lee. I'm. So..." Her eyes closed. She slumped against the dashboard.

Lee's crew helped remove her from the wreckage and laid her on the ground. Lee sat next to her, holding her head in his lap, his thoughts a jangled mess, willing her to take a breath and open her eyes. He ached to have her back. He didn't care that she was messing around with Brian. They could work it out. Just please wake up. He pressed his forehead to hers.

With no paramedics, no EMTs, and no CPR training in the fire department during the seventies, all they could do was wait for a rescue squad that carried oxygen, bandages, and a cot, but little else.

When Rescue Squad Four arrived, Sheri's dead body was delicately loaded onto their cot and lifted into the squad. After they pulled away, Lee turned to Brian. "Why?"

"We were just having a good time."

Rage crawled up Lee's insides. He clenched Brian by the throat, shaking hard. "You should be the one on that goddamn cot."

Lee's crew pulled him off. Brian gagged while rubbing his throat, then walked away. Lee called after him, "You killed her, you bastard."

The drunk who was driving the Cadillac was taken into police custody. Nobody said anything about Lee attacking Brian. Lee's crew knew Brian and Sheri. What could anybody say?

After only two years on the job, Lee had worked at countless scenes of tragic losses. In the blink of an eye, lives were forever altered. Now Lee was a member of that sad fraternity.

He never dated again.

* * *

The refrigerator hummed in the firehouse kitchen as the crew sat quietly mulling over the accident. Anderson said to Ralph, "You never said what went on with the chief and the boss."

Ralph told him about the accident and how Lee and Brian, who was now the chief of the department, had been the best of friends. Back then Brian was married and Lee was engaged. The couples did everything together, even went on vacations to Florida as a four-some.

When Ralph finished the story, Anderson said, "Damn. What did the boss do to him?"

"From what I heard, they stayed clear of each other after the accident. At least until the department bowling sweeper a few months later. The captain was hitting it pretty hard at the bar. When Brian walked in with his wife, he flipped out and slammed Brian to the floor. Went into a rant about Brian fucking his fiancée and killing her. The captain was Marine Force Recon in Nam. They're the Marine version of Navy Seals. Total bad asses. I heard their motto is 'Swift, Silent, Deadly.' I wouldn't even screw with him and I was a Ranger. Brian's lucky to be alive. It took six firefighters to pull the captain off. Brian made a hasty exit. His wife left him the next day."

"Man, that'll mess you up. I feel sorry for the boss. What do you have against him?"

"Almost got me fired. Back in '89, I decked another firefighter at a working fire. Jag tried to take my hose line. Turned out I broke his nose." Ralph pursed his lips. "Red snow everywhere. After the fire was out, our captain—who was my lieutenant back then—said he was writing me up for fighting. I told him to pound sand. It was our fire and I wasn't going to let that jag take it. Of course, Mr. By-The-Rules wrote me up and added insubordination to the charges. Damn near cost me my job."

"Heard there was a little more to the story," Crusher said, grinning. "Tell him the rest."

Ralph clicked his tongue. "Yeah, I kinda told the chief to go fuck himself when he read me the charges and said he was suspending me. He got pissed and said, 'Congratulations, you're now terminated.' The union saved my job, but that killed any promotions."

"Still don't think you should jam him up," Crusher said. "Just ain't right. The man's been through a lot."

"Part of the job, brother."

Chapter 7

The auto accident brought back the empty hollowness that Lee battled all too often.

Merle was in the front room watching *The Today Show* when Lee got home the next morning. Lee hurried past him to his bedroom. The tug of the 9mm Glock was strong. Lee opened the drawer and gazed at the gun. He pulled it from the drawer and ran his palm along the cold barrel.

"When you gonna get me some breakfast?" Merle shouted from the kitchen.

Lee took one last look at the gun and placed it back in the drawer.

Merle was waiting for him at the kitchen table when Lee came out of his bedroom.

"You sick?" Merle said. "Look like a ghost."

"I can't take care of you anymore."

"Throwing me out? Why? 'Cause I won't use that damn walker? I'll use it if that'll make you happy. Now, you gonna feed me? My stomach thinks my throat's been cut."

"It's not just that. You know you're losing it."

"Sometimes I can't remember shit. That don't mean I gotta be put away."

"Why is it my job to take care of you?"

"'Cause I'm your father."

Lee's face burned. He stuck out his arm and pointed at the top of his hand. "What kind of father does this to his own kid?"

"You know damn well why I did that."

"I'm done. Eat ice cream. I don't care what you do."

* * *

When Lee got up from his fitful morning nap, he found Merle seated at the kitchen table. The kitchen was spotless. "Why you gotta keep bringing up those scars?" Merle asked. "Can't you just get over it?"

"Why can't you just admit it was a damned mean thing to do to your son?"

"You never started another fire. Now you put 'em out. Should be thanking me."

Here we go again, Lee thought, looking to the ceiling. He blew out an exasperated breath. "You didn't do that to teach me a lesson."

"You could have burned our house down."

"Jesus. You have an excuse for everything. And what about Mom? You punched her so hard she lost my baby brother. And you blamed me. Like an idiot, I believed you. Maybe he was better off not having to grow up with a father like you."

"I wasn't that bad."

"Tell that to Mom."

"She was no saint, either, screwing around with that asshole, Albert."

"I don't need to hear about that again," Lee shouted. "She needed someone to talk to since you were such a son of a bitch."

Merle swatted at the air and pulled himself up with his walker. "They did more than talk." He shuffled to the front room.

Lee clenched his fists and gritted his teeth. Why did he let himself get drawn into these senseless arguments? They always played out the same, leaving Lee enraged and imagining driving his fist into Merle's face. Did he actually think one day Merle would plead for forgiveness for any of that or for the brutal beatings over the years? Lee had been beaten for everything from spilling his milk to wetting the bed. His mom would try to protect him, but if she tried to stop Merle from hitting him, Merle would turn on her. The beatings came to a stop when Lee grew into a hulking teenager well over six feet tall. The last time Merle raised a fist to him, Lee threw him to the kitchen floor. Standing over him, he stuck his index finger in Merle's face and said, "You ever touch Mom again..."

Chapter 8

The next work shift, Ralph, Crusher, Kenny, and Anderson gathered at the kitchen table after morning housework. Crusher slathered butter on his hard roll, examining it with the look of an artisan.

"You gonna make love to it or eat it?" Kenny asked.

Crusher waved his middle finger at Kenny and turned to Ralph. "Boss ever coming out of his office?"

Ralph sneered. "Fine with me if the jag never comes out."

"Be nice to know what's on the schedule."

"Screw that."

Crusher turned to Anderson. "Hey, cub. Go ask the boss what he's got on the schedule today."

Anderson sighed. "Why me?"

Ralph thrust his finger at Anderson. "Because you're the cub."

Anderson returned less than a minute later. "Oh, man. Boss wouldn't talk to me. That look on his face was weird like he didn't know who I was."

"Time to end this bullshit," Ralph said and stomped to the captain's office. He pushed the door open without knocking. The captain was sitting sideways at his desk in the darkened room with his head in his hands. Ralph slammed the door shut. No response. After a long pause, Ralph rapped his fist on the desk.

The captain's head snapped up. He glowered at Ralph. "What?"

"You ain't right, man."

"What's your beef?"

"In case you forgot, I damn near lost my job because of you."

"I had to write you up."

"And I have to write you up for attacking our drunk the other night. You would have killed the bastard if Crusher hadn't pulled you off. All I did was bloody a nose."

Barely above a whisper, Lee said, "I would not have killed him."

"Tell me you didn't black out. I'm guessing this isn't the first time you lost it like that."

The captain leaned back in his chair, looking to the ceiling. "So, now what?"

"Rules are rules. Right, Captain? Payback's a bitch, hey?"

"Do what you have to."

"Do us both a favor and pull the pin. You got plenty time on the job."

"Can't. I have…"

The fire alarm chimed. Ralph charged out the door.

* * *

Lee blew out a loud breath and followed Ralph, stopping at the computer for the printout. The dispatcher called out the responding companies including Engine 15, followed by, "Report of a fire at the school—15th and Meineke. Repeat..."

As they pulled out of quarters, a massive cloud of dark billowing smoke was visible in the distance. Crusher said to Lee, "We'll be first in."

"Thank God it's Saturday."

Crusher pushed the rig hard, racing up the opposite lane of traffic like a shiny red twenty-ton stock car, blasting the air horn at drivers who refused to get out of the way, and swerving around cars with inches to spare.

When they arrived on the scene, dark gray and black smoke belched from every crack and crevice of the aging structure that had once been a grocery store. Thick smoke curled from under the eaves of the roof and climbed into the crystalline blue morning sky. Snow had already melted off the roof.

Lee turned to his crew in the back jump seats. "Ralph. Kenny. Get a line laid out to that side entrance. Anderson, come with me. Let's see what we got."

Lee assessed the building as they circled it. Concrete block walls. No windows for ventilation or for making entry. They were slowed by heavy brush and knee-deep snow at the back of the building. The smoke was building fast.

Lee called into his radio, "Ralph, don't make entry until I check this out. I don't like the look of that roof."

As they came around the back, an immense bald Black man stumbled out a side door, hacking and wheezing, his white shirt smudged with soot. He grabbed Lee by the flaps of his smoke-stained yellow turnout coat. "My little girl. She's trapped in there. I couldn't get to her."

"Anyone else?"

"Just her."

"Where?"

"Last classroom. Back of the school."

"Anderson. Go help lay out the line."

Anderson ran back toward the rig.

The large man said, "Please hurry. It's real bad in there."

"Ralph," Lee said into his radio. "I'm going in. Got a little girl trapped in there."

"Hang on, Boss. We'll be right there."

"Can't wait. Back me up."

Lee pulled on his facepiece, positioned his leather helmet, reached around his back, and opened the air valve on the compressed air bottle. *Screw the rules,* he thought to himself. *There's a terrified little girl in there.* He crawled into the blackness on all fours, staying below the heat. He ran his gloved hand along the wall, searching for the hallway leading to the back of the school. *How in hell did this fire get going so fast?* Lee wondered. His knees grew warm. He called into his radio, "Ralph, we got fire in the basement. Watch yourself."

"Dammit. Wait for us."

Lee crawled deeper into the school. There was no turning back. He pounded the floor in front of him with his axe as he moved along the hallway to ensure it was sound. He called out in the darkness, "Little girl. Fire department. Where are you?" He thought he heard something coming from far down the hallway but couldn't make it out. He moved faster than he should to get to her, praying the floor wouldn't collapse and plunge him into the flames. He heard muffled coughing and gagging. He ran his gloved hand along the wall and found an open door. "You in there?"

From inside, came a high-pitched squeal followed by coughing. Lee crawled toward the fading coughs. He moved across the classroom, sweeping his hand over the floor, slamming desk after desk out of the way. He bumped into a large one, felt around it, and found the girl huddled underneath. He took one glove off and ran his hand over thick tight braids on the little girl's head. "You're gonna be okay. I'll get you out of here." Her gasping breaths were shallow. Lee took a deep breath, lifted the helmet from his head and slipped off the facepiece, placing it over the girl's face. Her breathing deepened. He snugged the helmet back onto his head.

Early in his career, Lee fought plenty of fires without a mask. It was macho to be a smoke eater back in the day. He knew he could last several minutes in this toxic atmosphere by keeping his nose and mouth close to the floor. The girl's breathing returned to normal.

"Are you with me?" Lee asked. He felt her head nod. "Good. Now, I'll need you to hold that mask to your face while I help you crawl out of here. Do not stand up. Understand?" She nodded again.

Lee draped his arm over and around her waist. They crawled along the floor, retracing the way down the ink-black hallway, staying low to protect the girl from the searing heat over their heads. A low rumbling intensified into a deafening crash. He hunched down, covering the girl with his body. Then, eerie silence. They continued crawling down the hallway toward the side entrance. Light from an open hole in the roof illuminated a maze of smoldering rafters and roofing that blocked their way. Lee struggled to pull the heavy rafters loose, gasping when bolts of pain flared down his back to his left leg. The rafters didn't budge. An orange glow erupted from the center of the pile.

The mask muffled the little girl's cries.

Ralph's voice came over Lee's radio. "Boss. Where you at? Part of the roof came down."

"We're trapped in the hallway." He activated the emergency alarm device at his waist that blared a high-pitched wail.

Lee could barely hear Ralph over the deafening wail of the device. "We're on our way."

There was no way his crew could get through that burning pile of rafters and roofing. The floor could give way at any time. They crawled back toward the classroom with Lee dragging his left leg, trying not to screw up his back even worse. Maybe one of the ladder companies could breach the wall from the outside. But no, it would take way too much time to get through the concrete block wall. He fought the panic and tried to control his breathing. Pinpoints of bright lights flickered behind his eyes. He was on the verge of passing out. “Try to hold your breath,” he told the girl. “I need the mask.”

After he took several breaths, he handed it back. The ringing bell from the regulator on his mask harness warned of only minutes of air left. Over the ringing of the bell and the wail of the emergency alarm device came the sound of water blasting against the wall from further down the hallway.

They continued toward the sound of the hose line. Or was it the sound of a ruptured water pipe? They crawled faster. Lee defied the stabbing pain shooting down his lower back, praying the floor wouldn't give way and drop them into the inferno below. They passed the classroom. Water showered down on them.

“We got you, Boss,” came from his radio. Seconds later, the girl was lifted from his arms. Someone pulled him along by his spanner belt. A fog stream from a hose line cooled him while they made their way out a narrow back door.

The bright morning sunshine momentarily blinded him. Paramedics rushed to Lee and the girl. Two tended to the little girl, who was sitting up and staring at Lee. Two other paramedics ran to Lee, who was on all fours. “We need to check you out, sir.”

He struggled to his feet, fighting the back pain. “I'm fine. Help with the little girl.”

Ralph jammed his finger against Lee's chest. “What the hell were you thinking going in alone? Next time, don't include us in your death wish.”

Lee slapped his finger away. “How did you find that back entrance?”

A loud explosion. Lee's insides jumped. The rest of the roof collapsed, sending flames raging into the sky.

The huge man who had told Lee about the girl appeared from the side of the building, sprinted to the girl, knelt, and pulled her into his thick arms. When he let go, she pointed at Lee. The man approached Lee and said, "Alexus said you saved her life. God bless you, my man, for saving my little girl." His overbite spread to an infectious grin.

The little girl was alive. He was alive. Lee should have been able to bask in the glow of the rescue, if just for a little while.

Chapter 9

The fire went to a second alarm and took until late into the night to fully extinguish. The exhausted crew returned to quarters close to midnight. After they finished repacking the hose and preparing their air masks for the next fire, the captain called them to the kitchen. "Just wanted to say nice job. That's all." He turned and limped back to his office.

"That's all?" Ralph said to Crusher.

"That's about as much of an attaboy as we get. Better than a bite in the ass."

"The captain was limping around pretty bad at the fire," Anderson said. "He could hardly get off the rig when we got back."

"Poor baby," Ralph said. "We all got screwed-up backs and knees."

Anderson shook his head. "I can't believe he found that little girl in there."

"He should have waited for us. If he goes down, we gotta drag his sorry ass out. Damn reckless."

Kenny chuckled. "C'mon, Ralph. Really? You'd do the same thing. You know it."

"Chief finds out he went in alone, he'll be in deep shit."

Crusher grimaced. "Jesus, Ralph. He saved that little girl."

"No. We did. If we hadn't found them, they'd both be crispy critters."

"How'd you know about that rear entrance?" Kenny asked.

"My bed's calling," Ralph said as he headed out of the kitchen.

* * *

Ralph marched to the captain's office early in the morning before the others got up. He didn't care if he woke him. He rapped on the door.

"What?" came from inside.

Ralph entered the dark office that smelled like the charred remains of the school. The captain was still in his soot-stained shirt, staring at the computer screen on his desk. Ralph took a seat across from him with his arms crossed. They sat in silence for several minutes.

The captain said, "That's it then, hey? Battalion Chief's coming by this morning. Can't stop you from spilling your guts."

"Yup. You know. Rules, hey? Might want to clean up before he gets here. You smell like burnt trash. Oh, and by the way, you're welcome."

Ralph headed to the kitchen and started a pot of coffee. The others wouldn't be up for another hour. He sat alone at the long wooden table contemplating what he was going to tell the battalion chief.

* * *

The captain entered the kitchen, followed by the white-haired battalion chief. The chief took a seat at the head of the table. The captain stood back against the wall with his arms crossed, gazing at the floor. Anderson set a cup of coffee in front of the chief without asking. "Thank you, son," the chief said. "The fire yesterday was arson. I need to know if any of you saw anything out of the ordinary."

They all shook their heads, except the captain. Ralph eyed him.

"That place was already rolling when we pulled up," the captain said. "Some guy came out the side door."

"You think he had something to do with it?"

"Doubt it. His little girl was inside. I did notice tracks in the snow behind the school."

"Be sure to put that in your report. Okay. Now I need to clear something up." The chief raised his eyebrows at the captain. "There's talk you went in alone. Any truth to that?"

The captain exhaled slowly. Before he could answer, Ralph said, "That's bullshit. We all went in together. It was by the books."

Kenny and Crusher glanced at each other, their eyes wide.

"That true?" the chief asked them.

Kenny answered first. "Absolutely, Chief. We're all about the rules. You know that."

The chief's head tilted. "Sure."

Crusher put his hand over his mouth, stifling a laugh.

The chief looked to Anderson. "That right, son?"

Anderson couldn't answer fast enough. "Yes, sir."

"That takes care of that. Now I have another issue. The drunk who killed those two kids the other night told the cops one of you attacked him and bashed his face in."

The room went silent. Crusher and Kenny looked sideways at Ralph. Anderson stared at the floor. The captain raised his hand. "So, yeah. It was…"

Ralph stood. "The lying bastard smashed his face on the steering wheel. Nobody attacked him."

Anderson jerked his head up and gawked at Ralph.

"That's what I figured," said the battalion chief. "Chief Peters said he wanted a thorough investigation. Said he'd be firing whoever did that." The chief rose. "Solid job on the rescue. Get me the details, Captain, and I'll put you all in for a commendation."

The captain followed him to the door.

"What just happened?" Crusher asked Ralph.

Kenny draped his arm around Ralph's shoulders and kissed him on the cheek. "Knew you weren't a total jag."

Ralph shoved him away.

Kenny crossed his arms. "Well, I never."

They all broke into laughter.

Ralph pushed away from the table. "Got some business to talk with our fearless leader." He strolled to the captain's office and opened the door without knocking.

The captain narrowed his eyes at Ralph, his face ashen. "Why?"

"You owe me big."

"What you want?"

"Nothing now. But if I ever need a favor or for you to look the other way..."

"I can't promise that."

"I lied for you. Twice. And pulled your ass out of that fire."

"You're asking too much."

Ralph raised his eyebrows. "I can always go to the chief and tell him you pressured me to lie. How bad you want to keep your job?"

The captain rubbed his forehead. Ralph waited.

"Looks like I have no choice," the captain said, his voice raspy.

"I have your word?"

"Yeah. Fine."

"Good."

The captain blew out a loud sigh. "Anything else?"

"You ain't right. And you know it. No telling what'll happen next time you lose it. Ain't fair to the crew. Deal with it or I will." Ralph headed back to the kitchen.

Chapter 10

"You ain't right," played over and over in Lee's head on the drive home. Ralph was right. He had blacked out at the car accident. It was only a matter of time before he lost it again, and that scared the hell out of him. He had to figure a way to control his rage before he did kill someone. Was it time for the Employee Assistance Program? After any mass casualty incident or fire death, a representative was brought in from the EAP to debrief the crews. Cards were handed out along with pleas to call for help if they experienced any signs of traumatic stress. Lee had heard the spiel too many times. He was terrified of sharing his darkest thoughts. Would they let him back on the job when they learned what was in his head? What crew would trust him if they knew he was seeing a shrink?

Merle was in the front room in his recliner when Lee got home. "Why you all hunched over?" Merle asked.

"Damn back."

Merle held up the *Milwaukee Journal-Sentinel* newspaper. "You're quite the hero."

Lee took the paper. On the front page was a photo of the little girl with the tight braids, her face smudged with soot, pointing at him. The headline read, "Dramatic Rescue at Odyssey School." The article quoted the battalion chief as stating the members of Engine Company 15 had pulled the little girl from the burning school seconds before the roof collapsed. The company had gone way above and beyond in their duties and bravery.

After reading the paper, Lee limped to his bedroom, drained.

Merle called after him. "What about my breakfast?"

Lee didn't answer and closed the bedroom door behind him. He couldn't stop trembling. Dammit, he had saved a little girl's life. He should be riding high. But no. Every major fire set off gut-wrenching emotions from a horrific fire early in his career where four firefighters lost their lives. These emotions were driving him toward what? Insanity? To the Glock? It was getting worse with each fire.

"I can't do this anymore," Lee snarled. He pounded on the dresser until he couldn't clench his fist. With his other hand, he opened the dresser drawer.

"Just do it," said the image in the mirror. Lee gave in to the magnetic pull of the gun and lifted it slowly from the dresser drawer. He clutched the gun, breathing hard. "Just do it," echoed in his head. His nerve endings crackled. His chest felt ready to explode from his hammering heart. He closed his eyes, took a deep breath—and bit down on the cold barrel.

"What the hell you doing in there?" Merle shouted from the front room.

Lee's eyes snapped open. He saw himself in the mirror with a gun barrel in his mouth. His eyes widened in terror. What the hell *was* he doing? He placed the gun in the drawer and slammed it shut. A shudder shook him to the core. Lee sat on the edge of his bed, his hand throbbing, his heart racing. He never came that close before.

"I need my goddamn breakfast," Merle shouted.

Lee ignored him and waited on his bed for the adrenaline to drain. After he calmed down, he fished a worn business card from his wallet. He took his cell phone from his pocket and dialed four of the numbers on the card, then stopped. What was he doing? He was always able to bounce back from these episodes. It just took time. Asking anyone for help was unthinkable.

He glanced up from the phone and sucked in a deep breath when he saw the vacant eyes staring back at him in the mirror. He called the number on the card. A woman answered. Lee moved the phone away from his ear and was about to end the call when the woman said, "Please don't hang up," as if she had read his mind.

He stared at the phone in his palm. The chaotic fog in his head cleared. It was only a matter of time before he swallowed a bullet.

The woman said, "Please let us help you."

"I'm a Milwaukee firefighter. I need to talk to someone. Today."

"Is this an emergency?"

"I need to talk to someone today."

"Got it. I can get you in to see Dr. Bennet at one o'clock at the VA. That's where most of the doctor's patients are."

"I'll be there."

He answered questions about name, age, and address but could not find the words to tell her why he needed to see the doctor.

* * *

Lee found Dr. Bennet's office tucked away at the end of a long hallway. He stepped into a small waiting room with four mismatched wooden chairs. The place smelled old, like the musty library at Washington High School. Nobody was seated behind the small beat-up desk that had a black phone on one side and a tiny fake Christmas tree with miniature red ornaments on the other side.

Lee coughed into his hand. A petite woman with huge black-rimmed glasses emerged from the open door behind the desk.

"I'm here to see Dr. Bennet," Lee said.

"That would be me. You're early."

"You're the doctor?"

She lowered her glasses on her nose and peered at him over the top.

Lee looked away. "Sorry. I...ah..."

"Thought I'd be what? Older? Or better yet. A man?"

"Yeah. I don't know."

She laughed and pushed her glasses back up her nose. "You're not alone. Most of my patients are older vets. I'm well over thirty, by the way. You should see my mother. She's sixty-five and could pass for my sister."

"Didn't mean to..."

"Don't worry about it. We're here to talk about you. Not me. Please come in."

Manila folders cluttered every open spot on the worn walnut desk that wasn't much larger than the one in the waiting area. More folders were stacked on the floor on each side of it. She motioned to the wooden chair with the rounded backrest in front of the desk.

"No couch?" Lee said, trying to sound clever as he gingerly lowered himself into the chair.

"You okay?"

"Messed my back up at a fire yesterday."

"The school fire?"

Lee nodded.

"That's you on the front page of the paper, isn't it?"

"I guess."

Dr. Bennet narrowed her eyes. "I see. Let's get started. A little about me. I've been researching PTSD or as I prefer PTS because I don't buy into post-traumatic stress as a disorder. The effects of a traumatic experience are expected and normal but vary widely. I've been working with patients at the VA to discover ways we can treat the effects of traumatic stress before they become debilitating." She waved her hand over her desk. "Every one of those files is a life altered due to a traumatic experience. Now, you. Tell me about yourself."

Lee glanced around the small room that was no larger than a walk-in closet. "This the Employee Assistance Program?"

"I'm one of the therapists."

"Okay, I'm confused. Are you even a doctor?"

She nodded once and smiled. "I'm even a doctor. Not a physician but a doctor of psychology." She leaned across the desk. "Can you tell me why you needed to see someone today?"

Lee twisted in the chair, trying to alleviate the stabbing back pain.

Dr. Bennet rested her chin in the cup of her hand and waited for an answer.

Lee clenched his fists, unable to meet her intense gaze. His heart pounded in his ears. "Sorry. This was a mistake." He pushed himself up from the chair, gritting his teeth from the back pain.

Dr. Bennet came from behind the desk and clasped his arm. "Sit. Let's just talk a bit."

She guided him back into the chair. After taking her spot behind the desk, she said, "Can you tell me about the fire?"

"This is all confidential, right?" Lee said.

She opened the top drawer of her desk, pulled out some papers, and slid them across the desk to Lee. "This is the confidentiality agreement I'm bound by."

Lee looked at the papers, then at her. Her warm smile and soft brown eyes calmed him. He told her the story of the rescue in a detached, emotionless way as if it were about someone else. When he finished, Dr. Bennet dabbed at her eyes. "That's an incredibly moving story. Had you not gone in alone when you did, that girl would not have survived. Risking your own life for another. I can't imagine what that must feel like."

Lee lowered his head. She was right. That should have been one of the best feelings in the world.

"Why does that make you sad? Am I missing something?"

"It's not that. It's just. I don't know. I can't do this."

"You know, some of my military patients have performed unbelievable acts of bravery on the battlefield. Instead of focusing on their accomplishments, they're haunted by visions, sounds, and emotions of horrific events. They relive those events and emotions over and over. This can lead to self-medicating with alcohol or drugs, alienation of family and friends, divorce ... and suicide."

The way she clenched her lips and studied his face after she said suicide, it was like she could see inside his head. Dr. Bennet folded her hands together. "I think I know why you're here."

How can you? Lee thought.

"In these first sessions, I'll want to get some background and history from you. Whatever you feel comfortable sharing. Before we address your past traumas, we'll work on coping skills to help you self-regulate your emotions. I shouldn't have asked about the fire. I assumed that was a positive memory.

It should have been, Lee thought and pinched his lips together.

"What do you do when you're not working?" Dr. Bennet asked.

"Take care of my dad and visit my mother in the nursing home."

"Anything you want to share about that? I know that can be quite a burden."

Especially when your father is an asshole, Lee thought and said, "No."

"Anything else I should know about you? Were you ever in the military?"

A vision of an enemy soldier, a young boy, collapsing to the ground flashed in his head. "Marines."

"Were you deployed?"

"Vietnam. '69."

"Is that something you'll want to address in therapy?"

"I put all that behind me."

She nodded and said, "Well, thank you for your service."

Sure as hell didn't get any thanks back then, he thought.

"You must deal with an incredible amount of trauma on your job. The human brain is not designed to constantly be bombarded with the things you experience on a daily basis. The cumulative effect of multiple traumatic events over the years can suddenly erupt into serious issues of post-traumatic stress for some. When we get into the therapy, we'll address whatever you feel is causing you the most pain and go on from there. Do you have any questions?"

Lee looked to the floor.

Dr. Bennet clasped her hands together. "Have you ever talked to anyone about any of this?"

He shook his head.

"I understand. We can work through this if you're willing. I know I can help."

"So I just tell you my problems, and they magically go away?"

"People used to spend years in what you might call 'talk therapy'. I've been using a different approach. It's called EMDR, which is Eye Movement Desensitization and Reprocessing."

"Eye movement, what? Sorry, but it sounds hokey."

"It's quite effective. I've seen improvement in a matter of weeks for some. You won't have to do much talking, but it would help if you could give me some background information on events that have been causing you pain. You want to give it a try?"

"I don't think so."

"Is what you're doing now working at all for you?"

Lee shrugged.

Dr. Bennet paused, then said, "You can quit at any time. What do you have to lose?"

"I need to think about it."

"Whatever you're dealing with is not going away. You asked to see me today. Please let me help."

Allowing someone to help him went against everything Lee believed in himself; that he always solved his own problems. It made him feel weak to think he needed anyone for anything.

Dr. Bennet leaned back in her chair, clasped her hands together, and said, "Please?"

Through gritted teeth, Lee said, "Fine."

"Good. We'll set up a schedule. I'd suggest you take some time off from the department so we can focus on treatment without distractions or triggering events from your work."

"I can't do that. If my crew finds out I'm seeing a shrink, they won't trust me."

"Shrink?" Her brow wrinkled. "Nobody will know you're here unless you choose to share that. The department will be notified you're taking time off. They won't be told why. The way you're bent over, I would say a back injury would be a plausible excuse if you need one. I'll let Employee Assistance know that you need time off for therapy."

"How long?"

"Let's start with two weeks. I'll see you three times a week."

"Anyone ever say no to you?"

She cocked her head and raised her brows.

Lee scanned the office. "Is this the best they can do for you?" He pointed to the doorway. "You don't even have a receptionist."

She grinned. "I'm on a tight research budget. Once I publish some results, maybe they'll move me. But I kind of like the coziness here. And they give me a receptionist on Tuesday and Thursday mornings until noon."

Looks more ratty than cozy, Lee thought.

"Before you go," Dr. Bennet said, "I need to ask you some tough questions." She paused, examining him over the top of her glasses. "Do you have a plan in place to end your life?"

Lee gasped and abruptly shook his head.

Dr. Bennet paused again before asking the next question. "Do you have any thoughts of taking your own life?"

Lee clenched his lips and shook his head ever so slightly.

"Do you fantasize about dying in a fire?"

All the time, he thought, staring at the floor. "No," he whispered. He was certain she saw through his feeble responses.

After several torturous seconds of silence, she asked, "Will someone be with you until we can meet again?"

Finally, a question he could answer honestly. "My father lives with me."

"Good. I'll see you in two days. Here's my card. Please call me if you need to talk before then. If you can't reach me, the number at the bottom of the card is a 24-hour crisis hotline. Don't hesitate to call."

Dr. Bennet followed Lee out of the office. A well-groomed gray-haired man seated in the waiting room saluted as Lee passed. Lee ignored him. As Lee walked out the door, he heard Dr. Bennet say, "You're looking dapper today, Colonel."

Chapter 11

Two days later, Lee entered the waiting room of Dr. Bennet's office. A mature woman wearing a blue Milwaukee Brewers baseball cap was seated in one of the old chairs. "Morning," she said curtly. "The doctor said you should go ahead on in."

Dr. Bennet rose when he entered and motioned for him to sit. "You look exhausted. Trouble sleeping?"

"Haven't slept through the night in years."

"Night terrors?"

If jerking awake in a cold sweat is night terrors, then yes, he thought. "I don't know. Maybe."

"I have to ask an important question—will you be comfortable talking to me through therapy?"

"Don't know."

"That's what I thought. Thank you for being honest." She turned to the doorway. "Brigid, please come in here."

The woman from the waiting room joined them. She lifted off her cap and ran her fingers through her curly red hair tinged with white streaks.

"Captain O'Brien," said Dr. Bennet, "meet Captain Garrison."

Captain O'Brien didn't wait for Lee to reach out his hand. She grabbed it and shook hard. "Forget that captain crap. I'm Brigid."

What the hell? Lee thought, looking to the doctor for an answer.

Brigid squeezed his hand. "Hey. I'm here."

"Um, yeah." Lee pulled his hand away. "But who...? Why...?"

Dr. Bennet came around her desk. "Brigid is one of our peer counselors. I know it can be difficult, if not impossible, to talk to us civilians. I don't have any firefighters as peer counselors yet, but Brigid's retired from the MPD. She spent a lot of time in the Core. I think you'll have plenty to talk about. I have to make some rounds, so take as long as you like." She left, closing the office door behind her.

Brigid turned her palms up and cocked her head.

"She coming back?" Lee asked.

"Nope. Just the two of us."

"So, you're a cop."

"So, you're a firefighter."

Lee's back flared. He grasped the top of the wooden chair. "I'm guessing the doctor doesn't know our departments don't exactly get along."

Brigid motioned for Lee to sit. "Take a load off before you tip over."

"I'm fine."

"No, you're not. Let's cut the crap and do this."

"Do what? I don't get it. You're a cop, not a doctor."

"First of all, I'm a retired cop. Second, I'm here for support. Dr. Bennet will be doing the therapy. She's found that having peer counselors offer her patients support helps speed recovery. I'm only here to talk. So, let's talk."

"Talk about what?"

"Would you sit down before you tip over?"

Lee wasn't about to take orders from a cop, especially a retired one, but his back couldn't take standing any longer. He lowered himself, blowing out a loud breath.

Brigid pulled a chair in front of him so they were facing each other. "You seeing a doctor about your back?"

"Nothing they can do. If I take it easy, it'll settle down in a few days. Been dealing with this for years."

"You should try yoga. Worked miracles for me."

"Oh? Throw your back out eating donuts?"

Her piercing green eyes drilled into him. "You do know I'm a volunteer. I don't get paid to take crap. If I wanted to hear that shit, I'd go back to my ex-husband."

Lee jerked back in his chair. "Jesus, it was a joke."

"You need to work on your shitty delivery." She shook her head. "Firefighters. Always the comedians. Now, I've got better things to do if you can't get over me being a cop."

Lee could see why she had risen to captain on the MPD. He was not easily intimidated, but she had him off balance. "Is this how you peer counselors treat patients?"

"I've been around enough firefighters on the street to know you don't want to waste time playing around with fake niceties." She leaned forward. "You know we see and deal with the same shit on our jobs. Can we start by agreeing on that?"

"I guess."

"Love your enthusiasm."

"Sorry. Jesus," Lee said.

"That was a joke."

"Maybe you should work on your shitty delivery."

Brigid smirked. "Touché. Now, let's get serious. I'll start." She told him how early in her career, she and her partner were ambushed in a back alley after chasing a drug dealer through an inner-city neighborhood. Her partner was shot in the chest. The attackers fled. She held his head off the cold ground, praying harder than she had ever prayed. His last words were, "Not your fault."

Her partner was a veteran and she was a rookie, but still, she should have seen it coming and reacted faster. How could she not blame herself? A wife and two little girls were left without a husband and father. After that, she worked tirelessly at gaining the trust of fellow officers but could not overcome the wall of guilt that prevented her from forgiving herself. She carried that all of her career until the trauma, pain, and suffering she saw on the job pulled her into a darkness she couldn't escape. The anger that surfaced without warning destroyed her two marriages and resulted in estrangement from her daughter. She took early retirement to heal but found herself falling deeper into depression until Dr. Bennet rescued her from herself.

Lee was well-acquainted with anger. Thoughts of what he might do to someone scared him more than thoughts of suicide. Ralph was right. He would have killed that drunk driver who ended the lives of those two people had Crusher not pulled him off.

When Brigid finished, she reached for a tissue on the doctor's desk. "It never goes away but it no longer controls me." She blew her nose, honking loudly.

Lee pointed out the window. "That male goose sure perked up."

She moaned. "Firefighter humor. Jesus. By the way, they're called ganders."

"That's tough about your partner. Sorry. "

"I know you firefighters don't like to play around the edges, so I'll ask, what keeps you up at night?"

"What about your daughter? You get along now?"

"We're working on it. Now, what's your story?"

Lee pointed at her Milwaukee Brewers cap on the doctor's desk. "So, you're a baseball fan."

"Very perceptive. You should be a detective. Now, talk."

Lee flared. "Damn, you're a ball-buster."

"You bet I am. And I know you have the balls to do this. You proved it when you rescued that little girl."

"Just doing my job."

"From the write-up in the paper, it sounded like you and your crew came damn near to buying it in there. You must have known the risk before going in. That took balls." She moved her chair closer. "Now talk."

"I could fill a book with the shit I've seen."

"I get that. But what keeps you awake at night?"

He felt like he was a probationer again going to his first major fire, adrenaline surging through his body, his brain short-circuiting. He was no coward and had never backed away from fear. But this was a different kind of fear, a paralyzing fear he had never confronted. At fires, there was always a plan. Here he had no plan. He felt like he was crawling into a raging inferno and had no clue how to put it out.

Brigid leaned back in her chair with her arms crossed. "Nobody makes it through this alone."

What keeps me awake at night? Lee asked himself, clenching his lips. Something he was not ready to share with anyone—a fire that took the lives of his entire crew when he was a firefighter.

Brigid waited.

Suck it up. Show this cop you're no coward, he thought. *Tell her about your fiancée.* That one he could try to share. Lee took a deep breath. "Thirty years ago." He took another deep breath. "We responded to an auto accident—it was two in the morning." Lee gritted his teeth, then said, "A car had been broadsided on the passenger side—it was bad. She was the passenger—my fiancée—with my best friend." He closed his eyes and saw the gaping wound on her forehead. Her last words played softly in his head, "Lee, I'm, so…"

Lee choked and gripped his forehead.

Brigid leaned forward and clasped Lee's other hand in both of hers and said, "She died."

Lee stared at her hands as the emotion of holding his dead fiancée in his arms sent him into the hollow darkness he was all too familiar with. He needed to leave. Get away from here. Get away from all of this. Lee jerked his hand away and stood. "I gotta go."

"Dr. Bennet saved my life. I can finally see in color again," Brigid said, rising from her chair. "Give her a chance." Their eyes met. She asked, "Do you have anybody you can talk to while you go through therapy?"

Lee looked away.

"You don't have anybody? Any friends or relatives?"

Lee's stomach tightened. His mom didn't know him and his dad was not someone he would ever confide in. The only other relatives were distant cousins he'd never met. He gave up needing friends many years ago.

He took a step toward the door.

Brigid moved in front of him. "If you can stand having a ball-buster to talk to," Brigid said, raising one eyebrow, "how about we get together the day after your therapy sessions?" She waited for an answer as Lee looked at the door. She fished a card from her back pocket and stuck it in his shirt pocket. "My number's on this. Call me anytime. I mean it. Call me. One more thing. Can I have your permission to share what we talk about with Dr. Bennet?"

"I don't know."

"How bad you want to get over this shit?"

All Lee wanted to do was to go through that door. "Sure. Go ahead. Tell her. Damn." He headed to the door.

From behind him, Brigid said, "See you in three days."

He shrugged and left.

Chapter 12

The house was quiet when Lee got home. His dad usually faded in the late afternoon and fell asleep in his recliner in front of the blaring television. Lee checked the front room, then Merle's bedroom. "Dad, where the hell are you?" He checked the rest of the house. The walker was gone along with Merle's shaggy winter coat.

Lee dashed outside and called out, "Dad, Dad, where you at?" He trotted down the sidewalk despite his aching back, calling out for him. Halfway down the block, he spotted footprints and the wheel tracks of a walker on a short section of sidewalk where the snow had not been cleared. He continued down the block and to the next one, calling for his dad and scanning the yards.

Merle had never wandered off but had become increasingly confused in the late afternoons. Lee pictured his dad lying frozen in some backyard. He'd seen this on the job where someone had wandered off and was found frozen solid as a chunk of ice. As much as his father disgusted him, he couldn't let that happen. He had to find him.

After scouring the neighborhood and knocking on neighbors' doors until darkness set in, he went home and called the police. He blew out a sigh of relief when he was told that someone had called two hours ago, reporting they had found an elderly man who fit Lee's description wandering through the neighborhood with his walker. The police were going to send someone over when they had an available squad, but they were backed up. It could be hours. They gave Lee the address and told him they would hold off sending anyone unless Lee requested it.

The home was one street over and three blocks away. Lee drove to the massive light purple Victorian house at the address the police had given him. He and Merle had driven by this pristine house countless times. It stood out among the decaying homes in the area. During the summer, lush flowerbeds surrounded it. Children of all ages would often be seen playing in the yard and hanging out on the porch. When Merle spotted them, he typically asked, "Why do these people have to have so many kids?"

How the hell did he get this far? Lee thought while limping up the stairs of the wide porch. He rapped on the door. He stood speechless when the towering bald Black man opened the door. The man's pronounced overbite spread into a broad grin. "This is certainly the good Lord's work," the man said, his voice deep and resonant. "The police said someone would be by and there you are."

"Yeah, I'm Lee Garrison. They said my father…"

"How could I forget you? You're the firefighter who saved our Alexus. God bless you, Mr. Garrison."

Before Lee could say anything, the man grasped his hand and snagged him into a bear hug. When he let go, the man's cheeks were wet with tears. "My Lord, this is such a blessing to meet you. I'm Clarence Williams. Everyone calls me Brother Williams. Please come in. Your father's in the kitchen. My wife's been tending to him. He's doing just fine, although a bit addled."

"How did he end up here?"

"I saw him two blocks over on 44th Street on my way back from church. He wasn't moving, just leaning on his walker. The way his legs were shaking, he looked ready to collapse. I pulled to the curb and asked if he needed help. He mumbled something and shook his head, but the look on his face told me otherwise."

"And he went with you?"

"Cussed me out a bit and struggled when I … ah … kind of urged him into the car. But he was too weak and cold to put up much of a fight."

It didn't surprise Lee that Merle refused to get in the car. He was that stubborn. "I should be the one God-blessing you."

"I couldn't leave him out there. This way to the kitchen."

The front room smelled like a pine forest. A Christmas tree laden with all manner of ornaments and multi-colored lights reached the tall ceiling. Presents of various shapes and sizes with shiny red and silver wrappings lay beneath the tree. Brother Williams stopped at the tree. "I love how excited the children get for Christmas. It's truly contagious."

Lee gazed at the white angel with a hand-drawn golden smiley face and glittery silver wings at the top of the tree.

As Brother Williams led him to the kitchen, the smell of baking bread and roasting beef had Lee salivating. When they entered the cavernous kitchen, Merle was seated at a long oak table with benches on each side, much like the firehouse kitchen. Merle's eyes widened when he saw Lee.

"Bernice, you'll never guess who the good Lord brought us," Brother Williams said. "This is the man who rescued our Alexus."

A petite woman seated next to Merle gasped, then said, "Oh, my Lord." She rose and rushed around the end of the table. "This a miracle for sure. I'm Miss Bernie, Alexus's momma." She wiped her hands on her dark purple apron and embraced Lee in a full-bodied hug. All this hugging felt awkward. Lee's arms hung at his side.

Miss Bernie guided him to the table. "Set yourself down. I was just gettin' ready to serve your papa some supper. We didn't know when somebody'd be by."

"Thanks, but we should get going. I want to thank you..."

Miss Bernie planted her hands on her hips. "You set yourself down while I put out supper. Least we can do is feed you and your papa."

Lee slid next to Merle on the bench seat. Merle asked, "What the hell is going on? Why we here?"

Lee put his finger to his lips. "Shh."

Merle opened his mouth to say something. Lee shook his head, frowning. Merle grunted.

Their attention turned to Miss Bernie, who went to the stove and pulled a huge blue-speckled roaster from the oven and spooned chunks of beef, potatoes, and carrots into three large serving bowls. She poured thick brown gravy over all of it and spread the bowls across the table. She went back to the stove and pulled a baking sheet of steaming biscuits from the oven. She guided the hot biscuits into two wicker bread baskets and placed them on the table. Three pitchers of grape Kool-Aid and three saucers of butter were added. At the end of the table, Miss Bernie placed a stack of plates, utensils, and mismatched plastic cups.

That's enough food for two fire companies, Lee thought, then whispered to Merle, "Where were you going today?"

Merle threw up his arms.

Lee turned to Brother Williams. "I don't understand how he could have walked that far. He can't even get himself up from the floor." Lee glanced at Merle, then said to Brother Williams, "He's never wandered off before."

"When you come to know Jesus, you learn there are no coincidences. I would tell you the good Lord wanted you both here. Never underestimate his power. Sometimes we have to trust he has a plan for us."

Lee was not a believer and was glad Brother Williams had not asked. But he had been involved in enough fires where inexplicable things happened that made him wonder. Like how had he found those two little girls in that burning basement last month so fast?

When he got back to the firehouse that night and went to write the fire report, the incident printout showed he got those girls out in under a minute. To find them in that pitch-black basement that quickly was beyond miraculous. He never missed a step going to their bed. He was convinced it was no coincidence. Something had pulled him right to those two unconscious little girls.

Miss Bernie patted Lee on the back while placing plates and utensils in front of him and Merle. "Let us enjoy the Lord's gifts. We can talk later." She turned to Brother Williams. "We're ready. You can call the children."

Brother Williams went to the living room and called out in a deep baritone, "Children, supper's on."

The floor above came alive with pounding feet and creaking floorboards, followed by rumbling from the stairway. Eight chattering children rushed into the kitchen, staring at Lee and Merle. Brother Williams held up his giant hand. The room went silent. "Children, Mr. Garrison here is the man who saved our Alexus. Before we eat, I want each of you to give him a hug and thank him."

The little girl with the tight braids who appeared to be around nine or ten years old wasted no time rushing up to Lee and resting her head on his chest while hugging him. "You save my life." She kissed him on the cheek. "Never forget you." Lee patted her on her shoulder, not knowing how to respond. She leaned back, studying him with her intense dark brown eyes. "You don't hug so good." She pulled up the pant legs on her jeans, exposing her knobby knees. "That floor was hot. Burned my knees. See? But I didn't cry."

"No, you didn't. You were very brave."

The rest of the children lined up in order from the youngest girl, who appeared to be around four, to the oldest boy, who must have been in his mid-teens. While all of this was going on, Merle stared across the room with a blank, zombie-like expression.

Once everyone was seated, Miss Bernie banged a serving spoon on the table. The children hushed and bowed their heads. Lee poked Merle on the arm. Merle wrinkled his brow. Lee tapped Merle's temple and pointed down. Merle lowered his head.

Miss Bernie grinned and cleared her throat. "Lord, bless this bountiful meal we're about to share with these two men you brought to our home today. Since Mr. Garrison and Alexus survived that awful fire, I know you have a grand plan for them. God bless all of us and guide us in your loving ways. Amen."

"Amen," the children chanted along with Brother Williams. The children passed plates and utensils around the table. Platters of food followed. Cups were filled with grape Kool-Aid.

As they ate, the laughter and chatter of the excited children grew louder and louder as they talked about Christmas and what they wanted for presents. When they finished eating, the children went to work clearing the table, sweeping the floor, and washing dishes. Each child, from the youngest to the oldest, had a job. Nobody whined. They all dove into the work with enthusiasm, laughing and talking the whole time.

Lee said to Brother Williams, "I can't believe how well-behaved these kids are."

"It's all about setting expectations and demanding they be met." He grinned wide. "I can be quite convincing. Works at my school and works here."

Lee could believe that. The huge man was an intimidating force.

Merle glanced around the room with a confused look on his face. He tugged on Lee's arm. "I need to go home."

"Not before you have some of my sweet potato pie and coffee," Miss Bernie said. "You men go on into the front room. I'll bring the pie and coffee. We can talk while the children finish with chores."

After two bites of pie, Merle's chin dropped to his chest. Within seconds, he was snoring. Miss Bernie took the plate from his lap and placed it on an end table, then removed her purple apron and draped it over her chair."

"I take it your favorite color is purple," Lee said to her.

"Purple's the color of hope. Something too many of the children around here have lost. Without hope, there's nothing. That's why we take in these children—to give them that purple hope."

Lee thought about what she said. Without hope, there's nothing. Had he lost all hope in finding peace or in any joy in living? Was Dr. Bennet the answer?

When Lee finished eating, he said, "You have a beautiful family." He pointed to an eight-by-ten photograph on the buffet cabinet that pictured Miss Bernie with what appeared to be a tall, gangly adolescent boy and a girl who looked like a teenage version of Miss Bernie. "Your daughter looks just like you."

Brother Williams glanced at Miss Bernie, who lowered her gaze to her folded hands.

Lee looked from Brother Williams to Miss Bernie. "I'm sorry. I didn't mean to…"

"No, no," Miss Bernie said, "I'm still paining over those two. They both gone. My boy, Jamal, kilt by a young man who was taken over by the devil." She looked to the ceiling, choking back tears.

Lee and Brother Williams sat in silence, waiting for Miss Bernie to collect herself. After several long minutes, she said, "And my girl, Lettie. My beautiful girl. She gone too." Miss Bernie went to the buffet and ran her finger over the image of Lettie. "You were such a blessing. Every day I pray the good Lord forgive me for being so hard on you and bring you back to me." She wiped at her eyes with a purple hanky and went to the kitchen.

Brother Williams told Lee how Miss Bernie's daughter, Latonya, whom everyone called Lettie, had run off after fighting with her mother about boys and running the streets. That was over twelve years ago. Miss Bernie never saw her again. She would be 26 now. The word was that she had run off to Chicago. Miss Bernie had made numerous trips there, pleading with the police to help find her daughter. She roamed the streets of the south side of Chicago, showing a picture of Lettie to anyone who would stop.

Brother Williams pointed to the handmade angel at the top of the Christmas tree. "Miss Bernie cherishes that angel. She and Lettie made that together when Lettie was eight."

"What was she, around 14 when she ran away? Were the police any help at all?"

"Sadly, lots of runaways around here. Police don't spend much time looking."

"That is so damn…"

"Yes, my man. Incredibly tragic. We're both praying the good Lord will reveal His plan to us. And just so you're not confused, Jamal and Lettie are Miss Bernie's children from a previous marriage. We've only been married for two years."

"Wait. So where did all these kids come from?"

Brother Williams' booming laughter echoed through the room. "Your confusion is written all over your face. We take in foster children. Tending to them gives Miss Bernie such joy. Helps ease the pain of her losses. We had to convert the upper flat to bedrooms for all these children."

"They let you take in this many kids?"

"The system is overwhelmed with Black children, especially older ones. They have nowhere else to place them."

It occurred to Lee, how firefighters were looked upon as heroes when they were just doing their jobs. Brother Williams and Miss Bernie were the true heroes, saving these children from being discarded. After giving this some thought, he said, "Do you have any idea who might have started the school fire?"

"I think somehow Sunrise Schools might have something to do with it. They've made it clear they want to take over the inner-city voucher schools in Milwaukee. They've already made substantial offers to me and others, but I didn't start this school for the money. I wanted to offer a place where our public schools could send at-risk children who were struggling and had little hope of graduating. These are very troubled, angry children who have seen too much violence and feel hopeless. Sunrise is not the answer. What would they know about helping these children? No amount of money will buy me out."

"You think they would burn your school down to get the vouchers?"

"The morning after the fire, I received an anonymous call, demanding I sell the school. This morning, I received another call that said time was running out. I needed to sell now before drastic action had to be taken."

"Do they mean legal action?"

"I don't know what that would be."

"Do the police know?"

"They're investigating."

"What now, with your school gone?"

"We'll start Christmas break early. When school starts again, we'll spread our students and teachers around to the churches in the area. They'll be more than happy to help until we can rebuild."

"Won't they just burn your school down again?"

"Pray they don't."

Lee rose from his chair. "I can't thank you enough for taking care of my father. And for the wonderful supper. We should go. Please thank Miss Bernie for me." He went to Merle and shook him by the shoulder. "Let's go home."

Merle opened his eyes and squinted at Lee. "Who are…? Oh, you."

"Time to go," Lee ordered as Merle struggled to get up. Lee helped him to his walker, wondering again how he was able to get as far as he did earlier.

When Lee got to the front door, a flurry of gunshots rang out from the street. The sound of shattering glass came from the second floor. Lee dropped to all fours, an instinctive move from years in the inner city. He motioned for Merle to get down, but Merle froze. Brother Williams rushed up the stairs. Lee cracked the front door open. A faded-green Buick Riviera drove off. "Stay back," he shouted at Merle and headed up the stairs.

Brother Williams peered out the shattered bedroom window. Bullet holes riddled the ceiling. "Thank the good Lord none of the children were up here."

Miss Bernie burst into the room, followed by the children. Brother Williams corralled them. "Everyone, back downstairs." The wide-eyed children gawked at the broken window as they headed to the stairway. Miss Bernie put her hand over her mouth. "Oh, my Lord."

"We better get downstairs, too," Brother Williams said to Lee and Miss Bernie. "We need to get the police. Keep everyone in the kitchen until we know it's safe."

When they got everyone to the kitchen, Lee said to Brother Williams, "The shooters were driving an old green Riviera."

"I saw it too. That's the One-Niners' car."

While they waited for the police, Merle kept asking what was going on. Miss Bernie answered patiently, explaining how someone had shot at their house. He would nod each time, appearing to understand, then ask the same question a short time later.

When the police arrived, a plainclothes detective with black hair neatly slicked back questioned Brother Williams. The detective assured them they would be patrolling the neighborhood all night. They'd also raid the crack house where the One-Niners were known to hang out.

The police wrapped up their investigation after nine o'clock.

After they left, Lee asked Brother Williams, "Why are the One-Niners shooting up your house?"

"Doesn't make sense. I was one of them once."

"What?"

"That's a story for another time."

Chapter 13

The next morning, Lee lay in bed thinking about the drive-by shooting and the heart-wrenching story of Miss Bernie's son and daughter. He couldn't get the grief-stricken look on her face out of his head. He desperately wanted to help her and Brother Williams. But how? A foreign sound coming from the kitchen pulled him from his thoughts. Laughing.

Across the kitchen table from Merle sat Alexus, chattering away. When she saw Lee, her eyebrows shot up and she ran to him, hugging him around the waist. Lee pushed her away and held her at arm's length. "Why are you here?"

"Your papa let me in. Momma Bernie said I could bring you chocolate chip cookies."

"Did you walk here alone?"

"Papa Williams walk me over. After last night, he don't want me on the street alone."

Cookie crumbs littered the front of Merle's shirt. He leered at Lee. "Now this is good eatin'. Not like that slop you feed me." He snatched another cookie from the wicker bread basket and stuffed half the cookie in his mouth.

Lee couldn't resist. He pulled a giant cookie from the basket and took a bite, savoring the gooey flavor of cinnamon, butter, brown sugar, and chocolate. Alexus took one for herself and said, "Momma Bernie showed me how to make 'em, but I did everything myself."

Lee flashed back to a memory of standing on a kitchen chair next to his mother, mixing a bowl of chocolate chip cookie batter and licking the spoon.

He asked, "Why do you call her Momma Bernie?"

"My real momma in prison for killing the man who was mean to me and my big sister. Momma Bernie took us in as foster kids and adopted me."

"Why didn't she adopt your sister?"

"She gone."

"What happened to her?"

"They say she's dead. I don't believe 'em. I know she still out there."

Lee choked on his cookie. After clearing his throat he asked, "Did she run away?"

"Where you keep your broom?"

The conversation was over. Lee pointed to the closet. "You don't need to clean up. I should take you home."

"If you didn't pull me out that fire, I wouldn't even be here."

"Just doing my job."

"I'm not gonna leave you and your papa living in all this mess. Least I can do." She went to the closet, pulled out the broom, and swept up the cookie crumbs.

Lee looked to Merle and shrugged. Merle said, "About time we got some help around here." He swiveled in his chair. "Hey, little girl, can you do the dishes too?"

"Name's Alexus, not 'little girl'. Mind your manners."

Lee snorted. "Yeah, mind your manners, Old Man."

After Alexus finished sweeping, she went about mopping the floor, then washed the dishes while Lee pondered what Brother Williams had said about the violence these children in the Core experience. Miss Bernie's son murdered, her daughter gone, Alexus's sister thought to be dead, their mother in prison for murder, and all these foster children needing a home. Does anyone outside the Core even care about these kids?

When Alexus finished, Lee walked her back to her house. Bullet holes riddled the second-floor purple siding. Plastic sheeting covered the broken-out window. Miss Bernie met them at the door. "See you finished off that girl's cookies. Hope she wasn't a bother."

Alexus pulled Lee's head down and kissed him on the cheek. "You my hero."

Lee straightened. "Just doing my job."

Alexus ran up the stairs.

Miss Bernie grasped Lee's hand. "The love of a child is precious. Embrace it. C'mon inside and warm up. We got someone coming by this morning for you to meet."

In the living room, two small boys squealed as they tried to pin an older boy to the floor. Above them, it sounded like a stampeding herd of buffalo.

"These kids get excitable during Christmas break," Miss Bernie said. "Best to let them blow off steam. I know they loud, but I surely love that sound."

Brother Williams was at the kitchen table. "Sit down, my man. You need to help me finish off that pie from last night."

Miss Bernie had a slice of pie slathered with whipped cream ready for Lee along with a mug of steaming coffee before he could say no. "Gotta finish up some sewing. I'll let you men talk." She went to the front room.

After a few bites of pie, Lee said, "Did you hear anything from the police?"

"Detective Boyle called this morning and said there was no sign of the One-Niners at the crack house. He assured me they would keep looking." Brother Williams ran his hand over his bald head and blew out a loud breath. "But what's troubling is they were seen around the school the morning of the fire according to the detective."

"He thinks they started the school fire?"

"This surely has me perplexed."

"Do you think that Sunrise hired them to burn your school down?"

Brother William stared at his coffee mug, gritting his teeth.

Lee finished off his pie.

Brother Williams got up from the table and took their plates to the sink. While Brother Williams rinsed their plates, Lee wondered how he had ever been involved with this violent street gang, a gang that shot up his house and possibly burned down his school. He couldn't imagine this gregarious gentle giant causing anyone harm.

When Brother Williams returned to the table, Lee couldn't hold back. "I have to say, I don't get it. You were a member of that gang? I mean, I don't know you that well, but still…"

"Well, my man, not something I'm proud of. I was a member many years ago. I joined when I was only sixteen. Like many, I grew up in a horribly dysfunctional home … It's no excuse for getting caught up in all of that. I was falsely convicted of murder when I was nineteen. A drug deal had gone bad and a young man lost his life. I wasn't a part of that, but a witness identified me as one of the assailants. Thank the good Lord for the University of Wisconsin's Innocence Project who tracked down the witness. He recanted his story, but I spent ten years in prison before being exonerated."

"Ten years in prison for a crime you didn't commit? How did you ever get over that?"

"I needed to see the darkness before I could see the light of our good Lord and dedicate my life to serving Jesus Christ and my community. Reverend Turner and my church helped me start

Odyssey School. That's why I will never give it up." Brother Williams clasped his hands together as if in prayer and nodded solemnly.

Lee wanted to know more, but Brother Williams looked lost in thought. The questions could wait. He said, "Miss Bernie said she had someone she wanted me to meet."

Before Brother Williams could reply, a young man wearing a weathered tan Carhartt winter coat and a faded green baseball cap with the John Deere logo on it strolled into the kitchen. He removed his cap and said, "I'm thinking that would be me."

Miss Bernie moved alongside him and pointed at Lee. "Mitch, this the man who rescued Alexus."

"She's not Lexi anymore?" Mitch asked.

"Said Lexi's a kid's name. Claims she's not a kid anymore."

Mitch grinned, then said, "Sounds like our Lexi."

Mitch reached out his hand to Lee. "Miss Bernie told me about you rescuing Lexi—I mean Alexus—darn solid. I had to drive in to meet you. I'm Mitch Garner."

Lee stood. While shaking Mitch's hand, he said, "You're pretty legendary around Engine 15. The front-page newspaper article about you still hangs in the firehouse."

"Ah, you know how that goes. I happened to be the firefighter in the right place at the right time. Any other brother or sister would have done the same thing."

Lee liked this young man already. Mitch had gone into the burning home across from Engine 15 alone without backup and nearly lost his life rescuing a child.

"Not sure I agree," Lee said, "but in any event, solid rescue yourself."

"How you getting along with my old crew?"

"They're all right," Lee lied.

"I had a blast with those guys. They taught me so much about fighting fires and other stuff I probably didn't need to know."

"I have to ask," Lee said, desperately trying to change the subject, pointing at a scar barely visible running across the top of Mitch's forehead. "You get that from the job?"

Mitch ran a hand over his disheveled jet-black hair. "Crashed a combine a long time ago."

"Combine?"

"We were harvesting wheat. I nodded off and rolled it down a ravine."

"I heard you moved back to the farm when you left the department. How's that going?"

"I loved fighting fires and helping Brother Williams out at the school on my off days. But farming is in my blood. That's where I belong. And I can still come back here a lot to help Miss Bernie and Brother Williams, especially in the winter, like now, when there's not much to do on the farm. I'm only an hour away. I've been working on finishing their basement and turning it into a game room for the kids. The older kids love helping."

"You men set yourselves down," Miss Bernie said as she placed a slice of pie and a cup of coffee on the table in front of Mitch. She rubbed his back and said to Lee, "Mitch rented my upper flat when he come to Milwaukee. He was such a blessing to all of us. Always doing for others."

"That's your fault," Mitch said, grinning. "You're the one who taught me all that." He turned to Lee. "So, Captain, how long you been on?"

"Thirty-two years."

Mitch whistled, then said, "When you planning to pull the pin?"

"Do I look that old?"

Mitch chuckled, then said, "No, but that's a lot of years chasing fires and running the streets all night long."

No choice, Lee thought, and nodded.

Brother Williams didn't appear to be listening, somberly sipping his coffee. Mitch said to him, "Miss Bernie told me it was the One-Niners who shot up the house last night?"

Brother Williams slowly lowered the coffee cup to the table, gazing at it. "Police think they also started the school fire."

"Holy crap. That don't make sense. The One-Niners have kids in your school."

Brother Williams stood. "High time for a sit-down with them."

Chapter 14

Mitch

After Brother Williams left to meet with the One-Niners and the captain went home, Mitch took his suitcase upstairs to the boys' room. When Miss Bernie had called Mitch at the farm to tell him about the drive-by shooting, he decided he would stay with them until he knew they were safe. His wife Jennie was also close with the family and reluctantly gave her blessing for him to stay with them as long as he promised not to do anything stupid and to let the police take care of the One-Niners. Miss Bernie had cleared out some dresser space for him and there was a spare bunk in the boys' bedroom.

He spent the rest of the day in the basement with two of the older boys, framing the concrete block walls with two-by-fours, so he could insulate and drywall the basement. He had taught the boys carpentry skills and he let them do most of the work. This was what he helped with at Brother Williams' school—teaching the children how to safely use power tools and work with wood.

When Mitch and the boys went upstairs for supper, he smelled ham. Miss Bernie was at the stove stirring a large kettle. He peered into it. "You make the best bean soup."

"It's them ham hocks that dress it up."

Mitch smacked his lips, then asked, "Have you heard from Brother Williams?"

"Said the One-Niners disappeared. No sign of them anywhere. Nobody's seen them since the morning of the fire. He's gonna keep on looking."

As soon as Mitch took a seat at the table, the children poured into the kitchen. Alexus plunked down next to him. "Can we come to your farm again next summer? I love feeding the baby cows."

The other children shouted, "Me too."

Mitch raised his hands and said, "Only if Miss Bernie says you were all good."

Every summer after Mitch moved back to the farm, the Boys and Girls Club of Milwaukee brought a busload of children there to camp for a week. They'd all get assigned chores in the morning and ride horses on the trails in the afternoon. Some days, they'd go for evening hayrides. At night, there'd be a huge campfire with singing and s'mores. Miss Bernie took care of meals and Brother Williams ensured the children behaved themselves. Mitch and his family enjoyed hosting them as much as the children loved coming.

The next morning when Mitch came down for breakfast, he asked Miss Bernie, "Did Brother Williams ever come home last night."

"Well after midnight. Went out again early this morning. Said he has to keep looking. Stop 'em before they do any more of the devil's work."

Mitch was anxious to visit with his old crew at Engine 15, but they wouldn't be on duty until tomorrow, the next redshift. It had been over a year since he stopped by. With Brother Williams out looking for the One-Niners, Mitch thought it best to hang around the house in case any more trouble cropped up. He spent the day working on the basement with the boys.

After supper, Mitch went to the front room with three of the younger children. They sat around the Christmas tree, telling Mitch who each of the gifts was for and what they were hoping to get.

Watching the excitement of the children got him thinking about how fun this Christmas would be now that his daughter was almost two.

It was after eight o'clock when Brother Williams trudged through the front door. The children ran to him for a group hug. His smile was strained and shoulders stooped. Miss Bernie came into the front room. "Children, let's give Papa Williams some peace. You go on upstairs now and get ready for bed."

The children scampered up the stairs. Miss Bernie went to Brother Williams and kissed him on the cheek. "C'mon in the kitchen. You look froze. There's some bean soup left over from last night. That'll surely warm your bones."

"Bless you."

Mitch followed them to the kitchen. He and Brother Williams sat while Miss Bernie filled a saucepan with soup.

"Any luck?" Mitch asked.

"No trace of them. I know some of their families and they haven't seen them in days. I'm at my wit's end."

"Maybe the cops will be able to track some of them down."

"Doubtful."

Brother Williams looked cold and exhausted. Mitch left him and Miss Bernie alone and went up to the boys' bedroom, where they were playing with Legos. Mitch joined them, building an intricate barn and farmhouse that delighted the boys. Alexus padded into the room wearing pink pajamas and clutching a Black Cabbage Patch Doll to her chest. "Why does Mr. Garrison look so mad all the time? It's kind of scary."

"Sometimes people only look mad, but they're not."

"Do you think he likes me?"

"Of course he does. And when he gets to know you better, I think he'll love you as much as I do."

"He don't act like it," she said and snuggled next to him as he watched the boys add to his Lego structures. As she drifted off, Mitch thought about all this little girl had been through with her mother in prison and her sister murdered.

Chapter 15

Mitch

After breakfast the following morning, Mitch headed to Engine House 15 in his brown Dodge Ram pickup. The roads were still slick from the snowstorm last week. In some areas, only one lane was open due to cars being snowed in. He pulled around back. It was before nine a.m. His old crew would be at the kitchen table for their morning bull session.

He pounded on the back door. Kenny opened it. Ralph, Crusher, and a lieutenant Mitch had never met were at the table. A skinny young man whom Mitch pegged as the cub was at the counter, pouring water into the Bunn coffee maker.

Crusher said, "Holy crap. Is that? No, it can't be."

Kenny went to his knees and bowed twice. "We're not worthy, oh, master. What brings you to our humble abode?" He rose, smiled wide, and clapped Mitch on the back.

"Yeah, yeah, yeah. Thought I'd stop by to check on you outlaws. I met your new captain the other day."

Ralph's lips hardened into a thin line. He studied the cigar he had been chewing on. "Total dickwad."

Mitch raised his eyebrows at him. "Oh?—Okay."

"About damn time you stopped around," Ralph said, then grinned. "Nice to see you, kid. Sit down. So, tell us. What kept you away?"

Mitch took a seat and immediately felt at home. He had spent many hours at this table with this crew. *Why didn't I come back sooner,* he chided himself, then said, "Ah, you know, farm work, family, helping Brother Williams at the school and Miss Bernie with the kids. Never seemed to have enough time."

"The school," Kenny said. "You won't be helping there anymore. Burned down last week."

"I heard you guys made a darn nice save."

"That was the captain," Kenny said.

Ralph lit the cigar he had been chewing on. "Asshole went in alone," Ralph said.

The lieutenant glanced at the lit cigar but said nothing.

Kenny pointed at Mitch. "Kinda like a cub going in alone at the fire across the street four years ago."

"Where is the captain?" Mitch asked.

"I'm filling in for him," the lieutenant said. "I was told he'd be off for a couple weeks."

"Know why?"

"Nope."

Kenny said, "Who cares? How about prime rib for lunch today to celebrate?"

Crusher patted his rotund belly. "You bet. Wife's been starving me. Says I'm getting too fat."

Kenny laughed. "Don't listen to her. You're a fine specimen."

Ralph said, "Specimen of what? A blue whale? Stay away from the beach. Someone'll roll your fat ass back in the water."

Laughter echoed off the walls. This camaraderie is what Mitch missed most about the fire service.

Ralph turned to the young firefighter. "Anderson, get our long-lost hero some coffee."

When Anderson placed a cup of coffee in front of him, Mitch said, "I'm Mitch Garner. How these animals treating you?"

"You're pretty famous around here," Anderson said, pointing to the newspaper article hanging on the wall.

"Forget about that. I was in the right place at the right time. How much time you got on?"

"Just got my year on. A group of us had a party two nights ago to celebrate. It was pretty wild."

"Got pictures?" Kenny asked.

Anderson pulled some photos from his back pocket and handed them to Kenny.

"Whoa. You had strippers? Nice."

As Kenny went through the photos, he passed them around.

Crusher pointed to a blurry photo of a man with his arms crossed, watching the crowd. The blood-red tattoo on his thick bicep appeared to say MOMMA FAILED. "Hey, Ralph. Isn't that your kid's tattoo?"

Ralph snatched the photo from Crusher. "Gimme that."

"What was he doing at a year-on party?"

Anderson said, "Hells Disciples were the bodyguards for the girls."

Ralph scowled at Anderson. "Need to keep your mouth shut, kid."

Mitch gasped when Kenny handed him one of the photos. "Holy crap. Where was this?"

"Backroom of the Crystal Palace," said Anderson.

Mitch grabbed his forehead. "I gotta keep this," he said and rushed out the back door breathless, his heart racing. He jumped in his truck and sped out of the back parking area, stopping in front of the vacant lot across the street. He clutched the photo in his shaking hand, not believing what he was seeing. He broke down, sobbing as the memories of the girl he loved as much as his own daughter flooded his thoughts. This was the girl he became close with through a department mentoring program. The girl he rescued from the house fire on this vacant lot that her mom's crackhead boyfriend had started after it came out he was molesting her. The girl whose mom went to prison for killing that boyfriend. The girl who was killed by the leader of the One-Niners for refusing to sell herself on the streets for him. Alexus's big sister.

But how? Mitch thought, staring at the photo. *Jasmine. It is you.*

He had to call Jennie, his wife. When she answered, he tried to talk but choked on the words.

"Mitch, honey, you okay? Talk to me."

He took two deep breaths, then said, "Jasmine. She's alive."

Silence.

"Did you hear me?" Mitch asked.

"Oh, my God. I can't believe it. Is she with you?"

"Not yet. I have to find her. She's with the Hells Disciples."

"What's she doing with that outlaw gang?"

"Dancing."

"You mean stripping?"

It was painful to admit the young girl he had mentored was now a stripper. "Jennie. I have to find her."

After a long pause, Jennie said, "I know. I hate to keep saying this, but please do not do anything stupid. You know what I mean. And let the police help. Do not do this yourself."

"I have to find her."

"Your daughter wants to say hi … Say hi to your daddy."

"Hi, Daddy. Santa's coming."

"I know. He's got some fun presents for you."

"Love you." Her little voice lifted his spirits.

"I love you too."

"Bye, Daddy."

"Bye, Sweetheart."

"What's your plan?" Jennie asked when she came back on the phone.

"Start asking around. Find out where they have her. Then figure out how to get her away from them."

"You know I love that girl as much as you, but you have a family to take care of. Let the police handle this."

During his time as a firefighter in Milwaukee, he learned that the MPD was short-staffed and overwhelmed. If they agreed to investigate, it would be a long process. He needed to get Jasmine away from the Disciples now. "I won't do anything stupid."

"And let the police handle it?"

"I won't do anything stupid."

After a long pause, Jennie sighed, then said, "Just don't do this yourself. Can you promise me that?"

"Promise."

"Good. Now go find our Jasmine."

Chapter 16

Lee

After breakfast, Lee headed over to Miss Bernie's house with his dad. She had suggested Lee drop his dad off at their place whenever he needed to get out. Brother Williams met them at the door and escorted them to the kitchen where the aroma of simmering tomatoes and cumin filled the room. Miss Bernie stood at the stove stirring a huge kettle of chili. "I hope you men are hungry."

"We already ate," Lee said. "But thank you anyway. I wanted to visit my mother over at Pleasant Manor. Is it okay to leave my dad with you?"

Miss Bernie looked over her shoulder at Merle. "You don't want to go see your wife?"

Merle stood at his walker, shaking his head. "She don't want to see me. Is that chili you're making over there?"

"Dad. We ate lunch already."

"Wouldn't call that swill you feed me lunch."

Screw you, Lee wanted to say, but not in front of Miss Bernie.

Miss Bernie waved her hand at Lee. "You go on now. We'll take care of your papa." She escorted Merle to the table. "Set yourself down."

Merle flashed a mocking grin at Lee and sat.

When Lee was about to get in his car, Mitch pulled to the curb behind him and leaped out of his truck. "I stopped over to the firehouse this morning. They said you were off for two weeks. Everything okay?"

"Back's acting up." *It's not really a lie,* Lee assured himself.

"I have some unbelievable news. Let's go inside."

"I gotta get going."

"Forget that. You need to see this."

Mitch raced up the steps with Lee following, knowing whatever the crew had told Mitch about him would be damn negative.

When they got to the kitchen, Mitch tossed a photo of a topless stripper onto the table. He had blackened out her bare breasts. "Miss Bernie. You have to see this."

Miss Bernie glanced over her shoulder, "Mitch, honey, can I look at your pictures later? I got to get lunch ready for these hungry kids."

"You'll want to see this."

Miss Bernie wiped her hands on her purple apron, took a seat at the table, and analyzed the photo. She clasped her hand over her mouth. "Oh, Lord. Can't be."

"That's what I said. But look at the scar on her neck."

"Jasmine!" Miss Bernie swayed backward.

Brother Williams moved behind her and rested his hands on her shoulders. "Alexus knew she was alive," he said.

"She was at a party at the Crystal Palace just two nights ago," Mitch said. He turned to Lee. "Ralph's kid was there. His club was providing girls for Anderson's year-on party."

"Ralph's kid was at the firehouse the other day. Total scumbag."

Miss Bernie continued staring at the photo. "How in the world did our Jasmine end up with that bunch?"

Brother Williams rubbed her shoulders. "All that matters is she's alive, bless the Lord."

"I'm going over to the Disciples clubhouse," Mitch said.

Lee rubbed his chin. "Hold on. That's a pretty rough group. I know you're ballsy, but you might want to think this through. Probably not a good idea to go storming in there. Let me help. See what I can find out. I gotta check in on my mother. The nursing home's expecting me. I should be back after lunch. Don't do anything till I get back."

Mitch picked up the photo, shaking his head. "I can't just sit here. I gotta do something."

"Wait for me. I won't be long."

Mitch put the photo back on the table. "Hurry."

* * *

When he finished his short visit with his mother, Lee rushed back to Miss Bernie's house. Mitch was pacing the living room when Lee returned.

"We gotta get her away from them, now," Mitch said.

"Let's see if Anderson knows anything."

Lee drove them to the firehouse. Anderson was in the front room monitoring radio transmissions when they showed up at the thick glass entry door. He scrambled to the door and let them in. "Hey, Boss. You okay? Lieutenant said you'd be off for two weeks."

"The rest of the crew down for the afternoon?"

"Yeah, I'm holding down the fort."

"Good. Let's go to the kitchen. We got some questions."

Anderson told them that one of his fellow probationers had an uncle who was a member of Hells Disciples. He arranged to have them supply four strippers for their private year-on party.

"Is that all the girls did was dance?" Mitch asked.

"There were some lap dances. I didn't go for any of that. Not my thing. But a few guys said the girls offered special services. As far as I know, nobody took them up on it."

Mitch clenched his lips. "Crap. We can't wait. We gotta get her away from those bastards."

"You sure that was Ralph's kid at the party?" Lee asked Anderson.

"I recognized him from that morning he stopped by the firehouse. I don't think he recognized me, though."

"You think your buddy could find out from his uncle where the girls are?"

"I'll give it a shot."

Ralph strolled into the kitchen and stopped when he saw Lee. "Thought we were rid of you for a while." He looked at Mitch. "So, what you all been talking about?"

Lee asked, "What was your kid doing at a year-on party?"

Ralph leered at Anderson. "Thought I said to keep your mouth shut."

"Lay off, Ralph," Lee said. "This is about your kid. Not him."

A recently promoted lieutenant Lee recognized rushed into the kitchen. "What's all the hollering…? Oh, didn't see you there, Captain. I'll let you gents finish your discussion." He went back to the office.

Mitch stepped between Lee and Ralph. "Look, Ralph, you need to know that your son's bike club is prostituting young girls. One of the girls is Jasmine, that girl from across the street we rescued. You need to help us find her."

Holy shit, Lee thought. The girl Mitch rescued was Alexus's sister Jasmine.

"That girl's dead," Ralph said. "Has to be someone else."

"No. It's her. You need to help us."

"Help you what? Bust my kid? Look, I don't know what the hell his club is doing and I don't want to know."

"But Ralph, what about Jasmine? You okay with that?"

Ralph pointed his finger at Mitch's chest. "We're done." Ralph spun and slammed through the double doors to the apparatus floor.

Mitch called out, "Ralph." The doors swung shut.

"Why didn't someone tell me it was Alexus's sister you rescued?" Lee asked Mitch.

"Assumed you knew, I guess."

"What happened to her?"

"We all thought she was murdered after she recovered from the fire."

"Damn."

"I'll tell you about it later. We need to find her."

Lee wrote his cell phone number on a slip of paper from the pad they use for grocery shopping and handed it to Anderson. "Call if you hear anything at all or if Ralph gives you any shit."

Anderson stared at the television on top of the refrigerator. His mouth dropped. "Boss, check this out." He went to the television and turned up the volume.

On the screen, a video showed the towering flames engulfing the Odyssey School. This faded to a press conference of Mayor Reynolds, Fire Chief Peters, Police Chief Werner, and a tall, graying blond-haired man dressed in a navy blue pinstripe suit and a blood-red tie. Mayor Reynolds said he wanted to update the media on the Odyssey School fire. He talked about the horrible tragedy of the most successful inner-city voucher school burning down. He thanked Chief Peters for the heroic efforts of his department in saving the little girl's life. After a long-winded talk about his record of support for the police and fire departments, he turned it over to Fire Chief Brian Peters, who thanked the crew of Engine Company 15 for their outstanding efforts, then extolled the policies and procedures of his administration that were critical for the rescue of the girl.

"Damn," Anderson said. "He's talking like he was responsible for rescuing the little girl. Didn't even mention your name."

"That jag couldn't find his way out of a dark closet," Lee said. "Much less crawl his fat ass through a fire."

A reporter asked Fire Chief Peters whether the fire was arson. Police Chief Werner went to the microphone and said they had evidence of arson and prime suspects but couldn't comment on the ongoing investigation.

Mayor Reynolds returned to the podium. He introduced River Hills State Senator William Decker. The senator in the pinstripe suit told the reporters he was a strong advocate of inner-city voucher schools. He wanted to give the inner-city children of Milwaukee an alternative to the struggling public schools. He promised to work with the mayor and the Common Council on ways the state could help fund these voucher schools.

When the four men were done patting each other on the back for the great work they were doing for the city of Milwaukee, the reporter came on and said, "We'll keep you updated on the investigation. Now let's see what we have in store for the weather."

"What a joke," Lee said. "That rich knob from River Hills could give a shit about inner-city kids. He's trashed Milwaukee for years. Lying bastards, all of them."

"More political bull crap. But what are we going to do about Jasmine?" Mitch asked.

"Let's see what Anderson can find out."

"That might take a while," Mitch said. "I can't wait for that. I gotta do something. Take me back to my truck."

"What you planning?"

"A visit to the Disciples."

"Okay. But let's be wise about this."

Chapter 17

Lee

After they left the firehouse, Lee took Mitch back to Miss Bernie's to get his pickup truck. Mitch followed Lee to an abandoned warehouse on the near south side of Milwaukee that was across from the Disciple's clubhouse. They parked two blocks away and walked to the warehouse. The door to the rear entrance was broken off the hinges and lying on the ground. Lee limped behind Mitch up the stairwell to the expansive second floor that was vacant except for several black fifty-five-gallon drums. The tall windows were broken out with glass fragments lining the frames.

From this vantage point, they could see the clubhouse was a concrete block, single-story building that had once been some type of small manufacturer common in the area. The windows had been filled in with the same concrete blocks the walls were made of. A rusting metal door served as the front entrance. The building had a flat snow-covered roof with two rectangular dome skylights.

The minutes dragged by with no activity at the clubhouse. "I'm going to circle around back of the clubhouse and see what that looks like," Mitch said.

"I'll wait here," Lee said, shivering from the frigid wind blowing through the broken-out windows.

Lee watched Mitch casually walk down the street one block and then cross over to the other side. He went across a vacant field next to the clubhouse and disappeared around the back. While waiting for Mitch, Lee thought about how close the Williams family and Mitch were and how they wanted to embrace Lee for rescuing Alexus. He would help Mitch find Jasmine but couldn't let this family become attached to him. Life was simpler that way. As he was thinking about this, pounding bass came from up the street, followed by four cars. They pulled in front of the clubhouse. Ten Hells Disciples got out and went inside.

Where the hell was Mitch? Lee had to warn him. But a Disciple waited in a car at the entrance to the clubhouse, watching the street. Even with the car's windows rolled up, Lee could hear the loud bass of what sounded like heavy metal. He'd have to go out the back door of this warehouse and trudge through the snow behind two other warehouses before crossing the street to make sure the Disciple didn't notice him, then find a way to the back of the clubhouse without being seen. This was going to take a while.

As he turned to leave, out of the corner of his eye, he saw movement on the roof. It was Mitch making his way toward the front skylight. Lee wanted to move out of the shadows and get Mitch's attention but couldn't take the chance the Disciple would see him. Mitch had to hear the music from the car and must have heard all of the car doors slam shut.

Mitch went to his knees and peered into the skylight. He stayed like that for a long while, then went to the front of the flat roof and glanced over the parapet wall at the cars below. He walked back across the roof to the back skylight as if he were walking on thin ice. *Smart,* Lee thought. *Make sure they don't hear you up there.* Mitch watched through the skylight for a while then disappeared over the back of the roof.

After what felt like a good half hour, Lee worried the Disciples might have grabbed Mitch at the back of the clubhouse. Maybe they did hear him on the roof. Or saw him looking down through the skylights. The Disciple in the car was still watching the street.

Lee went down the back stairway of the warehouse and out into the parking lot. He trudged through the snow behind the next warehouse when something hit him in the back, sending a rush of adrenaline through him. He went to his hands and knees, looked back, and saw the remains of a hard-packed snowball. Mitch stood twenty feet away, waving. Lee rose, made his way back through the snow, and said, "Nice arm."

Mitch grinned. "Nice reflexes. I didn't want to holler in case that Disciple in the car heard."

"What did you see?"

"What I didn't see was Jasmine or any of the girls. Just the Disciples who were drinking and smoking dope. The place looks like a strip bar."

"You go to a lot of strip bars?"

"I know what a strip pole looks like. Let's get back up there. Maybe they'll still show up."

When they got back to the second floor of the warehouse, Lee asked, "Don't you have to get back to the farm?"

"Nah. My dad and brother can handle things while I'm gone. Not much to do during the winter."

"Where you staying?"

"I'm bunking with the two older boys at Miss Bernie's place. She always has extra beds in case Social Services needs an emergency placement for a foster kid."

"How long you plan to hang around?"

"As long as it takes to get Jasmine home. What about you? Don't you need to get back to take care of your dad?"

"You said you went through some tough times. Something happen on the job?"

Mitch told Lee that before he joined the Milwaukee Fire Department, he had been a member of his small-town volunteer fire department and was first on the scene at a neighboring farmhouse fire. A little girl he knew perished in the fire. Mitch was unable to rescue her and blamed himself for her horrific death, wishing he had died with her in that fire. He nearly took his own life to end the guilt and hopelessness that plagued him. When he saw what the firefighters did on 9/11, he thought if he could do what they did and risk his own life to save others, maybe he could live with himself. He left the farm and joined the Milwaukee Fire Department to prove he wasn't a coward and a loser.

As the youngest member of the crew, he told Lee, he was assigned to work with children in the neighborhood on reading and writing skills through a fire department mentoring program. That's how he met Jasmine and Alexus. He became frustrated by his inability to connect with inner-city children and was about to give up.

"When I told Miss Bernie this," Mitch said, "she lit into me. I still remember exactly what she said to me, 'Well, let me tell you something, Mr. Mitch. Think the only way to save people is pulling them out of burning buildings? These kids around here are dying just like if they in a fire. They just dying slower. Want to be a hero, figure how to help those young'uns.' I never forgot those words. Miss Bernie was right. Helping inner-city children like Alexus and Jasmine overcome the challenges of growing up in the Core saved me."

Lee swallowed hard. Mitch's story triggered Lee's choking guilt. "I know exactly how you felt when you said you wished you had died with her."

"Can you talk about it?"

Although they just met, Lee felt a connection through their common story of pain and guilt. This was someone who would understand.

The pent-up story Lee had struggled to keep buried all these years poured out of him. He was the cub that day. They were first on the scene of a church fire and made entry to the basement where the fire was raging. As they were crawling through the searing heat in the pitch-black basement, the hose line snagged. The boss ordered Lee to follow the line out and free it. When Lee got outside, another company made entry into the church with their hose line to back up his crew. After they crawled inside, the air horns on the rigs blared, indicating all companies needed to back out immediately. Lee looked up to see flames shooting into the cloudy gray sky from the steeple. He had to get to his crew to help them back out. He crawled through the door just as the steeple crashed through the roof. The interior of the church exploded in flames. The blistering heat forced Lee back to the doorway.

Before stepping outside, he saw a section of the floor collapse into the basement. His crew and the backup crew were both down there. Fire companies arriving on the scene frantically laid hose lines to the church. The scorching heat blocked access to the trapped firefighters as fire crews desperately blasted the flames with torrents of water. The PASS devices—Personal Alert Safety Systems—of the trapped members wailed. After the fire was knocked down, Lee and the other crews dug through the debris, praying for a miracle.

The vision of the serene look on his good friend's face and his mangled body when Lee found him buried in the rubble burned into his memory. Lee would never fight another major fire where he didn't struggle with the suffocating anxiety he felt that day. He knew there was no way he could have saved his crew, but he should have died with them in that basement. The Red Devil took seven heroes that day. It should have been eight.

This crew had helped Lee get over some of the pain of losing his fiancée. They included him in social activities like Brewers baseball games, softball games, or just gathering at a bar to vent about the job. He was one of them.

Lee could never allow anyone to get close to him again. Not after this devastating loss. Never again. Life would be simpler that way.

When he became an officer, he pushed his companies relentlessly with training exercises in search-and-rescue techniques, hose layouts in challenging buildings, raising ladders properly, and on and on. He knew he was not well-liked for being so hard on his people, but he was obsessed with the fear of losing a crew member in a fire.

Lee was breathing hard when he finished. His head throbbed. "After the investigation, nobody ever talked about it again. That's what we did back then—sucked it up and forgot about it."

"There is no forgetting. We both know that. Even with Miss Bernie's help, I still struggled at times until I started working with a psychologist at UW Hospital in Madison when I moved back to the farm."

"That helped?"

"He uses this therapy called EMDR. And yeah, it works. You should try it."

Dr. Bennet's therapy, Lee thought, nodding.

As night fell, the temperatures dropped and the wind picked up, gusting through the open windows. Mitch had on his thick Carhartt coat, insulated gloves, and a camo ski mask.

Lee's whole body shivered, his teeth chattering.

Mitch said, "You want to go home and get something warmer to wear?"

"I should probably pick up my dad and take him home. You okay here?"

"I'm good. Us farmers are used to being out in the elements. I'll see you tomorrow."

Lee couldn't get to his car fast enough.

Chapter 18

Lee

The next morning, Lee called Brigid and asked to meet her for breakfast. When she entered Miss Katie's Diner, Lee stood and motioned to the booth. She eyed him. "Didn't take you for the gentlemanly type."

"Oh, I'm a real peach. You didn't notice?"

"Yeah, not so much. I'm glad you called. I got the feeling you were gonna bail on the therapy."

"I met a firefighter who recommended it."

"Sure. You believe another firefighter but not a cop?"

"That's not it."

"Sure it is. You seeing the doctor today?"

"Yeah, but that's not why I wanted to see you." He told her about Jasmine, who was only sixteen, and how he was sure the Hells Disciples were prostituting her.

"Let me tell you about the Hells Disciples. They're an outlaw biker club that morphed into an organized crime syndicate. They call themselves the Iron Horse Mafia. They still wear Hells Disciple colors and pretend to be bikers, but I don't think most have bikes or even ride anymore. Gives us real bikers a bad name."

"You're a biker?"

"Got a Harley." She raised an eyebrow. "You have a problem with that?"

Lee raised his hands and shook his head.

Brigid continued, "Drugs and sex trafficking are the Disciple's full-time gig. When the Italian Mafia in Milwaukee was broken up, the Disciples took over. They get support from a Chicago chapter. Believe me, the department has been investigating them off and on for years. I was assigned to investigate their Southeast Wisconsin operation when I was a detective. Witnesses disappeared or refused to testify. We've never been able to nail them. As far as this girl being sixteen, I guarantee those bastards have created a false identity and act as her manager for so-called exotic dancing engagements where other services are offered behind closed doors."

"How do the Disciples get their hands on those girls? I've worked in the inner city long enough to know there's no way the street gangs are going to allow white bikers or whatever they are to come into the Core and abduct young Black girls."

"Back then, the One-Niners sold girls to the Disciples as long as they stayed off their turf. Most of the girls were shipped to Chicago."

"If the department knew all this, how did they keep getting away with it?"

"Every time we got close, it was like they knew we were coming. We had one confidential informant who got deep inside the club. Just as we were about to indict them, he disappeared. My gut feeling is that they have or had someone inside the department tipping them off. Pretty much like how some cops were on the take from the mob back in the day. I have no proof. Just my suspicious nature."

"So the department just gave up?"

A waitress came to the table with two thick ivory-colored coffee cups and a full coffee pot. "Coffee?" she asked. They both nodded. She poured the coffee and asked, "You want to order?"

Lee waved her off. "Come back."

Brigid leaned across the table and said, lowering her voice, "I was damn pissed when the department dropped the investigation after we lost our informant." She stuck her finger in Lee's chest. "I fought like hell to keep the investigation open, but the fucking chain of command said no."

"All right, all right. Take it easy."

"Later, when I was captain, we received several missing-person reports of inner-city girls. Normally, we didn't dedicate many resources to searching for the girls, but one of the girls showed up at District Two, saying she had been abducted at the downtown bus station by a member of the One-Niner gang. She said this gangbanger took her to a house on the South Side and turned her over to some bikers. She crawled out a bathroom window late at night and ran to the police station.

"Two of my detectives worked the case until orders came down from the top that the case was being turned over to the gang squad. When I inquired how the case was going, I got stonewalled and was told the girl refused to testify. They were done. I went to the chief and demanded he let me follow up. He refused. With all the shit going on in my head, that was the final straw. I pulled my papers and retired."

"Sorry."

She stared at her coffee cup. "Me too."

"Any advice on how we get Jasmine away from them?"

"I didn't have many friends when I left the department ... I know, you're shocked, but let me see what I can find out." She motioned for the waitress. "Now, for some Eggs Benedict with a side of those incredible hash browns. You're buying."

* * *

The savory aroma of chili and baking bread greeted Lee when he got home. The vacuum cleaner blared from the front room. He found Alexus vacuuming their worn gray front room carpeting while Merle watched from his recliner. She turned it off when she saw Lee and smiled with her whole face. "Momma Bernie sent along some chili and biscuits for you and your papa. I got the chili heating on the stove and the biscuits warming in the oven."

"Alexus, you have to stop coming over here. You must have friends to play with."

"You my best friend now. But I don't know about your papa. He talks mean sometime."

Lee glared at Merle. "What did you say to her?"

"What you talkin' about?" Merle shouted.

Lee turned to Alexus. "What did he say?"

"Told me to get the hell out of his house. Kept on hollering, so I turn on the vacuum." She grinned. "He finally give up trying to yell over it."

"Jesus, Dad. What is wrong with you?"

"I don't know that kid."

"It's Alexus. The girl who cleaned our house the other day."

"Alexus who?"

Lee said to Alexus, "Please don't come over anymore."

"But I want to. You bring my sister home, I clean your house every day."

"They told you?"

"I always knew she still alive. Momma Bernie said some bikers got her, and you and Mitch gonna look for her." She clasped his hand in both of hers. "Please bring my sister home. Please. Please. Please."

Lee called over his shoulder, "Dad, stay put till I get back while I take her home."

Merle slapped at the air. Lee didn't bother telling Merle to keep an eye on the biscuits and chili. Instead, he turned off the oven and the burner to the chili before they left.

Alexus held Lee's hand on the way back to Miss Bernie's house. When they got to the house, she looked up at him. Her dark brown eyes misted with tears. She asked, "Why don't you like me?"

Her words hit like a gut punch. This little girl who adored him wanted him to like her, something he was not capable of. Lee had become adept at keeping people away. The loss of his crew and his fiancée had paralyzed his need to be liked or to care for others. "I'm not good at liking people."

"Then I teach you." She motioned with her finger for him to bend down. Her arms went around his neck, and she pressed her tear-soaked cheek against his. A warm glow spread through him. Alexus whispered in his ear, "Why you so mad all the time?"

"I'm not."

She tilted her head back. "Your face sure look mad."

It struck him that the anger simmering below the surface must be etched onto his face. "How can I be mad at you? See, you make me smile." For the first time in a long time, he smiled and meant it.

"Good." She ran inside and up the stairs.

Lee found Mitch, Miss Bernie, and Brother Williams in the kitchen. Lee asked Mitch, "Did I miss anything last night?"

"A few of the Disciples came and went."

"No sign of Jasmine?"

"Didn't see any of the girls."

Miss Bernie said, "Just can't figure how that girl would get mixed up with that bunch."

Brother Williams lifted her hand and kissed it. "For now, let's give thanks to the good Lord that she's alive."

"Did you see the update on the fire yesterday?" Lee asked Brother Williams. "That senator from River Hills said he was going to work with the mayor and Common Council on ways for the state to help fund inner-city voucher schools in Milwaukee."

Brother Williams cringed. "Decker. Don't know what that man is up to, but he's never done anything but savage our community. Man should be wearing a white hood the way he talked about our people. This whole voucher system has become controversial."

"I'm confused," Lee said. "I thought state politicians like Decker were all in on the voucher program."

"They were until our coalition of private inner-city schools started attracting a good portion of students away from some of the large private schools and the schools that were simply a sham. Anyone could open a school as long as they had students enrolled. There was little oversight on quality or how the voucher money was spent. Decker pushed the state legislature to cut shared-revenue funding to the city if the city didn't figure out how to cut funding to our schools or shut us down. He claimed our schools were shams, teaching our kids to hate whites."

"I didn't know about your coalition," Lee said.

"Others like myself recognized our children were not getting the education they needed with many of the private schools. We had numerous meetings with the superintendent of schools. He expressed his challenges with the cuts to public school funding due to the voucher program. Since the voucher system was here to stay, we organized our coalition with the approval of the superintendent and opened inner-city private schools that would take in some of the most at-risk children in the public school system—not turn them away as most of the private schools had been doing. Along with paid staff, we had to rely on volunteers for this to work. When we put out a call for help in the community, we discovered there were many who wanted to help our children but had no idea how. Without this volunteer help, I don't know what we would do. I have to believe God was at work here."

Mitch nodded and said to Lee, "Those kids at his school are amazing."

"Everyone in the coalition grew up in the Core," Brother Williams said. "We know the challenges and how to get through to these children. It's incredibly demanding, but the reward in seeing these children break through their pain and hopelessness surely fills my heart and soul."

Lee thought about this, then asked, "So what about Sunrise? Why wouldn't they just open their own schools instead of trying to buy you and the others out?"

"They need students and there's no way they'd be able to attract students away from our coalition now that we've built a reputation for providing critical education and counseling for our students." Brother Williams paused, then said, "It took years to build that trust. Our children have a graduation rate higher than the average of all Wisconsin schools. That's why we cannot let some for-profit outfit come in and take over."

"Is there that much money in it that Sunrise would actually burn down your school to get the vouchers?"

"Not if the money is spent on resources for the students instead of going into the pockets of the owners … Enough about that. What are we doing about Jasmine?"

"I have a retired cop looking into it. Mitch, why don't you check back with Anderson? See if he found out anything."

"How about I check with Ralph's kid?" Mitch said. "If he knew about Jasmine, maybe he'd help."

Lee grimaced. "He won't talk to me. If he knows you and his dad are friends, maybe. How about we meet here around four? I have a doctor's appointment this afternoon."

"About your back?"

Lee left without answering.

Chapter 19

Lee

Lee dropped Merle off at Miss Bernie's house while he went to his therapy session with Dr. Bennet. When he entered her small office, she wiped tear tracks from her cheeks.

"Should I come back?" Lee asked.

"No. Sit. We lost another veteran. Hung himself last night."

"One of your patients?"

"He was supposed to start therapy today."

Lee had no words.

Dr. Bennet blew out a loud breath. "Brigid said she met with you and you were able to share the story about your fiancée's tragic death. I'm so sorry. Thank you for sharing that. When we get into the therapy, that would be a good place to start, unless you want to address something else, although I can't imagine anything nearly as tragic as losing your fiancée like that."

I can, Lee thought. What about losing your crew, who were your best friends, in a church fire? The way his fiancée died fueled rage and anger that was under control most of the time but surfaced without warning. Being the lone survivor of his crew fueled an unceasing, crippling sense of guilt that made no sense. Much like Mitch not being able to save the little neighbor girl from her burning farmhouse and blaming himself. After their talk at the abandoned warehouse, Lee knew that Mitch understood but who else could? He wasn't ready to share that story with anyone else.

Dr. Bennet explained how the therapy would progress. Before they got into the desensitization phase with the eye movement technique, she would spend a few sessions getting to know Lee and creating a plan. Brigid would help with this if he didn't feel comfortable sharing some things with a civilian. As she explained the phases of treatment, Lee couldn't stop thinking about Alexus and her sister Jasmine.

"Are you still with me?" Dr. Bennet asked.

"Today's a bad day. Can we try this another time?"

"If you don't continue therapy, you'll have to go back to work."

"A young girl's life is on the line. I have to do what I can to help."

"What are you talking about?"

He told Dr. Bennet about Jasmine and what Brigid had told him about the Hells Disciples. When he finished, Dr. Bennet said, "I don't know. This sounds like a potentially dangerous and disturbing situation. You're already carrying a heavy load of past trauma and I'm worried it could trigger even more anxiety or worse. As your therapist, I highly advise letting the police handle this. I'm sure Brigid could arrange that."

Lee rose to leave. "No time for that."

Dr. Bennet stood and said, "Okay, then. But who's going to rescue the rescuer?"

Lee headed for the door. If she reported that he stopped therapy, he'd take an unpaid leave of absence if he had to.

"I'll cover for you," Dr. Bennet said. "But you need to check in with me and Brigid. When this is over, I expect to see you here ... good luck."

* * *

Lee entered Miss Bernie's house without knocking. She had told him to walk in whenever he came over. He was now family. Lee passed his sleeping father on the way to the kitchen where Miss Bernie, Brother Williams, and Mitch were seated at the table. Miss Bernie said, "Wait till you hear what Mitch found out."

Mitch said, "Yeah. So I headed over to Ralph's house. His son answered the door and I told him I used to work with his dad and thought I would stop by. He said his dad was working. I already knew that because I called the firehouse to get Anderson's phone number and asked who was working. I tried to strike up a conversation with his son by telling him how much his dad taught me on the job, and how much I respected him, and what close friends we had become. He kept putting me off. I finally asked if he knew that his club was prostituting a minor who I had rescued from a fire years ago. He said he didn't care if I was a friend of his dad or not, I needed to back the hell off. He shoved me out the door."

"So you didn't find anything out?"

"I parked a few blocks away and watched the house, hoping he'd want to warn the others about what I said since he made it clear he wasn't going to help. Sure enough, he jumped in his car. I thought maybe he'd head to the clubhouse. Instead, he drove to a house on South 22nd just south of Mineral Street, and ran inside. It's a long shot but maybe that's where they keep the girls. I hung around for a while and watched the house, but nothing was going on. While I waited, I called Anderson to see if he knew anything."

"And?"

"His buddy told his uncle, the Disciple, that he knew some people who might want to hire the same girls from the year-on party for another private party. His uncle told him those girls would be going back to Chicago right after Christmas. If these people wanted to hire them, they needed to do it now. He said there were plenty of other girls the club could provide besides those girls."

"Makes sense," Lee said. "A retired cop I know told me the Hells Disciples have a chapter in Chicago."

"I'm gonna head back over to that South Side house," Mitch said as he got up from the table. "I gotta get to Jasmine before they take her back."

"Give me a call if you see anything. After I get my dad tucked in for the night, I'll join you."

"You just leave him right here," Miss Bernie said. "Jasmine needs you. I can take care of your papa."

"I don't know. He can get pretty difficult."

"No stranger to difficult. Ask Mitch about how me and his papa went around that summer on the farm."

"I wouldn't say difficult," Mitch said, grinning. "More like impossible. But he was no match for that lady right there."

Miss Bernie stood. "Enough jabbering. You think you can get Jasmine away from those men?"

Lee said, "We'll find a way."

"Those men are surely doing the devil's work. He's cunning. You watch yourselves."

Chapter 20

Lee

They parked well down the block from the one-story light gray bungalow on South 22nd Street. Mitch got a pair of binoculars from the covered bed of his pickup truck.

Lee asked, "What else you got in there?"

"Us farmers try to be prepared for pretty much anything. These have night vision. They come in handy when coyotes are stirring up our cattle at night."

Powdery snow swirled through the tranquil residential neighborhood as darkness settled in. While watching the house, Mitch told Lee how Miss Bernie, Jasmine, and Alexus had come to the farm over the summer four years ago when his dad had a stroke. Miss Bernie nursed him back to health while the girls helped with chores. His dad gave her so much crap. He didn't care for Black people. But she gave it right back. By the time she and the girls had to go back to Milwaukee, his dad had recovered from his stroke thanks to Miss Bernie pushing him relentlessly throughout the therapy. He actually thanked her and the girls when they left.

After Mitch finished, Lee told him about his dad and the dilemma of taking care of an abusive father. When he finished, Mitch said, "That's tough. My dad and I went for years thinking we hated each other, only to find out we were both wrong. Crazy how we hang on to assumptions. We put that all behind us."

Lee pointed at the cigarette burn scars on his hand. "He did that to me when I was six. And beat the shit out of me more times than I could count. So, no fairytale ending for us."

"I'm no therapist, but going through my own therapy, I learned the only way to move on was to somehow figure out how to forgive."

"I can't see that happening. Man was a total bastard. Still is. Doesn't deserve my forgiveness."

"It's not for him; it's for you."

Mitch grabbed the binoculars. "Somebody's coming out of the house."

Lee squinted through the falling snow. "Can you tell who it is?"

"That's Ralph's kid and another Disciple. They got four women with them."

"Can you tell if they got Jasmine with them?"

"No. The women are wearing hoods."

"Let me take a look," Lee said. He focused on each of the women, who were wearing winter coats and tight-fitting miniskirts. They got in a black Escalade. "Let's see where they go."

They followed the Escalade to the Disciples' clubhouse. Cars, trucks, and vans were parked throughout the area. Some had Illinois license plates. Mitch parked well out of view. Even from this distance, they heard the pounding bass. The Escalade parked in an open area in front of the clubhouse that was being monitored by a Disciple with Prospect written on the back of his vest. The prospect opened the doors of the Escalade. Ace and the others dashed into the clubhouse.

Mitch pulled a rifle from the truck bed.

"What the hell is that?" Lee said.

"My Browning hunting rifle."

"I know what the hell it is. Served in the Marines."

"When?"

"Vietnam."

"Damn. You are old."

Lee raised his eyebrows.

"Sorry," Mitch said. "I was trying to be funny. You must have seen some pretty bad stuff."

Bad's not even close, Lee thought and said, "Nothing to talk about. Let me see your rifle."

Lee inspected the high-powered scope mounted on top of the rifle and a small laser sight mounted under the barrel. "You some kind of gun nut?"

Mitch laughed. "No. the scope comes in handy for hunting, but it's illegal to use a laser sight for that. Borrowed the laser from a neighbor who has quite an arsenal. When Brother Williams told me about the school being burned down by the One-Niners, I came prepared for anything."

The way Mitch said that and the look on his face convinced Lee that he was dead serious about being prepared for anything, even using the rifle. Lee said, "Glad you're prepared. I wasn't planning on spending the night up in that open freezer."

Mitch pulled an army-green blanket from the bed and handed it to Lee. "This thermal blanket will help. Use this in my deer stand. Gets darn cold up there." He reached into the truck bed and came out with two heavy brown mittens and a black ski mask and handed them to Lee. "Here. Don't want your teeth chattering like last time." Mitch grabbed the camp chairs and headed to the abandoned warehouse. Lee slipped the ski mask over his head, put the mittens on, and slung the binoculars from his neck. He followed, carrying the rifle and blanket.

When they got to the warehouse, Lee limped up the stairs behind Mitch, who asked, "Your back still giving you trouble?"

"I'll be all right."

Lee scanned the area with the binoculars while Mitch set up the camp chairs. When Mitch picked up the rifle, Lee asked, "That thing loaded?"

"Did you walk around with an unloaded rifle in Vietnam?"

"Good point."

They watched as more vehicles parked along the street.

A black Escalade identical to the one Ace was driving pulled into an open spot in front of the clubhouse. The prospect opened the doors. Two Disciples got out.

"You seeing what I'm seeing?" Lee asked.

"That bald giant with the black beard?"

"Not the big one," Lee said. "The smaller one next to him. Looks like Charles Manson."

"Who?"

"Charles Manson. He was a cult leader who ordered his people to slaughter an actress and her friends."

"Guess I heard of him, but I don't watch much news."

Lee focused on the Manson look-alike as a young woman got out of the SUV and grabbed his arm. She shouted something at him. He stopped, swung around, and slammed his fist into her midsection. She went to her knees. The huge black-bearded man kicked her in the side. She collapsed. Two other girls got out of the SUV and headed to the front door with the Manson look-alike and the black-bearded man. Their Milwaukee Hells Disciples colors were visible under the streetlight. At the top of the back of the vests, under Hells Disciples, scrolled in black letters, was "President" on the Manson look-alike and "Enforcer" on the black-bearded man. They left the young woman in a fetal position on the frozen sidewalk. The prospect made no move to help her.

"If that had been Jasmine," Mitch said, "those bastards would each have a thirty-aught-six slug in his head. We can't leave her lying there like that."

"Wait. There's another group coming up the street."

When the four men got to her, the colors of the Hells Disciples of Chicago were visible. One of them helped her to her feet. After an animated conversation among the men, one of them draped her arm over his shoulder, wrapped his arm around her waist, and walked her to his car. They drove off.

"She looked pretty messed up," Mitch said.

"Now we know what we're dealing with. Total slime."

"I gotta get back on that roof and see what's going on inside. Make sure they're not messing with Jasmine."

"Probably not a good idea. We don't even know if Jasmine is in there. And what would you do? Good chance all those bikers are armed. Let's just wait."

Mitch gritted his lips and nodded.

The temperature dropped to below zero and the gusting wind picked up as they watched groups of people continue to enter the clubhouse late into the night. Mitch was right; the thermal blanket kept Lee from freezing. He was still cold but not miserable.

It was after one in the morning when Mitch said, "How about I run up to George Webb's and get us some coffee and burgers?"

Coffee and burgers. What beautiful words, Lee thought and said, "You are a genius. I'll take three burgers with onions and the largest coffee they have."

When Mitch got back he asked, "Miss anything?"

"Two more cars from Chicago showed up, but that's about it."

Mitch handed Lee his bag of burgers. Grease had soaked through the bottom. Mitch set a badly dented stainless steel thermos down between them. "Help yourself to coffee."

"How much does that thing hold?"

"Half a gallon."

"I'll be pissing all night."

Mitch smirked. "At least you'll be awake."

Lee scarfed down the three burgers like a ravenous dog. After slugging down some coffee, he went downstairs and out back to relieve himself.

Shortly after Lee got back upstairs, Mitch nodded off.

Guess farmers aren't used to late hours, Lee thought as he settled under the blanket with the binoculars.

Music boomed from the clubhouse but traffic in and out slowed as the night wore on. Lee struggled to keep awake by drinking more coffee. He finally had to poke Mitch, who jerked awake and looked around like he was lost, then said, "How long was I down?"

"Couple hours. I gotta take another leak."

"You sure gotta go a lot."

"When I was your age, I could piss like a racehorse. Now I'm lucky to get it past my shoes. You'll see."

"Can't wait."

When Lee got back, Mitch said, "Go ahead and get some sleep. I'll take over."

The cold had sapped Lee's energy and he fell asleep more easily than he had in a long time. When he woke, the snow had let up and the sky cleared. The early-morning orange glow of the sun sparkled off the fresh snow cover. Groups of bikers with their women staggered out of the clubhouse shielding their eyes. Lee asked, "Any sign of the girls?"

"Not yet."

An hour later, only a few cars and vans were left along the street, including the Escalade. The rusted metal front door of the clubhouse swung open. Lee focused the binoculars on the group emerging from the doorway. "There they are."

"I think that's Jasmine," Mitch said, peering through the high-powered rifle scope.

"It's hard to tell with those parkas they're wearing. But that's Ralph's kid with them." Lee zoomed the binoculars in on the young woman who didn't have a hood pulled over her head. "Check out the girl next to him. Am I seeing things?"

He lowered the binoculars and the two men gawked at each other, speechless.

Chapter 21

Mitch

"We gotta move, now," Lee said.

Mitch took a last look through his rifle scope. The two Disciples and four women piled into the Escalade.

"C'mon," Lee said. "Let's grab your stuff and get back to your truck before they take off."

Mitch had to wait for Lee when they got outside. He was limping badly. Lee said, "Go ahead. I'll catch up."

By the time Mitch got to the truck and was loading the camp chairs and thermos into the bed, the Escalade drove off. He had to wait for Lee, who was carrying the blanket, rifle, and binoculars. By the time Lee got to the truck, the Escalade was out of sight. "Now what?" Mitch asked.

"We head to the South Side house."

Mitch sped through the congested city streets. When they arrived at the house, there was no sign of the Escalade, and the house was dark. "Crap," Mitch said. "We gotta find them."

"Let's just wait here a bit. You drove like a bat out of hell. Maybe we beat them here. Lee paused, then said, "What about that young woman we saw with them? Could it be?"

"I got a shiver when I saw her. Miss Bernie said she ran off to Chicago when she was a teenager."

"Sure looked like Miss Bernie's younger twin. But really, what are the chances?"

Maybe Brother Williams was right about there being no coincidences in this world, Mitch thought.

With no sign of the Escalade after a half hour of waiting, Mitch said, "I can't just sit here. Let's pay Ralph a visit."

"I don't know."

"I gotta think he'll help once I tell him what we saw at the clubhouse."

"I'm not so sure, but okay, let's go."

They found the Escalade parked in front of Ralph's house.

"Perfect," Mitch said. "If they've got Jasmine in there, Ralph knows her from when she lived across from the firehouse. He knew she was a good kid. I gotta think he'll tell Ace to let her go."

"What about the one who looks like Miss Bernie's daughter?"

"If she's in there too, I should be able to get a better look at her."

"Then what?"

"I don't know. I'll have to wing it and see what plays out."

"I don't know about this," Lee said. "From what we saw at the clubhouse, you might be putting yourself in a damn shitty situation."

"No way would Ralph let his kid mess with me."

Mitch got out of the truck. Before he closed the door, Lee said, "All right then. You know him better than me. I'll wait in the truck. If Ralph sees me, he'll probably slam the door in our faces."

Laughter and loud talking came from inside the house when Mitch trotted up the porch steps. He pounded on the door. It went quiet. He waited. He pounded louder. Someone pulled the front window curtain aside. The room was dark. Mitch couldn't make out the face peering out at him. He continued pounding on the door. The door cracked open. "Ralph, let me in."

"He's not here. Get lost."

"I'm not leaving without Jasmine."

Mitch put his shoulder into the door and shoved it open. He was greeted by the black barrel of an AR15 rifle pointed at his head. Ralph's son, Ace, grinned over the top of the barrel, narrowing his eyes. "I see we got a trespasser. Got every right to shoot your ass."

Mitch's chest pounded. He spread his arms wide. "I know you got Jasmine."

"Got no Jasmine here. Now haul your ass outa here before I light this bad boy up."

Mitch backed out of the doorway. "Your dad know you're prostituting those girls?"

Ace followed Mitch onto the porch, pointing the AR15 at him. A car door slammed. Ace glanced down the street. Lee hustled toward them, limping. Ace looked back at Mitch and growled, "Should have listened when I told you to back off. Now you're in deep shit." He waved the tip of the rifle up and down. "Get the fuck out of here and take your asshole buddy with you. See you around here again, your ass will be mine."

Mitch met Lee two houses away. "We gotta disappear, fast."

Ace watched from the porch with the AR15 at his side.

* * *

On the drive to Miss Bernie's house, Mitch told Lee about Ace threatening to shoot him and how he got a glimpse of four women.

Lee asked, "Could you tell if it was Jasmine?"

"No. Happened too fast."

"Should we tell Miss Bernie we think her daughter might be with them?" Lee asked.

"Better wait till we know for sure. Don't want to give her false hope."

When they got to the house, Lee, Mitch, Miss Bernie, and Brother Williams went to the kitchen, leaving Merle in the front room shouting at the late-morning news. The children would be coming downstairs soon for lunch. A kettle of sloppy joes simmered on the stove.

"My dad give you any trouble?" Lee asked Miss Bernie.

"I had a bed made up for him in the boys' bedroom, but there was no gettin' him in there. Said to leave him sleep in the recliner. He don't like being around kids. The way that man snores, I think those boys were just fine with that."

Mitch filled Miss Bernie and Brother Williams in on his encounter with Ace without saying anything about the young woman who could be Miss Bernie's daughter.

"Oh, my Lord," Miss Bernie said while clasping her chin. "The devil surely working through that man. Mitch, you watch yourself. No tellin' what that devil got planned."

Brother Williams said, "We need to report this to the police."

Lee clenched his lips, then said, "I don't know. According to my cop friend, these people are cunning killers. I don't think we want to risk them taking Jasmine back to Chicago if the cops start asking questions."

"Ace knows we're on to them," Mitch said. "I should have kept my mouth shut. Crap."

"Let's get back to the South Side house," Lee said, "We'll wait for them there. They don't know that we know about it."

"We can't take my truck. Ace saw it."

"Take the new school van," Brother Williams said. "It's got no markings on it yet."

The phone on the kitchen counter rang. Brother Williams put the receiver to his ear, "Williams' residence. How can I…?" His jaw went slack. He rocked back and steadied himself against the counter. "Who is this?"

Brother Williams lowered the receiver of the phone and stared at it.

Miss Bernie went to his side. "My Lord. What is it?"

"Said, 'Sell the school if you care about your family.' "

Chapter 22

Mitch

Lee helped Mitch empty the bed of his pickup truck into the rear cargo area of the extended white Chevy school van. Lee pointed at the camo clothing. "Planning on doing some hunting?"

"Isn't that what we're doing?"

Before they left, Brother Williams had demanded they concentrate on finding Jasmine. He would deal with the threats about selling his school. The police would be notified of the phone call, and Brother Williams would locate the leader of the One-Niners and get to the bottom of the threats.

Miss Bernie filled Mitch's thermos with coffee and packed ham sandwiches and a family-sized bag of Ruffles potato chips.

The Escalade was gone when they drove by Ralph's house. They continued to the South Side house and parked at the end of the long block. They watched the house through the back windows of the van.

The afternoon dragged into the evening with no sign of the Disciples. By seven o'clock, they had eaten all of the sandwiches.

Mitch yawned. "This sitting around is getting old."

"What else can we do? We leave here and go driving around, we could miss them."

Mitch asked, "What if they're already headed back to Chicago? Then what?"

"I guess we head to Chicago. I gotta think some of our brothers and sisters on the department down there would know something about the Chicago chapter."

Lee wasn't the most talkative person to be spending long hours with. As the night wore on, the oldies radio station filled the long gaps of silence.

When Lee began eating potato chips, crunching loudly, Mitch could barely stand the sound. Loud eaters had always grated on him and here he was cooped up in a van with one of the loudest. He resisted the urge to say something, instead telling Lee the rest of the story about Jasmine. Her mother's crackhead boyfriend had sexually assaulted her when she was twelve, and after being accused of the assault, he torched their house, which was across the street from Engine House 15.

Jasmine went into the burning home to get Alexus, not knowing Alexus had already run out. While searching for her sister, she succumbed to the heavy smoke and was burned, leaving permanent scars on her neck. Mitch was on watch at the firehouse that night. When he saw the house on fire, he alerted the crew and ran across the street without waiting for them. Jasmine's mother told him she was still inside. He didn't wait for his crew, crawling into the burning home without breathing gear. He found Jasmine unconscious in the second-floor hallway. While carrying her through the smoke-filled house, Mitch was overcome and went down. Ralph found them in the kitchen within feet of the back door and dragged them out.

That night, Mitch proved himself to Ralph, who became his mentor, teaching him how to read smoke conditions and how to be aggressive while watching for the Red Devil's lethal flashovers and backdrafts.

"Me and Ralph were tight," Mitch said, shaking his head.

"Never liked the guy," Lee said. "But he is one hell of a firefighter. Gotta give him that."

"Everyone was sure that DeAndre, the leader of the One-Niners back then, had killed Jasmine for refusing to prostitute herself for the gang."

"What happened to him?"

Mitch clenched his lips, then said, "I was out looking for her, and he jumped me. We got into it pretty good and the only way it was going to end was with one of us dead—and I'm still here."

Lee whistled and said, "Remind me not to mess with you."

"But how did the Disciples end up with her?" Mitch asked.

"My cop friend said the One-Niners sold girls to them."

Mitch thought about that and then how Jasmine had inspired him when she tried to rescue Alexus. After the fire, he dedicated himself to helping her through her recovery and her struggle with depression. This is when he discovered the power of love can overcome incredible odds. In saving her, he saved himself.

The two men took turns keeping watch while the other slept as the night dragged into the early morning with no Escalade in sight. Thankfully, Lee didn't eat chips while Mitch tried to doze.

At five a.m., Mitch asked, "Where the hell could they have been all night?"

"If they took the girls to a private party, it could be anywhere in the city."

"Or Chicago."

"How about we check out Ralph's place again," Lee said. "If they're there, we can follow them when they leave. Ace won't recognize the van."

Anything besides sitting here any longer, Mitch thought and nodded.

"Ralph should be home. Too early to leave for work," Lee said.

When they got to Ralph's street, they parked well down the block. Mitch said, "I gotta talk to him. Find out what he knows about his kid."

"Last person he wants to see is me. I'll wait here. Good luck."

Mitch headed up the sidewalk and paused at the front of the house, then silently climbed the steps and paused again at the front door, listening for any sign of Ace inside. The door swung open. Ralph stood in the doorway.

"How did you know I was here?" Mitch asked.

"Thought you might show up. Ace told me you and that asshole captain were snooping around yesterday." Ralph looked up and down the street. "He with you?"

"Did Ace tell you he put a rifle in my face or that he had Jasmine here?"

"My kid and his buddies stopped by to get some of his shit while I was gone. That's all. I told you before I don't keep tabs on him. He's got a place on the South Side."

"On 22nd?"

"How do you know that?"

"C'mon, Ralph. You gotta know something."

"Don't know shit. Rarely see him."

"What the hell, Ralph? You're a good man and a good friend. Why you doing this?"

"Doing what? Staying out of my kid's life?"

"You saw the photos of Jasmine. We both know that's her."

Ralph placed his hands on Mitch's shoulders, and said softly, "Go. Forget about all of this. Don't even think about calling the cops.

Those people are nobody to fool with. Go back to the farm while you still can." Ralph pushed Mitch away from the door and slammed it shut.

Mitch hollered, "Not without Jasmine. Ralph. Ralph, c'mon, don't do this."

Chapter 23

Lee

When Mitch got back to the van, he said, "That place on South 22nd is Ace's place. I can't believe Ralph is ignoring what his kid is involved in. Back when I was on the job, the crew told me that Ralph's kid had tried to get on the department a bunch of times, but he wasn't all that sharp and couldn't pass the written exam. They said it tore Ralph apart because his father and grandfather had been Milwaukee firefighters. The tradition ends with him."

"Who knows what Ralph is thinking? Hopefully, he comes to his senses before it's too late. Let's check Ace's place one more time, then head over to Miss Bernie's. I should check on my dad."

After swinging by Ace's house, Lee and Mitch got back to Miss Bernie's place in time for lunch. They were greeted by the smell of baking ham. When they entered the kitchen, the family was at the table, their plates filled with potatoes and ham in a creamy white sauce. Mitch shouted, "Yes. Scalloped potatoes and ham."

Miss Bernie waved them to the open spot next to Merle. "Still your favorite?"

"You bet."

Brother Williams asked, "Any luck?"

The children stopped chattering and looked to Mitch, who shook his head.

"We talk later," Miss Bernie said. "Now we enjoy God's blessings."

Alexus, who was never at a loss for words, had nothing to add to the chatter of the other children. She picked at her food with her head down. When they finished eating, the adults went to the front room while the children went about their kitchen chores. Merle went to the recliner and promptly fell asleep. The others spread out on the worn rust-colored sectional couch that spanned two walls and faced the Christmas tree.

Miss Bernie asked Mitch and Lee, "What you boys got planned?"

Mitch said, "We're still looking."

"You don't know where she at?"

"Not yet."

Alexus appeared in the entryway to the kitchen, tears streaming down her cheeks. "You said you'd bring my sister home. Where is she?"

Mitch said, "Soon as we find her, we'll bring her home."

"She's never coming home, is she?"

Anger rose in Lee's chest. He could hear blood rushing through his ears. Raging visions of bashing Ace's face flashed in his head. The words came out as a loud growl, "We will find her and bring her home."

Alexus gawked at him. Mitch said, "Whoa, Captain, pull back on the reins. That look on your face is scaring the crap out of her."

Lee snapped out of it and went to Alexus. She backed away. He knelt and opened his arms. "Sorry. I'm not mad at you. I'm mad at those men who have your sister."

She eased into his arms, her dark brown eyes glassy. "She's my sister. She need to be here. You bring her home. Promise?"

"Promise."

"Good." She kissed him on the cheek and ran upstairs.

He would do this, not because it was his job, but because there was no way he was going to disappoint this little girl who adored him and had already been through far too much pain and disappointment.

* * *

Lee and Mitch headed back to Ace's house on South 22nd Street in the white van. Mitch said, "You looked like you were crawling out of your skin back there. You okay?"

"Feel bad I scared Alexus."

"She's not the only one. You should have seen the look on your face."

Lee gripped his forehead. "Sometimes, I don't know, I get so pissed. It comes out of nowhere. I can't control it."

"That was me for years until I got help."

"That EMDR stuff?"

"Exactly."

When they got to Ace's house, Lee looked around the van. "Where did the potato chips go?"

Mitch shrugged.

They spent the afternoon watching the house in silence. Around six o'clock, Lee got a call from Brigid telling him to meet at his house. She was waiting by the back door when they got there. She told them she learned the department had no ongoing investigations into the Disciples. There would be no help from the police unless they could supply them with evidence of criminal activity. She explained how the department was struggling to keep up with the record number of homicides and escalating violence.

"Any ideas?" Lee asked Brigid.

"Even if you could supply MPD with info on the gang's activities, I don't know if that would be wise. If my hunch is right and they have someone inside the department tipping them off, you two could end up disappearing. These people are more evil than you could ever imagine."

I doubt that, Lee thought. The Disciples could never match the atrocities he witnessed in Vietnam. "We have to do something."

"You don't want to hear this, but the best advice is to drop it."

"Can't do that."

"They'll come after you."

Mitch said, "We're that girl's only hope. One thing I learned as a firefighter was to never give up, no matter how impossible things might seem. We're not giving up on her."

"Not sure what I can do to help but keep me posted." She flashed Lee a teasing smile. "I see why women find you firefighters sexy." She winked and left.

"You seeing her?" Mitch asked.

Lee felt the heat rise in his neck. "Let's get back to Ace's place."

Chapter 24

Lee

They went to the van. Before getting in, Lee said, "Forgot something."

When Lee got into the van, Mitch asked, "What was so important?"

Lee held up the 9mm Glock. "Had this in my dresser. Thought it might come in handy."

"Looks like things are getting real."

"Sure you want to get involved in this. You got a family to worry about."

"What about you? You got your mom and dad."

They won't miss me, Lee thought and said, "Things could turn ugly. I don't want you getting hurt."

"Noted. Now let's rescue Jasmine from those bastards."

On the way to Ace's house, they stopped at a McDonald's, where they ordered four Quarter Pounders and fries along with six large cups of coffee Mitch poured into his thermos.

When they got to Ace's street, they parked alongside some trees they could use for cover if they needed to relieve themselves while watching the house. There was no sign of the Escalade. The greasy smell of McDonald's burgers and fries filled the van as they scarfed down their dinner.

The street was quiet throughout the evening and well into the night.

"How long we gonna stay here?" Mitch asked when it got to be one in the morning.

"Even if they plan to go back to Chicago, I would think they have to stop back here to get the girls' things before heading back."

"If this is where they're staying," Mitch said. "And if they didn't already get their stuff and leave while we were gone."

"But remember what Anderson found out? That the girls would be here until after Christmas."

Mitch grimaced, then said, "That was before I told Ace we knew about his club prostituting them."

Mitch is probably right, Lee thought, losing hope. They watched the house in silence while Lee struggled to come up with a plan other than sitting here.

"There they are," Mitch said as the black Escalade went past them. "Let's rush 'em and grab the girls," Mitch said.

"No. We wait for the right time. Use our heads." Lee thought about the hours and sometimes days waiting for the right time to take out a target in Vietnam. Patience was crucial for a successful mission.

Mitch watched through his rifle scope while Lee peered through the binoculars. Two men and four women walked to the house. Within minutes, one of the men and two of the women emerged from the front door. The women each had what appeared to be a small carry-on bag.

Lee asked, "Can you tell if that's Jasmine?"

"Can't tell through the hood."

The girls climbed into the back seat of the Escalade.

Mitch asked, "What do we do?"

"Gotta follow them. You can bet Ace told the Disciples we're looking for Jasmine. If they think we went to the police, they'll want to get her back to Chicago."

The Escalade drove to I-94 and headed south. Traffic was sparse at this hour of the morning. Mitch stayed well behind. "Crap. They are heading to Chicago."

"Stay with them," Lee said. "Be hell to find them down there if we lose 'em."

Just before the Illinois border, the Escalade pulled into a truck stop. Mitch parked in the pitch-black shadow of a semi-trailer with the rear of the van facing the gas pumps. Rows of idling semi-rigs filled the truck parking area. The gas pumps and station were deserted except for a lone person inside at the counter. The truck drivers would be in their sleepers. Lee and Mitch watched as a skinny biker with a long brown beard got out of the Escalade and approached the pump.

"It's not Ace," Mitch said.

"Don't matter."

"What are you thinking?" Mitch asked, over the loud rumbling of the idling semi-rigs.

"Could you shoot the bastard if you had to?"

Mitch's mouth fell open. His brows knit together. "What the hell you talking about?"

"You haven't seen Jasmine in a long time. Don't know how she'll react. They could have her head pretty messed up by now. She doesn't know me. You need to cover me while I carjack them. I should be able to handle the biker, but if things go horseshit, I'll need you backing me up." As soon as Lee said it, he knew there was no way he could put that on Mitch. "Forget I said that. There has to be another way."

"We gotta do something before they get back on the road." Mitch put the binoculars to his eyes. "I can't see the girls through the tinted windows."

The biker began fueling the Escalade.

Mitch is right, Lee thought. *We have to do something fast.* "You got some way to disguise yourself?" Lee asked.

Mitch went to the back of the van and rummaged around. He came back wearing a camo jacket and carrying two ski masks, one camo and one black, both with openings for the eyes and mouth.

"Good," Lee said. "I'll cover you." The memory of a kill Lee had made in Vietnam flashed in his head. A boy, only a child, was guarding an enclosure with a rifle where friendly hostages were being held. It was up to his Marine Force Recon team to free them and it was Lee's job to take the boy out. The sniper shot hit the boy in the forehead. The boy collapsed to the ground.

Lee shook the memory from his head. Now the enemy was the Hells Disciples, and the mission was to free the girls at any cost. From what Brigid had told him about them murdering witnesses and prostituting young girls, there would be no remorse in killing one of them to free the girls if it came to that. Not like killing a child caught up in war.

C'mon. Focus, Lee thought.

"You okay?" Mitch asked.

Lee's head cleared. "Here, take my handgun. Tell him there's a sniper aimed at him. Tell him to look down. He'll see the red dot from the laser sight of your rifle on his chest. Take his keys and his gun if he has one and tell him to walk toward me. The girls might try to run. Put the gun on them and order one to drive. Act like you're one mean son of a bitch. Disguise your voice. Try to sound like Ralph but say as little as possible until we figure out what to do with them."

Mitch blew out a loud breath. "Holy crap. I can't believe we're doing this."

"Have the girl drive toward Milwaukee. Take the Highway C exit to the west. Lots of farmland in that area. Drive until you find a quiet stretch of road. Pull over and wait. Then follow me when I pass you."

"You sure? If this turns bad, we could get busted for kidnapping."

Lee was far from sure. What was he getting Mitch into? But they had to do something. If the girls got back to Chicago, their chances of getting them away from the Hells Disciples would be near impossible. Lee groaned. "You're right. This could turn bad. We should think of some other way to get the girls."

Mitch pulled the camo ski mask over his head. "No! Sometimes you just gotta jump the fence. Jasmine would never turn me in. And the Disciples won't want the cops involved. Let's do this." He handed Lee the other mask and pointed to the biker at the gas pump. "What do we do with him?"

"You got some rope I can tie him up with?"

"Something better. Farm stuff." He went to the rear of the van and came back with two rolls of gray duct tape and a bag of zip ties.

"Gotta give it to you, kid, you do come prepared." Lee pulled the black ski mask over his head. "Ready?"

"Let's do it."

The biker replaced the gas nozzle.

"Hurry," Lee said.

Lee cracked the back doors of the van open just enough to sight the rifle through it, training the scope on the back of the biker. His vest had the white rockers with Hells Disciples MC inscribed in black, but instead of Milwaukee on the bottom rocker, it read Chicago. Mitch casually approached him as he put his credit card back in his wallet.

A man in camo and a ski mask was not an unusual sight in Wisconsin in December. The biker pointed at Mitch and sneered, appearing to rant at him. Lee turned on the laser sight and watched as the man looked down, paused, and pulled a set of keys from his coat pocket. Mitch snatched them from him. The man's shoulders sagged as he trudged in Lee's direction, staring at the red dot on his chest. Lee kept the laser focused on him while keeping an eye on the Escalade. If the girls bolted, then what?

Mitch went to the passenger door of the Escalade and yanked it open, waving the gun at someone. After a few seconds, he climbed inside, slamming the door closed. Lee couldn't see anything through the tinted windows. The Escalade drove off with the biker glaring at it. When he approached the school van, Lee growled, "Turn around. We got you covered. Hands behind your back."

He slowly turned.

"Now walk backward towards me. I'll tell you when to stop."

When the man was in the shadows of the semi-trailer, Lee silently laid the rifle down in the van and stepped out. "Stop. My partner has you in his sights," Lee bluffed.

Lee pulled the man's left wrist behind his back. Before he could get the other one, the man swung around, clipping Lee on the side of his head with his fist, stunning him. The familiar red mist of rage blazed behind his eyes. Lee blocked the next punch, grabbed the man's windpipe, and slammed him against the semi-trailer. The man grabbed at Lee's throat. Lee instinctively went for his fingers and grasped the ring finger and little finger, forcing them back against the joints. The fingers snapped. The man went to his knees, clutching his fingers, shrieking. Lee pushed him to the ground and jammed his knee onto his throat to shut him up. His rage flared. He smashed his fist into the man's face. He cocked his arm for another blow. Light washed over them as the door of the sleeping compartment of the semi-cab banged open. A sleepy-eyed trucker glared at them, a revolver in his hand. "What the hell you assholes doing?"

The red mist cleared. The biker's matted beard was soaked in blood. Lee looked over his shoulder at the trucker. "This bastard's screwing my wife. I'm giving him what he deserves."

The trucker dipped his head and pulled the door of the sleeper closed, plunging them back into darkness.

With Lee's knee on his throat, the man could barely get the words out, "You're dead, motherfucker."

Lee leaned in, his face inches from the man's. "Go on, piss me off. We'll end it right here."

The man looked into Lee's eyes and gasped. Lee said, "Remember this look. Screw with me and it'll be the last thing you ever see." Lee turned him onto his stomach and grabbed a zip tie from his back pocket. "Hands behind your back." Lee forced the man's wrists together and yanked the zip tie snug. The man grunted. Lee helped him to his feet. "Now, into the van—on the floor."

After the man got into the back of the van, Lee stretched duct tape over his mouth and wrapped his legs together with three layers of tape. The man's bulging eyes looked like they were about to burst from their sockets.

Good. He thinks I'm going to kill him, Lee thought. He spotted a small pile of dirty rags under the back seat. He smiled to himself. More farm crap. He tied a greasy rag over the biker's eyes.

Lee slammed the back doors closed. He bent over from the pain in his back and took two deep breaths, the air thick with diesel exhaust, then limped to the driver's door and climbed into the van. The times he lost it on the job, he was devastated with remorse. But here, he felt strangely euphoric.

There was no turning back.

Chapter 25

Lee

Lee spotted the Escalade off the side of the road next to a barren snow-covered farm field. He passed it and flashed the brake lights twice to make sure Mitch knew it was him. The headlights came on and followed. They drove several miles until Lee saw a desolate side road bordered by thick woods. Lee turned off the headlights. Mitch did the same. They drove until the main road disappeared. When they stopped, Lee approached the passenger side of the Escalade.

Mitch rolled down the window and said, "Jasmine's not here."

"Damn. Better keep the ski masks on. Take the girls to the van. The biker's tied up on the floor. I'll drive this as deep in the woods as it'll go."

Lee was able to get it well off the road before it bogged down in the thick underbrush. He pulled the keys from the ignition and stuffed them in his coat pocket, then trudged back to the school van. Mitch was at the wheel. Lee took the gun from Mitch and checked out the young Black girls on the bench seat behind them. One had crimson-red dyed hair, the other raven-black hair. The heavy eye makeup on the crimson-haired girl didn't conceal her age. She had to be in her teens. The lighter-skinned black-haired girl next to her looked even younger. Neither one appeared scared. The crimson-haired girl demanded, "What gang you motherfuckers with?"

Perfect, Lee thought. *They think we're members of a rival gang.* He pointed to the back of the van. "Keep your mouths shut or you'll end up like him."

The crimson-haired girl said, "Chill, dude. Do what you gotta do, just don't get us killed with your crazy-ass bullshit."

Lee said to Mitch, "They even old enough to drive?"

The crimson-haired girl said, "Don't you worry your snow–white ass how old we are."

Lee ignored her and asked, "They have cell phones on them?"

Mitch shook his head.

The crimson-haired girl said, "You ignorant if you think Disciples let us have phones."

While Mitch drove back toward Milwaukee, Lee wracked his brain, trying to figure out their next move. He waved the handgun at the girls. "Who's at the house in Milwaukee?"

The crimson-haired girl sighed. "You ain't shootin' us. We valuable merchandise."

Merchandise, Lee thought. What kind of hell have these girls been through already in their young lives? Over his career, how many times had Lee responded to rapes, beatings, and murders of young women? One girl who was found nude in the tall weeds of an abandoned lot still bothered him. Only thirteen, she had been gang-raped by some classmates. While Lee and the crew treated her, she sobbed and asked Lee, "Why they do that? They my friends." The pleading look on her face was heart-wrenching. He had no answer.

No way were the Disciples getting these girls back. He had to figure out a way to get them, Jasmine, and the other girl, safely away from those predators. But how?

He lowered the gun and asked, "Who's—at—the house?"

"Now we can talk?" the crimson-haired girl said.

"Your choice. If not, I can get the tape out for the rest of the drive."

Mitch chimed in, playing nice guy, "Aw c'mon, brother. You don't want to do that." He glanced at them.

The girls looked at each other and crossed their arms. Lee waited several seconds, then grabbed the roll of duct tape from his coat pocket and ripped off a length.

The crimson-haired girl said in a flat voice, "They kill us if we say anything. So, go ahead. Tape me up."

"You're ours now. They'll never see you again."

"Soon as you let Snake go, they gonna come after us.

"Don't worry about Snake. He's gonna disappear."

A loud moan came from the back of the van followed by thrashing. Mitch swiveled his head toward Lee, grinning.

Don't laugh, Lee thought.

Mitch looked into the rearview mirror. "One of the girls have scars on her neck?"

The crimson-haired girl said, "You a half-wit? Told you, tape me up."

Lee rammed the tape into his coat pocket.

* * *

When they arrived at Ace's place, it was dark but morning was not far off. The only house with a light on was at the end of the block. The girls slept. Lee went to the back of the van and quietly opened the back doors. He rolled the biker toward him, put the gun to his temple, and whispered in his ear, "I'm gonna rip the tape off your mouth. It's gonna sting, but you need to keep your mouth shut. Nod so I know you understand."

Snake nodded twice. Lee ripped the tape from his mouth. Snake sucked in a deep breath.

"Where were you taking the girls?"

"Fuck you."

Lee reached behind Snake's back and clutched the fingers he had snapped and slowly twisted them.

"Aah," Snake groaned. "Okay, okay, okay. Back to Chicago."

"Anyone expecting you down there?"

Snake clenched his lips.

Lee clasped his hand over Snake's mouth and bent his fingers into a grotesque angle. His shriek was muffled by Lee's hand. Lee released the fingers and waited for Snake's breathing to slow. Lee lifted his hand from Snake's mouth.

"We were supposed to drop these two off at the Chicago clubhouse."

"How many girls did you leave behind at Ace's place?"

"Two."

"Why weren't you taking them back to Chicago with the other two?"

"Booked for a private party on Christmas."

"How many of your brothers are at Ace's place?"

"Six."

He pulled the blindfold from Snake's head and leaned in, their faces inches apart. The red mist rose behind Lee's eyes. "If you're lying to me, I'll rip those fingers right out of their socket. One more chance. How—many—brothers?"

"Ah, fuck. Just one."

"Ace?"

Snake clenched his lips, then said flatly, "Yeah."

"Who are the two girls?"

"Summer and Crystal."

"One of them have scars on her neck?"

"Summer."

This could work, Lee thought. The adrenaline rush Lee felt on missions in Vietnam coursed through his veins.

Chapter 26

Lee

Lee stretched duct tape over Snake's mouth and closed the back doors. He went to the driver's door and motioned for Mitch to lower the window. "Turn the radio on but not too loud." Kenny Chesney's "Summertime" softly played. Mitch leaned his head out the window. In a low whisper, Lee said, "You hear Snake? Ace and Jasmine are in there. The other girl could be the one who looks like Miss Bernie's daughter. What's her name?"

"Lettie. What we waiting for? Let's go."

"Give me a minute to think this through." Lee went around the other side of the van and climbed into the passenger seat. Both girls were still sleeping. They had to do something before the neighbors began to stir. "You stay with these girls. I'm going in."

Mitch picked the rifle off the front floor of the van. "What should I do if you don't come out?"

"Call the cops and tell them a man's been murdered at this address. Take the girls to my place. Here's the keys. I don't want you around when the cops arrive."

"You think Ace would kill you?"

From the bench seat behind them, the crimson-haired girl snickered. "Oh, he kill you all right."

Lee pointed his finger at her. "I told you to keep your mouth shut."

"Dude. Okay."

Lee turned to Mitch. "If I don't come out in fifteen minutes, things went horseshit. I'll want the police here fast."

"How about I tie the girls up and come in after you?"

The black-haired girl pleaded, "Why you wanna…?"

Lee flashed his hand in front of her face. She blew out a loud breath. Lee said to Mitch, "Too risky."

"And what you're doing isn't?"

"You ready?"

"Just don't get yourself killed."

Better than swallowing a bullet in my bedroom, Lee thought.

Lee approached the darkened one-story bungalow, his body humming with electricity, the 9mm Glock pressed to his chest. He didn't want to take the chance of squeaking floorboards on the porch. He went to the back of the house and peered into the kitchen window to get an idea of the layout. Making his way through a darkened house was something he'd done countless times as a firefighter. The challenge would be to do it silently.

Lee climbed the three concrete steps to the back door and pulled the set of keys out of his pocket that he had taken from the Escalade. He thumbed through the keys and found three house keys. The first one didn't fit nor the second one. His hand shook as he inserted the third key. It didn't work either. He turned it over and tried again. Still nothing. If he kicked the door in, Ace would be ready for him, and there was no way to know how the girls would react. They could shoot him. Risk was one thing, stupid another.

Lee went back to the van and opened the back doors. Both girls were awake, watching him. Lee rolled Snake from his side to his back and dug through his front pants pockets. He rolled him to his other side where he found a key chain hanging from a belt loop. After ripping the key chain from the loop, he rolled Snake onto his back. "Nod when I get to the house key. You screw with me, I'll dump your ass in Lake Michigan right now." Snake nodded when Lee got to the fourth key on the chain.

At the back door, Lee inserted the key and turned it excruciatingly slowly. The lock clicked. Relief washed over him. *So far, so good,* he thought. *Focus.* The door hinge squeaked as he pushed on the door. He stopped and listened, taking deep breaths to control the adrenaline and slow his heartbeat. After several seconds and no sound from inside, he edged the door open.

He took two steps inside and waited for his eyes to adjust. It was dark but nothing like the total blackness of a smoke-filled room. To avoid stumbling over unseen objects, he skimmed his feet across the kitchen floor. He entered the hallway and heard the muffled sound of a television. Light flickered from the space at the bottom of a closed door. The two doors across the hallway were open. He peeked around the corner of the first one, a bathroom. Nobody there. He went to the second open door. Squinting, he made out a bare mattress on the floor. He moved to the end of the hallway and peered around the corner into the living room. Nobody there. *Good,* he thought. *They're all in one room.*

The closed door to the bedroom opened, lighting the hallway with the flickering light from the television. Lee darted around the corner into the living room, pressing himself against the wall, holding the Glock to his chest. He stared at the entryway to the hallway, praying it wasn't one of the girls who was sure to scream when she saw him. If it was Ace, he'd have to move fast before Ace saw him.

A door latch clicked. Lee peered around the corner. The bedroom door was open and the bathroom door closed. He waited, listening for any movement from the bedroom. The minutes ticked by. He had to do something before Mitch called the cops.

The toilet flushed. The bathroom door opened. A burly red-headed naked man came out. Ace. Lee was on him before he had a chance to react, pressing the gun to his temple. He clasped his hand over Ace's mouth and whispered, "Please give me an excuse to put a bullet in your head." Lee didn't recognize the surreal voice coming from his lips. It was like he was possessed. He removed his hand from Ace's mouth and put his finger to his lips. He turned him around and marched him to the living room with the gun to the back of his head. Time was running out. "Lie down on your stomach," he whispered to Ace.

"You don't know who you're fucking with."

"If you wanna take another breath, lie down." The exhilaration he felt from this strange, possessed voice was intoxicating.

Ace went to the floor. Lee pressed his knee to Ace's neck while he pulled a zip tie from his back pocket. "Hands behind your back."

Lee stuffed the gun in his coat pocket and zip-tied Ace's hands together. "Now get up."

Ace struggled to his feet. Lee pointed to a chair in the corner of the room. "Sit."

"I don't think so," shrieked a high-pitched voice behind them. The ceiling light came on.

Lee spun. An AR15 was pointed at his chest. A nude young Black woman holding the rifle ordered, "Cut him loose."

"Lettie?"

The young woman winced. She waved the barrel of the rifle up and down. "I said, cut him loose. Now."

Lee's first instinct was to dive to the floor while pulling the gun from his coat pocket. But no. He came to save these girls, not shoot one of them. He prayed for the sound of sirens. Had it been fifteen minutes yet? He had to stall. "I'll need a knife."

The young woman hooted. "Ain't giving you no knife. I look like a fool?"

"I don't know what you want me to do."

A girl wearing a sheer pink nightgown emerged from the dark hallway.

"Summer, get that ski mask off his head," Ace bellowed at her.

As Summer tied her nightgown closed and moved around the young woman, the scars on her neck caught Lee's attention. She approached Lee and reached for the ski mask. Lee pushed her hand away. If Ace saw who he was, this would be over in seconds.

"He makes another move, shoot him," Ace said to Crystal.

From the hallway came the click-clack of a bolt-action rifle being cocked. "I wouldn't do that if I were you." Mitch moved into the light of the living room, still wearing his camo ski mask, training his hunting rifle on Crystal. "Hand him the rifle!"

Summer tilted her head at the sound of Mitch's voice. Her eyebrows knit together. Lee snatched the AR15 from Crystal, who had purple bruises running up her left arm. She said, "What you after? Drugs, money, what?"

"Get dressed," Lee said, then glanced at Mitch. "Go with them. I'll finish up with this asshole."

Mitch and Summer locked eyes.

Lee shouted at Mitch, "You hear me?"

"Yeah, yeah, I heard you. C'mon, ladies. Get some clothes on." Mitch followed them to the bedroom. Lee marched Ace to the chair and wrapped duct tape around his bare chest and the back of the chair, then taped his bare ankles to the legs of the chair. Through gritted teeth, Ace said, "You gonna be one sorry-ass mother—"

Lee slapped a strip of tape over Ace's mouth.

Mitch and the girls returned to the living room. Mitch's eyes were glassy. Summer kept looking back, studying Mitch with a piercing stare.

"Let's get them to the van," Lee said. "I'll stay with them while you drag Snake in here. We gotta hurry. Sun's coming up soon. Leave your rifle on the front seat of the van."

Mitch went to the back of the van to get Snake while Lee escorted Summer and Crystal to the sliding side door. Inside, the two other girls were zip-tied to the first row of bench seats directly behind the front bucket seats. Their mouths were taped shut. They leered at him with an intensity that sent a shiver up Lee's spine. He waved the AR15 at Summer and Crystal. "Inside."

Summer and Crystal slid onto the bench seats behind the other girls. Crystal said, "The Disciples be hunting you crazy fools down."

Summer stared at the floor, saying nothing.

Mitch hefted Snake over his shoulder and headed to the house.

We have the girls. Now what? Lee wondered.

Chapter 27

Lee

Lee put the AR15 and Mitch's hunting rifle in front of the passenger seat of the van while holding his Glock on the girls. When Mitch got back, Lee handed him the handgun and said, "Keep an eye on our passengers."

"Where we going?" Mitch asked while watching the girls.

"Everything good in the house?"

Mitch grinned. "They'll both be tied up for a while."

Lee spread his arms wide. "I told you to call the cops."

"Yeah. That. You should probably know that farmers tend to have a problem with authority. You're welcome, by the way."

One of the girls gasped from the back of the van. Lee waved his palm at Mitch and shook his head. Mitch clenched his teeth and nodded. He turned to the two girls on the bench seat behind him and gently removed the tape from their mouths. "Sorry I had to do that."

"That get you off? Know all about you bondage freaks," the crimson-haired girl said, spitting. "How about cutting our hands loose?"

"Gonna behave yourselves?"

"Long as you don't fuck with us."

"Here's the deal," Lee growled in a guttural voice while Mitch cut the zip ties. "There's going to be a gang war. We knew about you girls coming up from Chicago and didn't want you in the way when we blow up those bastards and their clubhouse."

Mitch coughed into his hand. Lee kept his eyes on the road, waiting for a reply from the girls. The back of the van remained quiet. *Good. Got their attention,* he thought and said, "Our club is taking over Milwaukee. You're ours now."

Lee pulled over ten blocks from his house and turned to Mitch. "I'm gonna need you to cover their eyes. Don't want them seeing where we're taking them. We gotta get them inside the house before the neighbors are up." He took the handgun from Mitch and waved it at the girls. "I don't want to hear a sound out of any of you." *God, I hope they're buying this,* he thought.

Lee turned the radio on. The guitar intro to "Stairway to Heaven" played. Lee whispered to Mitch, "Call Miss Bernie. Tell her and Brother Williams to come to the house."

Mitch got out of the van and walked around back. As the song ended, Mitch opened the back doors and rummaged through the pile of rags. He climbed into the van and tied rags around the girls' heads, covering their eyes.

When Mitch got back in the passenger seat, Lee used his guttural voice to tell the girls if they removed the blindfolds, they'd be getting their asses beat good. He handed the gun back to Mitch and drove toward his house.

Lee parked the van in the alley behind his house. The streetlight on the corner had been out for months. As dark as it was, there was no way the girls could know where they were. "Go ahead, take your blindfolds off." He took the handgun from Mitch. "Grab the rifles. I'll take them inside." He went around the van and opened the sliding door. "Let's go."

The girls climbed out.

"Into the house." He followed them to the back door and let them in. "Everyone to the front room."

On the way to the front room, Lee grabbed a kitchen chair. When they got to the front room, Lee pointed at the dark green couch against the wall. "Sit." The four girls squeezed onto it with Lee sitting across from them holding the handgun. He removed his coat and hung it on the back of his chair.

Crystal said, "When you blowing up their clubhouse?"

"They ain't blowin' up no clubhouse," Summer said. "They ain't members of any bike gang."

The three other girls gawked at her. Lee lowered the gun and slid it into the pocket of his coat. He removed his ski mask. "She's right. We wanted to get you away from the Disciples."

The crimson-haired girl screeched, "You motherfucker, wavin' guns at us, tyin' us up. What the fuck that all about?" She jumped up from the couch and charged at Lee, knocking him and his chair backward before he could react. She pounced on him. Her razor-sharp nails dug into his scalp. He caught her other hand as she tried to rake her nails over his face. Mitch charged into the room and lifted her off, holding her arms to her side. She screeched, writhing against his grasp.

Crystal rushed at Mitch, grabbed a handful of hair through his ski mask, and yanked his head back. "Get off her." She pulled the ski mask from his head, tossed it aside, and grabbed another handful of hair.

Lee sprang to his feet and tried to pull Crystal off Mitch. The room filled with grunts and groans.

From behind them, Summer said in a calm voice, "They won't hurt us. Leave them be."

Crystal scowled at Summer. "What you talking about, girl?"

"Trust me."

Crystal released Mitch. Lee sat back against the couch, rubbing his scalp, which was wet with blood. The crimson-haired girl stopped squirming.

"You okay, now?" Mitch asked.

"No, I ain't okay." She looked to Summer. "What kinda crazy shit going on here?"

Mitch let the crimson-haired girl go and said to Summer, "Jasmine, Oh, my God, Jasmine. I can't believe you're standing in front of me. You have to know we're only here to help."

"How he know your real name?" Crystal asked.

"Saved my life once."

"What he doing here?"

While staring at Mitch, Jasmine murmured, "Guessing he wants to save me again."

"You know that ain't happening. Disciples will hunt us down."

Mitch went to Jasmine and held her hands in his. The room went still. Everyone watched. After several seconds, Jasmine blew out a loud breath, looked down, and pushed his hands away. "You don't know what you got into. Get us back to the Disciples. They gonna track you down and kill you. Drop us off at the clubhouse. We'll tell them we never saw your faces."

"What about your sister? We promised her we'd bring you home."

Jasmine's face clouded. Barely above a whisper, she said, "The Disciples know about Alexus. They got pictures of her walking to school. Said if I caused problems, they'd hurt her. Now you're mixed up in this too. Take us back. Please. Before it's too late."

Crystal said, "We leaving. Can't stop us. C'mon, girls." She grabbed Jasmine's arm and headed to the back door. The two other girls followed, watching Mitch over their shoulders.

"Jasmine, no. Stay," Mitch pleaded. "We'll figure something out. Crystal—or should I say Lettie? I saw the bruises on your arm. How can you go back to that? Don't you want to go back to your mom, Miss Bernie? I don't get it."

"Don't know where you get that Lettie bullshit."

The girls rushed to the kitchen with Lee and Mitch following. Crystal went to the back door. It flew open as she reached for the knob. Miss Bernie stood in the doorway with Brother Williams towering behind her. Miss Bernie and Crystal locked eyes, staring at versions of themselves separated by time, their mouths gaping open in unison. Everyone froze.

Miss Bernie gripped her chest. "Lettie," she said and collapsed.

Chapter 28

Mitch

Mitch and Lee immediately knelt next to Miss Bernie, turning her onto her back. Mitch leaned in and shouted, "Miss Bernie. Miss Bernie. You still with us?" No response. Lee tilted her head back and put his ear to her mouth. He gritted his teeth, shook his head, and gave her two breaths mouth-to-mouth. Mitch placed two fingers on the side of her throat. His stomach clenched when he felt nothing. After several seconds he said, "Crap. No pulse."

Brother Williams dropped to the floor on all fours next to them, his perpetual smile sagging into gloom. Lee said to him, "Call 911. Tell them there's two firefighters performing CPR on a woman and we need a MED unit here."

Mitch gave chest compressions while Lee performed mouth-to-mouth breathing. Brother Williams made the call as the four girls rushed out the back door. He called after them, "Jasmine. Lettie. Please don't..."

They were out the door before he could finish.

Brother Williams returned to Miss Bernie's side. He held her hand in his, looking to the ceiling. "Please, Lord. Don't take my dear Bernice from me. I beseech you. Please." He drew her hand to his lips.

The crew from Engine 32 hustled in and took over CPR while attaching the defibrillator pads to Miss Bernie's chest. Within seconds, two paramedics rushed into the kitchen as the defibrillator analyzed her heart rhythm. One of the paramedics examined the read-out on the machine and ordered everyone to stay clear. Miss Bernie's back arched as a shock was administered. The kitchen became a flurry of activity as an IV was set up. Miss Bernie was intubated, and a doctor was called on the radio for instructions on which meds to give through the IV. The engine company resumed chest compressions.

"How long was she down?" the boss from Engine 32 asked.

Mitch was speechless, watching this lady he loved so dearly, near death, if not gone already. *You can't die,* he thought. *Not now. We will bring Lettie and Jasmine home to you.*

"We started CPR as soon as she went down," Lee said. "Couldn't have been more than a couple minutes ago."

Brother Williams gawked at the sight of Miss Bernie, the front of her blouse cut open with defibrillator pads attached to her chest, a tube sticking out of her mouth, and an IV needle taped to the top of her hand.

"Let's go to the front room where we can talk," Lee said, putting his arm on Brother Williams' back. He motioned for Mitch to follow.

Lee, Mitch, and Brother Williams plodded to the front room, followed by the lieutenant from Engine 32. They answered the lieutenant's questions for his report. When he was satisfied, he went back to the kitchen.

Brother Williams sat on the couch, his eyes closed, and his hands in prayer. Mitch sat next to him. "She's in good hands. She'll be fine. You'll see."

Brother Williams opened his eyes and placed his beefy hand on Mitch's shoulder. "The good Lord will have the final say on that, my brother. I pray He hears my prayers." He closed his eyes and went back to silently praying. Mitch was not a praying man but said some of his own.

They sat in silence as minutes clicked by on the round wall clock.

"Dammit. What was I thinking?" Lee said. "What a stupid, stupid idea to have her come here."

Mitch shrugged. "What else were we gonna do? You heard the girls. They're terrified of the Disciples. Miss Bernie would have been able to convince them to stay. I know it."

"But they didn't, and Miss Bernie's…"

Brother Williams stood with his hands on his hips. "I don't want to hear another word. You men were doing God's work. Who else was going to rescue those girls? They're both alive. You'll find them. Now we pray for Bernice."

The three sat in leaden silence. They all jumped when one of the paramedics shouted, "Clear." Over the next thirty minutes, this played out four more times. With each round of shocks, Mitch's hope faded.

Several minutes after the last shout of clear, the lieutenant came into the front room. "MED unit's transporting. Who's going along?"

Brother Williams sprang from the couch and followed him to the kitchen. Mitch and Lee were right behind. Mitch asked, "How's she doing?"

"They got a weak pulse back." He looked to Brother Williams. "You can ride along with the MEDs. Hurry before they leave."

Lee said to the lieutenant, "Thank you, brother. Nice work."

"Heard you're laid up."

"Bad back."

"Nice save at the school fire. They know who started it?

"They're thinking the One-Niners had something to do with it."

"Gotta get back in service," the lieutenant said as he headed to the door. "Take care of yourself."

After he left, Mitch said, "We better get over to Miss Bernie's and let those kids know what's going on."

Lee glanced around the kitchen. "My coat's gone. One of the girls must have grabbed it when Miss Bernie went down."

"You have another coat?"

"My gun was in it."

Lee went to his bedroom and came back with a well-worn, faded black coat. He followed Mitch out the back door. Mitch looked up and down the deserted alley. He shouted, "Crap. The van's gone."

"Now they've got the van and my gun."

"I can't believe Jasmine would take off like that. She loved Miss Bernie."

Lee opened his palms. "Who knows? Drugs, fear, brainwashing. She might not be the girl you knew. We're gonna have to watch our asses. Those girls run back to the Disciples, they'll come looking for us."

"Gotta hope they say they don't know who we are."

Lee frowned. "Jasmine might not say anything. But what about the others? They were pretty pissed."

"We'd better get over to Miss Bernie's."

"We'll have to walk. My car's still there."

"Your back okay to walk that far?"

"I'll stash the rifles."

* * *

The kids were gathered in the front room when they arrived. Merle lounged on the recliner in the corner. When he saw Lee, he said, "Get me out of here. These damn kids are driving me nuts."

"Pipe down. I don't have time to argue with you."

Merle swatted at the air. Mitch told the kids Miss Bernie had a heart attack and was at Sinai Hospital with Brother Williams. The room erupted with questions. Mitch told them they didn't know anything more but were going to the hospital and would report back to them. He asked the kids to keep an eye on Merle and not to let him wander off. They looked at each other as if they were being assigned to watch Freddie from the horror movie. Mitch and Lee headed to the front door. Alexus followed. "You take me along."

"I don't know if they let kids in the room," Mitch said.

"Don't care. I'm coming."

Mitch knew better than to try and convince her to stay. They piled into Lee's car. Mitch sat in the back seat with Alexus. As they pulled away from the curb, Alexus asked, "Momma Bernie gonna die?"

"I heard you don't want to be called Lexi anymore."

"Tell me! Momma Bernie gonna die?"

He had never lied to this little girl and as much as it hurt, he had to admit the painful truth.

"I don't know."

Alexus lowered her head and stared at her folded hands. Mitch searched for words of comfort as he draped his arm over her back and kissed the side of her head. All he came up with was, "We all know how strong Momma Bernie is."

Alexus looked up with tears streaking down her cheeks and said, "Momma Bernie told us they were going over to Mr. Garrison's house. What happened?"

Mitch saw Lee glance at him in the mirror, raising his eyebrows.

No more surprises, Mitch thought, and told her about finding Jasmine and Miss Bernie's daughter, Lettie, at Ace's place on the

South Side. He paused. Her face lit up. "She at the hospital with Momma Bernie?"

"Better tell her the rest," Lee said.

Mitch told her how they brought the girls back to Lee's house but feared the girls would run back to the Disciples. They hoped Miss Bernie and Brother Williams could help persuade them to stay. Mitch cleared his throat and told her how Miss Bernie collapsed when she saw her daughter and how the girls ran off.

When Mitch finished, Alexus's expression hardened. "That was not Jasmine. She'd never run off and leave Momma Bernie." She crossed her arms and sat back, shaking her head.

They drove in silence to the hospital.

At the hospital, they found Brother Williams sitting in the corner of the waiting room deep in prayer. Alexus ran to him and wrapped her arms around his waist. He caressed the top of her head with his massive hand. "Oh, my sweet girl. We must trust in the good Lord."

"Any news?" Mitch asked.

"A doctor came by a few minutes ago. Said they were taking Bernice to the cath lab. They may need to put stents in."

"How she doing?"

"All the good doctor would say is that they're doing everything possible."

Alexus looked up at Brother Williams. "Mitch said Jasmine was there when Momma Bernie fell out. Said she ran off."

Brother Williams leaned down and cradled her chin in his hand. "I think she just got scared."

Alexus pulled back, shaking her head hard. "Nope. That was not my sister."

Brother Williams pulled her back into his arms. "Let us pray for Momma Bernie."

Chapter 29

Lee

Late in the morning, a tall doctor wearing blue scrubs entered the waiting room. Everyone stood. "Mrs. Williams is in recovery. One of her coronary arteries had a substantial blockage. We inserted a stent to open the artery and restore blood flow to the heart."

Alexus ran to him. "She gonna be okay?"

The doctor smiled and nodded. He looked at Brother Williams. "Were you the one who started CPR?"

"No, it was these two men. God bless them."

"Any idea what might have triggered the cardiac arrest?"

My genius idea to have her come to the house, Lee thought and said, "Saw her daughter."

The doctor's brows knit together.

Mitch explained, "She was shocked to see her estranged daughter."

"Okay. But, no more shocks. She'll need plenty of rest."

Alexus tugged at the doctor's sleeve. "I need to see her."

The doctor knelt. "You her granddaughter?"

"I'm her daughter."

"Wait. I'm confused. You the estranged daughter?"

"Nope. I'm adopted."

"Sorry. Your mother is still in recovery. Once she recovers from the anesthetic and is stable, she'll be moved to a room. Then you can see her. A nurse will let you know." He looked to the men. "Any questions?"

Brother Williams wiped at his eyes, then reached out his hand. The doctor rose. Brother Williams grasped the doctor's hand and pulled him into a bear hug. "You are surely doing the good Lord's work here. God bless you, Doctor. I can't thank you enough."

Alexus joined in the hug and leaned her head against the doctor. As the three continued the group hug, a dry lump swelled in Lee's throat. Whatever it would take, he would get this family back together.

When the hugging was over, the doctor said to Alexus, "That's the sweetest thank you I can ever remember. Your mother is lucky to have such a loving family."

Alexus pinched her lips together, then said, "Nope. We're the lucky ones."

The doctor grinned and rushed out.

Mitch turned to Lee. "Now what?"

"You stay here. I gotta find the girls before the Disciples send them back to Chicago."

"No, *we're* gonna find them," Mitch said. "Jasmine doesn't know you. I might be able to talk her into staying. It's our only option."

"That is not Jasmine," Alexus said, jutting out her lower jaw. "Told you. She would never leave Momma Bernie like that."

Brother Williams rested his hand on Alexus's shoulder. "You men do what you have to do. We'll be here when Bernice wakes. May the good Lord watch over you and keep you safe."

* * *

Lee drove back to his house, parking two blocks away. They watched the house for several minutes. "No sign of the Disciples," Lee said and drove to the back alley.

When Lee parked the car, Mitch asked, "So, what's up?"

"Be right back. I'll run inside and get the rifles."

"Okaay? Then what?"

Good question, Lee thought, without answering Mitch. He went around to all of the windows, ensuring no Disciples were waiting to ambush him. He stepped inside the back door and stopped, listening. Hearing nothing, he got Ace's AR15 and Mitch's hunting rifle from behind his dad's dresser.

Mitch was standing by the car when Lee got back outside. "Should we call in a stolen vehicle report? Get the cops looking for them?" Mitch asked,

"Too many things could go wrong. If the girls run and there's a high-speed chase, there's no telling what could happen. And they have my gun. What if one of the girls gets crazy and starts shooting at the cops? Or, like you already pointed out, what if the cops pull them over and they say they were kidnapped by us at gunpoint?"

Mitch raised his eyebrows. "Copy that."

"I've been thinking," Lee said. "Ace is not that sharp, but he knows we were looking for Jasmine. Good chance he'll figure out it was us who took the girls. And he knows what your truck looks like. Better get it from Miss Bernie's and park it in my garage. Don't need those assholes showing up there looking for us."

* * *

After Mitch parked his truck in Lee's garage and got into Lee's car, he asked, "What now?"

"We make the rounds. Let's start with Ace's place." *What's the chance the girls would be there?* Lee thought. But they had to try everything. No assumptions.

On the way there, Mitch let out a loud groan. Lee asked, "What?"

"All my stuff is in the van. If the Disciples go through it, they'll find my address."

"You need to go back to the farm and protect your family. I'll take care of things here."

Mitch gripped his forehead and went silent.

Lee turned his car around. "I'm taking you back to your truck."

"And do what back at the farm? Wait and wonder if they're coming after me? We have to end this here. You're not doing this alone."

"What about your family?"

"I'll make some calls."

"How will that—?"

"I got plenty of well-armed neighbors who can shoot better than me. They're all hunters. Some are vets like you. They'll be more than happy to protect my family while we take care of this."

Take care of this, Lee thought. *Sounds simple. But how?*

They drove past Ace's house and Ralph's house with no sign of the van or the Disciples. Lee drove on to the clubhouse, frustrated at how close they had come to getting the girls and how he had screwed that up. He was pissed at himself for not thinking things through.

When they got to the clubhouse, Lee's frustration deepened. The area around the clubhouse was deserted.

"Crap," Mitch said. "Where do we go from here?"

Lee dug Brigid's card from his wallet and punched the numbers on his cell phone. She answered, "Start talking."

"It's Lee. You said to call anytime. Can I come over?"

"This a booty call?"

"Jesus, no."

"Very flattering."

"Look, if this is a bad time..."

Brigid laughed and said, "I'm screwing with you. C'mon over. I'm off Good Hope on 99th. Address is on my card."

Lee ended the call. Mitch asked, "That your cop friend?"

"You heard?"

Mitch's eyebrows knit together. "Booty call?"

"Need to shut your pie hole."

"Think she can help?"

"Got any other ideas?"

Chapter 30

Lee

Two massive pine trees bordered the asphalt driveway that led to a dark-brown ranch house with white trim. Lee pulled up to the garage and parked. Mitch followed him to the front door. Deep-throated barking erupted from inside. Before Lee pressed the doorbell, the door swung open. Brigid held the collar of a massive white pit bull baring its teeth.

Lee stepped back. "Why doesn't that surprise me?"

Brigid snapped her fingers at the dog and let go of its collar. The dog lay down with its head resting on its front legs. "Shame I can't train men like that. C'mon in."

The dog trotted behind them to the kitchen. Brigid motioned for them to sit at the beige tile-top table. "You both look like hell." She studied Lee for a few seconds. "I take it you're not here for peer counseling."

"Nice detective work," Lee said.

"Real clever."

"Just screwing with you."

"You two want to be alone?" Mitch asked.

Brigid ignored him and asked, "What kind of shit you two get yourselves into?"

Lee glanced at Mitch, then said to Brigid. "If I tell you we did some things against the law, as a retired cop, do you have to turn us in?"

"Depends. If you murdered someone, damn right I'd turn your asses in. If not, let's have it."

Lee told her about the attempted rescue of the girls. Throughout the story, she showed no emotion. It was like she was studying him for his reactions, her chin resting on her open palm. When he finished, Brigid kneaded her forehead.

Say something, Lee thought as the silence became unbearable.

"I'm gonna need a beer," she finally said. "What about you two?"

"A cold beer sounds good," Lee said.

Mitch raised his hand. "Me too."

She brought three bottles of Miller High Life to the table. "Now, what do you want from me?"

"Any ideas on what we do next?"

She twisted the cap off her beer bottle. "You kidnapped four women at gunpoint. Three are probably minors. That's some serious shit."

"What else were we supposed to do?" Mitch asked.

"Not that."

"You told us not to go to the police," Lee said.

"Also told you to walk away from this."

Lee leaned across the table. "I told you we can't."

"Too late for that anyway. If the Disciples find you, they will kill you. I gotta process this." She peeled the label from her beer bottle while Lee and Mitch sipped at theirs.

She clicked her tongue and said, "From what you told me, you still have no proof the Disciples are trafficking underage girls. Somehow you have to find the girls and convince at least one of them to testify."

Mitch shook his head. "Then they'll go after her and her family."

"Let me do some digging while you two see if you can at least track the girls down. No guns."

"If they're already on their way to Chicago, we're screwed," Lee said.

Brigid took a long sip of beer, set it down, and said, "Then get your asses in gear. Get out there and find them before that happens."

When they got back in the car, Mitch said, "Darn. She is tough. She'll give you a run for your money."

"What the hell you talking about? Ah, forget it. You need to haul your ass back to the farm. I don't want you going down with me if this turns bad."

Mitch's phone buzzed. "It's Brother Williams." He put the phone to his ear. "Yes, sir ... That's great news ... No, we haven't found the girls ... Okay, we'll check on them." Mitch lowered the phone. "Miss Bernie's awake. They're worried about the kids being alone at the house with the threats and the drive-by shooting." He peered out the side window. "I'm not leaving. Let's go."

"Wait. I gotta talk to Brigid."

Mitch smiled. "Unfinished business?"

Lee hustled to the front door. Before he pressed the doorbell, the dog barked. Brigid opened the door, smirking. "Second thoughts on the booty call?"

"Need your help."

"Okaay?" Brigid said.

Lee told her about the house getting shot up and the threats to Brother Williams if he refuses to sell his school. When he finished, he said, "Brother Williams saw the car that shot up their house. It's the One-Niners'. And the police have reports of One-Niners in the area when the school fire started."

"Anyone been arrested?"

"They've disappeared. The cops were protecting the house for a few days after the shooting but they're done. Somebody needs to protect those kids."

"Jesus. You do have a serious death wish. First the Disciples. Now the One-Niners. I'm afraid to ask. What you want from me?"

"Can you watch their house while we're out looking for the girls?"

"That I can do."

Lee wrote the address down and turned to leave. She grabbed his wrist. He turned back to her. She reached up, pulled his face to hers, beer on her breath, and said, "I gotta do this." She kissed him hard and pushed him away. "Now go. Find those girls. I'll watch the house."

Lee plodded to the car, his lips tingling. When he got in, Mitch asked, "Holy crap. What did she do to you?"

* * *

They parked down the street from Ace's place at the opposite end of the block from where they had parked the last time. A black van, a black Escalade similar to the one Lee drove into the woods, and two cars were parked in front of the house. "Must have ditched the school van," Mitch said.

"We don't know the girls ran back here. Any of the Disciples could have shown up and called the others."

Mitch pounded the dashboard. "Why did Jasmine have to run?"

"You heard her. Felt like she was protecting Alexus."

"What about Lettie?" Mitch asked. "Leaving her mother lying on the floor like that."

"We don't know what those bastards have done to them."

Mitch yawned and leaned his head against the window. The sun was just going down, but it didn't take long before he was snoring. Neither of them had slept much in the last two days. Getting by with little or no sleep was nothing new for Lee. He hadn't slept through the night in decades. There was no way he'd be able to quiet his mind tonight. And he didn't want to. He had to figure a way to find the girls, get them away from the Disciples, and somehow keep the Disciples from coming after them. The hours dragged on with no better plan than to sit here and wait.

Close to midnight, the bikers filtered out of the house. Lee poked Mitch. "Check this out."

Ace and Snake followed the Manson look-alike to the black van. He turned and began shouting something at them while ramming his finger into Ace's chest. Lee couldn't make out what he was saying. Ace and Snake hung their heads like a couple of schoolboys being dressed down by the principal. The Manson look-alike paused and appeared to be waiting for an answer. He pushed Ace against the black van. Ace made no move to defend himself. The Manson look-alike pulled a handgun from inside his black leather jacket, jammed the barrel under Ace's chin, and ranted something.

"Holy crap," Mitch said. "He's gonna kill Ace. Do we just watch this?"

Before Lee could reply, the Manson look-alike kicked Ace in the groin and stomped to the black Escalade waiting at the curb. Ace clutched his groin and dropped to the ground.

"Wow. Mr. Manson doesn't respond well to disappointment," Lee said.

Lee's phone beeped. "It's Brigid." He put the phone to his ear and asked, "Everything…?"

"You need to get over here, now," she said. "I got one of the One-Niners. He was prowling around the house."

"On our way." Lee ended the call.

"Holy crap," Mitch said.

"You heard that?"

"Let's get over there."

Chapter 31

Lee

They raced to Miss Bernie's house and parked behind Brigid's red F150 crew cab pickup truck. When they approached the passenger side, a thin Black man with spiked hair braids and a scraggly goatee peered out at them. Next to him, Brigid had a gun pointed at his head. Lee opened the door, grabbed the man by the collar of his black leather coat, and yanked him out of the truck. The red mist of rage rose, blurring his vision. "Burning down the school wasn't enough, you piece of shit?" Lee slammed his fist into the man's face.

Before he landed another punch, Brigid shouted from inside the truck, "Lee. Lee. Stop. Listen. He said he's gotta talk to Brother Williams. That's why he's here."

From behind Lee, Mitch said, "Holy crap. Deion. Peaches' dad. What the hell? I tutored your little girl. Why would you burn down her school?"

Lee lowered his fist and cocked his head at Mitch.

Spitting blood, Deion said to Mitch, his voice raspy, "'Course I know you. Peaches still talk about you and your farm."

"Why you doing this?"

"Get me Brother Williams."

"Better get him off the street," Brigid said. "Might be more of them watching."

Deion pointed at Lee. "If they was, this motherfucker be dead."

Lee raised his fist.

"Stop," Brigid ordered. "Let's get him inside."

Lee marched Deion up the porch steps with Mitch and Brigid following. When they went inside, the front room was dark, the Christmas tree a shadow in the corner. Merle snored in the recliner. "Let's take him to the kitchen," Lee said.

Brigid handed her gun to Lee. "I'll stay here and watch the front of the house. Try not to shoot him."

Lee saluted. "Yes, ma'am. There's a bunch of kids upstairs. Any of them come down, don't let them in the kitchen."

Brigid pointed at Merle. "What about him?"

"That's my dad." Lee nodded toward Deion. "This asshole's gang could shoot up the place again and my old man wouldn't stir." Before Deion could respond, Lee shoved him into the kitchen and pushed him down onto the wooden bench. Deion stretched a black hoodie over his head. He glared at Lee while wiping blood from his chin.

Mitch fished his cell phone from his coat pocket. "I'll let Brother Williams know what's going on." He went to the front room.

Lee fought the anger rising in his chest. "I was here when you animals shot up the house. You could have hit one of those kids, you piece of shit."

"Don't know nothin' about that."

"We saw your car."

Deion's eyebrows pinched together. "What the fuck you talkin' about, cracker?"

"That green Riviera. Hard to miss."

"Ain't talking to your saltine ass no more." Deion flashed his middle finger at Lee and crossed his arms over his chest.

Lee breathed deep, fighting the urge to go over the top of the table at him.

Mitch entered the kitchen and stopped, eyeing Lee. "Brother Williams and Alexus will be on their way here as soon as they get a cab. Said Miss Bernie keeps asking about Jasmine and Lettie."

Deion snapped his head around to Mitch. "You talkin' about the girl DeAndre killed?"

"Didn't kill her. Sold her to the Disciples."

"Damn. Thought for sure that girl dead."

"How many other girls you sell them?"

"Once DeAndre gone, we stop all that dirty business. Just deal our product."

"Selling drugs isn't dirty business?" Lee shouted.

Deion ignored Lee and said to Mitch, "You did us a favor taking him out. Dude's head was fucked from smokin' the glass dick." He scowled at Lee. "We don't force no one to take our product, jus' supply what they want. If we don't, someone else will. Know what I'm sayin'? And we don't sell to no kids." Deion leveled his index finger at Mitch. "Wasn't for me, you'd be in a box if I didn't stop the brothas from cappin' your ass."

"He's right," Mitch said to Lee. "He did call them off."

"I say you owe me," Deion said, wiping more blood from his chin.

"We should turn his ass over to the cops," Lee said. "Let them figure this out."

Deion cackled. "They ain't figuring nothin' out."

"Let's wait for Brother Williams. See what he thinks," Mitch said.

* * *

Brigid appeared in the doorway to the kitchen a half-hour later. "They're here."

Within seconds, Alexus dashed by her into the kitchen and up to Mitch. "You find my sister?"

He clenched his lips and shook his head. She went to Lee. "Why aren't you looking for her? You promised."

"We will. First, we had to make sure everyone here was safe."

She glanced at Deion. "That's Peaches' dad. He the one shot up our house?"

Deion snarled, "Didn't shoot up nobody's house."

From the entryway to the kitchen came the deep voice of Brother Williams, "Why you all hiding then?"

"We need to talk, Junior."

"Junior?" Lee asked Brother Williams.

"That's what they called me back in the day, long before this man was around." Brother Williams took a seat across from Deion. "You could have killed this little girl when you burned down my school." He pointed at Lee. "Thank the good Lord this man saved her."

"Why would I burn down your school? My Peaches goes there."

Brother Williams leaned across the table. "Your crew was seen there when the fire started."

"That's why we went underground. Knew the cops would be on our black asses."

"Why were they there?"

"A brotha got a call that one of our dealers was being jacked. Needed to get some people there fast."

"Who called?"

"Don't know. Everyone got burners."

Lee grabbed Deion's neck with one hand while pointing the gun in his face. "Sounds like a bunch of bullshit to me. What about you assholes shooting up the house?"

Brother Williams pulled Lee's hand off Deion's neck. "Let's hear the man out."

Deion rubbed his throat. "Cracker's got serious anger issues."

Brother Williams rested his elbows on the table. "We saw your car."

Deion claimed the green Riviera had been stolen from them over a week ago. They didn't report it because it came from a chop shop. Whoever stole the car was trying to set up the One-Niners for the drive-by and the school fire.

"Why should we believe scum like you?" Lee asked.

Deion said to Brother Williams, "Can we talk without Wonder-bread pointing that cannon at me?"

Brother Williams waved for Lee to lower the gun and said to Deion, "Why did you come here?"

"You needed to know we didn't torch your school. You know that don't make no sense."

Brother Williams leaned back, rubbing his chin. Lee looked at Mitch, who turned his palms up. They all waited for Brother Williams to say something.

Alexus pushed between Lee and Deion. "Your daughter's a friend of mine. Said you not a bad man. Why you let DeAndre take my sister and do her like that? Now those bikers got her."

"That was all DeAndre. Had nothing to do with it. I knew Jasmine. She a good kid."

"He was in your gang. You need to get her back from those bikers."

Brother Williams rubbed his bottom lip. "She's right. Your crew owes that to this family."

"You believe this scumbag?" Lee asked. "We should turn his ass in." He looked back at Brigid, who was still standing in the doorway. "Am I right?"

She clicked her tongue, then said, "One-Niners have a better chance of finding her than you two. And you don't want the police involved. You don't know what those girls will say. Too risky. You know what I mean."

"Listen to the bitch," Deion said. "Turn me in, good luck gettin' Jasmine back from the Disciples. You think the cops give a shit about missing Black girls from the 'hood? Those girls white? It'd be all over the news. Simple fact."

"Let him help," Alexus pleaded.

Brother Williams clasped his hands together as if in prayer and looked to the ceiling. After a long pause, he said to Deion, "I believe you, brother. Go find Jasmine. She'll be with three others. One of them is Miss Bernie's daughter."

"Gotcha, Bro. I'll put word on the street to watch for the Disciples and the sisters." Deion scowled at Lee. "We'll be settling up later."

Mitch fished the photo of Jasmine out of his back pocket and handed it to Deion. "This should help."

Deion examined the photo. "We'll find her."

Chapter 32

Lee

After Deion left, Brother Williams escorted Alexus upstairs to her bedroom, leaving Lee, Mitch, and Brigid in the kitchen. Lee asked Mitch, "What was that gangbanger's daughter doing at your farm?"

"Brother Williams brought some kids from his school to my farm for a week. Had a great time."

Brigid wasn't listening and said, "How did I let myself get pulled into this insanity?"

Mitch grinned. "Probably couldn't resist the charms of our captain."

The heat rose in Lee's face. "We need a plan," he said, desperately trying to change the subject.

Brigid grinned. "Yes. A plan. What do you have in mind?"

"I was hoping you might have an idea."

"From what you told me about the altercation at Ace's house, it would appear the girls haven't shown up yet. But if and when they go back or are found by the Disciples, chances are they'll tell them who took them and where you live. You can't go home."

"What do you suggest we do?" Lee asked.

"The One-Niners are out looking for the girls. The police are investigating the school fire and the drive-by. I would suggest you step back and crash at my place for a while and clear your head."

"Can't. I gotta keep looking."

"Have it your way. I'm heading home. Let me know if you change your mind."

After she left, Mitch grinned at Lee. "How can you pass that up?"

"We gotta find the girls. You coming?"

On the way to Lee's car, Mitch said, "She's right, Captain. You should get some rest. If you don't mind my saying, you're looking pretty rough."

"I do mind," Lee said as he opened the car door.

"Okay, I'll keep my mouth shut. Where to?"

"Since everybody cleared out of Ace's house, let's check the clubhouse."

"Wish there was something else we could do," Mitch said. "This sitting and watching is mind-numbing."

"I'm open to any ideas."

They drove to the clubhouse in silence. When they got there, Mitch peered at the vacant warehouse. "That thermal blanket is still in the van. You gonna be okay up there?"

"I still got those mittens and ski mask. It's pretty calm out tonight. I should be fine as long as that wind doesn't kick up."

Lee carried the AR15 he had gotten from Ace to the second floor of the abandoned warehouse. Mitch followed with his hunting rifle. "You're not walking like an old farmer anymore."

"Still hurts like hell, but it's tolerable."

"How long has it been bad?"

"Seems to have flared up more the last six months."

Mitch found some pallets and stacked them next to the open window for them to sit on. Mitch dozed off several times. Lee couldn't quiet his mind enough to sleep. A few people came and went but no sign of the girls or Ace and Snake. Lee was losing hope fast.

"I don't think I could be a cop doing stakeouts," Mitch said. "This is awfully boring."

"Don't you hunters sit up in tree stands for hours on end?"

"Not through the night when we should be sleeping. How long you wanna stay here?"

"Where else we gonna go?" Lee asked.

"Then I'm going to get some chow from George Webb's."

"Just get me coffee."

After Mitch got back and ate his burgers, he stretched out on the pallet and promptly fell asleep.

How the hell does he just drop off like that? Lee thought. *Must be a farmer thing.*

When the orange glow of the rising sun cast light beams across the rutted heavy-timber flooring, Lee had all but lost hope of the girls showing up here or anywhere in Milwaukee. Since they belonged to the Chicago club, they might have run back there with the van. Maybe it was time to head to the Windy City.

Clomping from the stairwell sent a jolt through Lee. He shook Mitch and whispered, "Someone's coming. Get behind that fifty-five-gallon drum."

"What about you?"

"I'll stand off to the side of the doorway."

"The Disciples?"

"Gonna find out real soon."

Lee hurried to the side of the entrance, waved his hand at Mitch, and put his finger to his lips. Lee slowed his breathing and focused on the growing rumble from the stairwell. He held the AR15 tight to his chest, blending into the shadows from the support columns, waiting to ambush them from behind once they entered the room.

Two figures in black hoodies carrying AK47s sauntered into the room. The taller one said, "When you gonna let me get a taste of your fine sister?"

"When you let me at your fine momma."

The big man placed his hand on the shorter man's shoulder and hooted. "She eat you up and spit you out, little man."

"Stop," Lee shouted while pointing the AR15 at them. "Drop your guns. Don't turn around."

The tall one said, "You know who you're fuckin' with?"

"One more time. Drop the guns."

"How about you drop yours, cracker," came from the doorway. Lee looked back to see two more figures in black hoodies emerge from the doorway with AK47s trained on his back.

Dammit. How could I be so stupid? Lee fumed. He raised his left hand in the air and bent to place the AR15 on the floor. "Look. I thought you were the Disciples."

"We look like a bunch of raggedy-assed bikers?"

"No. I…"

"Everybody slow down," Mitch said, peering over the top of the fifty-five-gallon drum, aiming his hunting rifle at the two men in the doorway. The big man spun and pointed his AK47 at Mitch. His short partner did the same. For a brief second, Lee considered diving to the floor while swinging the AR15 up and taking out the two who were distracted by Mitch. If they had been Disciples, there would have been no decision. But who were these people? Everyone froze.

Another figure in a black hoodie came around the two in the doorway who had their AK47s pointed at Lee and said, "Who we got here?"

Lee couldn't make out the face but there was no mistaking the raspy voice.

Deion slipped his hood back. "I know these crackers." He pointed at Lee. "I owe that one." He pointed to Mitch. "That dude's straight."

The tall gangbanger asked, "What we do, Deion?"

Deion glared at Lee. "Junior say you okay. I got to respect that for now. Someday, we settle up." Deion motioned for the gang members to lower their rifles. Mitch stood and lowered his rifle. Deion approached him. "So, I save your ass again."

"No. You saved theirs." Mitch tilted his head toward the tall gangbanger and his partner.

"Okay, dude. I give you that. What up?"

"No sign of the girls."

"What about you?" Lee said from behind Deion. "You said if they're in town, you'd find them."

Deion said to Mitch, "Get his nasty ass out of here. Don't trust that mean-eyed motherfucker. We'll take over."

The red mist rose. Lee took two steps toward Deion. The gangbanger next to Deion pointed his AK47 at Lee. Mitch moved in front of Lee. "C'mon, Captain. Let's get out of here. Let these gents take over."

Deion eyed Lee, then said, "Yes, let us gents take over."

As much as Lee wanted to get at Deion, he knew Mitch was right. Lee picked up the AR15 and followed Mitch to the stairwell.

When they got back to the car, Mitch said, "You sure got a way with people."

"Scum like that should be locked up."

"That scum is our best chance of finding the girls. They got this. How about we check on Miss Bernie?"

"I'll drop you off at the hospital. I should check on my dad."

Chapter 33

Mitch

Mitch found Miss Bernie's room and cautiously entered, not wanting to wake her if she was sleeping. She was sitting up watching a cooking show on the wall-mounted television. When she saw him, she reached out her arms. He couldn't get to her bed fast enough. She groaned as he hugged her. He stopped and pulled back. Through the dry knot in his throat, he croaked, "Did I hurt you?"

"My ribs a bit sore. Seems that some strong young man was pressing on my chest yesterday morning." She grasped his face between her hands and kissed him on the cheek. "You save my life."

Mitch swallowed hard. "Brother Williams tell you what happened?"

"Clarence filled me in. Said the girls ran off when I fell out. You find 'em?"

"It's all my fault. I should have told you they were at Lee's house."

"Stop that foolishness. Doctor says I was lucky you and Mr. Garrison there. Said a artery to my heart was clogged up bad. It would likely give out sometime soon. If nobody was there, I'd be paying a visit to the good Lord. He made sure you were there when it stopped." She patted the bed next to her. "Now sit yourself down and tell me about my Lettie and Jasmine."

Mitch told her how he and Lee had found the girls and taken them to Lee's house, hoping she and Brother Williams could persuade the girls to stay and not run back to the Disciples. He told her how the Disciples had photos of Alexus and warned Jasmine if she left, they would hurt her.

When he finished, Miss Bernie wiped at her eyes with a Kleenex. "Oh, my poor Jasmine, carrying the weight of the world on her shoulders. I had a dream about her last night. She was standing over me, crying her eyes out, not saying anything. Then she was gone. I pray you can bring my Jasmine and Lettie home. You be careful, though. The devil's working his evil through those people."

"Peaches' dad turned up at your house last night. Said it wasn't the One-Niners who started the school fire or shot at your house. Brother Williams believes him. Alexus convinced him to help find Jasmine since it was his gang leader who abducted her."

"I know Peaches' dad, Deion. Watched him grow up. Another young man from the neighborhood pulled into the devil's work."

"He has people all over the city looking for the girls."

Miss Bernie nodded. "God bless him for that. I pray he finds the Lord someday."

"When can you go home?"

"How that Mr. Garrison doing?"

"Okay, I guess."

"I worry about him. He's carrying around some awful pain and anger." She paused, then said. "A lot like someone I used to know before he discovered the power of doing for others."

"Yeah, I was pretty messed up for a while."

"And you the perfect man to help Mr. Garrison. God bless you both."

"What about you? When can you come home?"

"Two more days. Thank the good Lord I'll be home to celebrate the birth of Our Savior."

* * *

Lee

While Mitch was visiting Miss Bernie, Lee decided to go to Ace's place instead of checking on his dad. He watched the house through the morning, struggling to come up with his next move. Mitch was right. The One-Niners had the best chance of finding the girls but no way could he sit and wait. Should he break into the clubhouse during the day when there were few Disciples around? And then what? Torture them? That wouldn't turn out well. Would Ralph help once he knew about their encounter with Ace and Snake? Mitch claimed they had been good friends. But would Ralph turn against his own kid?

An older woman wearing a thick tan coat and a gray scarf tied tightly over her head came out the front door of the house next door to Ace's. She looked up and down the street from her porch, then worked her way down the steps, one at a time. Lee rushed up to her. She spotted him and clutched her jumbo purse to her body. She waved her finger at him as he neared. "You stay back or I scream."

Of course, she took him for a mugger the way he had run up to her. He probably looked like a crazed psychopath after the last couple of days. He stopped and waved his hands in the air. "Sorry, lady. I don't mean to bother you. Just wanted to ask you about your neighbors."

"Just stay back, I say."

"I'll stay right here. I just want to know if you've seen anything strange next door."

She tilted her head and squinted. "Those two had four colored girls staying with them all week. Looked like girls you pay for ... but none of my business what people do."

"Did you see them last night?"

"There was quite a ruckus. All those cars coming and going woke me. No respect for others these days. Then they all left around midnight."

"Did you see the girls?"

"Never saw them. Went back to bed."

"Before last night, did you see anyone at the house besides the girls and the two men?"

"An older man stopped by a few times. Had bug eyes. Wore a blue baseball cap with some kinda design in red lettering on the front. Couldn't make it out."

Lee opened his coat to show her his blue sweatshirt with the red Milwaukee Fire Department Maltese Cross. "Did it look like this?"

"Oh, yes. That's it. You a firefighter?"

That had to be Ralph, Lee thought. *Son of a bitch.* He closed his coat and said, "Those people are up to no good. Please call me if you see anyone come back to the house. Do you have a pen and paper I could use?"

She fished around in her purse while watching him. After several seconds of digging, she brought out a Bic pen and a yellow Juicy Fruit gum wrapper. He took them from her and wrote his number on the wrapper. "No need to call the cops. It's a private matter."

"Good. I don't like to get involved." She took the pen and wrapper and stuffed them back in her purse. "Knew something wasn't right, but I don't snoop."

Lee headed to Miss Bernie's house, getting there after noon. When he entered the front room, four of the younger children were gathered around Merle in the recliner. He was reading to them. Brother Williams motioned for Lee to come into the kitchen where the older children were finishing the noon dishes. Alexus stood on a stool at the sink scrubbing a dinner plate. She handed the plate to the next child, who rinsed it and handed it to the next child, who dried it. Another child put it away. The chatter and laughter of the children lifted Lee's mood.

"How in the world did you get my dad to read to the kids?" Lee asked.

"I told him everyone in this house has a job and his job would be to read to the little ones."

"He didn't argue?"

Brother Williams' mouth widened into a full-toothed grin, then said, "I'm quite persuasive."

Lee told Brother Williams about their encounter with the One-Niners at the warehouse. After Lee finished, Brother Williams said, "Thank the good Lord nobody was harmed. Might be best to let the One-Niners find the girls."

Alexus dried her hands on the light purple hand towel. She approached Lee and asked, "Where's my sister?"

Brother Williams rubbed her back. "They'll find her. Takes time."

She shook her finger at Lee. "You shouldn't make promises you can't keep."

Lee swallowed back the knot in his throat. He wanted to hug this child and tell her he would never stop looking. The look on her face did not invite a hug.

Brother Williams said, "I need to check on Bernice. I'll take Alexus and three of the older children. Will you stay with the others till I get back?"

"You bet. Mitch should be there."

"You're a good man."

If only I could believe that, Lee thought.

After Brother Williams left with the four older children, Lee joined Merle and the four young ones in the front room. The colored lights from the Christmas tree and the pine scent gave the room a warm glow. Under the tree was a pile of shiny red and silver-wrapped gifts. Lee fell asleep listening to Merle read some book about a hungry caterpillar.

The kitchen phone rang. Lee shook his head clear and went to answer it. He picked up the receiver. A crusty voice said, "Last chance. Sell the school." Before Lee could say anything, the call ended.

Chapter 34

Lee

Shortly after six o'clock, Brother Williams, Mitch, and the four older children burst through the kitchen entryway. Lee, Merle, and the four younger children were at the table eating pizzas and drinking sodas. The older children cheered when they saw pizza boxes and scrambled to place more plates around the table.

"Didn't know what to feed them," said Lee. "Figured all kids love pizza."

"Old men too," said Brother Williams as he scooped up a slice with strings of mozzarella hanging from it.

The chatter stopped while the children scarfed down every last crumb of pizza. When they finished, they thanked Lee and went about cleaning the kitchen and washing the dishes.

The men went to the front room where Merle immediately began snoring in the recliner.

Lee said to Brother Williams, "Got another threat on the phone. Said, 'Last chance. Sell the school.' "

"Somebody has to know who's up to this," Mitch said. "We know Sunrise Schools has something to do with it."

Brother Williams ran his hand over his bald head. "Somebody always does. Just a matter of finding that somebody."

"What if it was the One-Niners?" Lee asked. "I don't trust that leader. Maybe they had a money offer from Sunrise they couldn't refuse."

"Deion is certainly doing some bad things," Brother Williams said, "but I have to believe him when he says he wouldn't burn down the school his daughter goes to."

"I believe him too," Mitch said. "He's nothing like DeAndre. That man was pure evil. The One-Niners are no saints, but they're nothing like they were back when he was their leader."

Brother Williams left the room, returned with his bible, and began reading. Alexus came into the room and approached Lee with her head hanging. "Sorry the way I talked at you," she said softly. "I want my sister back so bad it hurts my heart."

Lee's chest ached from the child's anguish. He whispered, "Can I hug you like you taught me?"

She leaned her head on his chest, sending a warm glow through him.

She looked up at him and said, "I been praying hard for Jesus to bring her home by Christmas like Papa Williams told me to do."

Brother Williams looked up from his bible and said, "The good Lord surely hears your prayers." He turned to Lee. "You look exhausted. You and your father are free to stay here tonight."

"If it's okay with you, I'd like to leave my dad here while I check with Brigid. See if she knows anything more. I don't know when I'll be back."

Mitch raised an eyebrow.

Lee said, "Don't say it."

* * *

Lee drove to his place for a quick shower and shave. Before going inside, he circled the house, looking inside the windows. He pushed the door open slowly and went inside, waving the AR15 back and forth as he scanned the kitchen. He flicked the light on. Nothing was out of place.

His thoughts turned to Brigid. Her kiss stirred a deep yearning in the pit of his stomach. He got a bottle of Korbel brandy from the cabinet and poured a small splash into a coffee cup, hoping to take the edge off the thoughts ricocheting in his head. He sat at the kitchen table, sipping brandy, torn between going to Brigid's house or combing the streets. *I should be thinking about how to find the girls,* he thought. *Not about a retired cop.* After all these years alone, was he even capable of a relationship?

"About time you got here," came from the darkness of the front room.

Lee snatched the AR15 from the table and jerked it in the direction of the voice.

"Take it easy," Ralph said as he moved into the light of the kitchen.

"How long you been here?"

"You got a broken lock on one of your windows. Might want to replace it. Never know who might break in. If you're not gonna shoot me, how about putting the rifle down?"

Lee laid the rifle on the table. "You know what Ace is involved in, don't you?"

Ralph sat across from Lee. "Been here all day waiting for you."

"Your kid is involved in some serious shit."

"I don't keep tabs on him or his club."

Lee glared at Ralph. "You were seen at Ace's place last week when they had the girls there."

"You—owe me. I need you to walk away from this."

"What did your kid tell you?"

"You made a big mistake taking those girls."

A cold shiver crept up Lee's spine. "You know."

"Didn't take a genius to figure it out. Even my idiot kid got it. Mitch was looking for the girl and Ace recognized your bat-shit crazy eyes through the ski mask."

Bile rose in Lee's throat. "Should have never let Mitch get involved."

"Pass the bottle. I'm gonna need some of that." Ralph sipped from the bottle, wiped his mouth on his sleeve, and said, "Their President beat the kid. Told him to get those girls back before Christmas or he'd turn him over to the Enforcer. According to Ace, that Enforcer is one cold-blooded monster."

"So they know it was me and Mitch who took the girls."

"Ace is terrified of what they'll do to him if he can't get the girls back. He was just doing what he was told … to help Snake with the Chicago girls. I told him I'd find out where the girls are if he didn't say anything about you and Mitch taking them. If they kill Mitch, I'd never forgive Ace or myself." Ralph leaned across the table, grimacing. "You need to tell me where the girls are."

"Ralph, what the hell are you doing?"

"If you had a kid, you'd understand." Before Lee could react, Ralph snatched the AR15 and aimed it at Lee. "Where the hell are the girls?"

Lee couldn't help chuckling. "Go ahead. Do me a favor and shoot. You said yourself, I got a death wish."

"You are one sick fuck," Ralph said.

"If the girls go back to the Disciples, you know they'll tell them me and Mitch took them and they'll come after us."

Ralph laid the AR15 on the table and took another drink of brandy. Lee crossed his arms and waited. Ralph finally blew out a loud breath and said. "I got no love for those bastards. They sucked my kid into their sleazy club. I blame myself. When I got back from Nam, I was pretty screwed up."

"You had quite a reputation when you got back. Didn't they call you the Jawbreaker of South Milwaukee?"

"I was tough on the kid and he rebelled. Who wouldn't? He tried to get on the department three times but couldn't get past the entrance exam. Of course, I rode the hell out of him. Family tradition and all that bullshit. Then my wife went through hell with MS. After she died, me and Ace took it out on each other. Now he considers the Disciples his family." Ralph groaned and said, "I gotta figure a way to keep him out of jail … or alive. You should have walked away when I told you."

"You think it's right what they were doing to those girls?"

"How do you know those girls didn't join up on their own?"

"Jasmine was abducted and sold to the Disciples. Does that sound like she did it on her own?"

Ralph shook his head slowly. "What a fucking mess."

"Talk your kid into helping us."

"What can he do without ending up in the slammer?"

"He must have enough dirt on the Disciples to put them away. I have to think the police would give him immunity for testifying."

Ralph stared at the bottle of Korbel, drumming his fingers. "If he lived long enough to testify."

Ralph is probably right, Lee thought.

"I'll take that," Ralph said, pointing at the AR15. "The kid might need it back."

Lee grasped the rifle. "I need it more."

Ralph rose from the table, stared at the rifle, then said, "My head's ready to explode with all this shit." He headed to the back door.

"Talk to your kid," Lee said. "That's our only way out of this."

Ralph paused at the door. His head drooped as he opened the door and left.

There has to be another way, Lee thought. Relying on Ace to come through was too long a shot. Even if Ralph appealed to him, what was the chance he'd do what his father asked? They were about as close as Lee and Merle.

Chapter 35

Lee

After showering, shaving, and agonizing over what to do next, Lee headed to Brigid's house. When he got there, she opened the door, wearing an oversized blue Milwaukee Brewers T-shirt and saggy gray sweatpants. The white pit bull stood at her side, edging forward, baring its teeth, growling low. She snapped her fingers and the dog stopped. "I see you cleaned up. Decided to take me up on my offer?"

Lee's face warmed, remembering her lips on his. He had to get that out of his head. "I uh. Just wanted to talk. You know, about what to do."

She stood in the doorway, analyzing him. "Um-hmm."

He couldn't remember feeling this awkward. She had him totally off balance and not knowing what to say. "I really do need to talk."

"Okay. Let's talk."

Lee followed her to the living room. He sank into the overstuffed beige couch while she went to the kitchen. She came back with two tumblers filled with amber liquid. The ice cubes clinked as she handed one to him. "Jack Daniels. You look like you can use a drink. Since you had a beer the other night, I figured alcohol wasn't an issue."

"No. Plenty of pickles on the job, but I never had a problem with that." He sipped at the whiskey, waiting for the liquor to spread its calming warmth through him.

She sat across from him on the matching loveseat. "Pickles?"

"Alcoholics."

"Right. You people." She shook her head. "You wanted to talk. Now, talk."

He told her about his encounter with Ralph. When he finished, she said, "Ralph's in a tight spot. It's either his kid or you and Mitch. From what you told me, I would guess he'll go with his kid. Don't know what to tell you. This is getting more complicated by the hour."

"I should be back on the streets looking for the girls."

"Oh, no, you don't. You look ready to break. I know the look. You're not leaving until you get some rest. When was the last time you slept?"

"I have to find them."

"The One-Niners are taking care of that. You won't be any good to anyone if you fall apart."

She moved to the couch and rested her hand on his. Her warm touch sent a tremor through him. Lee scanned the room, avoiding her gaze. "No Christmas tree?"

"Let's get your mind off things for a while. Can you tell me about your dad? I got the feeling you don't get along so well with him."

Lee relaxed, took a long sip of the whiskey, and told her about Merle burning him with cigarettes when he was a kid. He went on to tell her how Merle beat him and his mom, sometimes using a belt, and how Lee put a stop to it when he threw his dad to the floor.

When he finished, she said, "I noticed those scars at the doctor's office. I didn't want to ask. Scars can be triggers. Thanks for sharing. We've both been through a lot. I think we can help each other." She took the tumbler from him and placed it on the glass-topped end table. "Let's relax for a while and decide what to do when our heads are clear." She pulled his face to hers and kissed him, softly this time. Her mouth tasted of sweet whiskey. His stomach clenched. She stopped and leaned her forehead against his. "What do you think?"

He put his lips to hers. He lost himself in a yearning he had not felt in way too many years. When he stopped she rose and led him to her bedroom.

* * *

Lee jerked awake in a cold sweat and sat up, his heart pounding. The room was dark. A soft hand caressed his shoulder. "You're okay," Brigid said and kissed his cheek.

When he caught his breath, he said, "Damn. Sorry I woke you. What time is it?"

"Don't worry about it. I spent years struggling to sleep through the night, waking up just like that most nights. You hardly moved until just now. It's almost five."

"Holy shit. I haven't slept like that in years."

"It's not like we slept the whole time." She grinned, ran her hand over his chest, and kissed his neck. "You got one hell of a bod for an old fart." She glanced at the bulge in the sheets. "Good morning down there." She threw the sheet off and moved on top of him. The smooth warm skin of her naked body pressing against him quieted his brain. He was in a place he could stay forever. She put her face to his, their eyes inches apart, and made slow intoxicating love to him. She awakened passions he had not felt since before his fiancée died.

When they finished, Brigid laid her head on his chest and asked, "I didn't hurt your back, did I?"

"Didn't feel a thing."

She lifted her head and said, "Didn't feel a thing? You sure seemed to be enjoying yourself."

"No, no, no. About my back."

Brigid chuckled. "You have to learn when I'm messing with you. This was nice."

"This part of the peer counseling program?"

"Did it work?"

"Seriously. Aren't there rules against counselors having relationships with patients?"

"Are we in a relationship?"

"Well. I uh…"

"I can't help myself. I love yanking your chain. Dr. Bennet would not be happy to know we slept together. But who's going to tell? Besides, I'm a volunteer. What they gonna do? Fire me? Let's get some coffee and figure out how to keep you out of jail. I need more nights like that. It's been a while." She rolled out of bed, went to her closet, and turned the light on.

He had never imagined what she would look like naked. She kept her slim figure well hidden under worn jeans and loose-fitting sweatshirts. He couldn't take his eyes off her. He wanted to tell her making love to her was beyond incredible. Instead, he said, "Work out?"

"That some kind of backhanded compliment?"

"No, no. I…"

"I have got to control myself. You're way too easy." She smirked. "You're not bad yourself. I might have to keep you around if Roscoe agrees."

"Roscoe?"

She pointed to her white pitbull standing in the doorway, eyeing Lee.

Brigid slipped on a dark blue robe. "You coming?"

He dressed and went to the kitchen. Roscoe watched him take a seat while Brigid got a box of Eggo Waffles from the freezer and held it up. "Sorry, this is about all I have. I don't get many overnight guests."

"Haven't had those since I was a kid."

Brigid loaded four in the toaster and took a seat across from Lee. She took a deep breath and said, "How you gonna handle not getting Jasmine and Lettie back home if that's how this plays out? You're already carrying around a shitload of pain and trauma. I'm worried you won't be able to come back from it."

He had to do this. Not because of any obligation like taking care of his father and not because it was his job or duty. Alexus and her family had made him feel alive for the first time in years. After Lee had lost his crew and his good friend in the church fire, he lived by a simple code: keep others at a distance to avoid that kind of pain ever again. That led to a lonely, joyless existence that he accepted until a little girl shattered the emotional shell he hid behind. She opened his eyes and his heart to the lie he had been living.

What he would not be able to come back from was the crushing guilt of breaking his promise to Alexus and walking away from this family.

Brigid reached across the table and covered his hand in hers. "What you're doing is … I don't even know how to say it, but you may not be able to save them. You're putting a hell of a lot of pressure on yourself. I'm sure you've seen plenty of tragedy on the job you couldn't do anything about. I know I have. Sometimes there's nothing we can do to change the outcome. We have to accept that."

"Let's eat," Lee said.

They ate in silence with Brigid glancing at him between bites. When they finished, she got up and went behind him, wrapping her arms around his chest. "I'm not telling you to stop looking. I know you won't. I'm just worried about you." She kissed the top of his head. "I'm going to get dressed. Don't leave without saying goodbye."

You don't know how much I want to stay, Lee thought as he watched Roscoe follow her out of the kitchen. His thoughts turned to Jasmine and Lettie. Somehow he had to figure a way to get them home and then protect them from the Disciples. In Vietnam, there were times when the fighting was so fierce, he was sure he wouldn't survive. His team's one-word motto was "endure." His die-hard refusal to give up saved his ass and others. He had made a promise to Alexus, and by God, he was going to keep it. There was no accepting any other outcome.

Chapter 36

Lee

Before Lee left to meet up with Mitch and plan their next move, Brigid went to her basement and brought back a small black handgun. "Here. Take this. It's a compact '45.' Fits in your pocket but packs a hell of a punch." She handed him the gun and kissed him hard. "Now. Go. Do what you have to do. I'll check back with you later."

When Lee got to Miss Bernie's house, Merle was in the front room recliner by himself. "Where the hell you been?" he shouted at Lee.

"Don't worry about it, Old Man."

"Get me the hell out of here. Can't stand all this ruckus."

Lee ignored him and went to the kitchen, where the children were finishing the morning dishes. Brother Williams and Mitch were at the table drinking coffee. Mitch grinned and said, "You look refreshed. Relaxing night?"

"I stopped by my house on the way to Brigid's. Ralph was there. He told me Ace knows it was us who took the girls. He was in charge of the girls and if he doesn't get them back, he's in deep shit. Ralph actually held the AR15 on me and demanded I tell him where they are. He's totally screwed up."

"Crap. The Disciples know it was us."

"No. Ace didn't tell them—at least not yet. Ralph told him he'd find out where the girls are if Ace kept us out of it. But if Ace can't get the girls back, I gotta think there's a good chance he'll give us up to save his ass. And if the Disciples do learn it was us…"

Brother Williams said to Lee, "Thank God the girls didn't go back to the Disciples."

"Not yet. Did you get any more threats about selling the school?"

"I called Detective Boyle this morning and told him about last night's threat. He said they were talking to the other inner-city voucher schools but could not connect Sunrise with the threats. The One-Niners are still their prime suspects. I didn't want to tell him that Deion showed up here. We need him and his crew on the streets looking for the girls. You men worry about finding them. I'll worry about this school business."

The children finished the dishes and left the kitchen. Alexus stayed. She went to Lee and rested her head against his shoulder. "Papa Williams says you and Mitch risking your lives to find my sister." She kissed him on the cheek and left.

Lee swallowed the stone in his throat and said to Brother Williams, "You okay with my dad staying here until I can figure something out?"

"He's not much bother. Sleeps a lot. The kids like to pester him to read to them. He acts like he's irritated, but I think he enjoys having something to do."

"Hard to believe, but I'll take your word for it."

"Sometimes we don't see those closest to us."

Close is not a word I'd use, Lee thought and said to Mitch, "Let's hit the streets."

"Where to?"

"The van was low on gas when they took it and they have to eat. Let's start by asking around the gas stations … and fast-food places."

Brother Williams said, "Best tell them you're friends of mine. Around here, some might not be eager to talk with a couple of white men."

* * *

Lee and Mitch spent the day roaming the city, beginning in the Core. Everywhere they went, people knew Brother Williams. They were eager to help and agreed to keep a lookout for the girls and the van but no one had seen them. Late in the afternoon, Lee received a call from Brigid, saying they needed to meet. Lee suggested his house now that he was comfortable with the fact that the Disciples didn't know about him yet.

Lee and Mitch waited in the kitchen. Lee motioned for Brigid to come in when she appeared at the back door window. She waved a manila folder as she came through the door. "This might be of interest." She laid it on the table. "Names of Disciples and their last-known addresses. Includes their leader, Charles Kaczmarek." She opened the folder and pointed at a mugshot. "Goes by Manson."

Mitch glanced at Lee. "That's the name of the guy you said he looks like."

Of course. What else would he go by? Lee thought and picked up the file, examining it. "All he needs is the swastika on his forehead and he'd be a dead ringer."

"And just as evil," Brigid said. She lifted another mugshot from the folder of a grisly, square-faced bald man with a thick black beard and no neck. "This one's just as bad, if not worse. The club enforcer. It's thought he does a lot of the dirty work. They call him Warlock."

"Where'd you get these?"

"A friend on the gang squad ... Yes, I do have a few friends." She lifted a photo from the folder of a gray-bearded man built like a fire hydrant. "This one's called Tank, he's the Sergeant at Arms.

Don't have much on him, just this surveillance photo. No criminal record.

Lee examined the mugshot of Warlock. "What good is all that now? The girls aren't with them."

"We need to keep all options open," Brigid said. "They could turn up at any time at one of those locations."

"I suppose you're right."

Brigid grinned. "Could you say that one more time? I love the sound of it."

"You can't stop yourself, can you? Mitch, take my car and keep asking around. Me and Mrs. Right will keep our options open by checking out some of these addresses in case the van turns up."

"Brilliant," Brigid said, chuckling. "Let's go."

On the drive to Manson's place, Brigid filled Lee in on his background. He had spent seven years in prison for beating to death a teenager who backed into his motorcycle. According to prison records, nobody messed with him. Presumably, he was feared because he was known to belong to the Hells Disciples. When he got out, it didn't take long for him to become the president. There were three rival gangs in Milwaukee when he took over. Now, there is only the Hells Disciples.

Homes of several members of the rival clubs were bombed. In one, a mother and two children were killed. The presidents of the two other clubs went missing. Months later, when the ice melted off the Milwaukee River, their bloated bodies floated to the surface. Both were mutilated and missing their genitals and tongues. Their gang colors had been cut from their vests. MPD had an informant who was sure this was the handiwork of Warlock. There was never enough evidence to convict any of them. The informant turned up missing before they could nail them. He's never been found. She finished by saying, "These people are ruthless."

Visions of mutilated bodies in Vietnam flashed in Lee's head. "If those bastards do anything to Jasmine or Lettie, I won't need evidence for what I'll do," Lee said.

Brigid rubbed his shoulder. "Just don't do something you can't come back from."

They crossed into Shorewood and pulled to the side of Lake Drive. Brigid gazed at a massive two-story Old English Tudor-style house with white stucco gables. The house sat on a huge lot surrounded by tall, dense arborvitae trees. "That's it."

"How the hell…?"

"I know, right? The only thing bordering the back property is Lake Michigan. Conveniently private. It's owned by Allure Property Investments, an LLC. Manson and Warlock have been staying there for years. The Milwaukee gang squad worked with Shorewood PD to investigate the connection. My buddy said—off the record—they were ordered to drop it and concentrate their resources on inner-city gangs."

"Living large like that mafia character on TV, Tony Soprano."

"Except this Iron Horse Mafia has no code of honor," Lee said. "They gotta be doing more than selling drugs and girls."

"You should have been a detective." She laughed and said, "Why didn't I think of that?"

"Funny. You should have been a comedian."

She kissed him on the cheek. "Thought you firefighters had thicker skin."

"The van's not here. Let's keep moving."

"I love it when you give orders."

He couldn't help smiling. Her wry sense of humor was growing on him.

The twenty other Disciples they had addresses for were scattered over the city with most on the South Side. They checked out the addresses of the known gang officers. With no sign of the van at any of the locations, they headed back to Miss Bernie's house.

Merle was alone in the front room, dozing in the recliner. With Christmas Eve one day away, the pile of gifts under and around the tree covered an entire corner of the room. Lee and Brigid went to the kitchen where Brother Williams was nursing a cup of coffee and reading his bible. The floor above them squeaked and groaned. Brother Williams said, "Kids are getting excited. We let them open one present tomorrow night. There's some leftover burgers if you two are hungry. Kids already ate supper. Any luck finding the girls?"

Lee clenched his lips, then said, "No sign of them. We plan to go out again later tonight. I hate to ask, but can my dad stay here while we're out looking?"

"Of course. Can you stay with the kids while I take some things to Bernice? She's coming home tomorrow, thank the good Lord."

Chapter 37

Lee

Lee and Brigid sat on the front room couch of Miss Bernie's house soaking in the pine scent of the Christmas tree and the soft glow of the colored lights. Lee stared at the angel with a hand-drawn golden smiley face and glittery silver wings at the top of the tree. *Any time you're ready,* he thought. *We could use some help down here.* Brigid moved closer. "It's been a while since I enjoyed any holidays, much less Christmas. This is nice." She leaned her head against his shoulder.

Lee was lost in thought about the Disciples. In Marine Force Recon, he was trained to kill. Lines of morality faded in the chaos of war. The government sent him to Vietnam to kill people he knew nothing about and he came back burdened with guilt. If he had to kill in this war with the Disciples, there would be no guilt.

Brigid poked him in the ribs. "Where you at?"

Before he could answer, Alexus trudged down the stairs, stopped, and gawked at them. "My sister never coming home, is she?"

The forlorn look on her face tore at Lee. He had no words to comfort her. Brigid slid over and patted the cushion between them. "C'mon over and sit with us."

Alexus wedged herself between them with her arms crossed and head down. Brigid pulled one of her hands loose, rubbed it, and said, "Tell me all about your big sister."

Alexus shared story after story about how Jasmine took care of her when their momma got sick. She protected her from the mean man who stayed with them, the one their momma killed when she found out he hurt Jasmine. She took care of the house and made sure Alexus had school clothes and lunches. Jasmine was smart and planned to go to college. Alexus smiled at the memories while telling the stories. Brigid smiled along with her, telling her what an amazing girl Jasmine must be.

Watching Brigid comfort Alexus, Lee wondered how she could be estranged from her own daughter.

The front door swung open. Mitch stopped when he saw them on the couch. Alexus ran to him, hugging him hard around the waist. "You excited about Christmas?" he asked.

Her sad look returned. "Not without my sister."

Mitch went to his knees. "You keep praying like Brother Williams said, and we'll keep looking."

She shrugged and said, "I been praying all day and I'll keep on praying till Jesus hears my prayers. I best get upstairs and get back to it." She looked over her shoulder. "I'll be praying for all of us." She trudged up the stairs.

Mitch grinned. "You two look comfy. Want to be alone?"

Merle grunted and woke. He looked around the room, jerking his head from side to side, stopping when he got to Lee. "Where the hell am I? Get me out of here. Now. You take me home."

"Can't. You need to stay here another night."

"You do what I say. You're supposed to take care of me. You promised your mother."

Lee rose from the couch and stomped to Merle. "Look, Old Man. I gotta a lotta shit going on. I don't have time to take care of your sorry ass. This family is counting on me."

"Fuck them."

Rage clawed its way inside Lee's head. "No. Fuck you, you selfish bastard." Before he could say anything more, Brigid was between them.

"Let's go." She turned Lee around and pushed him toward the kitchen. Merle shouted a string of profanities. Mitch followed them. Brigid sat Lee down and faced him. "Slow down." She grasped his chin. "Look at me. Now's not the time to lose it. Focus on the girls."

"He is such a—"

"I get that. Let it go. Take some breaths and think about this family."

Lee clenched his teeth.

Brigid put her hands on each side of his head and shook. "Look at me. Slow the fuck down."

Lee's head cleared. "Is that the way a peer counselor is supposed to talk?"

"Good. You're back."

"Jesus, could I be any more screwed up? You should run while you have the chance."

"You're not a lost cause," Brigid said with a slight grin. "Not yet." She let go of Lee and grabbed the folder off the table. "Let's get to work."

While they were going through the addresses, mugshots, and surveillance photos of the Disciples, Brother Williams returned from the hospital. He said Miss Bernie would be discharged tomorrow morning. She was in good spirits and wanted Brother Williams to tell them she feels incredibly blessed for what they're doing to bring her girls home. Every waking hour, she prays for the good Lord to look over all of them. When he finished, he excused himself and headed upstairs to check on the children.

Brigid went back to the pile of mugshots. "Let's separate them into locations north and south of the Menomonee Valley."

Lee was not used to letting anyone take over, but she was the detective. He did what she asked. When they had the mugshots separated, Brigid handed Mitch the ones with South Side locations. "How about you start checking out some of these addresses?"

Mitch groaned. "More stakeouts? There must be something else we can do."

"Right now," Brigid said, "this is all we have to go on. My contact is going through the missing person's reports for girls around the ages of the other two. If we can locate their families, there's an outside chance they could turn up there. I don't think we want to sit on our hands and wait for that. So, yes. More stakeouts. Me and Lee will start at Manson's house."

* * *

Lee and Brigid parked within sight of the huge house. "What are the chances they'd bring the girls here?" Lee asked.

"Pretty slim. But we might see something that could lead to answers. That's how investigations play out. We keep asking questions and trying different approaches until there's a breakthrough."

After they settled in and finished their supersized cups of gas-station coffee, Brigid ran her hand up Lee's thigh. "I've never had sex on a stakeout."

"Seriously? What if a Shorewood cop comes by?"

She kissed him on the cheek. "God, I love messing with you."

"Glad I amuse you."

"Oh, c'mon. Lighten up."

Lee pointed at a silver sports car entering the driveway of Manson's place from the opposite direction. "Looks like our man's getting some company."

The car disappeared into the shadows at the side of the house.

"Could you make out the plate?" Brigid asked.

"Too far away."

Brigid put the truck in gear and moved closer.

Twenty minutes later, the car drove out of the drive. The vanity plate said POWR.

"Nice ride," Lee said. "A Porsche Carrera. Manson has rich buddies."

"That's the state senator from River Hills, Decker. What the hell would he be doing with Manson?"

"From what Brother Williams said, that license plate should probably read white power."

"I've heard."

Brigid waited until the silver sports car was two blocks away before following. Red and blue lights flashed from behind them. She pulled to the curb and slammed her palm against the steering wheel. "C'mon. What the hell?" She had her wallet out the window with her badge displayed when the officer approached the car. When he got to the car, she said. "Retired Milwaukee Captain."

"Please remove your license from the wallet," the officer ordered.

"For Christ's sake. Why?"

"Please do as I say."

She ripped the license from her wallet and shoved it at him. He said, "I'll be right back."

"Thanks to Barney Fife, we lose Decker. Asshole."

"Thought you cops took care of each other," Lee said.

"Not this prick."

"Check this out," Lee said, pointing to a black van moving out of the shadows at the side of the house and inching down the drive.

"That's the van we saw Ace and Snake driving. I'm sure of it. Has a dented front panel."

The van headed south on Lake Drive.

A short time later, the officer returned to the truck, handed Brigid her license, and said, "Sorry, but our protocol is to run everyone we pull over."

"Why the hell did you pull me over?"

"A neighbor was concerned about a parked truck with occupants lingering this late at night. I was watching you from down the street. What are you doing here?"

"You don't have anything more important to do than harass a fellow officer?"

"It's not Milwaukee, so no, I didn't have anything better to do. Have a good night … Captain." He headed back to his patrol car.

"That asshole was mocking me." She opened her door and turned to get out.

Lee grabbed her arm and pulled her back. Smirking, he said, "I see I'm not the only one with anger issues."

"You a therapist now?"

"Hey, maybe you're the one who needs to lighten up."

Her eyes narrowed. After several seconds she broke into laughter and wagged her head. "Call Mitch and tell him to get over to Ace's place in case that van shows up there. I'll try to catch them."

"After your little squabble with Barney Fife, you may want to follow the speed limit around here so we don't end up in the Mayberry jail."

"Funny."

Once they got to Milwaukee, Brigid stepped on it. They never caught sight of the van. Lee checked with Mitch, who was now at Ace's place. So far, nothing. They flew over the city streets to South

22nd Street and pulled behind Mitch. Lee went to his car. He told Mitch about seeing the senator leave the Manson house minutes before the black van left. Mitch asked, "You think that senator has something to do with their sex trafficking?"

"Ace and Snake should have been here by now. Stay here. We'll check out the clubhouse."

"One-Niners are probably watching the place. Make sure you don't piss them off. You're not exactly their favorite honky."

"On second thought," Lee said. "Why don't you check out the clubhouse? We'll watch this place."

* * *

Mitch

Mitch climbed the stairs to the second floor of the abandoned warehouse across from the Disciple's clubhouse. When he entered, two AK47s were leveled at him. He shouted, "Deion knows me. Mitch Garner."

Deion moved out of the shadows. "What up?"

The two One-Niners turned back to the broken-out windows.

Mitch told Deion about Ace and Snake showing up at Manson's house, then asked, "What about you? See anything?"

"My crew's been all over the streets. Got nothin'. All we been seeing here are a few Disciples come and go. I'll send some brothas up to that Manson dude's crib."

"I don't know. Captain said a cop's been patrolling the area. Your crew might not blend in that neighborhood."

Mitch's phone chimed. "Mitch, you gotta come to the house now," said a young male voice. "It's on fire."

"Where's Brother Williams?"

"Still inside. Gave me his phone to call 911. Hurry."

"What about the kids and Mr. Garrison's dad?"

The call ended.

Deion said, "Heard that. Gimme your phone. I'll put my number in. Let me know what's up. We can't be anywhere near there."

Mitch called Lee's cell phone.

Lee asked, "What's up?"

"Miss Bernie's house is on fire. I don't know how bad, but Brother Williams is still inside."

"What about the kids and my dad? Are they out?"

"Don't know. I'm heading there now." Mitch ended the call and sped to Miss Burnie's house, blowing through two red lights. Before he saw the house, he smelled the acrid mixture of burning wood and furniture. He turned the corner. Fire rigs crowded the street in front of the house. Their rotating red and white strobes flashed across neighboring homes. Half the roof was burned away.

Mitch parked and sprinted toward the house. Bursts of water shot through a broken-out first-floor window and through the open roof as fire crews wet down the last remaining burning embers. Other crews were tearing off the remaining roof and tossing burned mattresses and furniture out the windows.

Across the street, in front of a large crowd, Miss Bernie's children huddled together, the smaller ones wrapped in blankets, the older ones only in pajamas, all eyes fixed on the smoldering remains of their home. Alexus saw Mitch and ran to him, white puffs of breath trailing her. She wrapped her arms around his waist. He held her head against his chest as he stared at a steaming rubble pile that had once been brightly colored Christmas gifts. Next to that were the remains of the Christmas tree wrapped in bare wires and blackened bulbs. At the top of the tree was the angel with the hand-drawn golden smiley face now blackened with soot, missing its wings. From inside the front room, someone called out, "Look out below." The skeleton of the recliner Merle slept on flew through the broken-out front window, crashing next to the Christmas tree.

"Where are Brother Williams and Mr. Garrison's dad?" Mitch asked.

Alexus looked up, her eyes glassy, and pointed to the dark vacant lot next to their home. A yellow plastic sheet covered a large body. She struggled to get the words out. "Papa. Williams."

Chapter 38

Mitch

A gray-haired woman wearing a red vest with the Red Cross insignia escorted Mitch and the children to a waiting city bus at the end of the street. A battalion chief and a police detective with black hair neatly slicked back followed. The detective introduced himself as Detective Boyle and questioned the children about what they had seen and heard.

The oldest boy, whom Mitch knew as Alonzo, told them he woke to a screeching smoke alarm on the second floor. When he opened his second-floor bedroom door, the smoke from the hallway choked him. Brother Williams ran from room to room shouting for the children to get up and run outside as fast as they could. He followed the children. When they were all out, he gave Alonzo his cell phone to call 911 while he went back in to get Lee's dad.

Brother Williams and Lee's dad didn't come out until the firefighters carried them out.

Detective Boyle said to Mitch and the chief, "Let's talk outside." He turned to the Red Cross lady. "Can you stay with the children?"

"Of course," she said, her chin trembling.

When they got outside, Detective Boyle asked the chief, "So, tell me about the fire."

The chief told Detective Boyle when he arrived on the scene with Engine 32, every floor was showing heavy smoke. Flames were shooting through the roof. A burning car that had been parked too close to the house had ignited the back of the house and extended inside. He was told by the older kid there were still two people inside, probably in the front room. Three firefighters made entry through the front door with a hose line. Despite the blinding smoke, they were able to locate and get one of the occupants outside. One of the firefighters stayed with him to assess and treat his injuries. The other two went back to search for the other occupant. As they were making entry, the room flashed over, the entire room erupting in flames. They had to back out. One line was not enough to fight and control that much fire.

As they backed out, a ladder truck, a paramedic unit, and another fire engine arrived on the scene. The second engine company was ordered to get another line on the fire, and the ladder company was ordered to assist with search-and-rescue operations. The paramedic unit transported the first occupant to St. Mary's Hospital.

With two lines on the fire, they were able to knock it down and gain entry to the front room. They found the second occupant, a much larger man, and carried him to the adjacent vacant lot, away from the burning house. No medical assistance was needed. He was burned beyond recognition.

Detective Boyle asked Mitch, "How are you connected to the family?"

"A friend."

"Anything you can tell me about the occupants that I should know?"

"Just that they were good people. Did you run the VIN?"

"It's been altered and the plate's a fake."

"Any idea what kind of car?"

"Not much to go on. All we got is a burned-out frame. Best guess is a mid to late nineties Riviera."

* * *

Lee

Lee and Brigid had to park over a block away from the house. Without saying a word, Lee leapt from the truck and charged to the scene, ignoring his back pain. The fire was out. Crews were tearing off the remaining roof boards. A burned-out mattress flew out a second-floor window. Lee ran around the smoldering remains of the house, praying not to see any of the damned yellow sheets. Seeing none, he breathed a sigh of relief.

A burned-out shell of a car was at the back of the house. All that was left of it was the blackened frame. Brigid moved alongside him. When he turned to her, he caught a glimpse of the ME in the dark adjacent lot, standing over a yellow plastic sheet that barely covered the huge body beneath it.

When Brigid saw what Lee was staring at, she said, "Jesus, no."

The sight sucked the breath out of him as he ran to the covered body. Two enormous bare feet, blackened and charred, protruding from the bottom of the yellow sheet, triggered the blistering memory of the charred remains of his crew and best friend at the church fire. He knelt and slid the yellow sheet over Brother Williams' feet. Brigid knelt beside him, resting her chin on his shoulder.

The red mist blurred Lee's vision. "Killed you for your school," Lee growled, gritting his teeth. "Those animals *will* pay."

Lee marched up to the chief, who was giving orders into his portable radio.

"Where are the kids and the other adult?" Lee demanded.

The chief continued talking into his radio.

Lee spun him around. The chief started to say something, then pointed to the bus at the end of the block. Lee rushed to the bus with Brigid right behind. He pounded on the closed door. It slammed open. The driver pointed to the back and watched Lee scramble up the steps. The children were huddled together, hugging and rocking. Mitch stood, his chin quivering, and said, "The kids are fine. But Brother Williams…"

"Where's my dad?" asked Lee.

"Took him to St. Mary's."

Brigid clutched Lee's hand.

Mitch cleared his throat and said, "Brother Williams got all the kids out and went back in for your dad. The crew from Engine 32 got your dad out but couldn't get to Brother Williams in time."

"Died going in after my dad? Son of a bitch. How'd it start?"

"A car fire next to the house got into the walls. By the time the chief and Engine 32 arrived, every floor was showing heavy smoke with part of the roof gone. It must have been going a while in the walls and attic. When it burned through the inside walls and triggered the smoke alarms, it sounds like it was rolling. The kids barely got out."

Mitch paused while wiping his nose with the back of his hand. Sobs and sniffles echoed through the bus. Alexus stared at the floor, expressionless. Brigid pushed by Lee and Mitch and knelt in front of her. "Oh, honey," she said wrapping the child in her arms.

"What the hell was a car doing back there?" Lee asked Mitch.

"I know. The kids said nobody ever parked back there. Get this. The car was an older Riviera."

Lee gasped, "Holy…"

"Yeah. I know," Mitch said.

Brigid looked up from Alexus. "What?"

"Whoever stole the One-Niner's car," Mitch said, "is setting them up again."

Alexus scowled. "Why they *do* that? Now Papa Williams gone."

Mitch, Brigid, and Lee looked at one another. Nobody had an answer.

After several long minutes, the Red Cross lady said, "I can see how much you all loved Papa Williams. I wish there were words to…" She swallowed hard. "What I can do is offer you lodging and food. I'll have to split you up since there are so many of you."

Lee raised his hand. "Nope. They need to stay together. They'll be staying at my house."

"Are you family?"

"Close friend of the family."

She asked the children, "That okay with you all?"

Their heads bobbed.

"I'll have to check out your house," she said to Lee, "then we can do this as an emergency placement for now. I can take some of the children there, but I don't have enough room for all of them in my van."

"Mitch," Lee said, "take the rest of the kids to my place in my car. Me and Brigid will meet you there later. We got some digging to do."

* * *

Lee

As they approached the smoldering house, Lee spotted a plain-clothes detective and a firefighter in clean mustard-yellow turnout gear in the vacant side yard. They were standing over the bright yellow plastic sheet covering Brother Williams. Brigid said, "I know that detective. Boyle."

"That's the same one who investigated the drive-by. He's with the arson inspector. Let's see what they know."

Detective Boyle studied Brigid as they approached. "It's you."

"Nice to see *you* too," she said.

"Right."

Lee asked the arson inspector, "What you got so far?"

As the fire inspector told him everything he already knew, Lee stared at the yellow sheet covering Brother Williams' body. *Why did I leave my old man here?* Lee thought. "I am so, so sorry," he said to the remains of Brother Williams, choking back the knot in his throat.

Brigid, as if reading his mind, whispered in his ear, "Do *not* blame yourself. Direct that anger at who did this."

Brigid asked Boyle, "What you got so far?"

"Don't have time to chat with a nosy civilian."

Her mouth twisted into an angry sneer. "You son of a bitch. I should…"

Lee pulled her away, then turned to Boyle. "My father was in there, you dick." Lee clenched his fists. Boyle flinched.

The arson inspector moved between Lee and Boyle. "Whoa, Captain. Take it easy."

Lee and Boyle glared at each other like a pair of rabid pitbulls ready to go at it. Brigid tugged at Lee's arm. "Stop."

Lee yanked his arm away. Brigid shouted, "I said stop. Snap out of it."

"All right, all right. Take it easy."

Detective Boyle said to Lee, "I recognize you. You were at this house when it got shot up."

"Let's cut the shit," Lee said. "Who you looking at for this?"

The scowl on Boyle's face eased. "Sorry about your dad. The night of the shooting, Mr. Williams informed me that the One-Niners shot up the house. The description of the car they were in fits the one at the back of the house. Soon as we grab their asses, the case'll be closed."

Brigid asked, "Did he say he actually saw the One-Niners or just the car?"

No answer.

She continued, "Doesn't that seem a bit too obvious to you, Einstein? Ever think the One-Niners are being set up? You think they would be stupid enough to be seen shooting up the home of a man who's respected throughout the community?"

"Yes, I do. Just a matter of how much someone offered."

"And who would that someone be?" Brigid demanded.

"We're looking at Sunrise Schools. We nail the One-Niners, we should be able to get to Sunrise."

"Maybe it's not the One-Niners."

"You know something we don't?"

Brigid tugged Lee's hand. "Let's get out of here. I'm sick of talking with this pea brain."

Detective Boyle said to Lee, "Wait. I need some info on your father."

"Sorry," Brigid said. "He doesn't have time for some nosy asshole detective."

As they walked away, Brigid flashed her middle finger over her shoulder at Boyle.

"Old friend?" Lee asked.

She stopped and faced him. "Don't need you fighting my goddamn battles."

"Okay. Okay. Got it. You looked ready to lose it."

"*You* worried about *me* losing it? You gotta be kidding. You'd have decked him if I hadn't pulled your ass away."

He smirked. She was right. They were quite the pair.

Her expression hardened. "Not so funny if you got locked up."

"I get it. Can we move on?"

Brigid huffed and said, "Boyle was my asshole boss at one time. After I outscored him on the captain's exam, I became *his* boss. He had a bit of trouble taking orders from a woman. One of the Neanderthals. Said the only reason I got the promotion was because I was a woman. Called me a stupid cunt. I took it personally. One thing I'm not is stupid."

Lee had to laugh.

Brigid continued, "I put him on charges. He'll never be promoted again with that in his file."

This got Lee thinking about his history with Ralph and how Ralph was never able to get promoted because Lee had put him on charges. Now he owed Ralph because Ralph hadn't put Lee on charges for attacking the drunk who killed the young couple.

"Why didn't you tell him what we know?" Lee asked.

"I don't trust him. If I told him we had contact with the One-Niners without informing MPD, he'd figure a way to screw me."

"Do we know it's not the One-Niners?"

"You need to get over your little spat with your spiked-hair buddy."

"You don't trust Boyle, I don't trust that gangbanger."

Chapter 39

Lee

The dark streets were quiet as they drove to Lee's house in the early morning hours. Brigid kept glancing at him. She asked him once if he was okay. He didn't answer. She didn't ask again. He fought the darkness and rage closing in on him. Images of the skeleton of the burned-out home, the charred Christmas tree, and the smoldering rubble pile of burned presents flashed through his head.

What had him on the verge of totally losing it was the image of Brother Williams' feet and what he knew the rest of his body looked like after being incinerated in the fire. The only thing keeping him from going over the edge was knowing he had to keep it together to avenge Brother Williams' death and bring Miss Bernie's girls home. Lee pressed his lips together, swallowing his rage.

When they arrived at Lee's house, Brigid rested her hand on his shoulder. "Please let me in. I'm here. You're not alone in this. Let me help."

Lee got out of the truck and said, "I'll be okay. Let's go inside."

The corners of Brigid's mouth turned down. "Right."

* * *

The children were gathered in the front room. Lee, Mitch, and Brigid went to the kitchen. Brigid put on a pot of coffee. Mitch said to Lee, "I'm supposed to bring Miss Bernie home from the hospital today. How am I going to...?"

Brigid joined them at the table. "We gotta think this through. When I saw Decker pulling away from Manson's place, it got me thinking. His opponent in the last election released a list of Decker's campaign donors. One of the major donors was Sunrise Schools. Sunrise also aired independent commercials supporting Decker. Their mission statement is to give all children a good old-fashioned American education. Whatever that means.

"Here's the kicker. Decker's been pushing for the state to help fund inner-city voucher schools, which he's fought against for years. If Sunrise takes over these schools, all that funding goes to them. And they'll have control over the curriculum. They don't have to follow the rules for choice schools in Wisconsin. Milwaukee's voucher program is independent of the state. What the hell do they know about the challenges of inner-city students? Victory Schools tried the same thing a while back." Brigid shook her head.

"I remember Victory Schools wanting to take over Brother Williams' school," Mitch said. "The City Council planned to condemn his school until a bunch of us firefighters brought it up to code with a new roof and other repairs. It was all over the news. Brother Williams was on *The Today Show*, talking about his school."

"Two aldermen," Brigid said, "went to jail for taking bribes from Victory."

"What happened to Victory?" Lee asked.

"Their legal team got them off with an agreement to stay away from Milwaukee."

"So you think Decker is taking bribes as legal campaign donations and paying them back by hiring the Disciples to force the voucher schools to sell?"

She threw her hands up. "What do you two think?"

Lee's eyebrows knit together. "What about the One-Niners?"

"Think about it. We have them at the scene of the school fire and their car at the drive-by shooting and the house fire. That's just too damn obvious. Brother Williams knew these people and he believed Deion's story. What do we know? We now know there's a connection between Decker, Sunrise, and the Disciples."

"Isn't *that* too obvious?"

"You and I are the only ones who saw Decker leave Manson's place. So, no."

Mitch said, "If you're right, they killed Brother Williams and almost killed some of the kids just to get the vouchers? … That's beyond evil."

Lee knew what evil looked like up close. It had been all around him in Vietnam. He clenched his lips and said, "They need to be gone."

Brigid cocked one eyebrow. "I don't like that look on your face. What are you planning?"

"I gotta get to the firehouse before redshift goes home."

* * *

Lee drove to Engine 15, fighting the rising red mist. He had to put a stop to the Disciples. He couldn't wait for the police to figure this out. If witnesses were found, they'd likely never make it to court. If the Disciples ceased to exist, the girls wouldn't have to fear going back to their families, and the inner-city voucher schools would no longer be terrorized.

There were times in Vietnam when he and his team were forced to commit acts of violence most civilians would find revolting. Those acts were crucial for their survival. That was not a war fought by the rules. And taking down the Disciples would not be by the rules.

Brigid and Mitch could not be involved. If things turned south, he would take the fall and keep them out of it.

Lee went to the back door of the firehouse and heard the loud bull session of the redshift crew. The kitchen went quiet when he entered. Ralph was not at the table. The lieutenant who was filling in for Lee while he was off stood and asked, "Hey, Cap. How's the back?"

Lee pointed at Kenny. "Gotta talk to you. Let's go to the office." He looked to the lieutenant and asked, "That okay?" Without waiting for an answer, he headed down the hallway.

When they got to the office, Lee said, "Something about that school fire's been bothering me. Did you guys ever do a fire inspection of the place?"

"No. We only did the factories and warehouses in our area that had hazardous materials."

"What about fire drills?"

"Sure. We did two a year."

"Did they use that small door at the back of the school to evacuate?"

"First time I saw that back door was at the fire. It wouldn't have been used for evacuation because you'd have to go through the boiler room to get to it."

Lee rubbed his chin. "How did you guys find it at the fire? When I circled the building, I didn't see it."

"It was concealed by heavy brush."

"So, how did you find it?"

"When you called on the radio and said you were trapped, Ralph told us to follow him. He knew a way in. We ran to the back of the school and he pushed some bushes aside, exposing that small door."

"How would he know that?"

"I asked him and he blew me off."

Lee mulled this over, then asked, "Ralph say why he's off today?"

"Last work day he said he had family business to attend to. He's off for two weeks on trades. What's up, Cap?"

* * *

When Lee got to Ralph's house, he stomped up the porch steps and pounded on the door. "Ralph. Goddamnit. Open this fucking door." He stopped and listened. Hearing nothing from inside, he turned and gave the door a fierce mule kick. The door flew open. Lee barged through the doorway into the murky lighting of the living room. All the window shades were drawn. He called out, "Ralph! Where the hell are you?"

Lee moved down the hallway to the kitchen. At the table in the subdued light from the drawn shades sat Ralph, his face gaunt and expressionless. Lee charged him, knocking him off his chair. Then Lee pounced on top of him, the red mist raging. "What did you have to do with that school fire?"

Lee saw the thick coffee mug in Ralph's hand an instant too late. It slammed into his temple, clouding his vision. Pinpricks of light flashed behind his eyes. He fell back, shaking his head, fighting the fog. Ralph straddled him, pressing his knees onto Lee's upper arms and clasping Lee's throat with both hands.

"You sick psycho," Ralph said. "What the hell is wrong with you?"

The fog cleared. Lee could barely breathe with this bear of a man on his chest. In gasping breaths, Lee said, "You had something—to do—with that school fire. Almost killed—that little girl."

"You both would have been crispy critters if I hadn't saved your asses."

"Your kid's gang—started that fire."

Ralph gasped. "That was the One-Niners."

"Bullshit—and you know it. Get—off me." Lee squirmed under Ralph's weight.

"Sure. And let you go all Recon on me. I've seen that movie." Ralph tightened his grip on Lee's neck. Lee stopped breathing and slowly closed his eyes. After several long seconds, Ralph leaned forward so their faces were inches apart. "You should have walked away from this."

With everything he had, Lee rammed his knee into Ralph's ass, knocking him off balance. Lee twisted hard and threw Ralph off. Before Ralph could react, Lee turned him onto his stomach and pinned him to the floor. He twisted Ralph's right arm behind his back. With his other hand, he gripped the back of Ralph's neck and mauled his face into the floor, crushing his nose. Lee forced Ralph's arm up until the shoulder popped. Ralph howled.

"Jesus, Ralph. What the hell? You were gonna kill me."

"Hell no. Just wanted you to pass out. I saw that crazy-assed look in your eye."

"Last night, your kid's gang burned down Brother Williams' house. Killed him and put my dad in the hospital. Nearly killed some of those kids. I swear if you had anything to do with that I'll…"

"Jesus. Didn't know nothing about that. You gotta believe me. I'm not some kind of monster."

"Then tell me about the school fire."

Ralph squirmed. Lee forced Ralph's right arm further up his back. Ralph gasped and said, "All right, all right."

Lee released the pressure on Ralph's arm, pulled Brigid's compact "45" from his coat pocket, and pressed the barrel to the soft spot on the back of Ralph's neck just below the base of his skull.

"Let's cut the shit. We both know the Disciples started the school fire. And your kid is one of them." Lee pressed the barrel of the pistol harder into the back of Ralph's neck. "Start talking."

"Ace had no choice. Do what he was ordered or that goon they have for an enforcer would convince him. They knew I was a firefighter. That's why they put it on him to burn the school down. Ace said if he screwed it up, the enforcer would make an example of him and me. He was terrified. Pleaded with me to help. Promised he'd make sure nobody got hurt."

"So, you checked the place out, found that back door, and told your kid how to get a fire rolling in the basement. Or did you start it?"

"You going senile? I was on duty."

"You could have set it up early in the morning with timers—or had your kid light it up later when you were at work so you had an alibi. Your kid's gang wanted to make sure it looked like arson by the One-Niners. No need for a fancy cover-up."

"I didn't start any fires. And you're damn lucky I was on duty. You and the girl would not have made it out."

Lee struggled to keep from losing it. "I'm supposed to thank you? Are you shitting me?"

"Just pointing out that I saved your ass."

"From a fire you helped plan. Now who's the psycho? Anything else I should know?"

"Just that my idiot kid never saw the girl and her dad go in. They must have gone in the side door when he was out back."

Lee leaned forward, putting his mouth next to Ralph's ear. "Your kid will be up for murder if he was a part of last night's fire. You need to convince him to help the cops bring down the Disciples before it's too late."

Ralph groaned. "Dammit, Ace."

"How in hell did you let yourself get pulled into this?"

"I promised my wife before she died that I'd take care of the kid. It was my fault that he went horseshit. Somehow I had to fix him. But there was no fixing. This comes out, I'm toast." Ralph blew out a loud breath and stopped squirming. "If you're done beating the shit out of me, how about getting off?"

A part of Lee felt a tinge of sympathy for Ralph. His kid had put him in an impossible situation. Lee was still damn pissed but not roiling with out-of-control rage. He got off Ralph, put the gun back in his coat pocket, and helped him to his feet. Blood ran from Ralph's nostrils, dripping off his chin. Lee grabbed a dish towel from the sink and handed it to him. They both limped to the table like a couple of battle-worn soldiers. Ralph squeezed his nose with the towel. "You broke my goddamn nose."

Lee wiped the side of his head and examined the blood on his palm. "You got me pretty good too."

Ralph put the towel down and held his right arm tight to his chest. "Took my shot. Don't get a second chance with you Recon freaks." The top of Ralph's right shoulder had a prominent bulge.

"Sit down," Lee ordered. He placed one hand on the top of the bulge and with the other hand, he grabbed Ralph by the elbow and lifted his arm while pulling hard. Ralph grunted as the shoulder popped into place and the bulge disappeared.

"Aren't we getting a little old for this crap?" Ralph asked, rubbing his shoulder.

The pain in Lee's lower back flared as the adrenaline drained. "You and your kid's only hope is to turn himself in. Help the cops take down the Disciples."

"You promised to look the other way," Ralph said. "You owe me."

"If your kid testifies, he could keep you out of it. And nobody would have to know you were involved. That's the best I can do."

Even as Lee said this, he knew the chances were slim that Ace would live to testify if he decided to help.

Chapter 40

Mitch

Miss Bernie was sitting on the edge of her bed, wearing her violet Sunday dress when Mitch and Alexus entered her hospital room. Her head was bowed and hands clasped in prayer. Alexus ran to her and buried her face in Miss Bernie's bosom, sobbing. Miss Bernie pulled her close and rocked. Mitch stood in front of them, his arms hanging at his side. The minutes ticked by. A nurse came into the room and asked, "Is Bernice ready to go?"

Miss Bernie kept rocking Alexus. Mitch said, "Give us a few minutes."

The nurse smiled. "Stay as long as you need."

Mitch sat next to Miss Bernie and rubbed her back. "You know."

Barely above a whisper, Miss Bernie said, "Felt Clarence leave me last night."

Words stuck in Mitch's throat. He thought about how Brother Williams had been a mentor to him. When Mitch was still in Milwaukee, Brother Williams asked him to help at the school, showing kids how to use tools and build things. Helping the inner-city children helped Mitch find peace. As much as he loved that man and how devastated he was, Mitch couldn't imagine how Miss Bernie was feeling. She was an incredibly strong woman who relied on her faith to carry her through tragic times that would have destroyed most people. Her first husband had left her to raise two little children on her own in the Core. Her daughter, Lettie, had run away as a teenager, and her son, Jamal, was murdered by a gangbanger. She eventually found peace in raising foster children with the love of her life, Brother Williams. How would she ever get over losing him?

Miss Bernie stopped rocking. "Take me home."

"Umm," Mitch said. "You don't know about the fire?"

She didn't answer.

How could he tell her? He searched for the right words.

Alexus stopped sobbing and said in a deep voice Mitch didn't recognize, "Those bikers burn down our house and kill Papa Williams."

Mitch jerked his head back. "How do you know that?"

"Heard you all talking in the kitchen."

Miss Bernie's eyes widened. "The children!"

"They all got out," Mitch said.

She went back to rocking Alexus with her eyes squeezed shut.

Jasmine, Lettie, where are you? Mitch pleaded. *Miss Bernie desperately needs you.*

* * *

Miss Bernie and Alexus sat together in the back seat of Brigid's truck that Mitch had borrowed. Mitch glanced at them frequently through the rearview mirror when he heard Alexus sniffle. The far-away look on Miss Bernie's face never changed, sending a chill through him. He had never seen her like this.

When they got to Lee's house, the children ran to her. Miss Bernie stood in the middle of the front room with the children enveloping her. She looked lost. Mitch took her hand and guided her to the couch. The children pleaded for answers with their eyes. Before he could answer, Alexus said, "Momma Bernie just real tired." She looked to Mitch. "Ain't that right?"

"Yes, yes, she is. She'll be fine after she gets some rest," Mitch said, praying Alexus was right.

This seemed to make sense to the children as they nodded their heads.

Brigid, who had been standing at the back of the room, pointed to a stack of cots next to her and said, "The Red Cross dropped these off with some bedding. Why don't we set them up in the bedrooms upstairs for the kids? There's two bedrooms down here. Maybe Miss Bernie would like to take one of those and get some rest."

Mitch asked Miss Bernie, "Would you like to lie down for a while?"

She didn't respond, the far-away look never changing. Did everyone have a breaking point? And was this hers?

Mitch took her hand and walked her to the first bedroom next to the front room. The queen-sized bed was unmade, the rumpled sheets and pale-blue comforter in a pile. He gently guided her onto the bed and pulled the comforter over her. He kissed her on the forehead. "I love you. We all love you." He patted her folded hands. He could barely get the words out, "Rest easy, sweet lady."

She stared at the ceiling.

Mitch met Brigid in the kitchen. She said, "Miss Bernie looks like she's in shock."

"What do we do? Do we take her back to the hospital?"

"Let her rest for now. I'll check with my therapist and see what she thinks."

"I should check on the captain. He looked more pissed than usual when he left this morning."

"That's an understatement. He looked ready to explode."

"You think he's going after Manson?"

Brigid shrugged. "Damn him. He can't do this himself."

Mitch dialed the number and a cell phone chimed from the back bedroom. "Crap. Left his phone here."

Brigid groaned, then said, "What the hell is that man up to?"

Chapter 41

Lee

After leaving Ralph's house, Lee decided it was time to meet Manson. He needed answers and he knew how to get them. In Vietnam, his team was well-schooled in interrogation techniques, both those taught by Marine Force Recon and those picked up during the chaos of jungle warfare. Lives depended on getting information fast, whatever it took. The Hells Disciples had to be defeated. He'd start with the leader and the enforcer and see where that led him. Having a plan, at least the start of one, eased his sense of helplessness. There was no time to wait for the cops to figure out the Disciples were behind the fires or for the One-Niners to find the girls. He had to act.

When he got to his car, Lee fished his keys out of his coat pocket and realized his phone wasn't there. *Maybe that's best,* he thought. *I don't need any distractions.* His back aching, he gingerly moved onto the driver's seat.

The cold barrel of a gun pressed into the back of Lee's neck. "Don't be stupid," Ace said from the back seat. "Hand me the keys with your right hand and keep your left on the wheel."

The compact "45" buried deep inside Lee's coat pocket was so close but so far away. He held the keys up so Ace would have to reach for them. When Ace went for them, Lee would jerk his head to the side, grab the gun, and twist it from Ace's hand before he could react.

Ace cackled as the gun barrel moved away from Lee's neck. In the rearview mirror, he saw Ace lean back, just out of Lee's reach, waving a silver-barreled handgun at him. "You were thinking about taking my heat, weren't you? My old man warned me about you. How about you lay those keys on the seat for now."

Lee's first instinct was to roll onto the floor while pulling the pistol from his pocket like a western gunslinger. Getting the gun from deep in his coat pocket would be a challenge, and Ace would have the advantage, but he didn't seem all that sharp. Lee slowed his breathing, ready to make his move. Out of nowhere, the black van pulled alongside. Snake leveled an AR15 at him through the open window.

"Get in the van," Ace ordered. "And leave the keys."

Lee glanced down the street as he got out of the car. It was Sunday morning quiet, Christmas Eve Day. With the car and van blocking the view, neighbors would have no clue as to what was happening.

"Keep that burner on him," Ace said. "He's some kinda bad-ass Marine vet."

"Check his pockets," Snake ordered.

Ace pulled the compact "45" from Lee's coat pocket. Over his shoulder, Lee saw Ace wave the two pistols. "Now I got me two heaters." He pointed the "45" at Lee's head, his face turning to an evil scowl, and said, "I would like nothin' more than to blow your miserable brains all over the road with your own piece."

Snake said, "Not now."

"I know. He's got something of ours." Ace slipped the pistols into his coat pockets and opened the sliding side door of the van. He kicked Lee hard in the ass. "Now get in there."

Snake backed into the driver's seat, pointing the rifle at Lee's chest, his finger on the trigger. Lee edged onto the bench seat behind Snake, his mind reeling with a plan to take them both out. This could be his last chance. He'd have to act fast. They were in close quarters now. When Ace climbed into the van, he'd grab Snake's rifle by the barrel, yank it forward, and force the barrel away from him and at Ace. Chances were good that Snake would involuntarily pull the trigger when Lee yanked the rifle. He'd have to do this in one quick motion.

Ace went to the back of Lee's car and opened the trunk. "Christmas come early. Looky what Santa brought me." He leered at Lee and raised the AR15. "I believe this is mine." He reached into the trunk and lifted Mitch's rifle out. "What you planning on shooting with this bad boy?"

Lee glared at Ace. "Animals."

As Ace got into the van, Snake slid over to the front passenger's seat, derailing Lee's plan. Snake was smarter than he looked. Lee set his jaw. The red mist rose, not at Ace and Snake, but at himself. *How the hell did I let these two idiots take me?* he chided himself. *I gotta keep my head straight. They'll screw up at some point.*

Snake took a roll of duct tape and a zip tie from the glove compartment. He raised his hand with the ring finger and little finger wrapped together in white tape. "You gonna pay for this." He tossed the duct tape and zip tie to Ace and said, "You got two good hands. You know what to do."

While Snake held the rifle on Lee, Ace zip-tied Lee's wrists together and stretched duct tape over his mouth. Ace went back to Lee's car and rummaged through it. He brought back the black ski mask Mitch had given Lee. Ace held it up. "Might come in handy." He tossed it in the back of the van.

"There's a vacant lot two blocks over," Snake said. "Ditch his car there and leave the keys. Chances are somebody'll take off with it. Hurry. Time's running out."

* * *

When they got to Ace's place, Ace slipped the ski mask over Lee's head. "Don't need any nosy neighbors seeing your nasty face. Might just be the last time anyone sees it. Follow Snake and keep your hands in front of you at your waist. Don't think I won't take you out. We'll be long gone by the time the neighbors come out and see your body."

They entered through the back door. Ace lifted the ski mask off Lee's head and pointed to the open basement door. "Get your ass down there." They had to duck under the low ceiling when they got to the bottom of the stairs. The swampy-smelling basement was like a cave, the stone walls covered in greenish-black mold. Gaping cracks and crevices meandered across the buckled concrete floor. Two dim light bulbs hung from wires at the front and back of the room. Four small glass-block windows were painted black. On Lee's right were three decrepit wooden chairs next to a battered kitchen table lying on its side missing one of the thick legs. A rusty bed frame leaned against the back wall with musty bedding and clothing next to it. Piles of junk were strewn along the other wall. Lee focused on the junk while trying not to be too obvious.

Ace scraped one of the heavy wooden chairs across the floor and placed it beneath the hanging light bulb at the back of the basement. While Snake held the AR15 on Lee, Ace sat him on the chair, leaving his coat on him. He wound duct tape around each of Lee's ankles and the legs of the chair. Ace sneered as he wrapped the tape around the back of the chair and around Lee's arms and upper chest. "Learned this from you."

Didn't learn all that good, you idiot, Lee thought.

"This might sting," Ace said, cackling. "Real sorry about that." He ripped the duct tape from Lee's mouth.

"What kind of animals are you?" Lee roared. "Kill Brother Williams and nearly kill a bunch of kids for what? To get his god-damn school?"

"What the hell's he talking about?" Snake asked.

Before Ace could say anything, Lee said, "You gonna tell him how you burned down a school and almost killed a little girl? How you shot up that little girl's house, then burned it down, killing her dad? All those kids barely got out, you miserable punk."

"Yeah? I know where you live. Maybe I burn your house down." Ace latched onto Lee's shoulders, hurling him and the chair backward. The back of Lee's head cracked against the concrete floor. Ace jumped on top of him, grabbed his neck with both hands, and squeezed. As the lights faded, Lee felt strangely at peace. There was no fighting it.

Snake yanked Ace off. "What kinda shit your chapter involved in? Disciples can't be associated with killing kids. My pres will be hearing about this."

The color drained from Ace's face. He stammered and said, "Dude's making shit up. Trying to distract us. Let me beat his ass. He'll tell us where those girls are."

"Cool it. My brothers in Chicago already have issues with your chapter and they won't be happy to lose four girls. It'll cost your club big and you know your pres won't be happy with you if you don't deliver Crystal and Summer to that fancy Christmas party tomorrow. Those other two were supposed to be back in Chicago four days ago."

Lee's mind raced. If he was going to finish this mission and take out the enemy, he had to keep them convinced he knew where the girls were.

Snake set Lee and the chair back up and said, "You tell us where the girls are and we're all happy. You refuse? We turn you over to the club and you get your ass tortured by their enforcer. Then we all lose. Should be an easy choice. Now. Where are the girls?"

"You think I'm going to let you get your miserable hands on them?"

Snake laid the AR15 on the floor and slammed his good fist into Lee's stomach. Lee dropped his chin to his chest, acting like it hurt like hell, and gasped. Snake could pound away all day and not hurt him the way he was punching him. If Snake knew anything about hand-to-hand combat, he would have struck higher at Lee's solar plexus. Lee slowly lifted his head as if he were struggling to catch his breath. Snake hit him again. Lee groaned and said, "Okay, okay."

Snake grinned. "Now. Where you got the girls?"

Lee spit at him and said, "Fuck you and your simple buddy there." He wanted to enrage them. That's when mistakes were made. Snake was smart enough to know they needed to keep Lee alive if they were ever to find those girls.

Ace picked the AR15 off the floor and put the barrel to Lee's forehead. *Good. He was getting to them*. "Go ahead. I guarantee you'll never find those girls and you'll be the one getting your ass tortured by that enforcer, what do they call him, Warlock?"

The butt of the AR15 slammed against the side of Lee's head. The room went dark.

Chapter 42

Mitch

Brigid went through the kitchen cabinets while Mitch called Kenny to see if he had seen Lee. Kenny told him about their conversation at the firehouse and about Lee's concerns about Ralph knowing where the back door to the school was the morning of the fire. Before ending the conversation, Kenny asked, "You think Ralph had something to do with that fire?"

"Don't know what to think, brother." Mitch ended the call and said to Brigid, "I think the captain went over to Ralph's house."

"Yeah, I heard."

"I'm going to head over there. Can you take care of things here?"

"Sure. But there's not much food. Those kids are going to get hungry."

"Depending how this goes, I'll try to pick up some groceries. Did you talk to your therapist?"

"She said to monitor Miss Bernie and let her rest for now. She needs time to process her grief. Better for her to be here surrounded by family than in a hospital room."

"I'll need your truck again."

"These poor kids. Hell of a way to celebrate Christmas."

"We gotta find a way to bring those girls home."

* * *

There was no sign of Lee's car or the Disciples when Mitch pulled onto Ralph's block. At Ralph's door, Mitch listened for a sign of a struggle. Hearing none, he knocked. No response. He knocked harder. Still nothing. He turned the knob and opened the unlocked door. "Ralph. Ralph, you here?"

Ralph stepped out of the shadows of the dark hallway, holding a wadded-up dishtowel to his nose, the front of his navy blue T-shirt stained with blood. "You come to finish the job?"

"Holy crap. The captain do that?"

"Jesus, kid. You need to haul your ass back to the farm. This ain't no place for you."

"Where's the captain?"

"Get the hell out of here. You don't know what you're getting into. This is about more than that girl."

"You had something to do with that school fire, didn't you?" The defeated look on Ralph's face told Mitch all he needed to know. "What about the house fire? Did you…?"

Ralph lowered the blood-soaked dishcloth from his broken nose. "Had nothing to do with that."

"Ace?"

"I hope to hell not."

"Ralph, you gotta help us before anyone else gets killed."

Ralph headed to the kitchen without answering.

"What happened to you?" Mitch called after him. "I looked up to you."

Ralph stopped and turned back to Mitch. "You need to go. Run. Get the hell out of here before they come for you."

"Can't. Just like you taught me at fires. There's no giving up."

Ralph turned and headed to the kitchen. Mitch watched, shocked at how his friend and mentor now disgusted him. When Ralph disappeared into the darkness of the kitchen, Mitch shouted, "I looked up to you," and left.

On the way to Brigid's truck, Mitch called her and told her about Lee's attacking Ralph. When he finished she said, "I'm worried about him. He's on a razor's edge. There's no telling what he might do."

"He knows Manson must have ordered the Williams' house to be burned. I gotta think that's where he's heading next. I'll go up there. How's things going at the house?"

"Too quiet. Miss Bernie just stares at the ceiling. The kids wanted to gather around her, but I didn't want them to see her like this. I told them she needed to rest. Later, I found Alexus snuggled next to her, telling her how she loved her more than anything in the world and to please not leave her. I went to the kitchen and bawled my eyes out."

Mitch parked two blocks from Manson's house and waited, thinking about Alexus and all she had been through in her short life. Her father left the family years ago. Her mother was in prison for killing the man who molested her sister, Jasmine. And now the Disciples were prostituting Jasmine. Her beloved Brother Williams was dead, and the person she loved most in the world, the woman who took her and Jasmine into her home, was drowning in grief.

It was nearly noon when Mitch's phone chimed. Brigid said, "Anything going on up there?"

"No sign of Lee. Think I'll head to Ace's place."

"Stop by Lee's house on the way. You won't believe what's happening."

"What are you talking about?"

"Just get back here, now."

* * *

Women and children Mitch didn't recognize were gathered on the front porch of Lee's house when Mitch pulled up. He went around to the back door and smelled cinnamon. When he entered the kitchen, Mitch gasped. Deion was at the table with Brigid, drinking coffee, both stuffing their mouths with gooey cinnamon buns. The folder of mug shots of Disciples lay open between them. Mitch glanced around the kitchen. The counters were filled with Christmas cookies and all sorts of baked items. Brigid said, "You should see everything in the refrigerator. Had to freeze some of it. Grab a cinnamon bun. They're still warm."

"Umm. What? How?"

"Deion, you fill him in," Brigid said.

"Put the word on the street about Junior—Brother Williams. All the crews respect that man."

"So, who are all these women and kids?"

Deion grimaced. "What? You don't think bangers got families?"

Mitch raised his hands. "Sorry. Are they all from your gang?"

"From crews all over the city."

Brigid said, "Check out the front room."

Mitch went to the entrance to the front room. A tall Christmas tree decorated with multi-colored blinking lights stood in the corner with a white angel at the top looking down on them. The children were gathered around the tree chattering while separating and piling gifts under it. A short, older woman with a little boy around five and a girl around Alexus's age next to her pulled a small present from her large shopping bag and handed it to Alonzo, the oldest boy, and said, "This one for you." The woman pulled out a larger present with a grinning Santa Claus on the red wrapping paper and handed it to the four-year-old girl who squealed. Mitch asked the woman, "Where did you get all these presents?"

"When my boy told me about these poor kids losing their papa and their house, I walked the neighborhood, telling ever one, asking if they might have one or two things they could spare."

"Your son Deion?"

"Umm hmm." She pointed to the girl and little boy who was missing a front tooth. "These his kids, my grandkids."

He looked closer at the girl and said, "Hi, Peaches. I remember you from when you visited my farm."

"I love feeding those baby cows. When can I come back?"

"How about next summer?"

Peaches grinned, then asked, "Where's Alexus?"

"I don't know where she is." He looked to her grandmother. "How did you guys get that tree here?"

Before she could answer, the gray-haired Red Cross lady came forward. "Our volunteers contacted Home Depot out on Capitol Drive. They sent someone down with one of their decorated trees. Walgreens sent gifts and candy. I was going to see what you and the kids would need for food." She waved her hand toward the women and children crowded behind them. "But these folks have been bringing all kinds of wonderful food for you all. The pastor at their church stopped by and said the congregation would provide plenty more food as long as needed."

Mitch reached his arms out to Deion's mother. "This is so … I don't even have words."

She pulled back, eyeing him suspiciously.

Mitch dropped his arms. "Sorry. I didn't mean to…"

"No need. Not used to getting hugged by a white. Only whites that show up on my street wear badges. Plenty more gifts coming for these kids. Deion spread some cash around and said to get whatever this family needs."

What this family needs more than anything, Mitch thought, *is Jasmine and Lettie home and the Disciples behind bars.*

Mitch knelt and shook the little boy's hand. "Thank you for sharing your gifts."

The boy grinned and slinked behind his grandmother.

"And thank you, Peaches," Mitch said.

She smiled and followed her grandmother to the door.

Mitch turned to the Red Cross lady. "And thank you for everything you're doing … Sorry I don't even know your name. I'm Mitch. I assume you already met Brigid."

"Dorothy, but please call me Dot."

"Well, nice to meet you, Dot. I don't know what we would do without your help. Can I hug you?"

She welcomed Mitch into her arms.

After thanking each person in the crowd, Mitch went to the kitchen and asked Brigid, "Where's Alexus?"

"In the bedroom with Miss Bernie."

Mitch entered the darkened bedroom. Alexus was snuggled next to Miss Bernie, who was staring at the ceiling.

"Did you see all the presents these people are bringing?" Mitch said to Alexus.

"Don't feel like Christmas."

"Peaches was here, asking about you."

No response.

"Miss Bernie," Mitch said. "You should see the tree they brought. It's beautiful."

She continued to stare at the ceiling. Alexus snuggled closer to her.

Mitch sat on the bed with them in somber silence for half an hour. He rubbed Alexus's back before leaving, then went to the kitchen. "I feel so damned helpless. What do we do?"

"Just be here for them is all we can do," Brigid said.

Deion appeared lost in thought. To him, Mitch said, "You know it was the Disciples who started those fires and set your gang up."

"Lady B, here, fill me in."

Did B stand for bitch or Brigid, Mitch thought but didn't ask. He grabbed a cinnamon bun, glanced at it, and put it down. "How're we gonna get evidence to prove the Disciples are behind the fires?"

Deion wiped the white frosting from his lips with the back of his hand. His eyebrows pinched together, forming a deep furrow. "Got all the evidence I need."

Brigid studied Deion, nodded, and pushed the folder of mug shots across the table to him.

Lee's cell phone chimed. Mitch raced to the bedroom and snatched it off the dresser before it stopped chiming. When he answered, a woman said, "You the firefighter stopped by my house the other day?"

He thought fast, not wanting her to hang up. "Yes. Yes, I am."

"You told me to tell you if I saw those men bring those girls back to their house."

He gasped in a rush of excitement. *Finally,* he thought. "Are they there?"

"No. Saw them bring a man wearing a ski mask to the house. I could see the husky one behind him had a gun. Figured you might want to know that."

"Was the man with the ski mask wearing a black coat?"

She nodded. "Looked pretty shabby."

"Did you call the cops?"

"You told me not to."

"Right. Anything else?"

"Wait. I see the husky one. He's leaving."

"Is he getting in the black van?"

"No, he's taking that old gray car they drive sometime."

"You know what kind of car it is?"

"Don't know cars. It's old and gray. Has four doors. That's all I can tell you."

Mitch ended the call and took the cell phone with him to the kitchen. "They got Lee at Ace's place. I gotta get down there."

"I'm coming along," Brigid said.

"You should stay with the kids."

She shook her head. "I'll see if Dot can stay and keep an eye on things."

"What about the Disciples? No telling what they got planned next. If all these people know we're here, the Disciples must know too."

Deion stood. "Don't worry about those raggedy-assed bikers. I'll have eyes on this place. They show up, they disappear."

Chapter 43

Lee

As Lee regained consciousness, he kept his eyes shut and stayed limp. Snake said, "You stupid fuck. What if the asshole doesn't wake up? He's our only chance to find those girls."

"I didn't hit him that hard," Ace said.

"He better come around soon. We don't deliver those girls to that Christmas party tomorrow night, your pres will want answers. I wouldn't want to be you."

"What about you? You're the one got jacked."

"But the girls were taken from your place. And your club ain't gonna mess with a Chicago brother. They know better. They'll take it out on you. And if those girls aren't back in Chicago the day after that Christmas Party, my club will want to know why. So, if we don't find them, your sorry ass is fried. And I won't be going down with you."

Footsteps came toward Lee. A hand clutched the bottom of his chin and lifted his face. Lee remained limp. He could feel hot breath on his face and resisted turning away from the sour smell. Ace said, "You need to wake your ass up." Ace released Lee's chin and rapped him alongside the head. Lee fought the urge to laugh at him and spit in his face.

You did me a huge favor, you idiot, Lee thought.

Snake said, "You think that's gonna wake him up, you moron? Jesus."

"Then you figure out how to wake him. I gotta run to my old man's house quick. Said he needed to talk. Matter of life and death. Whatever the hell that means. I'll take the car."

When Lee heard Ace's boots climb the stairs, he felt a rush of relief. Only one of them to deal with. He'd have to wait for the right moment. A few seconds later, a hand gripped his chin and shook his head. Snake said, "If you can hear me in there, tell me where the girls are and I'll let you go. I can't see letting that asshole kill a fellow vet, even though you busted my fingers." He released Lee's chin. "Ah, shit. He nailed you good. Lucky to be alive."

Footsteps headed across the basement and up the stairs. This was it. The zip tie that Ace used on his wrists was the cheap type used for bundling automotive wires. Ace had done him another favor by tying his hands in front of him instead of behind his back. Lee bit the loose end of the zip tie and pulled it so that the locking mechanism was on top and centered between his wrists. He tugged it with his teeth, eliminating any slack. Ace had duct-taped his upper chest and arms over his coat to the back of the chair. A surge of adrenaline electrified Lee's body. He twisted his upper body in the chair, loosening the duct tape just enough to free his arms. Lee lifted his arms over his head and spread his elbows wide. With everything he had, he chicken-winged his arms down and back. The zip tie snapped.

The toilet from above flushed.

Lee clawed at the duct tape around his chest while thrashing in the chair until he was able to get enough play in the tape to force it over his head. He unwrapped the duct tape from his right ankle, then scratched around the tape on his left ankle with his thumb, searching for the end. "Dammit, come on," he said to himself as the floorboards above him creaked.

He found the end of the tape, picking at it frantically. He finally got a grip on the end and unwrapped it. Lee scrambled to the pile of bedding and grabbed two musty pillows and an old shirt. He stacked the pillows on the chair and draped the shirt over the top one. The hinge on the basement door squeaked. One of Snake's black engineer boots appeared on the first step. The low basement ceiling blocked his view.

At the bottom of the junk pile, barely visible, was the end of the missing leg from the battered table. Lee had spotted it when they first brought him down here. As Lee slid the heavy leg from the pile something thudded as it settled. Lee gasped.

Snake pounded down the stairs.

Lee went to the chair and unscrewed the hot bulb above it, darkening the back of the basement. He rushed to the wall and knelt behind the overturned table as Snake appeared at the bottom of the stairs, pointing the AR15 at the shirt and pillows on the chair. "What the…?"

Lee charged across the basement, letting out a blood-curdling scream. Snake froze for a split second. As Snake turned the rifle toward him, Lee slammed the table leg against his left arm. Snake yelped. The rifle dropped to the floor. Lee grabbed Snake by the neck and slammed his head against the rock wall. Snake's eyes glazed. Lee punched him hard in the solar plexus. Snake gagged and bent at the waist.

"That's how you do it," Lee said.

Snake took several short breaths and straightened, holding his arm. "I know that. I was making it look good for Ace. No way was I going to let that miserable piece of shit kill a fellow vet."

"What the hell you talking about?"

"You broke my arm."

Lee picked the AR15 from the floor and put the barrel under Snake's chin. "Tell me why I shouldn't kill you."

"That would be a mistake."

"Tell me why."

"I had nothing to do with those fires. My club's been having issues with the Milwaukee chapter. They're playing too loose. That leader is living way too large. Only a matter of time before he draws the attention of the feds. When I tell my club about them burning houses down and shooting up houses with kids inside, good chance we'll be cutting 'em loose."

Lee pressed the barrel of the rifle under Snake's chin. "But your club is okay with trafficking young girls? Give me a break. For you to bring those girls up here, there must have been some big deal going on besides a small party for a bunch of firefighters."

"Private party with big spenders tomorrow. We been bringing girls up here for years when they needed extras for their parties. One of their members was bragging to me once that the leader, Manson, has been accumulating videos and photos of some important people that come to these parties in, let's say, compromising positions. And he can't be touched because they have these important people in their pocket."

"What kind of depraved shit you make those girls do?"

"Don't make them do anything. I transport the girls and stand by as a bodyguard. Make sure they get back to our club the way they came."

"Some of those girls are just kids. They have families."

"Just doing my job. Why you want them?"

"Tell me again why I shouldn't kill you?"

"You'd kill a fellow vet?"

"Yup."

"Look, I figure you got some connection to those girls. Maybe if you'd stop busting me up, I'd have no problem telling my club those girls disappeared and put it on these Milwaukee losers. I'd love to see these assholes go down. Sick of being around them."

Lee contemplated this. The Chicago Disciples still had photos of Jasmine's sister. Would they come looking for Alexus to find Jasmine? What were the chances Snake would even try to convince his club to forget about the girls? It was too long a shot.

After duct-taping Snake to the chair, Lee went through the house. Ace had left the AR15 and Mitch's hunting rifle behind but must have taken Brigid's compact "45." He grabbed the rifles and stashed the black ski mask in his coat pocket, then drove the biker's black van to the vacant lot where Ace was supposed to have ditched his car. This early in the day, the street people wouldn't be out. His car was still there. Lee stashed the rifles in the trunk.

He twisted up some newspapers that were hanging in the brush, went back to the van, took off the gas cap, and stuffed the newspapers down the gas pipe, leaving a portion hanging out. He lit the end, ran to his car, and sped away. In the rearview mirror, he saw the van erupt in a fireball.

Ace should be at Ralph's house by now, Lee thought, and headed over there. Whatever it took, Lee was not going to let Ralph stop him. Ace had threatened to burn his house down. That was not happening. Lee would tie him down with Snake. That should give him enough time to take out Manson and his ogre of an enforcer before they were found. The most effective way to bring down an enemy was to take out the leaders.

From the end of the block, Lee spotted a rusting gray Impala parked in front of Ralph's house. Lee got the AR15 and the black ski mask from the trunk of his car. He pulled the ski mask over his head and slipped the rifle under his coat in case any neighbors might be watching. He would have to take Ace by surprise and hope like hell Ralph didn't get in the way. There was a good chance Ace had the "45" with him. If he wanted a shootout, so be it.

Lee crouched below the windows while making his way to the back of the house. The kitchen was right off the back door. When he got to the back of the house, he stopped and listened. It was too quiet. He couldn't see inside. All the shades were drawn. If they were farther inside the house, it would be near impossible to surprise them.

Time was running out. There was no telling what the Disciples might have planned next. Lee needed to act. He slowly opened the screen door and checked the inside door. It was locked. He heard Ralph shout, "Did you start that fire that killed Brother Williams?"

"He was warned."

"Turn yourself in before it's too late. Agree to be a confidential informant. Good chance they'll let you off easy."

"Fuck you, Old Man. I ain't turning myself in."

"It's your only chance," Ralph pleaded.

"Screw that. Manson would have me killed before it ever went to court. I took care of your captain, and I'll take care of the other one when I get the chance."

"Can't let you do that."

"What you gonna do? Turn me in?—That ain't happening."

The crack of a gunshot rang out. Lee turned his back to the door and with a ferocious mule kick, slammed the door open. He spun into the kitchen waving the AR15. Ace bolted out the front door. Lee shouted after him, "Go ahead. Run. I'll find your ass."

Ralph gawked at him with the bewildered look Lee had seen on the wounded in Vietnam. "You're alive," Ralph said. "Didn't think the kid could take you out."

Lee took his ski mask off. "You okay?"

"I can still cloud a mirror." Ralph looked down at his blue T-shirt that was dampening with blood. "Bastard shot me."

"Let's take a look." Lee grabbed a knife from the countertop and cut the shirt off. "He got you just below the shoulder blade. I'll call 911."

"Don't do that. You'll get tied up in an investigation. I need you to stop Ace. I can't let him go after Mitch. I'll get myself to the ER and give them some lame excuse about accidentally shooting myself. I'll be okay. The idiot kid couldn't even do this right. He was gonna take another shot when you broke in. Ran like a chicken shit." Ralph grimaced, then said, "You saved my ass from my own kid. Guess we're even."

"You sure you're okay?"

"Go. Stop him. Whatever you gotta do."

The gray Impala was long gone by the time Lee got outside. He headed back to his house.

Chapter 44

Mitch

Brigid and Mitch sped to Ace's place in her truck. They slowed when they came to the house, watching for any sign of Ace and Snake. Neither the black van nor an old gray four-door car was in front of the house. Brigid parked the truck one block over. They jogged back to Ace's street.

An old woman stared at them through the front window of the house next door to Ace's. *Could that be the caller?* Mitch wondered. With Brigid leading the way, holding her Glock to her chest, they edged their way along the side of Ace's house, peering into the windows.

Brigid stood to the side of the back window and glanced inside. "It's quiet. Check the door."

Mitch turned the knob. "It's open."

"Follow me in and stay low," Brigid said. "This could turn bad, fast."

They entered the kitchen and made their way down the hallway with Brigid swinging her gun back and forth as they checked the first bedroom. When they moved back into the hallway, the floor squeaked. They froze. From the basement, they heard a muffled groan. "They got the captain down there," Mitch whispered.

"They know someone's here, but they don't know who. We have to act fast. You with me?"

"You bet."

"I'll go down and tell them I'm here to read the meter and that the owner said it was okay to let myself in. If they're unarmed, I'll draw my weapon. When you hear me shout 'Police!' you come down and back me up."

"What if they're armed?" Mitch asked.

"I'll pretend I didn't know anyone was down there and apologize for interrupting them. Act like I didn't see the guns. I'll tell them I can read the meter later."

"You think they'll buy that?"

"Let's go," Brigid said. She opened the basement door. The muffled moaning turned frantic. She made her way down the stairs and shouted, "Meter reader." The moaning stopped, followed by silence. Mitch strained to hear what was going on. Why wasn't Brigid saying anything? Why wasn't Ace or Snake saying anything? *I gotta do something,* he thought.

Laughter echoed up the stairway. It was Brigid. Was this her way of diffusing things?

"Mitch, c'mon down. You gotta see this."

When Mitch ducked below the low ceiling, he saw Snake duct-taped to a chair at the back of the basement with Brigid standing next to him. She said, "Looks like Lee's been here." She ripped the tape from Snake's mouth. "Where'd he go?"

"Bastard broke my arm."

Brigid pressed the barrel of her Glock against his temple. "Where'd—He—Go?"

"How the hell do I know?"

Mitch asked, "What about Ace?"

"Went to his old man's house."

"You bastards killed a good man in that fire," Mitch shouted.

"Told your buddy, that was all the Milwaukee chapter. I had nothing to do with it."

"And prostituting young girls? You had nothing to do with that either?" Mitch wanted to beat the hell out of this miserable piece of humanity but heard the words of his mentor, Miss Bernie, in his head, "Do not let that devil move you to violence."

Snake said, "I don't know what you and that firefighter want with those girls, but I could give a shit less about getting them back to Chicago. You want them, you can have 'em. I'll give my chapter some story about them being abducted and blame it on the Milwaukee chapter."

"You ain't blaming shit on us," boomed from the bottom of the stairwell. Mitch and Brigid spun together. A bald, square-faced man with a thick black beard glared at them over the top of an AR15. Warlock. Next to him, Manson grinned diabolically. The blood drained from Mitch's face.

"Put that pea shooter on the floor and kick it toward me," Manson said to Brigid.

She paused, eyeing Warlock with a look that could cut glass. He sneered, his finger on the trigger of the rifle. "Go ahead, bitch."

Brigid gritted her teeth, lowered the gun to the floor, and kicked it toward Manson. He picked it up and examined it. "I heard you were snooping around that fire."

"Who told you that?"

Manson approached her, pointing the pistol between her eyes. "Where's that fireman that was with you?"

Warlock moved alongside Manson.

Brigid's face reddened. "Rot in hell."

Manson slammed the pistol against the side of her head. Mitch reached for Manson's arm. Warlock rammed the butt of the rifle into

Mitch's gut, sending him to his knees, gasping for air. Mitch looked up in time to see a black engineer boot coming at his face. He blocked it with his arm. Warlock poised the rifle butt above Mitch's head.

Manson waved his hand at Warlock while watching Brigid. "Are we done playing?"

Mitch rose from the floor. Brigid glared at Manson, her eyes blazing.

"Dust them here, Boss?" Warlock asked. "Or we have a little fun with them first?"

"We don't have time for that. I gotta find out how they know we burned that house down and who else knows. We need to go. Too many neighbors around here."

Manson went to Snake. "Where's the whores?"

"Dude there and his partner took them."

Dread overwhelmed Mitch as Manson turned to him. "What you want with them?"

"To get them away from you animals."

Manson's coal-black eyes smoldered. "Where you got them?"

"I tell you, you'll kill me right here."

"If you don't, I'll let Warlock take you apart piece by piece until you beg him to kill you."

"All right. All right. I'm supposed to meet my partner later. He'll have the girls with him. If I don't show up, he'll know something's wrong and disappear."

"When and where?"

"Six o'clock."

"Where?"

"I'm not stupid. I'll take you there."

Manson grinned. "You bet your ass you will." He went back to Snake. "Where'd Ace go?"

"To his old man's place."

"Fucking loser," Manson growled. He pointed at Mitch and Brigid. "Your phones."

They handed their cell phones to him. "You won't be needing these anymore." He dropped them to the floor and stomped on them, grinning at Brigid. "Just in case any of your cop friends planned on tracking you."

"And you," Manson said to Snake. "Maybe you disappear and I tell your chapter that you ran off with their whores." Manson glanced at Warlock. "Let's get them out of here."

Chapter 45

Lee

As Lee pulled up to his house a crowd was milling around the front porch. He went on high alert. The mission would have to wait until he knew everyone was safe inside. He drove around to the alley.

Lee approached the house with the AR15 under his coat. He crouched below the kitchen window and glimpsed through the lower corner. Inside, the Red Cross lady was seated at the table focused on the doorway to the front room. Everything looked calm. He took the AR15 back to his car. The kids didn't need to see him with the rifle. He put it back in the trunk.

As he turned to head back to the house, a gangbanger carrying an AK47 appeared from the side of the garage. Lee ducked below the back of the car, grasping for the keys to open the trunk. The gangbanger called out, "Chill, dude. I'm here to watch your crib."

When Lee stood, he saw it was the tall gangbanger from the warehouse, he asked, "What are all those people doing on my porch?"

"Don't know, but they sure ain't Disciples. Know what I mean?"

Lee couldn't bring himself to thank a gangbanger. He nodded and went to the back door and quietly opened it, trying not to surprise the Red Cross lady. When he stepped inside, he heard children chattering in the front room. The Red Cross lady's head jerked his way. He raised his hand and whispered, "Everything okay?"

"What happened to the side of your head?"

"Minor scuffle. What's all the noise about?"

She pointed to the doorway to the front room. The youngest foster child clutched a package wrapped with red Christmas paper to her chest. Her full-faced smile eased Lee's jittery nerves. The little girl ran across the room to him and said, "Look what those nice people brought me, Mr. Garrison."

"You are one lucky girl," he said, thinking how untrue that was. She seemed satisfied with his response and skipped back to the front room. After all that kid had lost, Lee was shocked she could feel any joy. He could learn something from this four-year-old.

"Um, what's going on?" Lee asked the Red Cross lady.

She led him to the crowded front room and while he took in the festive scene of women and children sorting gifts, she explained what had been going on all day. When she finished, Lee asked, "So all these gifts and food are coming from gangs across the city?"

"Not all of it. Some came from their church. But most of it came from the gangs. Who would have ever thought, hey?" She grinned. "Kinda like gangland Toys for Tots."

Lee pondered this while they watched the kids sort and pile gifts under the tree. These gangs, who over the years had fought violent wars with each other, had come together to honor Brother Williams. This man must have touched the lives of so many children throughout the inner city. What a legacy he was leaving behind. Who would fill that void?

"Where are the other two?" Lee asked the Red Cross lady.

"They left. Asked if I would stay with the kids. Told me the house was being watched. Not to worry. I think that gang member who was here might have something to do with that."

"What did he look like?"

"His hair was all in spikes."

Lee flared. *Holy shit,* he thought. *That gang-banger was here. In my house. Uninvited.* He blew out a loud breath and said, "You must want to get back to your family, but can you stay until the others get back?"

She frowned. "Got no family. I'm a widow. Never had kids. That's why I volunteer. Spending Christmas Eve with these children would be such a blessing. Do what you must. I'll stay as long as I'm needed or until I'm kicked out"

Lee smiled and said, "Nobody'll be kicking you out. I'm Lee, by the way. Can't thank you enough for…"

"No need. I'm Dot. You go do what you have to do."

He went to his dad's bedroom and peeked inside. Miss Bernie and Alexus were snuggled close on the bed. "I will not let anybody hurt you two," Lee said to himself. He had promised that little girl he would bring her sister home. And Miss Bernie desperately needed her daughter to help get her through the loss of her beloved Brother Williams and her home. He had no idea how to find them. What he could do is protect this family. He had to admit, he was glad Deion had the One-Niners watching the house. If Lee could bring down the Milwaukee club, at least this family and the girls would be safe from them. The Chicago club would still loom as a deadly threat if Snake told them Lee and Mitch had taken the girls.

Lee went to his bedroom, got his cell phone, and dialed Brigid. The ringtone rang and rang, then stopped and went to her voicemail. Lee said, "Where the hell are you two? Call me back when you get this." He dialed Mitch next, got the same result, and said, "Dammit, Mitch. Pick up. Ace is out there looking for you."

Lee walked back to the kitchen, his brain spinning. Had Ace gotten to Mitch and Brigid? Or were they inside a building like a hospital where cell phones didn't work? Why would they be in a hospital? That wouldn't be good. He stopped and took a few breaths. All he could do at this point was to keep trying to call and hope they got his message. He shifted gears. The mission. He needed to strike the Disciples before they made another move.

Dot was sitting on the front room floor surrounded by the kids and greeting people as they made their way inside with their gifts. She looked up, smiled at Lee, and said, "Merry Christmas, Mr. Garrison." The children looked his way, all of them grinning, and shouted, "Merry Christmas, Mr. Garrison."

Lee stopped at the back door, soaking in the joy and warmth radiating from the front room. The Disciples had already taken so much from this family. They would take no more. He needed to act fast, but it was critical to plan his next move wisely and not let his seething hatred for the Disciples force him into making a deadly mistake.

Chapter 46

Lee

It was the middle of the afternoon when Lee parked at the Pleasant Manor Memory Care Unit. He couldn't let Christmas go by without visiting his mom. This would give him time to think out his next move and hear from Mitch and Brigid. *Please be a good day,* he implored, knowing this could be the last time she would see him if the mission went sideways.

The woman at the desk greeted him with a smile and said, "She'll be so happy to see you."

"Me? Or someone else?"

She grinned wide. "You."

He rushed to his mom's room and found her seated on her bed looking through an old photo album. "Merry Christmas, Mom."

"Oh, my. What happened to your face?"

"It's nothing. I'm fine."

She patted the bed next to her. "Come sit. I was just going through some old holiday pictures. What happened to your face?"

She's repeating herself, he thought, hoping he wasn't losing her already. He repeated, "It's nothing. I'm fine."

The last thing he wanted to do was go through a bunch of photos reminding him of his childhood. In the past, he would simply refuse. But today, with her alert—at least for a little while—he wanted nothing more than to please her. She spread the album over their laps and slowly paged through it. There was a picture of him as a toddler, wearing a sagging white cloth diaper. His bright red

T-shirt had a smiling Santa on the front. The Christmas tree he stood next to was laced with silver strings of tinsel and multi-colored lights. He proudly held up a yellow Tonka Truck to the camera.

His mom said, "You loved that truck. Never let it out of your sight."

When she got to the pictures of him holding his high school wrestling trophies, she said, "I was so proud of you. Merle was too."

Lee couldn't help himself. "He always called me a loser." As soon as he said it, he regretted it. A shadow passed over her face. "Sorry, Mom. I know he was proud of me," Lee lied.

She turned the page to a photo of him standing next to the Christmas tree in his green fatigues. "You never wanted to talk about your time in the Marines," she said.

"Nothing to talk about."

"That's what your dad said about the army."

Lee knew that Merle had been in the Second World War but never asked him about it. He didn't ask Merle about anything. Mostly just kept his distance. When Lee got back from Vietnam, Merle never asked him about that, which was fine with him. As his mother paged through the album, making comments about how cute he was and how much fun they had when he was a kid, he noticed the far-away look on his father's face in one of the photos. There it was—the thousand-mile stare he had seen on other vets.

Since she had mentioned his dad, maybe it was time to talk about him—not about the beatings and abuse but whatever his mom would like to share. Seeing that look on his father's face piqued his curiosity. There was no telling if this opportunity would ever come up again. "Did Dad bring anything home from the war?"

"He brought back the letters I sent him, along with some medals and pictures of him and his army buddies. I put them in one of his old lunchboxes he used when he worked for A.O. Smith. I added the letters that he wrote back to me. There were only a few. And they were short. He always said he was fine and that he … loved me … and missed me." Her eyes misted. "I loved that man so."

"Does he still have it?"

She pulled some Kleenex from the box on the nightstand and dabbed at her eyes, then nodded. "He wanted to burn everything. I hid it from him in the basement crawl space. When you brought me here, I snuck it out in one of my suitcases. I didn't want him asking questions about what I was doing with an old lunchbox and finding the letters. I like to read those letters once in a while when I'm … feeling like myself. They remind me of who I was … and who he was." She put her hand on Lee's. "You never knew him before the war. That's the man I fell in love with. I'm sorry what he did to you." Silence hung between them.

Lee felt the anger rise for what his father had put them both through for all of those years. He wanted to tell his mother how much he hated him for that. Instead, he gripped her hand and said, "Not your fault, Mom."

She whispered, "I wished I could have had the strength to leave him and protect you. I kept praying … he would go back to the man I married. Then … all of sudden you were grown and he couldn't hurt you anymore." She leaned into Lee and sobbed into his chest.

He held her head and hugged her like Alexus had taught him and said again, "Not your fault."

When she sat up, Lee took a Kleenex from her nightstand, wiped the tears from her eyes, and asked, "Do you still have those letters?"

"Mm-hmm."

"Could I see them or are they too personal."

"Under my bed."

The dented black lunchbox with the curved top was nestled between two suitcases—suitcases she would never use again. He sat back on the bed with the lunchbox on his lap. His mother watched him snap the latch and tilt the top open. Lee carefully removed the neatly folded letters. Underneath the letters was a black-and-white photo of five skinny bare-chested soldiers with slight smiles that were more grim than happy standing on a beach surrounded by palm trees. Lee knew the look of forced smiles for the camera. His mom pointed to the short soldier in the middle and said, "That's your dad. Wasn't he handsome?"

Lee stared at the photo, wondering what kind of hell they had gone through. "Do you know where this was?"

"Merle was only nineteen when he joined the army. The year after they bombed Pearl Harbor."

More he didn't know about his father. "What about these pictures? Do you know where he was?"

"All I know is that it was some island in the Pacific fighting the Japanese."

Lee scooped the rest of the photos from the lunch box and gasped. At the bottom of the box were two medals. He gazed at the bronze cross with an eagle on the front attached to a red, white, and blue ribbon. Next to this was a heart-shaped medal with a profile of George Washington attached to a purple ribbon.

He lifted the medal with the bronze cross from the box and shook his head. "Damn. The Distinguished Service Cross." He looked to the other medal. "And a Purple Heart."

A slow smile spread across her face.

Lee cradled the Distinguished Service Cross in his palm. "Mom, the only award higher than this is the Medal of Honor. Do you know what he did to receive this?"

"Only thing he ever said was he got a bad concussion when most of his company got killed. He wouldn't say anything more. He'd get mad if I asked him about it. You know how he gets."

Lee understood why his father never wanted to talk about any of that. The brutal conditions and savage battles that soldiers endured in jungle warfare in the Pacific Islands and in Vietnam had plenty in common. Merle had to have done something way above and beyond the call of duty to receive that medal. His dad was a true hero.

Lee could never forgive his father for the way he treated him and his mom. A man was responsible for his actions regardless of his history. Merle never once said he was sorry for any of it. Not for killing Lee's baby brother in the womb when he viciously punched his mother, not for scarring Lee for life with cigarette burns, and not for the beatings he dished out to Lee and his mom. He always had an excuse that put the blame on them. There was never any remorse. No, Lee could never forgive him, but now he understood.

The thought occurred that he should probably check on his father. He was lying in the hospital suffering from carbon monoxide poisoning and probably some serious burns. But he would have to wait. The enemy was lurking out there somewhere, planning.

Lee placed the medals back in the box and picked up the stack of letters. He leafed through them and found a yellowed and faded note his father had sent his mother. At the bottom in bold letters was *You are my everything, Love Merle*. He looked at her and asked, "Okay if I read this?"

"Of course but not now. Let's chat some more."

Lee was desperate to get back to the mission but couldn't leave his mom. They laughed and talked through the afternoon, basking in each other's company. She told stories from her childhood and he told stories about some of the lighter responses from his career. There was so much he didn't know about her. On the rare occasions in the past when she was lucid, they had nice talks, but nothing like today. It was as if she knew she might never have another chance to tell him about herself. *We should have had these talks years ago,* he chided himself. *Why did I wait?*

As the afternoon wore on, gaps of cloudy silence drifted into their talks. Lee wondered if now was the time to tell her about Merle getting burned in the fire. There was no telling when she would be lucid enough again to understand.

"Hey, Mom. I got something..." he started to say, then thought, *But why?*

"Not now, my love," she said, her eyes clouding. "I'm tired and need to rest."

My love. That's how she referred to him when she thought he was her lover from long ago. He put the photos and letters back in the black lunch box and slid it under the bed. They were done.

As he left the nursing home, he decided it was time to take out the leadership of the Disciples. He'd have to work out the rest of the mission plan later.

He headed to Manson's place.

Chapter 47

Mitch

Warlock and Manson walked Mitch, Brigid, and Snake to the black Escalade. Manson had Brigid drive. He sat in the front passenger seat holding her gun on her. Mitch and Snake sat in the next row of seats with Warlock behind them with the AR15.

When Brigid pulled away from the curb, Manson said, "You make the slightest move I don't like, I'll part that red hair with a cap. Head up to Lake Drive." Manson didn't seem concerned that they would know where his place was. Mitch knew what that meant. He glanced sideways at the door. The safety lock was on. They all bounced in unison as they hit a deep pothole. Snake groaned and shifted his broken arm against his chest. Warlock said, "Be glad to put you out of your misery. Just sayin'." He cackled like it was the funniest thing ever said.

Brigid glanced in the rearview mirror at Mitch, her eyes dark. Manson poked her arm with the gun. "Watch the road, bitch." They passed a McDonald's with two squad cars parked in the lot. "Don't even think about it," Manson said. "Keep it under the limit."

They drove north with Manson directing Brigid where to go. Mitch's mind raced. Time was running out. At some point, he'd have to make a move. He had to hope they bought into meeting Lee and the girls at six o'clock. There was no room in the Escalade for all of them, so there was a good chance one of them would go with Mitch to get the girls and one would stay at the house with Brigid and

Snake. Then it would be one on one. If Manson went with him, he liked his odds. But Warlock? He was massive, twice the size of Mitch.

As they crossed into Shorewood, Manson pointed to a driveway lined with dense arborvitae trees. "Turn in there."

They drove to the back of a massive two-story, red-brick Old English Tudor-style house with white stucco gables. The entire backyard was enclosed by the same tall arborvitaes that lined the driveway. "Welcome to my humble digs," Manson said. "Shame we don't have time for cocktails and a tour." Manson's lips hardened into a thin line. "Let's go."

Manson led the way to two doors lying at an angle to the ground that were butted against the back of the house. They looked like the root cellar doors to old farmhouses. Manson unlocked the chain that was wrapped around the handles and flung the doors open. He disappeared into the darkness and flicked on a light.

"Get your asses down there," Warlock growled, poking Mitch hard in the back with the AR15. They made their way down the cement steps into a musty room with graying wooden shelves lining the walls. The floor was black hard-packed clay. *We're never leaving here,* Mitch thought, fighting the panic coursing through his veins. Manson slid a floor-to-ceiling section of shelving away from the wall and entered what looked like the opening of a cave. "We got a nice surprise waiting for you," Manson said, looking over his shoulder.

"Follow him," Warlock barked.

They followed Manson single file down a narrow curved tunnel lined with wooden planking, illuminated by a string of red lights. Brigid went first, followed by Snake and Mitch. Warlock brought up the rear. Mitch glanced back at the enormous man, who had to turn sideways to fit through the tunnel. Warlock rammed the butt of the AR15 into Mitch's back.

Brigid stopped at the end of the hallway. "What—the—hell?"

Manson turned and leveled his vacant coal-black eyes at her. "Your very own Disneyland."

Warlock shoved Mitch into Snake, who groaned while clutching his broken arm. Warlock shoved Mitch harder. "Move it."

They entered a cavernous room with concrete walls and an arched ceiling. Four spotlights were trained on the center of the room, highlighting a king-sized four-poster bed covered in red satin sheets and giant pillows. Two black hoods were at the foot of the bed.

Mitch sucked in a breath as he tried to process what he was seeing. Next to the bed was a black dental chair outfitted with straps on the armrests, footrests, and a headrest. Next to that, scattered over a stainless steel tabletop, was a macabre assortment of knives, scalpels, pliers, vice grips, and a pruning shears. Under the table were bottles of liquids and a box of rubber gloves.

A cold shiver crept up Mitch's spine. A camera on the arched ceiling was focused on the bed. A large-screen television stood against the far wall with unmarked wooden crates stacked next to it. Along the wall to his left, bookcases from floor to ceiling were filled with bundles of cash and stacks of DVDs. In the corner was a gray four-foot safe. Mitch glanced at the other wall and his mouth dropped. Brigid looked at Mitch and mouthed, "Fuck." Four sets of handcuffs hung by chains from the ceiling. Directly below them, steel O-rings anchored ankle straps to the floor.

Manson reached for the AR15 Warlock was holding. Mitch resisted the overwhelming urge to rush them. They were too far across the room. He'd have to wait. Manson took the AR15 and waved it at Brigid and Snake. "You two against the wall. Warlock, hook 'em up."

"What about the other one?"

"He'll take you to get the whores and you can grab that nosy-assed firefighter."

Mitch felt a twinge of relief. They bought his story.

Warlock pushed Snake against the wall, securing the handcuff on his right wrist. "You won't be telling your club shit." When he lifted and twisted Snake's broken left arm, Snake wailed and passed out. Warlock secured the other handcuff and attached the ankle straps. Snake's limp body swayed in the restraints, his chin against his chest.

"Get your coat off," Warlock ordered Brigid.

After she dropped her coat to the floor, Warlock grabbed her wrist. "Please fight me."

"So you can get your rocks off? Fuck you."

"You'll get your wish soon enough." He twisted her wrist while securing the handcuff. She clenched her lips, keeping her eyes trained on him while he attached the restraints. When he finished, she stood spread eagle. Warlock ran his hand under her blue Milwaukee Brewers sweatshirt and mauled her breasts, sneering.

Brigid's steely eyes narrowed.

Warlock removed his hand and went to the stainless steel table. Mitch's heart pounded in his ears. They were living a horror movie and he was helpless to stop it. It took all of Mitch's control not to charge across the room and tackle Warlock. Manson would shoot him before he got anywhere close. Warlock picked the pruning shears from the table and went back to Brigid. He held up the shears and said, "Never filmed an old broad like you. Let's take a look." He cut the sweatshirt off her. "This is going to be a riot." He snipped the front of her bra and the shoulder straps. The bra dropped to the floor. Warlock stood back. "Damn. Not bad." He squeezed and twisted her nipples hard enough to bring tears to her eyes. His sinister laugh echoed off the walls. "Might be a market for a female cop getting fucked and snuffed. What do you think, Boss?"

"Snuff films?" Bridget shouted. "You sick bastards."

Warlock leaned into her, their faces inches apart. "And you get to be the next star."

"Enough of that," Manson said. "Let's see if Tank can solve our little problem." Manson punched a number on his cell phone. After a pause, he said, "Get ahold of Boyle and get the address of that firefighter who was snooping around the fire. He grabbed the whores from Chicago." He listened for a few seconds and said, "Go to his place. If he has them, bring 'em all to my place, including that firefighter." He listened again and said, "Don't leave any witnesses. You know what I mean. I want that son of a bitch." He ended the call and leered at Mitch. "If the whores are there, won't need you anymore."

A wave of nausea rose from Mitch's stomach. He swallowed back the bile, imagining what these monsters would do to that houseful of kids and Miss Bernie. "You're wasting your time going there. He's smarter than to bring the girls there. Plus the police are watching his place."

"We'll see how smart he is when we get him down here. Tell me where you were supposed to meet him and I'll call off Tank."

"If you don't call him off, I won't be taking you anywhere."

"Maybe you don't understand where you're at. If I let Warlock at you, you'll tell me anything."

Warlock let go of Brigid's nipples and roared with laughter. "Let me at him."

"We don't have time. It's almost five. Take him to the whores. Call me at six." To Mitch, he said, "If they aren't there, I'll be cutting this red-headed bitch up into little pieces."

"They'll be there."

Warlock grabbed Brigid by the crotch. "I'll be thinking about you, sweetheart."

Brigid's mouth twisted into a scowl. Was that the look of rage or terror? Mitch couldn't tell. Warlock let go and marched Mitch out to the Escalade.

Warlock pointed to the driver's side. "Let's go. You drive. The whores better be there."

"What happens after we pick them up?" Mitch asked.

Warlock threw his head back, cackling loudly.

Where the hell could Mitch take him? Maybe he could drive off one of the bluffs overlooking Lake Michigan or slam the Escalade into a light pole and hope Warlock was injured more severely than him. But somehow he would have to get back to Manson's place before six. Crashing the Escalade wouldn't work. What if he blew a stoplight and got broadsided on Warlock's side? That was a plan. He would drive down Lake Drive, turn west on Locust Street, and watch for his chance. Yes. That could work. Mitch would snatch the rifle from Warlock when the airbags deployed. The massive Escalade should be able to take a broadside hit and still be drivable. He'd order Warlock to drive them back to Manson's place and march Warlock down the cave, take Manson by surprise, and free Brigid and Snake.

Mitch headed south on Lake Drive.

At Locust Street, he went west. The intersection of Locust and Sherman Avenue would be perfect. This intersection was known as one of the most frequent sites of major accidents in the city. The park would be to the north, giving Mitch a good view of traffic coming down Sherman Avenue.

When they were two blocks from the intersection, Mitch slowed and watched for southbound traffic that would hit the Escalade on Warlock's side. In the distance, he spotted a city bus approaching. His chest pounded. He'd have to time the traffic light and blast through the intersection on a red light just as the bus barreled through. But would the Escalade be drivable after being hit by a bus? No time to worry about that. He focused on the bus and the traffic light, which had turned red.

Chapter 48

Lee

Lee parked four blocks away from Manson's house. Lake Drive was Christmas Eve quiet. It was after five. The sun had set, but the luminous December moon glimmered over the upscale neighborhood. He slipped Mitch's hunting rifle under his coat. The scope would come in handy if it was necessary to take a long shot at the enemy. Lee strolled toward the house. He ducked behind a large shrub when he saw car lights in the distance. He didn't need that Shorewood cop asking questions.

When he got to the house, he crept along the row of arborvitae trees to the backyard, crouching low. The arborvitaes cast ghostly swaying shadows across the lawn. He stopped when he had a good view of the back of the house. He pulled the rifle out from under his coat and scanned the back of the house with the high-powered scope, trying to determine the best entry point. He paused at each window, hoping to see one of them. If he could take one of them out from outside, his chances of a successful mission improved dramatically. He scanned the first-floor windows and noticed two open doors leaning at an angle next to the house. He focused the scope. They were cellar doors. He flushed with excitement. Perfect. There was his entry point.

They couldn't have made it easier.

He crept across the lawn, keeping an eye on the windows. As he approached the open doors, he went to his stomach and crawled the rest of the way to the opening. He peered inside. There was a light on. Nobody there. Good. He inched down the steps, waving the rifle back and forth. At the bottom, he scanned the room and spotted a shelving unit pulled away from the wall. Behind the shelving was the opening to a passageway, illuminated by red lights. He flashed back to the tunnels of the Viet Cong. He wasn't one of the tunnel rats who would fight their way into these tunnels to search for intelligence and caches of weapons. Lee was too large but had been in some of the intricate tunnels that housed underground hospitals and living areas for the enemy after they had been taken over by the tunnel rats.

He shook the vision from his head. It was critical to stay focused on the mission. Lee made his way down the narrow curved tunnel one silent step at a time. Before he saw the end of the tunnel, he heard Manson say, "You won't be going back to Chicago, asshole. And neither will those whores. You'll disappear and those whores will star in our next production. We'll make some serious bank off that. And you're the one gave me the idea to tell your club you ran off with 'em. Ain't that a bitch."

Someone groaned. Manson continued, "Who else knows about the fires?"

"Why don't you ask your fucking informant?" Brigid said. A loud slap echoed down the tunnel.

Brigid. What the hell? Lee thought. And who was groaning? Could it be Mitch? He had to keep the red mist under control and use his head. He worked his way silently down the tunnel, resisting the urge to rush ahead, wondering how many Disciples were down there.

"Don't matter," Manson said. "I'll let Warlock get that out of you. But, maybe I have a little fun first. Bet those little tits of yours stood up firm and proud back in the day. How about I carve my initials in them?"

At the end of the tunnel, Lee could see part of a bed in a brightly lit room. He couldn't see more of it due to the curve of the tunnel. A primal shriek reverberated through the tunnel, sending a chill through Lee. He couldn't wait any longer. He'd have to rely on surprise. They'd never hear him coming with the unrelenting shrieking. Adrenaline surged through his veins, heightening his senses. It was go time. He'd only have microseconds to react to whatever was in that room.

He raced to the opening and burst into the room, crouching, pivoting the rifle from side to side, his finger coiling the trigger. The shrieking stopped. It was Snake, hanging by his arms, his bulging eyes trained on Lee. The room went silent. Brigid was hanging by her arms, topless, next to Snake. The side of her face was bright red, one eye swollen. Manson was in front of her, holding a scalpel to her breast. He spun and flashed Lee a diabolical sneer. "You don't know who you're fucking with. I'll cut this bitch."

"You make a move and I'll blow your head off."

Manson's sneer resembled the skull on his colors.

Lee pushed the barrel of the rifle forward. "Put—it—down. Now!"

Manson's eyes twitched.

The room took on a red tinge as Lee flared. He bared his teeth, growling, about to squeeze the trigger when Manson's evil sneer evaporated. He dropped the scalpel. His hand moved to his vest.

"He's got my gun," Brigid shouted.

Lee glared at Manson. "Go ahead. Go for it. I'm jumpy as hell."

Manson immediately raised his hands.

"Now, put the gun on the floor. Keep it slow and smooth."

Manson took the gun from inside his vest and lowered it to the ground. "You the firefighter took our whores. Give 'em back, we're all good."

"You killed a good man, you piece of shit."

"This won't end here. Even if you have the balls to kill me, my club will hunt you down."

Brigid coughed. "Um. How about getting us down?"

Lee waved the rifle at Manson. "You heard the lady."

Manson reached up to unlock Brigid's handcuffs. She tilted her head toward Snake. "Get him down first. Bastard's about to pass out again."

Manson ripped off the Velcro ankle straps and unlocked the cuffs from Snake's wrists. Snake gripped his broken arm and slid onto the floor with his knees drawn up to his chest, rocking. Manson went to Brigid and unlocked the handcuffs, then reached down and undid the ankle straps.

Lee pointed at Brigid's swollen face. "He do that?"

As Manson straightened, Brigid picked up her gun from the floor and slammed it alongside his head. "Payback's a bitch, hey?" She rammed her knee into his crotch. He bent at the waist. She stepped back and kicked him in the head, laying him out.

"Guess that answers my question," Lee said.

"So, you gonna keep looking at my tits or hand me my coat?"

Lee shook his head, chuckling to himself. She couldn't resist working on him even now. He picked her coat and her sweatshirt off the floor and handed them to her. She inspected the cut-up sweatshirt and tossed it back on the floor. "You know how much I paid for that?" Her eyes narrowed. "Looks like someone tried to mess up your pretty face."

"Where's Mitch?"

She slipped on her coat, zipped it, and pocketed her gun. "He went with Warlock to meet you and the girls."

"What are you…?"

She waved her open palm. "Mitch convinced Manson that he was going to meet you at six. If the girls aren't there, this prick threatened to cut me up." Manson glared at them from the floor. She kicked him in the stomach. "He sent one of his other henchmen, that guy Tank we saw in the mugshots, to your place to check for you and the girls. Told the bastard to make sure there were no witnesses."

The red mist rose. *Focus. No mistakes,* Lee thought. "So Mitch is with Warlock and Tank is on his way to my place."

"Deion has people watching your place, so everyone should be safe."

"I was there. Only saw one banger. If that Tank guy takes help along, I don't know how safe they are."

He handed the hunting rifle to Brigid and glared at Manson.

"From the look on your face," Brigid said, "God only knows what you're planning, but there's some rubber gloves under that table. Put them on and hand me two."

Lee snapped on the gloves, went to Manson, and with one hand, clutched Manson's upper arm, yanking him to his feet. Lee towered over the short man. Lee's other hand went to Manson's throat. It took all of his willpower not to squeeze the life out of him. He shoved him against the wall under the cuffs. "Attach the ankle straps." After Manson velcroed the straps to his ankles, Lee growled, "Raise your arms." Lee clicked the cuffs tight on Manson's wrists.

Manson said, "You're good as dead. My club knows who you are. And your bitch there too."

"They know who we are because of Boyle," Brigid said. "He's their informant." She leveled the butt of the rifle at Manson's face.

Lee stepped between her and Manson. "First we need some answers."

Manson guffawed. "Yeah. That ain't happening."

"We'll see." Lee went to the stainless steel table and grabbed the pruning shears.

Brigid gasped. "You're not thinking of…"

"He wanted to take a knife to you. Maybe I make him a eunuch. No, better yet, I cut off his balls *and* his dick." Lee took a black hood from the foot of the bed and slipped it over Manson's head. "I can't look at your miserable face any longer."

Manson's breathing quickened, his breath sour.

Lee pointed at Snake. "Keep an eye on him. I don't trust that little bastard." He went back to the table. "Let's see what else they got here." He rummaged through the lower shelf and found a bottle of sulfuric acid. "Perfect. I like this better." He poured some into a large glass measuring cup. The smell of rotten eggs wafted from the cup. Brigid's jaw dropped as Lee crossed the room to Manson and pulled the bottom of the hood open. He put the cup just below the opening and said, "Smell it. You know what this is?"

"Fuck you. You're dead, motherfucker."

"Good. Let's get started." Lee opened the top of Manson's engineer boot and dribbled several drops of acid inside. Manson shrieked, shaking his head violently.

Lee waited a few seconds and said. "You're going to call Tank and call him off."

Manson grimaced. "Fuck you."

"I can't even imagine what it'll feel like when I dip your dick in acid. Gotta hurt like a son of a bitch. Let's find out."

"Seriously?" Brigid said, furrowing her brow.

"Let's give him a minute to think about this while the acid burns into his foot." Lee went to the table and filled another measuring cup with distilled water and went back to Manson.

Brigid grinned and said, "Let me." She placed the rifle on the table. Snake glanced at it.

"You get off the floor," Lee said, "I'll break your other arm."

Brigid went to Manson. She removed the black hood. "I want you to see this." She yanked his pants down and snickered. "So, it's true what they say about small hands. Let's see how fast that little pecker will dissolve." Lee handed her the measuring cup. Manson curled his lips as if challenging her. She lowered the cup, grinning wide until it was inches from his limp member. "My turn to have some fun."

He gritted his teeth. "Okay, okay, okay. Stop."

"Good boy." She turned to Lee. "He's all yours."

Manson had the desperate look of a defeated enemy. "That wasn't so hard, was it?" Lee asked. He looked at Manson's crotch. "Maybe hard's not the right word." Lee fished a cell phone from Manson's pants. "Password."

Manson groaned and said, "Six nine, six nine."

Lee punched the numbers on the phone. "How do I dial Tank?"

After Manson told him how to find and dial Tank, Lee said, "You're going to tell him you found the girls and tell him not to go to my place. I have any doubts about you convincing him and whoever might be with him, I'll let this lady finish the job."

Lee punched the number. It continued to ring until it went to a robotic voicemail message. Lee whispered in Manson's ear. "Tell him what I told you." He put the phone in front of Manson's face. Manson repeated what Lee had told him to say. Lee ended the call.

"Now we call Warlock and tell him to get his ass back here with my partner. Tell him that you need him alive."

Warlock answered the call. Manson told him what Lee had ordered. While he was talking to Warlock, Brigid wiggled the cup inches below Manson's limp member, grinning. Warlock said they were still on the way to the meeting place. He'd head back and should be there in twenty minutes. When the call ended, Brigid said to Lee, "One of us should get to your place in case that Tank character doesn't get the message."

"I need to finish things here. You go. Watch for Ace. He's still out there somewhere." Lee handed her the keys to his car. "My car's four blocks south on Lake Drive."

She looked around the room. "I don't know what you got planned, but don't leave anything behind."

"Go. Hurry. There's a houseful of kids relying on you. Oh, and there's an AR15 in the trunk that might come in handy."

She grabbed him by the back of the neck and kissed him, then held him at arm's length. "You can't do this alone."

I have to, Lee thought and said, "Go."

She grabbed her sweatshirt and bra from the floor and left.

Chapter 49

Mitch

The city bus was one block from the intersection and had the green light. Mitch would have to time this perfectly to make sure the bus driver didn't have time to react when Mitch blew the red light. He would swerve just as the bus hit them, lessening the impact, hoping the damage to the Escalade would not be severe enough to make it undrivable but violent enough to injure Warlock. Mitch swallowed hard. This had to work.

Warlock's phone chimed. He answered, "What's up, Boss?" He listened, then said, "Got it. We're on our way back."

"What happened?" Mitch asked.

"Don't worry about it. Turn around. Now."

They were too far from the intersection to run the red light. No telling what Warlock would do if Mitch tried speeding to the intersection from this far away. The man was powerful and had a rifle trained on him. He'd never make it. Crashing the Escalade on the way back could still be done. Mitch struggled with how he could do this. If he drove into a tree, chances were the SUV would not be drivable. If he tried to get a car or truck to broadside them on Warlock's side, there was a good chance the occupants of the other vehicle could be seriously injured. Mitch decided the risk of injuring or possibly killing the occupants of the other vehicle was too great. He'd wait until they got to the back of the house to make a move.

* * *

At the house, Mitch parked in the dark shadows of the arborvitae trees. When Warlock turned to wedge his massive body out of the Escalade, Mitch ducked and rolled out of the driver's seat. He dashed into the darkness at the back of the SUV.

Warlock shouted, "Motherfuck." He slammed the door. "You won't get ten feet from here before I grease your ass." Mitch peered under the Escalade, watching Warlock shuffle toward him at the back of the vehicle. Mitch silently scampered around the front, crouching low. As Warlock peeked around the back of the Escalade, Mitch ran at him and knocked him to the ground. He pounced on the hulk's back, grabbed a handful of greasy hair, yanked his head back, and draped his free arm around Warlock's thick neck. He squeezed with everything he had, struggling to choke him off. The AR15 was pinned under them. Warlock struggled to his feet and clawed at Mitch's arm while swinging him back and forth like a loose backpack. Mitch wrapped his legs around him and held on. *Just a few more seconds. He'll pass out.*

Warlock threw himself backward, landing on top of Mitch. Mitch's head cracked on the frozen ground, stunning him. He couldn't breathe. His grip weakened. Warlock rolled off and picked up the AR15. "Nice try, little man. If the pres didn't want you alive, you'd be dead. Get your ass up."

I was so close, Mitch thought, nauseous with dread. As Mitch rose to his feet, stabbing pain shot through his chest. He knew the feeling from his farm accident in the combine. Warlock had cracked some ribs when he fell on top of him.

"Back inside," Warlock ordered, waving the rifle toward the opening to the cellar.

As they headed down the tunnel, Mitch planned to charge Manson when they got to the room. There was no way he would watch them torture and kill Brigid. He'd rather take a bullet.

The narrow opening to the room was in sight. His heart raced. He was ready.

When he got to the opening, he stopped. Manson was hanging by the cuffs in the ceiling, his pants around the ankles of his pale skinny legs with a black hood over his head. From behind the dental chair, Mitch's hunting rifle was trained on him, the red dot of the laser sight, glowing. Warlock pushed Mitch into the room.

Lee called out, "Duck." Mitch dropped to the floor. The deafening crack of a gunshot echoed through the room. Mitch couldn't tell where the shot came from. Stillness enveloped the room. Lee rose from behind the chair, nodding. "Way to follow orders," he said, his voice sounding far, far away. "The ringing will let up."

Mitch looked back at Warlock, who was lying on his side, gasping for air, clutching his chest, and hacking crimson blood onto his black beard. Mitch kicked the AR15 out of his reach. He asked Lee, "Where's Brigid?"

"Went to the house in case any Disciples show up. You should go, too."

"The One-Niners are watching the place," Mitch said.

"You trust them? I was there. I only saw one of them … I don't want you involved in this. I can take care of things here."

"Yeah, that's not happening. I'm already involved and even if you don't think so, I might be able to help."

"So much for following orders," Lee said, then grinned. He went to the table and pulled a wad of rubber gloves from a box. He tossed some to Mitch. "Put these on. We can't leave any traces behind."

What the hell is Lee planning? Mitch thought.

While Lee snapped on the rubber gloves, he told Mitch about Ace shooting Ralph and taking off.

"What changed Ralph's mind?" Mitch asked.

"You."

"What do you mean? I wasn't able to convince him to help."

"Ace threatened to kill you. Ralph couldn't let that happen."

A surge of relief swelled in Mitch. "Told you he wasn't all bad."

Lee raised his eyebrows. "Surprised the hell out of me."

Mitch pointed at the bruise on the side of Lee's head. "Ace do that?"

"The idiot and that one on the floor jumped me."

"What we gonna do about him?" Mitch asked, pointing at Snake.

"Have to worry about that later. Let's get to work. First, we see what these degenerates have down here. I think I know what's on those DVDs, but we have to be sure."

"I think I already know," Mitch said, examining one of the DVDs. "Snuff films."

Lee gritted his teeth, shaking his head, then said, "I don't want to see that shit, but we gotta know for sure what's on them. See if you can figure out how to play it." Lee went to the wooden crates along the wall, took the top from one of the long ones, and raised an AR15 in the air. "You planning on going to war?" he asked Manson, who didn't answer.

On the shelf next to the television was a bank of electronics. One looked like an expensive version of Mitch's DVD player. He pressed the power button on the television, then the power button on the DVD player, and loaded the DVD. On the big screen, a naked Black girl was tied to the bed. A naked skinny white guy wearing a black hood entered the frame. Mitch couldn't watch. He joined Lee at the wooden crates. Lee opened one of the smaller crates and held up a bundle of orange dynamite sticks. "Check this out."

"Holy crap," Mitch said. "How many cases they got of that stuff?"

"Enough to blow up half of Shorewood."

"Guns, Dynamite, DVDs, and all that cash. What the hell is going on here?"

"Time we get some answers," Lee said. "Grab your rifle and cover me while I get this animal down." He took the black hood off Manson. While Lee unlocked the cuffs, Manson never took his eyes off his enforcer, who was lying on his side at the entrance to the tunnel. The big man gasped and went still.

"Pull up your pants," Lee ordered. "I don't need to see that anymore. And take off the ankle straps. We got some talking to do." When Manson freed his legs, Lee grabbed him by the arm and marched him to the dental chair. "Sit." Manson had no fight left. Lee strapped his arms and legs to the chair and then strapped his head to the headrest. "Now we talk. First question, what does Senator Decker have to do with all of this?"

"I don't know any Decker."

Lee gripped Manson's chin, forcing his mouth open. With his other hand, he grabbed the measuring cup that contained the acid and held it next to Manson's open mouth. Manson's eyes grew wide. "You lie one more time and this goes down your throat. I saw him leave your place."

Manson stared at the cup that was inches from his mouth. "He's the distributor of the films."

"Who's he sell them to?"

"I don't know that."

Lee pushed the cup against Manson's lower lip. He gagged. Lee pulled the cup away. "Try again."

"All I know is there's a market overseas. They pay big bank for them."

Lee pointed to the stacks of money on the shelving. "That's where the cash came from?"

"Most of it."

"What does Sunrise Schools have to do with any of this?"

"All I know is Decker hired us to get the voucher schools to sell to them. Whatever it took."

"So you burn down the school, shoot up the brother's house, then burn his house down and kill him. And set up the One-Niners. I got all that right?"

"He should have sold."

Lee put the cup back on the stainless steel table, clutched Manson's windpipe, and squeezed until Manson's bloodshot eyes looked ready to burst. A vein on the side of Lee's neck bulged. The look of animal rage on Lee's face stunned Mitch. He didn't know what he should do. He shouted, "Don't kill him, Cap. We still need him."

Lee yanked his hands back and shook his head, staring at his open palms. "No. No. You're right." He took the cup from the table and waved it in front of Manson's face. "Let's start again. What about that investment company, Allure, that owns this place?"

"You're going to kill me, aren't you?"

"Not if you tell me everything. On my word."

Shrieks of terror came from the television, sending a wave of revulsion through Mitch.

Lee shouted, "Turn it off."

Mitch couldn't get to the television fast enough.

Lee pushed the cup against Manson's lower lip. "Allure."

There was no more resistance from Manson who answered without pausing. "They launder the cash."

Mitch glanced at Snake, who was sitting on the floor gripping his broken arm to his chest, rocking back and forth, groaning. He looked to be in shock from either the pain or what was happening in front of him or both.

Lee continued, "What about the videos you got of so-called important people? Where are those?"

"In the safe."

"The combination?"

Manson didn't hesitate telling them. Mitch went to the safe, opened it, and pulled out a stack of DVDs and CDs. He placed them on the table, went back to the safe, got two thick manila folders, and brought them to the table. The DVD and CD cases were inscribed with initials in black marker.

"Who you got on those?" Lee asked.

Manson grinned as if he were proud of what he was about to say. "Your police chief."

"Who else?"

"Decker and a bunch of rich assholes."

Lee pointed to the bed. "Down here? Doing that?"

"Hell no. They don't know nothing about this, except for Decker, but he didn't want to know anything about how we made the films."

"But he knew what was on them?"

"Hell, yeah. He had to okay them. All he was interested in was how much he could sell them for."

Lee picked up a DVD. "So, what's on these?"

"Got the police chief and the others with our whores ... doing some pretty kinky shit."

"Decker know about these?"

"Oh, yeah. He wanted insurance in case the chief or any of his rich buddies decided to turn on him." A sinister grin spread over Manson's thin lips. "But Decker don't know about the one with him on it. Made sure he was with an underage one ... That's my insurance. I got more. I tell you, you keep your promise. Right?"

"My word actually means something to me. Not like you degenerates."

"Decker and the chief belong to the Guardians."

"That political action committee? What does that have to do with anything?"

"They call themselves Guardians of American Values. They talk shit about Hitler and how they have to stop Blacks and Mexicans from taking over. They like to brag about how the morons with the FBI will never be able to trace their laundered cash."

"Surprised you weren't one of those Nazis, considering you call yourself Manson."

"I got tagged with that when I was a prospect. Don't mean nothin'."

"How do you know about all that with the Guardians?"

"We provided girls for their parties. Always wanted young Black ones. They'd have some kind of meeting before the party while we were setting up, always behind closed doors. They'd get loud when they got fucked up. We could hear 'em through the closed doors. I had the whore's bodyguards record them talking their shit. I don't trust any of 'em. Figured those CDs were more good insurance."

Bastard's bragging, Mitch thought. Probably has no fear of prison but is terrified of Lee. Who wouldn't be?

"Who were some of the others in the Guardians?" Lee demanded.

"I don't know who they were, just that they were a bunch of rich fucks."

While Lee interrogated Manson, Mitch went through the folders.

"Back to Decker," Lee said. "How is he connected to the Guardians?"

"He's the leader. The money he gets from the films funds their shit."

"Does he know about the recordings of the meetings?"

Manson shook his head and said, "Decker told me his buddies would keep the heat off my club if I did their dirty work. Things were going just fine until he told us to force those voucher schools to sell to Sunrise. Stupid fucking move. What kind of dough is in those schools? On one of the CDs, they talk about their plan to control education. Stupid. Now our whole operation is coming down … Thanks to your nosy ass."

"How'd you recruit Detective Boyle?" Lee asked.

"Turned up at a private party. Not one of the Guardian's parties. Some cop party. Didn't know who he was so we videoed him. Found out later he was a detective. He liked that dominatrix shit. We sent a little jack his way to keep him happy."

"Does the police chief know Boyle is your informant?"

"Hell no. We had him keep tabs on the chief in case he decided to come after us. Can't have enough insurance."

The sinister grin appeared again, disgusting Mitch. He held up one of the folders. "This might show where the money is coming from and where it goes."

"That right?" Lee asked Manson, who nodded without hesitating.

Lee said to Mitch, "Let's get Mr. Manson here on DVD. You know how to use that camera on the ceiling to record some DVDs?"

"I don't know."

"Tell him how to do it," Lee said to Manson.

"Put a blank one in the same unit you played the DVD on and press 'record.' Everything's already set up. Hit 'stop' when you're done."

Mitch found two cases of blank DVDs in the cabinet below the big-screen television along with two black Sharpies and a cache of cell phones. "Hey, Cap. There's a bunch of cell phones under here."

"What are those for?" Lee asked Manson.

"They're burners."

Lee held up Manson's cell phone. "This a burner too?"

Manson nodded.

Mitch adjusted the camera on the ceiling so it was trained on Manson. He ejected the DVD of the girl being brutalized and inserted a blank DVD into the unit. "Let me know when you're ready, Cap," Mitch said.

Lee removed the head strap from Manson. "Your turn to be recorded. Tell the camera everything you told me and I'll keep my word. Everything. Do not leave anything out." Lee circled his finger in the air. Mitch hit record. With Lee glowering at him, Manson began.

While Manson talked into the camera, Mitch took a look around the huge cavern. In a hollowed-out enclave, he spotted a pile of clothing: jackets, shorts, shoes, tops. All of it girl's clothing. He lifted a small pink backpack from the pile. He swallowed back the bile rising in his throat. He wanted to throw it against the wall. Instead, he searched through the pockets and found a laminated card. A student ID card from Washington High School. The girl in the photo smiled wide, oblivious to her future. He jammed it back in the pocket of the backpack, gritting his teeth.

Mitch took the backpack to Lee and handed it to him without saying anything. Manson was still talking into the camera. Lee clutched the backpack, his face pinched in rage. If Lee lost it, Mitch wouldn't stop him this time.

When Manson finished, Mitch stopped the recorder and said to Lee, "There's a pile of girl's clothes in the back corner." Lee held the backpack in front of Manson's face, shaking it, his knuckles white. "Where are the bodies?"

"Cremated."

"How?" Lee shouted.

"Decker owns a string of funeral homes."

Lee dropped the backpack and paced the cavern, breathing hard. Mitch watched, his thoughts consumed by the image on the ID card. He'd never forget the beaming face of the innocent young girl whose remains would never be found.

Lee stopped pacing and stood in front of Manson, his hands on his hips, his face taking on a savageness that shook Mitch. Snake stopped groaning, his attention fixed on Lee. Manson closed his eyes as if awaiting execution. Lee stood there, silent, not moving. The stale air in the cavern grew thick as Mitch waited, wondering how Lee was going to kill Manson.

In a demonic voice, Lee finally said, "Tell me why I shouldn't kill you right now, you useless piece of shit."

"Said your word meant something to you," Manson whispered without opening his eyes.

Mitch waited for Lee to explode. He was shocked when Lee's body relaxed. The deep furrows on Lee's forehead eased as if a switch had gone off in his head.

Lee went to the table and got one of the burners. He punched the numbers and said, "Brigid, it's Lee. Everything okay there?" He listened, then said, "Got it. We'll do that. Meet you back at the house after we get rid of some dead weight. " Lee ended the call and said, "We gotta get rid of any traces of DNA and fingerprints."

"But we had gloves on."

"Not ours. Brigid's. She was in the cuffs. And Warlock was running his hands all over her. She doesn't think she came in contact with anything else or left prints on anything, but let's not assume. There's some rags and rubbing alcohol under the table. I'll start wiping everything down. Can you make copies of the DVD?"

"I don't have a clue. But they must have a way to make copies."

Lee went to the dental chair and released the straps on Manson's arms and legs. "We need six copies. Now. You fuck around, deal's off. I will kill you." Lee glanced at Mitch. "Keep an eye on him."

Mitch grabbed his rifle and marched Manson to the shelf with the bank of electronic equipment. Mitch watched the lights of the units come on as Manson inserted the DVDs and worked the controls.

The room filled with the pungent scent of rubbing alcohol as Lee went to work, first dousing Warlock's hands with the alcohol, then wiping down any surface Brigid might have come in contact with. He wiped down Manson's cell phone used to call Warlock and Tank, dropped it to the floor, and stomped on it.

Manson's testimony was short and concise. It didn't take long for him to make the copies.

"How should I label them?" Mitch asked Lee.

Lee went to Manson, grabbed him by the arm, and walked him back to the dental chair. He strapped his arms down, then asked, "Your real name, asshole."

"Kaczmarek."

"That's right. Now I remember. Charles." He looked at Mitch. "Put Charles Kaczmarek on the DVD cases. And this address. Need to make sure the right people find this place."

While Mitch helped Lee finish wiping the room down, Manson stared blankly at his dead enforcer. Snake stayed quiet, rocking back and forth holding his broken arm to his chest.

When they finished, Mitch asked, "Now what?"

"We pack up and get out of here."

"What we taking?"

"The DVDs of Charles here spilling his guts ... and let's take four of those burners."

Mitch pointed toward Snake and Manson. "What about them?"

"I know a good place to dump 'em. Oh, and let's take some dynamite."

"Um. Okayyy." Mitch's stomach tightened, dreading what Lee planned to do with the dynamite—and Snake. He'd have no problem with whatever Lee had planned for Manson but what about Snake? He had to ask, "What do you...?"

The manic look on Lee's face stopped him cold.

Chapter 50

Lee

Lee drove the Escalade south with Mitch in the last row of seats behind Manson and Snake. Now that Warlock was eliminated and Manson soon to be taken care of, Lee was feeling better about the mission. He wasn't too worried about Ace. Ralph's kid wasn't all that sharp and he was a coward. But how would he stop the rest of the Disciples from coming after him and Brigid? By now, they were sure to know where he lived. He couldn't take them all out at once. When they realized their leader had gone missing, they were sure to go underground and remain a threat.

Mitch asked, "Where we heading, Cap?"

"We gotta get rid of this trash."

"You planning on…?"

"You gave your word," Manson said, his voice raspy.

Lee answered, "I'm not killing you."

Snake groaned. "What about me? I didn't have anything to do with their sick shit. You know that. How about giving a fellow vet a break?"

Snake was right, but the best way to guarantee their safety was for Snake to never make it back to Chicago; to disappear. Lee pulled to a stop one block from the clubhouse. He looked back at Manson and said, "Welcome home."

Mitch's face clouded. "I don't get it."

Lee gave Snake a long look and said to Mitch, "Stay with Snake."

"You want my rifle?"

"I won't need it."

Manson cried out, "You gave your word."

Lee was done talking. He grabbed a bundle of dynamite and marched Manson, limping on the foot burned by the acid, to the vacant warehouse across from the clubhouse. When they got inside, Lee shouted up the stairwell, "Got something for Deion." A bright flashlight shined down on them.

"Bring him up," echoed down the stairwell.

Lee shoved Manson up the steps.

They passed through the opening to the frigid second floor. Moonlight spilled through the tall broken-out windows, starkly lighting the broad expanse of the vacant warehouse. They were immediately surrounded by four of the One-Niners holding AK47s. Deion approached, examining Manson. Lee said, "Thought you might want to have a chat with the president of the Disciples."

Deion squinted at Lee and said, "I was lookin' forward to stompin' your cracker ass after the way you disrespected me at Brother Williams' crib." Deion moved closer, examining the side of Lee's head. "Looks like someone beat me to it ... Guess we'll call it even."

"He's all yours. And this too." Lee held up the dynamite and nodded toward the clubhouse. "I think you know what to do with this. Anyone in there?"

"Place been dead. We're about ready to fly. Got business to attend to ... but first, we attend to that." He pointed at Manson. "Take the peckerwood's colors. Throw that nasty shit on the floor."

The heavy bald One-Niner behind Manson yanked Manson's vest off and tossed it toward Deion's feet. Deion unzipped his pants and pissed on the face of the sneering skull while grinning at

Manson, who watched, expressionless, his shoulders slumped. After Deion finished, he said, "You a fool. You stay away from the hood, we got no problems. But no, you kill a brother and try to fuck me. That man had the respect of every crew in Milwaukee … Now you pay."

"You kill me, the Chicago club will be on your asses," Manson said barely above a whisper.

Deion let out a loud grunt, then spit in Manson's face. "Nice try. They dumb enough to come into our hood, they won't make it out."

Spit dripped from Manson's eyebrow as his face drooped.

Lee handed Deion the dynamite. "Good place to drop that would be through the skylights. If that was something you were thinking of doing."

Deion narrowed his eyes at Lee. "Shame you not a brother. We could use a badass like you." Deion held out his fist. Lee bumped it with his. "Respect," Deion said, nodding once.

"Some of the Disciples might show up at my place. I gotta get back."

"I got a brother watching your crib."

One might not be enough, Lee thought, then said, "We got one of the Disciples' cars. Can one of your people drive us to my place in that? Then make it disappear?"

Deion turned to a tall, slender man with dreadlocks down to his waist. "Dreads, take the man to his crib. Then take the ride to the chop shop."

Did Lee have a premonition when he told the girls he was going to blow up the clubhouse? He grinned to himself and left, thinking the Disciples clubhouse being destroyed by their own dynamite was some kind of poetic justice.

When Lee slid into the front passenger seat of the Escalade followed by Dreads in the driver's seat, Mitch's face pinched into confusion. "Where's he taking us?"

"To my place. But first, we gotta stop by Ace's. Our prints and DNA have to be all over it. Dreads, take us to South 22nd Street, south of Mineral Street."

"Don't worry about it," Dreads said. "That'll be taken care of." He gripped the steering wheel. "Shame we gotta trash this bad boy."

"Taken care of. How?"

"Can't talk about it."

Probably a waste of time anyway, Lee thought. Where would they start? They'd be there all night. As they drove away, Lee kept looking back, watching. When they got five blocks away from the clubhouse, he told Dreads to pull over. If he was right about Deion, this shouldn't take long.

"Why we stopping?" Mitch asked.

Lee pointed out the back window. "Watch."

Several minutes later, an orange ball rose into the sky behind them at the same time the Escalade shook from a thundering explosion. Probably didn't need that much dynamite.

"Holy crap," Mitch shouted. After the shock wore off, Mitch pointed to Snake. "What about him?"

"Yeah. He's kind of a problem," Lee said, checking the dashboard display, which read 8:15.

Lee turned to Dreads. "Okay, let's go."

On the way to his house, Lee struggled with his next move. The first leg of the mission was complete; the elimination of the Disciple's leadership. The rest of the club had to be neutralized before they learned about it. But how? And a decision had to be made about Snake. Killing a veteran went against Lee's sense of duty; the same thing that drove him to take care of an abusive father. But if he let Snake go and he ran back to Chicago and told them everything, they were screwed. Maybe Brigid would have a solution. But was it fair to involve her in this, especially if the Chicago Disciples came after them, or the cops somehow connected them to the scene at Manson's place?

He was lost in the sludge of agonizing decisions when Mitch said, "That underground room. It was huge. How did the Disciples excavate that without attracting attention?"

"That had to have been there when Manson moved in. Back during Prohibition, beer barons created underground caverns to store beer and liquor. Some of them used the caverns for speak-easies. They'd be turning in their graves to see what those animals have done with it."

"Now what?"

"Hoping Brigid will have some ideas."

Nobody was on the porch as they approached the house. Lee told Dreads to drop them off in the alley. As they were getting out of the Escalade, Lee turned to Dreads and said, "Tell Deion not to go anywhere near Manson's place."

Dreads stuck his thumb in the air and drove off.

Lee gripped Snake's good arm and led him up the back walk with Mitch following. Brigid watched from the kitchen window. She met them at the door cradling her gun, eyeing Snake. "Why would you bring him here?"

"We need to talk," Lee answered.

She frowned. "I guess we do."

"Dot still here?"

"In the front room with the kids."

"Let's go downstairs before anyone sees him."

Chapter 51

Lee

When they got to Lee's dimly lit workout area, Brigid said, "Now what?"

"I was hoping you might have some ideas," Lee answered.

"What did you do with Manson?"

"The Iron Horse Godfather is no more."

"You kill him?"

"Less you know the better."

"Bullshit. Stop thinking you're in this alone. Tell me."

Lee knew better than to hold anything back when she was in interrogation mode. After he finished, she said, "We need to be careful with our next move. This could go sideways any number of ways."

"Do we take a chance on getting the cops involved?" Mitch asked.

Brigid shook her head. "Don't think that's wise just yet. Keep an eye on Snake. I need to talk to Lee without him listening."

They went to the laundry room. Brigid said, "I don't want MPD involved. Fucking Boyle could tip off the rest of the Disciples, and we have way too many loose ends. If MPD finds the girls and they say that you and Mitch kidnapped them at gunpoint, we both know the two of you could go away for a long time."

She's right, Lee thought, nodding. "Where do we go from here?"

"Even if the girls decided to testify against the Disciples, there's no guaranteeing their safety long term. Or, if they go back to Chicago and tell that club you and Mitch took them and also killed a brother biker, I don't see how you'd ever be safe." She gritted her teeth, then said, "Now I see why the department rarely followed up on runaway girls in the Core. Our chief was on the take." She furrowed her brow. "You left all the DVDs and CDs at Manson's?"

"Everything except five copies of Manson's confession. Left one there on the table. Also grabbed four of their burners."

"Brilliant. Thinking like a cop ... Sorry ... Probably the last thing a firefighter wants to hear." She paused, then said, "Our best bet is for all of this to blow up without us being connected in any way."

"Is that even possible?"

Lee waited in silence while she mulled this over. The furnace blower kicked on. She finally said, "I've got some ideas. Where are the DVDs of Manson's confession?"

"Mitch has them."

They went back to Lee's workout room. Brigid asked Mitch, "Where are the DVDs?"

"In my coat pocket."

"You touch them?"

"Had rubber gloves on."

"Good. Got any more gloves?"

He pulled two rubber gloves apart from the wad he had in his coat pocket, put them on, and handed two to her. After she snapped on the gloves, he handed her the DVDs. She examined them. "These aren't admissible in court but in the right hands, they could bring down some of the Guardians, including the chief and that sick bastard, Decker. I got an idea where they should go." She handed two back to Mitch. "Find a good place to stash these." She turned to

Lee. "Hand me the burners. We'll each keep one. There's an extra in case we need it. We'll use these to make any calls from now on. I'll put the number of each phone in the others.

After she finished programming the phones, she asked Lee, "What about your phone? Did you use it at any time down there or anywhere near there?"

"It's been off. It's an antique. About all I can do is talk on it."

"Good. Leave it off and use the burner."

"After I drop off the DVDs, I'll call in a murder at Manson's place, then I'll ditch this phone. They'll be going over every inch. I hope to hell you didn't miss anything."

"We wore gloves the whole time," Lee said.

Brigid shook her head and said, "Mitch wasn't wearing gloves when they first took us down there."

"When they were cuffing you and Snake," Mitch said, "I was standing at the back of the room. Never touched anything. I did get into it with Warlock before we came in, but no blood. Fat bastard cracked my ribs."

Lee added, "And we went over everything you said you came in contact with twice."

"Can we trust the One-Niners to take care of Ace's place?" Brigid asked. "My blood's on the basement floor."

"Said they would."

"Like how they took care of the clubhouse?"

Lee shrugged and asked, "What about the AR15 in my trunk?"

Brigid nodded. "Who knows where that came from or if it was used in any murders? I'll ditch it. Take my gun. I won't need it." She headed to the stairs. "I'll have to take your car. My truck's still over by Ace's."

"Where are you…?"

Before he could finish, she was halfway up the stairs.

* * *

Mitch

After Brigid left, Mitch pointed toward Snake, who was still sitting on Lee's workout bench, and asked Lee, "You decide what to do with him?"

"Can't hide him. Kids would find him eventually. I got some rags on my workbench. See if you can make a sling for him. I'll get a shirt to put over his colors. We'll tell the kids he's my nephew and joining us for Christmas." Lee looked over his shoulder at Snake. "If he wants to stay alive, he'll go along with it."

Snake didn't respond.

When Lee went to get a shirt, Snake said, "He's insane. You know that. Just look at him."

Lee was looking pretty rough, Mitch thought.

"He'll never let me go," Snake said. "At some point, he'll either kill me or turn me over to the gangbangers. You let him do that, it'll be on you. Let me go and I'll tell my club what Manson was doing and that he killed the girls in snuff films. Give me one of those DVDs to show them. They won't want to come anywhere near Milwaukee when this all blows up."

Mitch pondered this while tying rags together to fashion a sling. If Snake was telling the truth, the girls would no longer be in danger from the Chicago club. If he was lying, they would come after him, Lee, and Brigid.

Lee rumbled down the stairs holding a red and black flannel shirt. Mitch asked, "You decide what to do with him yet? I mean after tonight."

Lee shook his head.

"He said if we let him go, he'll tell his club that Manson killed the girls in those films. What do you think?"

"We'd be putting our lives in his hands."

Snake looked up at Lee from the workout bench. "You saved my life. Manson was gonna kill me. I know that. On my honor as a vet, I won't turn on you."

"Let's go upstairs."

When they got to the kitchen, Lee shoved Snake toward a chair at the table and said, "Sit."

Mitch went to the front room where Dot and three of the younger children were on the floor chattering and playing *Chutes and Ladders*. *It's a Wonderful Life* played on the television in the corner. Dot smiled at Mitch. "The older kids went upstairs. I didn't know when anyone would be back, so I told the kids they could open one present tonight. One of the presents was this game."

"Thanks for staying. You must want to get back to your family."

"I told Mr. Garrison, I have no family. Spending Christmas Eve with these kids has been such a blessing. I need to thank you."

"Then please, stay as long as you like."

"Bless you."

Mitch went to the bedroom, wishing he had something he could tell Miss Bernie that would help soften the pain of all she had lost. There were no words. All he could do was be there for her. Alexus was snuggled up next to her. Mitch watched them as the red numbers on the digital clock by the bed shifted ahead minute by minute. After a while, he lost track of time, his mind reeling with the events of the last few days.

"Mitch, get out here. Now," Lee hollered from the kitchen, pulling Mitch from his thoughts.

Crap. The Disciples are here, he thought.

When Mitch entered the kitchen, he froze, not believing what he was seeing. Those emerald eyes and cinnamon-colored skin. Jasmine. It was her, wearing baggy jeans and a heavy red sweatshirt with a W on the front. She had none of the heavy makeup on that she had worn when he and Lee had brought her and the other girls here. He crossed the floor without realizing it. Before he could say anything, she said, talking fast, "I heard about Brother Williams and the fire. I had to come. But I think it's a mistake. I should go. The Disciples will be coming after me and they'll kill all of you." She pointed at Snake. "He knows."

"Slow down. Let me look at you." Without makeup, she looked like a typical sixteen-year-old. The joy Mitch felt when he first saw her crumbled when he looked into her eyes. The sparkle had faded. "We have a lot to talk about but first, there's two people who need to see you."

"They're here?"

"In the bedroom."

She looked to the back door, hyperventilating. "I don't know if I can do this."

Mitch took her hand. "Deep breaths. We've been through a lot together. I'll be at your side. You know you can trust me." He led her to the bedroom. Mitch flicked the light switch on. Alexus looked over her shoulder at them, squinting. Her eyebrows shot up. She spun off the bed and ran at her big sister, almost knocking her over. Jasmine hugged Alexus's head to her waist. Alexus looked up and said, "Knew you'd come back to me. 'Cause you my sister."

Jasmine kissed the top of Alexus's head over and over.

"They told me you run off when Mama Bernie fell out," Alexus said. "I told them it wasn't you. You'd never do that ... Right?"

Jasmine choked.

Miss Bernie sat up on the bed. The vacant look on her face vanished as her eyes grew wide. She mouthed, "Jasmine," stood, and opened her arms. Alexus and Jasmine rushed to her and embraced in a three-way hug. They broke into choking, raspy sobs. Tears of joy clouded Mitch's vision. They were finally together again.

When the sobbing ebbed, Miss Bernie held Jasmine at arm's length. "My beautiful Jasmine. You really are here."

Jasmine looked to the floor. "I'm not beautiful. I'm disgusting."

"Oh, child."

"I don't know how you can look at me the way I ran out on you when you fell out."

Miss Bernie clutched Jasmine by the chin and lifted her face to hers. "You done nothing wrong, child. You got scared. Mitch told me why. You were worried sick those men would hurt Alexus. The good Lord will take care of them."

With the captain's help, Mitch thought.

Jasmine shook her head. "I was terrified that if I stayed, the Disciples would find me here. It doesn't make sense, I know. I freaked." She wiped away tears with the heel of her hand. "And now Brother Williams is gone and your house burned down. News said the police are looking for the One-Niners. Why?"

Miss Bernie pulled Jasmine back into her arms. "Only thing matters is you back. We all surely thought you passed, but Alexus here knew you were still with us somewhere. We don't know what you been through, but the good Lord brought you back to us. Ain't nobody taking you away."

"I can't stay. The Disciples will keep looking for me until they find me. When they do, they'll hurt you all."

Mitch cleared his throat, then said, "Wasn't the One-Niners who burned down the house and killed Brother Williams. It was the Disciples."

"What? How? I don't understand."

"I'll explain later. Trust me, you can't go back to them. Me and Captain Garrison will make sure they don't hurt anyone."

"You think the two of you can stop the Disciples?"

"I don't think all of them could stop the captain."

Miss Bernie grasped Jasmine's shoulders. "You stay with us. Let them boys do what they gotta do."

Do what we gotta do, Mitch thought. If they only knew what that would be.

Jasmine asked Mitch, "What happened to Snake?"

"Had a little skirmish with the captain. I got a question for you. What do you know about Snake? Would you trust him?"

"He always treated us girls good. Never tried to take advantage and protected us at parties. Not like Ace, who couldn't stay off us." She turned away from Miss Bernie and frowned at Alexus. "Sorry, Lexi. You shouldn't hear this."

"I'm not a kid anymore. I'm almost ten."

Jasmine nodded. "No. You're not a kid anymore."

"Like to be called Alexus. Lexi's a kid's name."

"Of course." The trace of a smile crossed Jasmine's lips. "My little sister is all grown up."

Mitch had to ask, "What about Crystal? Did you know she was Miss Bernie's daughter?"

"First time I saw her, that's what I thought. But when I asked her about it, she laughed at me and said she didn't know any Miss Bernie or anyone else in Milwaukee. Said she grew up in Chicago."

Jasmine paused, examining Miss Bernie. "I'm sorry. You probably don't want to hear this."

"I do need to hear it," Miss Bernie said.

"Okay. I remember when I was little, I saw Lettie around the neighborhood but she was a lot older than me. When you took me and Alexus in, I saw your pictures of her, and I was so sad when you told us she had run off. That's all I knew about her. After Crystal said she didn't know you, I just thought how weird it was that she looked so much like you. Never asked her about it again. Then when I saw you and her face to face, I knew she was Lettie. I told her that and she got pissed. Sorry. I mean mad. Said I didn't know what I was talking about. Didn't say another word all the way to Madison."

"Is that where she is now?" Mitch asked.

Jasmine nodded. "Tiffany and Shanice too."

Chapter 52

Mitch

Mitch stood back as Miss Bernie pleaded with Jasmine to take her to her daughter. Jasmine looked at Mitch, who said, "Looks like we're taking a drive to Madison. How did you get here?"

"Borrowed a car."

"Good. We'll take that. Where's the school van?"

"In Madison."

"All my stuff still in it?"

"Didn't let the others touch none of it."

Alexus clung to Jasmine's side. "I'm going along."

Mitch knelt next to her. "Me and Miss Bernie will bring your sister back. Promise. But we need to get Miss Bernie's daughter and her two friends. We won't have room for you."

She looked up at Jasmine. "It's okay you run off when Mamma Bernie fell out. That don't matter now. I'm scared you never come back. You even said you couldn't stay."

"I was wrong. I will be back. I promise." She unwrapped Alexus's arms from her waist and held her hands. "I promise, little sister."

Alexus looked to Miss Bernie. "Please tell them to take me."

"Oh, child. You heard Mitch. There's no room. We'll be back before you know it."

Alexus stepped back and crossed her arms. "Just so you know, I'm not going to bed till you get back."

* * *

Miss Bernie and Jasmine sat in the back of a tan rusted-out Buick Century with Mitch driving. On the way to Madison, over the drone of the loud muffler, Jasmine told them how Lettie wanted to go straight to the Disciple's clubhouse when they got away from Mitch and Lee. Jasmine told her and the other two how Mitch had saved her life and had been like a father to her. She was terrified the Disciples might find out he had taken them. She convinced them to wait.

Tiffany suggested they go to Madison and see if her sister would let them stay with her for a while. The Disciples would never find them there. Tiffany's sister loaned Jasmine the clothes she was wearing. When she saw the news on television about Brother Williams dying in the fire, Jasmine told them she had to get to Milwaukee. Tiffany's sister let Jasmine use her car.

More worried about me and her sister than herself, Mitch thought. This was the Jasmine he remembered.

"I dreamt about you when I was in the hospital," Miss Bernie said.

"That wasn't a dream. I called around the hospitals that night. Sinai said you were there but couldn't give out any information. I borrowed this car and drove in. I had to see you."

"Bless you, child ... How did you get mixed up with those bikers?"

"DeAndre tried to rape me. I fought him with everything I had. I dug my nails into his chest, screaming that I'd never let him sell me on the street. He could go ahead and kill me ... He tied me up and sold me to the Disciples. They sent me down to Chicago where nobody would know me. If I ever see him again, I'll kill him with my own hands."

Mitch coughed into his hand and said, "That was taken care of."

"What you mean?"

"We were out looking for you after he abducted you. He cornered me and Jennie. He was going to kill us."

"What happened?"

"He's dead."

Mitch watched her reaction in the rearview mirror. She blew out a long breath and sat back, slowly shaking her head. "Who took over the gang?"

"Deion."

"Peaches' dad. I remember him. He wasn't so bad."

"If it weren't for him, I wouldn't be here. After I killed DeAndre, the One-Niners could have killed me. He stopped them. When Deion took over, the One-Niners stopped selling girls to the Disciples. They still sell drugs but not to kids. Not making any excuses for them, but they aren't anywhere near as bad as when DeAndre was in charge. Deion said most of the club did what DeAndre wanted because they were all terrified of him, including Deion. Actually thanked me for killing him."

"You said it was the Disciples who killed Brother Williams. Why?"

Mitch should never have told her and Miss Bernie that. He'd have to be careful what he said, leaving out most of what he, Lee, and Brigid had learned and how they learned it. "Some cop friend of Captain Garrison told him that," Mitch lied. "That's about all I know."

Glancing in the rearview mirror, Mitch saw Miss Bernie take her purple handkerchief from her purse and dab at her eyes. "I'm a forgiving woman, but there's a place in hell for what them evil men did to our family." She pulled Jasmine close. "For what they did to this sweet child."

The woman who religiously preached forgiveness had been pushed beyond the limit to forgive in the face of unimaginable evil. And she didn't know just how evil they were.

For the rest of the drive, Jasmine wanted to hear stories of Alexus. The mood in the car lightened as Miss Bernie shared stories of their little spitfire who took no guff from anyone. The laughter coming from the back seat gave Mitch a sliver of hope draped in worry. If things went south, he could end up dead or in jail for kidnapping. He'd never see his family or the farm again.

As Mitch's mind whirled with the terrifying possibilities, Miss Bernie and Jasmine hooted over something Miss Bernie had said. The laughter and knowing he was going to reunite Miss Bernie with her daughter stiffened his resolve. He'd have to trust Lee and Brigid to know what to do.

Jasmine directed Mitch to a trailer park on the south side of Madison. When they turned onto Marigold Drive, he saw the white school van. He pulled behind it. "All of you staying in that little trailer?"

"It's pretty nasty," Jasmine said. "Tiffany's sister been nice, but her boyfriend wants us out. They knew what we were when we showed up. Who wouldn't, the way we were dressed? Tiffany had to go and tell them the Disciples were looking for us. They freaked out."

Miss Bernie asked Mitch, "You think Mr. Garrison would let those girls stay at his house with us till I find a place?"

"You betcha," Mitch said, thinking about the brawl they had there. Would they even go with him?

"I need to see my Lettie," Miss Bernie said, her voice cracking.

Jasmine led the way, clanking up the metal grating steps. They followed her inside. The place reeked of marijuana and mildew. The crimson-haired girl and the black-haired girl, Tiffany and Shanice, peered at them from a blue couch with black-stained armrests, smoking a joint. They wore baggy jeans and sweatshirts. Across from them on a black recliner that listed to the side, wearing the same baggy clothes, was a young version of Miss Bernie.

Lettie glared at Jasmine. "Why you bring her here?"

"You're her daughter. You need to talk to her."

"I don't need to do nothin'. Get her the fuck out of here."

Miss Bernie approached Lettie, who stood and shouted, "Stop. I don't want to see you. I can't."

Miss Bernie grabbed Lettie's hand and put it to her chest. "My heart stopped when I saw you. I couldn't believe it was you. Please, Lettie. Please."

"You don't get it. I'm not her anymore. She doesn't exist."

Miss Bernie lifted Lettie's hand to her lips and kissed it. "You were just a child when I run you off with all my preachin', thinking I had all the answers. I was scared to death. You were so young and beautiful, I knew the boys would be after you. Fear makes you stupid. Shoulda been listening to you instead of hounding at you about every little thing. Please try and forgive me. Don't go back to those men."

Lettie yanked her hand away. "We don't have a choice. They'll come after us and you too. You need to go."

Mitch said, "We can protect you. Just come with us back to Milwaukee."

Tiffany laughed. "You and what army? That big honky I jumped on? We go with you and the Disciples find us, they beat our asses. I don't think so."

Shanice set her jaw and crossed her arms.

Crap, Mitch thought. *Now what?* Before he could think of what to say, a skinny shirtless Black man charged down the hallway, waving a pistol at them. He shouted, "You a fucking Disciple?"

Jasmine waved her hands. "No, no, no. This Mitch. The man I told you saved my life."

The man wavered back and forth, his eyes glazed and pupils dilated. He pointed the shaking gun at Mitch while staggering toward him.

Holy crap. He's gonna shoot me, Mitch thought.

Tiffany jumped up from the couch and got between them. "Put that down, you fool. He look like one of those bikers to you?"

He slapped her. "Don't you be talkin' shit to me."

Mitch lunged at him and knocked him to the floor. The man struggled to point the gun at Mitch. It went off with the bullet going through the ceiling just over Miss Bernie's head. Mitch twisted the pistol from the man's grip and handed it to Jasmine. He helped the man to his feet. "I'm not a Disciple. Didn't you hear the girl? Damn near killed this lady."

A stout young Black woman with black braids swishing over her face staggered toward them from the hallway. "What the hell going…?

"Tell your nasty-assed sister and that other trash to get out my crib," the man hollered. The man raised his fists at Mitch, dancing from foot to foot. "I'm gonna kick your motherfuckin' ass."

Mitch shook his head and shoved the man onto the couch. He took the pistol from Jasmine and stuck the barrel in the man's mouth while gripping his neck with his other hand. "Stay." The man collapsed back onto the couch, raising his hands to the ceiling.

Tiffany's sister knelt next to the man. "Sorry. Sorry. Sorry. He high. Don't shoot my man."

"Everybody. Grab your coats. Out to the van before the cops come," Mitch ordered. "Who's got the keys?"

"I got 'em," Jasmine said.

Miss Bernie reached out to Lettie, sobbing. "Please give me another chance, child."

Lettie pushed her away and turned her back. Miss Bernie clasped her hands in prayer. "Please come home."

"C'mon. We gotta go, now," Mitch shouted.

Jasmine grabbed Lettie's hand, pulling her toward the door. "We need to go. We can decide what to do on the way."

When they all got outside, Mitch scanned the street. It was eerily quiet. "I can't believe nobody heard that gunshot."

"Gunshots going off all the time around here," Tiffany said. "Nobody gonna come outside. Summer said you save her. You gonna save my black ass too?"

Mitch blew out a loud breath. "Just get in the van."

"Where you taking us?" Tiffany asked.

"Back to the house in Milwaukee," Mitch said.

"Where we gave you and your honky partner a beat down?"

Mitch grinned, shaking his head. He slid the van door open. "Just get in."

They piled inside. Miss Bernie sat between Jasmine and Lettie on the bench seat behind Mitch. Tiffany and Shanice sat on the bench seat behind them.

"Where's my brother?" Lettie asked Miss Bernie.

The van went quiet. Mitch adjusted the rearview mirror to see why. Miss Bernie stared at the purple hankie she was wringing in her hands.

"What?" Lettie asked, her voice shrill.

"Jamal is with our Lord," Miss Bernie said in a whisper as she tried to hug Lettie, who grabbed the top of her head with both hands and shrieked, "No. No. No. He can't be gone. No."

Chapter 53

Lee

After Mitch, Miss Bernie, and Jasmine headed to Madison, Alexus joined Lee and Snake at the kitchen table. She pointed at the bruise on the side of Lee's head. "How you do that?"

"Wasn't paying attention to what I was doing."

She asked Snake, "You a fireman too?"

Snake looked to Lee, who answered, "No. This is my nephew, Bert, from Chicago. Come to spend Christmas with us."

"The pony I got to ride on Mitch's farm was Bert. He was real nice." She stared at Snake's sling. "What happened to your arm?"

"Fell on a slippery sidewalk."

"Does it hurt?"

"Gotta say it does."

She patted his back and kissed his cheek. "Kisses always make it better."

Snake's face reddened. "Thank you."

"My sister come home. We gonna have the best Christmas ever. You wait and see." She turned and skipped to the front room.

"I'll put on some coffee," Lee said, "It's going to be a long night."

* * *

The laughter of small children echoed through the house. Lee and Snake sipped coffee at the kitchen table while Dot played *Chutes and*

Ladders in the front room with Alexus and the three younger children. "What's with all the kids?" Snake asked.

"Foster kids from the house your partner burned down."

"Told you, he's no partner of mine ... Were those girls I brought up from Chicago foster kids?"

"Crystal is Miss Bernie's daughter. Summer was her foster child before you animals got a hold of her. Their real names are Lettie and Jasmine, as if you give a damn. The other two, I don't know." Lee struggled to control the anger rising in his chest. "How do you live with yourself? See how that little girl kissed you on the cheek? How long before your club would want to put her on the street? Disgusting pieces of shit. All of you."

Snake stared at his coffee mug, grimacing. "What you gonna do with me?"

"You think you deserve to live after what you've done to those girls?"

"Told you. I only transport and protect them at parties."

"You're still a part of all that evil shit."

"If I could stop it, I would."

Lee ignored him, obsessing about the mission. How was he going to take care of the rest of the Milwaukee Disciples and evade the Chicago chapter? He couldn't eliminate all of them.

Snake leaned across the table. "You're a hell of a warrior. Ace said you were a Marine. I take it you served in Nam. Must have seen some shit. I did a tour in Iraq. Saw how you didn't hesitate taking out Warlock. You won't hesitate taking me out either, will you?" He paused, then said, "That would be a mistake. I can help you solve your dilemma."

Snake wasn't talking like an outlaw biker. He sounded more like a lawyer pleading a case.

Lee stuck his index finger in front of Snake's face. "I know what you said. You'll go back to your club and tell them Manson killed the girls. How do I know you won't tell them I took their girls and took out one of their brothers? I'd be an idiot to put my life in your hands."

"Got any better options?"

Alexus came into the kitchen. "The other kids getting tired. Can you come play with us?"

Lee's head pounded. Might be a good distraction to take his mind off things for a while. And how could he say no to the imploring look on her angelic face? Lee peeked into the front room. Three small children slept on the floor next to the tree, covered in a faded gray blanket. Dot said, "Now that the little ones are sleeping, any chance you have some games for us older kids?"

Lee got Monopoly, his mom's favorite game, from the hallway closet. He and his mother would play it for hours.

Lee set the game on the kitchen table. Dot joined them. Alexus took the Scottish Terrier piece. "I love dogs. Mitch had a dog on his farm, Billy, who saved me when I almost drowned in the pond. Jasmine loved him too."

Snake said, "I had a dog when I was a kid. Dogs are the best." He looked over at Lee. "They don't judge people."

Lee held back his anger in front of Alexus. Dot counted out the money. Alexus said, "I like playing with Momma Bernie and Papa Williams. They let me win sometimes. The older kids never let me win." She frowned and looked up at Snake. "Can't play with Papa Williams no more. He in Heaven. Those bikers burn down our house and kill him. They burn down my school too. Why they gotta do that?"

Dot leaned over and put her arm around Alexus. Lee glared at Snake, who lowered his head, covering his eyes with his good hand. Alexus asked him, "What was your dog's name?"

Snake cleared his throat and said, "Otto."

"That's a funny name for a dog."

"He was a funny-looking wiener dog."

"Wish I had a dog."

As the game went on, they made sure Alexus would win. Whenever someone landed on her property, she jumped up and down, squealing. Her joy was infectious. They all laughed along, a welcome distraction for Lee, if just for a little while.

Chapter 54

Mitch

Jasmine talked the others into going to Lee's house to give them time to decide what to do. Lettie stopped protesting after learning about her brother. As they drove along I-94 toward Milwaukee, Jasmine told them about the Disciples burning down the school and burning down Miss Bernie's house, killing Brother Williams. After Jasmine finished, Miss Bernie got the girls to open up. She had that effect on people. When Mitch was living in her upper flat and struggling with depression, she had forced him to talk to her and share things he had never told anyone, things he was ashamed of. She opened his eyes to the power of forgiveness, starting with himself.

As the girls talked, he learned when Lettie had left home twelve years ago at the age of sixteen, she went to the Greyhound Station in downtown Milwaukee where a young handsome Black man sweet-talked her into going to his place for the night. He turned out to be a One-Niner. They sold her to the Milwaukee Hells Disciples, who sent her down to the Chicago chapter.

Tiffany and Shanice met at a temporary foster home. They had both been in foster care for most of their lives. As teenagers, the chance of getting a permanent placement was slim. They stole money from their temporary foster parent and took a bus to Chicago where they fell into the hands of the Chicago Hells Disciples.

***

As they approached Milwaukee, Lettie asked Mitch if they could stop by the scene of the fire. She needed to see for herself the place where she had lived with her brother and mother. It was after midnight when they got there. Yellow strips of police tape swayed from the tree by the street in the frigid breeze . They got out of the van and stood in the front yard, taking in the charred skeleton of the house.

One day ago, this was a home filled with children excited about Christmas and a man and a woman who loved them all dearly. Now, all that was left was a pile of rubble and ashes, their loving home devoured by the insatiable flames that mercilessly took their beloved foster father from them.

Mitch watched the quiet street, dimly lit with streetlights, worried the Disciples might show up.

Miss Bernie asked Mitch, "You see him when they brought him out?"

"He was out when I got here."

"Where?"

Mitch walked her to the side yard. He pointed to an indentation in the snow where Brother Williams had lain, covered with a bright yellow plastic sheet. Miss Bernie knelt and ran her hand over the packed snow. She looked to the heavens. "The pain of losing you broke me, my love. I prayed for the good Lord to take me too. His answer to my prayers was to bring these precious girls home."

Lettie and Jasmine knelt next to her at the altar of Brother Williams. The snow sparkled as the moon peaked from the clouds. They draped their arms over her as she continued to run her hands over the bed of snow that had cradled the love of her life.

Tiffany and Shanice stood next to Mitch. Tiffany sniffled. Shanice hugged herself against the cold. A vision of Brother Williams with his overbite and broad smile flashed in Mitch's head. He looked to the sky. His chest tightened.

Before they left, Miss Bernie went to the pile of rubble in the front yard and took the charred angel from the remains of the tree. The wings were gone, but the hand-drawn golden smiley face had survived, slightly smudged. "We made this together when you were eight," Miss Bernie said to Lettie. "You insisted we put it at the top of the tree every Christmas. And we have ... every Christmas."

Lettie took the charred angel from her and ran her hand over it ever so gently. She leaned her head against Miss Bernie and moaned. Mitch thought he heard her say, "Momm."

* * *

They arrived at Lee's house around one in the morning. Before going in, Mitch said, "Snake's in there. I need you all to pretend you don't know him. There's a house full of kids and they think he's a nephew of the captain."

"What the hell?" Tiffany said. "You said you were gonna keep us away from them."

"Don't worry about him. He can't hurt anyone."

Mitch led the way in. Seated at the kitchen table were Lee, Snake, and Alexus. As soon as Jasmine entered, Alexus ran to her and buried her face in her red sweatshirt. Jasmine said, "Told you I'd come back." She pointed at Lettie. "This is Miss Bernie's daughter, Lettie."

"You gonna stay with us too?" Alexus asked.

"Would that be okay?"

Alexus took Lettie's hand. "You want to see all the presents we get to open tomorrow?"

"I would love to."

Mitch whispered to Lee, "Where's Brigid?"

"No idea. Tried calling her burner but no answer."

They followed the others to the front room where three of the children slept on the floor at the foot of the Christmas tree. Dot was asleep on Merle's recliner.

Miss Bernie said, "No sense waiting. It's Christmas Day. Get everyone up." Alexus tore up the stairs and hollered, "Everybody. Get up. We opening presents now."

While they waited for the children to come down, Miss Bernie took the white angel from the top of the tree and replaced it with the charred angel with the missing wings. She looked at Lettie. "Every year when I put your angel on the tree, I prayed for the good Lord to bring you home for Christmas. Today … he answered my prayers."

The children clomped down the stairs. The little ones who were sleeping under the tree sat up, bleary-eyed. When everyone was there, Miss Bernie went to the center of the room and said, "Today is Our Lord and Savior's birthday. I see no reason to wait until morning to celebrate. And we celebrate our family being together after all these years. Before we open these gifts brought to us by the love of our neighbors, we need to carry on Papa Williams' tradition of singing Christmas hymns. Sing loud so he can hear you. She looked up. "This is for you, my dear Clarence."

The adults lined the back wall while the children gathered around the tree. They started with "O Come All Ye Faithful," followed by "O Little Town of Bethlehem" and "Hark! The Herald Angels Sing." When they finished, Miss Bernie turned off the lights, leaving only the multi-colored lights of the Christmas tree glowing. She moved to the center of the room and said, "Now we sing Papa Williams' favorite." She began singing "Silent Night." Everyone joined in, holding hands, swaying to the music. Alexus stood between Jasmine and Snake at the back of the room. She clasped both their hands. Mitch thought he saw Snake's lips moving ever so slightly.

While they sang the last verse, Lettie went to Miss Bernie and embraced her. Jasmine joined in the embrace followed by Alexus. Before the song was over all of the children had crowded around Miss Bernie, taking turns hugging her.

I'll never forget this, Mitch told himself. Later today, if Lee didn't need him for anything, he was hoping to head back to the farm to be with his family. He needed to hug his wife and little girl. He had called his wife, Jennie, yesterday and promised he'd be home for Christmas Day. She had grown close with Miss Bernie, Jasmine, and Alexus when they spent the summer on the farm. If he couldn't make it back, she understood. They would celebrate Christmas when he got home. He had told her about searching for Jasmine but didn't go into detail about the fires or the grave danger he was in.

He was not a praying man, but as he watched the children hugging Miss Bernie he prayed to himself, "If you can hear this, God, please help us."

After they finished singing, the older children handed out the gifts that had been labeled with the appropriate ages. Once the gifts were distributed, the four-year-old girl opened hers first, squealing with delight over the brown-skinned, brown-haired Cabbage Patch Kids Doll.

Snake moved to the couch next to Lettie and said, looking down at his hands, "Sorry."

Lee motioned for Mitch to follow him to the kitchen. When they got to the table, Lee said, "Brigid's still not answering the burner. Why the hell didn't she tell us where she was going?"

Miss Bernie came into the kitchen. "Gonna have some hungry kids before long." She went to Mitch and kissed his cheek. "God Bless you for bringing my girls home." She went to Lee and rubbed the wound on the side of his head. "And God Bless you, Mr. Garrison, for all you done. Never forget how you saved our Alexus."

Miss Bernie turned the oven on and took two large casserole pans from the refrigerator that were covered in aluminum foil. She slid them onto a rack in the oven and went back to the front room.

Before long the smell of potatoes, ham, Italian spices, and mozzarella cheese mingled with the smell of burnt coffee. Lee poured the coffee that had been on the burner for hours into two cups and handed one to Mitch, "This mud should keep us awake."

They sat in silence listening to the hum of the excited children in the front room that went on for over an hour before things calmed down. Miss Bernie came into the kitchen and pulled the two large casserole pans out of the oven. When she removed the aluminum foil, Mitch salivated. One was lasagna and one was scalloped potatoes and ham. She set them on the counter and asked Lee, "You got some plates?"

"Not enough for all the kids. I have paper plates and plastic forks in the cabinet next to the oven."

Miss Bernie is back in her glory, Mitch thought. Serving others always brought her joy. He remembered all the hearty meals she had made when he rented the upper flat from her. It was only five years ago but seemed a lifetime. Today seemed a lifetime.

Miss Bernie piled the paper plates and forks next to the casseroles and put out a tray of Christmas cookies. She called the kids to the kitchen. They lined up, filled their plates, and took them to the front room where they spread out over the floor. After the children had all served themselves, Miss Bernie demanded everyone else eat up. Dot and the girls lined up at the counter, filled their plates, and went into the front room. Snake had passed out on the couch.

Lee stayed seated at the table.

"Aren't you gonna eat?" Mitch asked.

"Maybe later."

Mitch went to the counter, heaped a pile of scalloped potatoes and ham on his plate, and grabbed three cookies. When he was done, Miss Bernie served herself and joined her girls and the children in the front room.

The house went quiet. The children didn't last long after they ate. They filtered out of the front room and went up the stairs to the cots, carrying their gifts. Miss Bernie and Alexus waved at Mitch and Lee as they headed to the bedroom. The glow on their faces left Mitch breathless, unable to get words out as they passed.

Mitch was taking a massive bite from his fourth cookie when his burner chimed. It was from Brigid's burner. "Finally," he said and answered, holding the phone between him and Lee. "You okay?"

"Listen close, asshole," Ace said. "You bring me the girls and I won't splatter this bitches' brains all over the ground. I want you to bring them to me, not that crazy-assed partner of yours. I see him, she dies."

"I need to talk to her."

"Mitch," she said. "He threatened to have Lee's house shot up if I refused to call. Sorry."

Before Mitch could answer, Ace came back on the line. "Deliver the girls and she lives. It's that simple."

"I don't have the girls."

"Then she dies. And maybe we burn down your partner's house after we shoot it up."

Lee twirled his index finger in the air, urging Mitch to keep talking. Mitch thought for a second, then said into the phone, "What do you want me to do?"

"Bring them to Washington Park. When you get close, I'll tell you where to go. If there's anyone following you, she dies. I'll give you fifteen minutes to get here."

"I can't get there in fifteen minutes. It's too far," Mitch lied.

"You at your asshole partner's place?"

"Told you. I don't have the girls. I gotta pick them up. Give me twenty minutes."

There was a long pause. "Twenty minutes. Not a second longer. You better not be fucking with me." The call ended.

Chapter 55

Lee

G*oddamnit,* Lee thought. *Never underestimate your enemy.* He rubbed his chin. "Didn't think he had the balls for this. We should be able to pull this off. He's not that sharp."

"How we gonna do it?"

"I grew up playing in Washington Park. You take the girls in the van. I'll take your truck and park a few blocks away. Then go in on foot. There's plenty of brush for me to duck behind. Get the girls. We'll need them."

Mitch went to the front room. When he brought the girls to the kitchen, Lee explained how his friend, Brigid, was being held hostage by Ace. He was demanding that Mitch bring them to him in exchange for Brigid. He assured them they would not be in danger. Ace needed them alive. He told them how he had been a sniper in the Marines and would be able to shoot Ace before he ever got near the girls. They were decoys to distract him.

After Lee finished, Mitch said, "If we don't do this, he's gonna kill her and shoot this place up. Maybe burn it down."

Tiffany said, "I'm not gettin' in the middle of that crazy shit."

Shanice shook her head. "Me neither. Rather go back to the Disciples. At least I'll still be alive."

Lee said, "You all know what snuff films are, right?"

"What you talking about?" Tiffany asked.

"You need to know the Disciples planned to use you girls in one of those films."

Tiffany scowled. "That's crazy talk. Our club would never do that."

"Not yours. The Milwaukee chapter. You must have met their leader, Manson. You trust him?"

The girls looked at each other. Mitch said to Tiffany, "It's true. We saw one of the films where they killed a pretty girl just like you."

"We gotta go. Who's coming?" Lee asked.

Jasmine came forward. "I'll go."

"Me too," Lettie said.

Tiffany shook her head. "Not me."

Shanice crossed her arms. "Nope."

"Take the van with Lettie and Jasmine," Lee said. "Better take Snake along too. Don't want him running off and warning anybody or talking these other two into going with him. Tape him down. Have Jasmine and Lettie walk slowly toward wherever he's holding Brigid so he knows you have the girls. Tell him you'll let the other girls go when he lets Brigid go. As this is happening, I'll position myself so I can get a clean shot with your rifle. Has the scope been sighted in recently?"

"Last fall for deer hunting."

"Good. You need a gun in case things go horseshit?"

Mitch grinned. "A nice guy in Madison donated one to me."

Lee raised his eyebrows at Mitch and handed him a cell phone. "This is the extra burner. Put yours on speakerphone and have one of the girls hold this one close enough to yours, so I can hear. I'll stay silent on this end to make sure Ace doesn't hear my voice. I'll take a footpath to the middle of the park. You circle the park a few times. Drive slow. That way I can get to wherever he sends you in time to take him out."

He went to his bedroom, stripped down, and put on the thermal underwear he used on duty, then put on black pants and his warmest sweatshirt. He still had the black ski mask Mitch had given him and a pair of gloves. He never thought of getting his winter coat—the one the girls had taken—from the van. They were already gone. His old black coat would have to do. He was used to working outside in freezing temperatures at fires but that was wearing thick, heavy turnout gear.

He sped to the park in Mitch's truck, parking in a quiet alley off North 40th Street. His shoulders tightened as the frigid air hit him when he got out of the truck. He was relieved to see nobody was out in the brutal weather. A few cars went by on West Lisbon Avenue, but that was two blocks to the north.

He jogged into the park, ducking behind trees and shrubs. His black clothing stood out against the white snow cover whenever the moon appeared from behind the clouds. It was slow going, but if Ace spotted him, the mission would be compromised. Lee didn't think Ace would kill Brigid until he had the girls, but the man was unpredictable and a special kind of stupid, which made him dangerous.

"We've circled the park twice and haven't heard from Ace yet," Mitch said over Lee's burner. Seconds later Lee heard Mitch's burner chime. "Where you want us to go?" Mitch asked.

"Come in on 45th Street north of the park," Ace said. "I'll tell you where to go once you're inside the park. I see that asshole partner anywhere near here, the bitch dies."

Lee headed to the lagoon, where he could blend in with the overgrown vegetation. It wasn't long before Ace said, "Go to the rear of the band shell."

Lee had to hustle. They'd be there in less than a minute. He tried to sprint, but his back flared. He gritted his teeth and moved as fast as he could without aggravating it into a full-blown spasm. He was two hundred yards east of the band shell and could see the side of it. An old gray Impala was the only vehicle parked in the rear lot. He'd have to work his way around back. Lee stopped and bent over to relieve the stabbing back pain, puffing white clouds of steam. He straightened and peered through the scope of the rifle. The van inched down the drive. "Nice job, Mitch. Keep it slow," he said to himself.

Lee moved along the lagoon. When he got close, he crawled on his stomach, taking no chances Ace would spot him. Crawling took some of the pressure off his back but the chill of the icy snow cover seeped through his pants and thermal underwear. Once he stopped, the frigid temperatures would soon have him shivering. He needed to get a precise headshot off that would take Ace down instantly. Shaking hands would add a level of difficulty above an already risky shot.

The van entered the parking lot behind the shell and stopped as Lee moved into position. He took his gloves off, peered through the high-powered scope, and found Brigid standing in a corner, out of sight of the van, duct tape over her mouth. Ace was behind her, using her for a shield. With them up against the back wall, there was no way for Lee to get in position for a better shot. He'd have to wait for the exchange. As Lee watched them through the scope, Ace said, "Pull up right next to the back of the building."

"Can't do that," Mitch said. "I'm gonna park at the far end of the lot. You won't get any of the girls until I see Brigid's okay."

"No. Park where the fuck I told you."

There was a long pause, then Mitch said, "Fine. I'm outta here. You ain't getting the girls."

The van headed back up the drive. It went twenty feet before Ace said, "All right. Stop. Park wherever the fuck you want."

"You want the girls, you do what I say. You shoot Brigid, I shoot you with my hunting rifle. I don't miss."

Lee was impressed with how Mitch was handling this—bluffing Ace and calling Ace's bluff. The van pulled back into the lot and parked over fifty feet from the back of the band shell. Mitch said, "I'll let two of the girls go. When you let Brigid go, I'll let the other two go."

Lee focused on Brigid, waiting for Ace to expose himself enough for a kill shot. Lee tensed and relaxed his muscles, warding off the chills as he lay on his stomach in the icy snow. "Hurry up. Let's do this," Lee said to himself. He prayed Brigid knew to keep still and not move. Lee couldn't see but assumed Ace had a gun to her head or her back. He slowed his breathing and was in sniper mode, elbows resting on the ground, gripping the frigid stock of the rifle with his bare left hand while caressing the trigger with his right trigger finger. After several long seconds, the side van door slammed open. Lettie stepped out, followed by Jasmine.

"Now let Brigid go," Mitch ordered.

Brigid didn't move as Jasmine and Lettie walked across the parking lot.

"I'm not letting the other two go until you let her go," Mitch shouted.

When Jasmine and Lettie got behind Ace and Brigid, Mitch said, "Let her go. Now."

Dead silence. Ace made no move to let Brigid go. It was a standoff. Ace wasn't so stupid. Lee waited for his shot.

"Just give me the fucking whores and you get the bitch."

"Can't do that," Mitch answered.

"You ain't getting her till I get them."

"I gotta think this over," Mitch said.

"Ain't got time for this shit."

C'mon, asshole, give me one clear shot, Lee thought, clenching his lips.

A shot rang out.

Lee gasped. "Oh, no, no, no!"

Chapter 56

Lee

Lee fought the red mist. *Keep it together,* he pleaded. *Take the bastard out* ... He waited for Brigid to fall.

Ace dropped to the ground.

Mitch sprang from the van and ran across the parking lot. Lee struggled to his feet and followed, limping. When Lee got to them, he turned Ace over and saw blood oozing from the side of his head. He looked up at Jasmine, her arm hanging at her side, clutching a handgun.

"You okay?" he asked. A dazed look clouded her face. He took the gun from her. It was his 9mm they had taken from his house when Miss Bernie went down.

Brigid moaned through the duct tape. They had all been gawking at Ace. Brigid's hands were zip-tied behind her back. Lee gently removed the tape. Brigid spit a few times and said, "We gotta get out of here. There's a cop station close by. If somebody reports shots in the area, they'll be on our asses."

"Take the van back to the house," Lee said. "I'll meet you there. Is that your gun he was using?"

She raised her eyebrows. "Um, yeah. The one I loaned you." She waved her arms behind her back. "Got something to cut these?"

"In the van," Mitch said.

Lee handed Mitch the rifle. "Take this. It'll slow me down."

"Aren't you coming with us?"

"I left your truck in an alley off 40th Street. We need to split up in case you get pulled over leaving the park. If that happens, I'll speed by, hoping they follow me."

"Enough talking, you two," Brigid said. "Mitch, grab my gun and the phone next to the shit bag."

Lee headed toward the lagoon. The red taillights of the van disappeared up the drive. Distant sirens grew loud. The flashing red and blue lights of a squad car came over the bridge leading into the park from 47th Street. Lee ducked behind tall vegetation at the shore of the lagoon. Another siren from the opposite side of the park drew his attention to flashing red and blue lights moving down 40th Street. More sirens sounded from the north of the park, where the van exited.

The squad car on 40th turned onto the walking path Lee had come in on, playing its spotlight over the area. Lee hunkered down in the heavy brush. The moon broke through the clouds and cast a luminous glow over the snow-covered park. He waited in the subzero cold, shivering uncontrollably. Despite having gloves on, his fingers grew numb. All he could do was watch the squad cars move through the park, illuminating it with their high-powered spotlights, and wait for his opportunity to get the hell out. He watched a squad pull into the parking lot behind the band shell. It wouldn't be long before they found Ace's body. Within minutes, the park would be swarming with more cops. They'd be there for hours, probably until morning. There was no way he could last that long in these temperatures.

He had the 9mm in his coat pocket. What the hell was he thinking? He couldn't get caught with that. Was hypothermia messing with his head? He had to figure out what to do with it, fast.

He couldn't toss it in the frozen pond. If he tried to hide the gun, there was a good chance they'd find it, and it was registered to him.

C'mon, think, he thought, trying to shake the fog from his head. He could say Ace tried to rob him and he shot him. But that was way too lame. They'd have lots of questions he had no good answers for. Not yet, anyway. As he struggled to come up with an alibi, the spotlights went off and the squad cars raced away.

Lee ambled out of the park, hobbled by stabbing back pain. Before getting in Mitch's pickup, he heard the sirens and air horns of fire rigs going off from all directions.

***

Mitch

Mitch parked the van in the alley behind Lee's house. Brigid and the girls rushed inside as Mitch cut Snake loose. When Mitch and Snake entered, the house was quiet, the smell of baked casseroles and burnt coffee still lingering in the air. Dirty paper plates overflowed a kitchen waste basket.

"What did I do?" Jasmine asked, shaking her head.

"Saved our asses," Brigid said, clasping Jasmine's shoulders, looking into her eyes. "And killed a man who needed killing."

"Now what?" Jasmine pleaded. "The Disciples will be coming for us."

"No they won't," Mitch said.

"How do you know?"

"I gotta check on the kids." He hoped they didn't see the doubt on his face.

Christmas tree lights cast a warm glow over the front room. Dot was still sleeping in Merle's recliner. Nobody else was in the room. Mitch went to the first bedroom and peeked inside. Miss Bernie snored lightly with Alexus huddled next to her under the covers, her eyes closed. He went to Lee's bedroom. Tiffany and Shanice were asleep on the small twin bed. Back in the kitchen, he asked Brigid to join him in the basement. Lettie and Jasmine could keep an eye on Snake. He was not much of a threat with his broken arm and broken fingers.

When they got to the basement, Mitch asked, "What happened?"

"As far as I can tell, Ace must have followed me after I left here in Lee's car. Probably figured he was following Lee. I never spotted him. I don't know why he didn't jump me after I made my first drop. Maybe surprised it wasn't Lee when I got out of the car and didn't know what the hell to do. I made my last drop-off at Channel Four. Figured they would run with the DVD or at least put some reporters on it. I parked two blocks away so nobody at the station would see the car. I wrapped a scarf around my face in case they had security cameras. While I was walking back to the car, I called the station's hotline and told them a DVD had been dropped off and they needed to see it immediately.

"Then I called in the shooting at Manson's place. While giving the dispatcher the address, Ace jumped me from behind and forced me into his car. When we got to Washington Park, he made me call you. If it wasn't for this house full of kids, I would have told him to get fucked. He could do whatever he wanted to me, but I couldn't take the chance that he'd send some henchmen over here to shoot up the house. I know Deion said they were watching the place. Just couldn't take the chance. I figured Lee probably dealt with hostage situations in Vietnam. At least I hoped to hell he had."

"Did Ace hear you make the 911 call?"

"If he did, he didn't say. He was pretty jacked up."

"Where did you take the other DVDs?"

"Let's just say I still have contacts I can trust who worked with me when the Disciples were being investigated. One's MPD and one's FBI. They needed to be at Manson's place when the shit hit the fan. They both know to keep me out of it. Where the hell is Lee? He should be here by now."

"Yeah, I know," Mitch said. "Think the cops got him?"

"From the sound of the sirens, we got out of there just in time. It was more than one squad but it's a big park. I gotta think Lee evaded them."

"Then where is he?"

Brigid pressed her lips together, then said, "Who knows? The man's a cowboy. Wants to do everything himself his way. If the cops did get him, we got more problems to deal with."

When they got back upstairs, they heard distant sirens and air horns. Brigid said, "Must be one hell of a fire going somewhere."

"Sounds like more than one."

Chapter 57

Lee

Lee parked Mitch's truck in his garage and went inside. Brigid, Mitch, Jasmine, Lettie, and Snake were seated around the oval kitchen table. Brigid went to him with open arms. "What took you so long?"

"Cops surrounded the park. I was freezing my ass off. I think hypothermia was messing my head up."

"How would anyone know?" She smirked and wrapped her arms around him.

"You never stop, do you? I gotta change clothes. Pants got wet from lying in the snow."

She pulled his head down and kissed his lips, then said, "How about some hot coffee? There's food left in the fridge. I'll microwave some while you get changed."

"You'll have to be quiet," Mitch said. "Tiffany and Shanice are sleeping in your bedroom."

By the time he got back to the kitchen, a cup of coffee and a steaming plate of lasagna were waiting for him. Between bites, Lee said, "I was totally lost on what my next move would be. I couldn't wait them out. Then the cops just left. Sirens were going off from all over."

"We heard those too."

"So how did Ace find you?"

"Just eat. I'll explain later." She pointed at Jasmine. "This girl saved my ass. Our asses."

Lee nodded, thinking of the gut-wrenching feeling he had when he thought Ace had shot Brigid. If Jasmine had not taken him out, the mission could have gone south any number of ways.

"Yes," Lee said to Jasmine, "you did save our asses. Well done. That was damn amazing. And you are one incredibly heroic young lady."

Jasmine's weak smile faded as quickly as it appeared.

Brigid tilted her head toward Snake, who was slumped in his chair, sleeping. "What we doing with him?"

"He always treated us good," Lettie said, looking at Lee. "You aren't going to kill him, are you?"

They all waited for Lee to answer. Could he kill him? If it guaranteed the safety of the rest of them, he could. He continued eating. Lettie and Jasmine went to the front room, leaving him, Mitch, Brigid, and Snake at the table. Brigid filled him in on how Ace jumped her. When she finished she motioned toward Snake and said, "So what are you going to do with him?"

"Where's my car?"

"Couple blocks from Channel Four."

"Take me and Snake there."

"What you got planned?"

Lee didn't answer.

* * *

Silence hung heavy over them as Brigid drove Lee and Snake to Lee's car. On the way, they were passed twice by squad cars and fire engines. When Brigid pulled alongside his car, she said, "Please don't do something you can't come back from. I'm begging you. I can't lose you."

Lee got out of the truck without looking back and shoved Snake into the passenger seat of his car. As he was getting in, Brigid called out, "Come back in one piece. That's an order." Lee slammed the door closed. He couldn't look at her. He had to do this.

He drove to Atwater Park and parked in an isolated area. Snake bowed his head. "This is it then."

Lee held his 9mm in his lap. A hollowness spread through his chest, thinking about what Brigid had said. Would he be able to live with himself? "Tell me why I should let you live?"

"You heard Lettie. I never abused those girls. You're right. It's still shitty to be a part of what was going on. I don't like it. Let me live, you won't be sorry. Trust me."

Trust, Lee thought. That was something to be built over time with actions, not words. Like the trust he had in his Marine unit, the trust he had in his fire companies, and the trust in his mother's love before dementia set in. Now Alexus and her family had to trust him to make an impossible decision. The lives of Brigid and Mitch also hung on this decision. His head pounded.

Lee had made countless life-and-death decisions weighing risk and reward as a fire officer and had to live with the ones that went bad. If he screwed this up, there would be no living with it. If he let Snake go back to Chicago and he told them everything, none of them would ever be safe again. If he killed Snake, who was pretty much helpless right now, he feared the guilt might take him back to his bedroom with the barrel of the 9mm in his mouth. What would that do to Alexus and Brigid?

Snake sat in silence, staring at his broken arm while the battle over what to do raged in Lee's head. He needed to decide soon. The Disciples would still have to be dealt with before they found out Manson and Warlock had been killed.

Lee gripped the gun, running his hand over the barrel.

"If I trust you and you turn on me, I will hunt you down till the day I die. What I did to Manson will be nothing compared to the horror I'll put you through."

"Thanks, brother."

"Don't call me brother. Where should I take you?"

"My car's down the block from Ace's place."

* * *

As Lee crossed over the 16th Street Bridge, red and blue flashing lights came up behind them, the siren blaring in short bursts. He slowed and pulled to the side of the road, his nerve endings crackling.

The cop car sped past. Snake looked over at him. "I thought for sure we were screwed."

"There's no 'we.' Keep your mouth shut."

Lee stopped the car when he turned onto South 22nd Street. A fire engine and a ladder truck were in front of the smoldering remains of Ace's house.

Snake said, "Looks like the bangers took care of that."

"Where's your car?"

Snake pointed to a dark blue Ford Explorer parked two cars away.

Lee said, "Go. Before I change my mind. Don't make me regret not killing you. If you put that family and those girls in danger by spilling your guts, I will hunt you down."

Snake left, clutching his broken arm to his chest. When he got to his car, he turned and saluted.

What did I do? Lee thought, remembering trusting a girl in Vietnam who promised not to tell anyone she had seen them. They lost three members of their detachment when they were ambushed. Trust is a dangerous game.

Lee watched Snake drive away and then headed to St. Mary's Hospital. As he drove east, the sun came up over Lake Michigan, casting a reddish-orange hue on the sides of the downtown high-rises.

* * *

A nurse at the ICU Burn Unit greeted him at the reception desk. When he told her his father's name, she said, "Let me get you Dr. Stevens. He's been treating Mr. Garrison."

"Is he all right?"

"Talk to the doctor. He'll be right here."

A tall white-haired doctor hustled up the hallway to Lee. He reached out his hand, "I'm Dr. Stevens. You're Mr. Garrison's son?"

"Is he okay?"

"I'm glad you're here," Dr. Stevens said and dropped his hand. "We did everything we could. I'm sorry. His brain was without oxygen for too long. He has pulmonary edema and his organs are failing. No easy way to say this. The best thing for him is to take him off life support."

Lee appreciated the doctor's concise almost terse report. When Lee had to inform families that they were not able to save a loved one, that's how he did it. No long explanations. Short. Concise.

He thought about all the beatings and abuse he and his mother had suffered over the years and how many times he wished his father would just fall over dead. Now all he wanted was one more chance to connect on some level. "Can I see him before you take him off life support?"

"Of course. This way."

The doctor took him to Merle's bedside. Merle's face was swollen, his lips blue. His chest rose and fell as the ventilator blew air into his failing lungs. Although Lee had seen plenty of death on the battlefield and on the job, the sight of his father lying there should have triggered an emotional response. What he felt was more like a pang of regret, not the crushing grief he felt when he had held his dying fiancé in his arms or the rage he had felt when he saw the body of Brother Williams barely covered by the plastic yellow sheet.

"Spend as much time as you like. Let us know when you're ready," the doctor said and left.

"What the hell is there to say, Old Man? We never liked each other much. Wish I could have heard some of your war stories and what you did to earn that Distinguished Service Award. Must have been something damned courageous. I don't know what you did or saw over there. I do know that shit never goes away. Guess that's why you were the way you were."

Lee pulled a chair from against the wall and placed it next to the bed. He sat, lost in thought about how soldiers coming back from war had to deal with the horrors on their own. Merle had taken it out on those closest to him.

The ventilator hissed and clicked. Lee watched Merle's chest rise and fall. "I can never forgive you for the hell you put me and Mom through ... but I get why." Lee paused, studying Merle's face for a reaction. "You should know Mom kept all your letters. Don't know what else to say ... ah, shit. You're not in there anyway."

Dr. Stevens was chatting with the nurse at the nurse's station when Lee left his father's bedside. "You can take him off life support," Lee said, flatly.

The doctor pinched his lips together and then said, "Sorry for your loss."

The nurse asked, "Would you mind filling out some papers? The paramedics only had his expired driver's license."

"I have to go."

"Can you at least sign this one giving us permission to end life support?"

Lee signed the paper and went to his car. Halfway to his house, a wave of emotion swept over him. He pulled over, sobbing. *Jesus, what the hell is wrong with me?* he thought. *I hated the bastard.* Then it hit him like a sledgehammer—what his mother had told him about his father.

Before the war, he was a kind loving man who loved her dearly and would have been a fine father. The man who came back from the war was angry and sullen, nothing like the man who left, but she held on to the hope she could help him overcome the darkness that festered inside him.

Was Lee following in his father's footsteps the way he treated his crews? He knew he was despised throughout the department but told himself he was being hard on his crews to make them better firefighters. If Lee had had a kid would he have been like his dad? The thought terrified him.

When this was all over—if this was ever going to be over—he needed to go see Dr. Bennet at the VA.

Chapter 58

Lee

Lee returned to the house around six a.m. and entered through the back door. The kitchen was quiet. When he entered the front room, Mitch and Brigid were glued to the television screen. Nobody else was up. Brigid said, "You got to see this."

"My dad died."

Brigid rushed to him while Mitch stared in shock. She cupped Lee's face in her hands and peered into his eyes. "How you doing with that?"

"You saw how I ripped into him the last time I saw him alive. How am I supposed to deal with that?" Lee blew out a loud breath and said, "I couldn't even smile at my dying father. What the hell's wrong with me?"

"Want to talk about it?"

"Not now. What do I need to see?"

Her eyes narrowed. "What about Snake? Did you…?"

"He's on his way back to Chicago. I'm going to regret that. I know it."

"Could you live with yourself if you killed him?"

Lee didn't answer.

"We will talk this out later," Brigid said. "When you're ready."

"Where's Dot?" Lee asked.

"She went home."

On the screen, a blond female reporter interviewed a woman standing across the street from a burning house. Through sobs, the woman said, "They busted in and ordered us out at gunpoint. Beat the hell out of my old man. Took him away. Who the hell did this?"

"Did you get a look at them?" the reporter asked.

"Hell, no. They all had masks over their heads."

"Your jacket says property of Hells Disciples. Was your man a member of the club?"

"Damn right. He was an officer. Sergeant at Arms." She looked into the camera and said, "Whoever did this, you'll pay."

"Holy shit," Lee said. "They got Tank."

The television cut to an aerial view from News Chopper Twelve. The camera scanned burning homes scattered throughout the city. Some were smoldering ruins and others had flames shooting through the roofs into the clear morning sky.

"Damn," Lee said. "There must be at least eight or nine fires going."

"You need to see what they got on Channel Four," Brigid said and changed the channel.

Veteran anchorman Charlie Robbins was at the news desk, saying, "We have plenty more to report. The fire department has been fighting numerous fires around the city. There was also a massive explosion in the valley last night. We're told it was the clubhouse of the Hells Disciples. It appears there was some kind of gang war going on. Let's get an update from Susan Davies in Shorewood."

A young, black-haired reporter appeared on the screen across the street from Manson's house. The entire area was awash in red and blue flashing lights. She said, "Thanks, Charlie. We received information early this morning about the Hells Disciples allegedly being involved in human trafficking at this location. If the accusations are true, there were some incredibly horrific things going on in that house. By the time we arrived, police from Shorewood and Milwaukee were on the scene along with the FBI. The authorities aren't sharing any information. That's all I have for now."

Brigid said, "Before you got here, they gave some locations of the fires around the city. I recognized them from when we were checking out the Disciple's places. The Hells Disciples are history."

"How did the One-Niners know where they lived?" Lee asked.

Brigid pursed her lips, then said, "Someone ... might have given them the mugshots with the addresses."

"Did you know they were going to do this?"

"Figured the addresses would help them find the girls ... That's what you wanted, right? I have to say I'm feeling damn good about it. They're running the Disciples out of town just like the Disciples ran the other outlaw clubs out of town. Street justice took care of its own tonight."

"You didn't answer my question," Lee asked, his chest tightening, anger rising. "Were you in on the plan?"

"I knew you'd never rest until you eliminated the threat of them coming after us and the Williams family, even if it meant sacrificing yourself. I couldn't let that happen ... I can't lose you."

"What the hell were you thinking? How could you know there would be no collateral damage? And what if those police files show up? This could all come back to bite you in the ass. ... Dammit, Brigid."

"Okay. Slow down. Take a breath. Deion promised no family members would be harmed. And the files have already been destroyed."

Brigid clasped his shoulders. "I can't lose you."

Lee was speechless.

Brigid leaned back, studying him. "Say something."

"You could have told me," he shouted.

"No way would you have let me do this. Tell me I'm wrong."

Lee's anger and frustration faded as her words resonated in his head; *I can't lose you*.

Brigid pulled him close, resting her head on his shoulder.

He cupped the back of her head and said softly, "I got you into this, and the thought of you going down to protect me is … more than I can handle."

Brigid whispered into his ear, "I'm not going down."

"Sometimes you just gotta jump the fence," Mitch had said when they were deciding whether to carjack the girls. Those words set in motion everything that followed.

It was time for Lee to jump the fence he spent years building around himself and care for this woman like she deserved, this woman who had risked it all for him. "I'm not good at this stuff, but … I do care about you … a lot … I guess you're stuck with me."

"Then kiss me, you fool."

Mitch coughed into his hand and said, "Before you two start making out, I just wanted to say what an awesome team you make … How Cap took out the leadership of the Disciples and you helped the One-Niners finish the job."

"And you brought the girls home," Brigid said, stepping back from Lee, poking him in the ribs. "See, Mr. I-can-do-everything-myself. You needed our help. And we all needed Jasmine's help. Admit that I'm right."

"We back to that again. Yeah, okay. You are right."

"I love those three magical words. Could you say that again?"

Lee shook his head, gritting his teeth.

Brigid kissed him and said, "Have I ever told you how god-damned amazing you are?"

"Could you say that again?"

The three of them broke into laughter.

* * *

As they watched more newscasts come in, Miss Bernie joined them in the front room, followed a short time later by Alexus, Lettie, and Jasmine. They watched in silence as the events of the early morning hours played out on the screen. *The Today Show* picked up the news feed from Channel Four for their national audience.

Before long, everyone was up and sitting in front of the television. Miss Bernie went to the television, turned it off, and said, "Don't need to see any more of that. I want you all to know how blessed I am to have you here with me. I know Papa Williams is looking down on us all with such love and pride. Family is everything and you are all my family, including Tiffany and Shanice who I pray will stay with us."

She went to the couch where Brigid was sitting between Mitch and Lee. "I can't thank you all enough for everything you risked in bringing us together. You were truly doing the work of Our Lord Jesus Christ whose birth we celebrate today." She looked at the wide-eyed children on the floor. "Now, I need you children to help me prepare our Christmas feast with all of the generous bounty our neighbors brought us. But first I want every one of you to personally thank our heroes, Mr. Garrison, Miss Brigid, and the young man I always considered a son, Mitch."

The three of them rose as Alexus came to them and said to Lee, "Thank you for keeping your promise, and I'll keep mine to clean your house." They hugged. Alexus said, "You hug good—just like I taught you."

Words caught in Lee's throat. He wanted to thank her for saving him from himself. She forced him to accept her and awakened a long-dormant yearning to care, opening the way for him to have the courage to finally let Brigid in.

Alexus hugged Mitch and Brigid next. Jasmine joined her little sister, and said, "No way to thank you all enough."

"No," Lee said. "We can't thank you enough. You're our hero."

After all the children had thanked and hugged the three of them, Miss Bernie took her turn and held each one of them in a long, warm embrace and then said, "God bless you and God Bless us all."

Chapter 59

One week later, an intimate funeral service for the family and friends of Clarence (Brother) Williams was held at Miss Bernie and Brother Williams' church, The New Hope Baptist Church. Two weeks after that, a celebration of life was planned. As the story of Brother Williams' tragic death and inspirational life played out on national television, it became clear there would be a massive crowd in attendance. Arrangements were made by the mayor to hold the event at the Wisconsin Center Grand Ballroom. The large space would allow the inner-city community along with those from around the state the opportunity to pay tribute to this incredible man who had touched the lives of so many struggling children and families.

* * *

Lee

When Lee and Brigid arrived at the Wisconsin Center, the parking ramps were full. They had to park several blocks away in the parking lot of Firehouse 2 at 7th and Wells. A steady stream of people headed toward the center. When Lee and Brigid got there, the lobby area was crammed with people waiting to get into the ballroom. Thankfully, the event organizer had told Miss Bernie to let family and friends know they could enter through a back entrance.

"Do you ever wonder who would show up for your funeral?" Lee asked.

"Jesus, no. That's a morbid question. That something you think about?—And this isn't a funeral. It's a celebration of life. So, let's celebrate."

"You're right."

"Say that again."

"You're right. You satisfied?"

"For now."

Lee chuckled, thinking this lady would keep him on his feet. Exactly what he needed to get through the months of therapy ahead with Dr. Bennet.

They found the back door and were directed to a side entrance to the ballroom. When they got inside, Lee was awed by the size of the crowd. People were lined up out into the hallways. Groups of gang bangers were seated among nervous-looking white people. Off-duty firefighters, groups of teenagers, and children with their families were scattered throughout the packed ballroom.

The acting police chief had put out an order that on this day all were welcome at Brother Williams' celebration. No attendees would be targeted.

Lee spotted Deion sitting next to a girl around Alexus's age, a little boy around five, and an older lady. Lee nodded. Deion pointed at him and gave a quick nod back.

"That's Deion's mother and his kids. The little girl is Peaches, the girl Mitch talked about," Brigid said. "They dropped off presents at the house when you were gone."

Miss Bernie stood and waved at Lee and Brigid to join her in the first row. At the end of the row was Dot, who smiled at them as they went by. Next to her was Mitch, who stood and said, "Can you believe the turnout? Must be a couple thousand here."

"We had to park at the firehouse," Lee said.

Mitch turned to the young woman with short auburn hair standing next to him and said, "Jen. This is the captain I told you about." He turned back to Lee. "This is my wife Jennie." He pointed to the little girl with jet-black hair next to Jennie and said, "This is our daughter, Jasmine." Mitch must have noticed the look on Lee's face. He said, "Yes. We named her after Jasmine."

Jennie pulled Lee into a tight hug. "I can't thank you enough for protecting my husband." When she let go, she had tears in her eyes. "Thank you, thank you, thank you," she said and kissed Lee on the cheek.

Brigid moved alongside Lee. "Hi, Jennie. I'm Brigid."

"Yes. Let me hug you." When Jennie released her, she said, "I just ... I don't know how to thank you and Captain Garrison enough for all you did."

Brigid raised her eyebrows at Mitch and said to Jennie, "I bet he didn't tell you that he's the one who brought the girls back home. We couldn't have done that without him. He's probably the only one who could have talked them into coming back."

"I'm just so happy everyone's safe," Jennie said, rubbing little Jasmine's back.

But are we? Lee thought. If Snake lied to him, the Chicago Disciples would be coming for them.

"Everyone, please be seated," blared from the loudspeakers.

Lee and Brigid moved down the row. Lettie and Jasmine were seated on each side of Miss Bernie. Alexus was next to Jasmine. Alexus stood and waved at Lee to come sit next to her. When Lee and Brigid took the two open seats next to Alexus, they were greeted by waves from Jasmine, Lettie, and the foster children who filled out the row. Alexus leaned her head on Lee's arm and said, "Miss Bernie says Papa Williams is smiling down on us all. We're supposed to be happy that he's with the good Lord, but I still feel sad. I miss him."

"Me too, Alexus. Me too."

The mayor took the stage and thanked everyone for coming to pay their respects to Brother Williams. He expressed his deep regret for appointing the corrupt chief of police and promised to clean up the department. Lee's thoughts wandered during the talk, wondering how long they'd have to live with not knowing whether Snake had kept his promise.

When the mayor finished, he introduced Governor Thomas, who promised to push the state legislature to increase funding for both public and alternative voucher schools in Milwaukee through increased shared revenue to the city. His administration would work with the mayor and the Common Council to ensure the voucher money only went to schools that offered programs for the most at-risk children, not the for-profit companies that were taking over so many of these schools in large cities.

Next to take the stage was the United States Senator from Wisconsin, Jerome Kaufman, who shared his love of Milwaukee—the city he grew up in—and pledged to donate his own money to rebuild Brother Williams' Odyssey School.

Although they all paid due respect to Brother Williams, they still sounded like political speeches Lee had heard way too many times.

When the politicians were done, the president of the NAACP gave a stirring talk about the extraordinary success of Brother Williams' school in a city that has the lowest high school graduation rate in the country for African-American children. When he finished, he introduced Reverend Turner, who went to the podium and informed the audience that he had a long, long history with both

Miss Bernie and Brother Williams. He had married them at his church and performed the funeral service when they laid Miss Bernie's son, Jamal, to rest.

He told the story of how Brother Williams came to him in search of peace after ten years in prison for a crime he didn't commit. He went on to say how Brother Williams had to live in darkness before he could see the light; the light that came from dedicating himself to helping others. He told stories of miracles that Brother Williams' love of children had wrought; stories of children growing up in crushing poverty and violence who beat the odds and went on to college or became tradespeople or civil servants.

He asked those in attendance who had gone to or who are going to Brother Williams' school to stand. Hundreds of young people of all ages stood, including Alexus and Jasmine. The crowd clapped. Cheers rose to a deafening level.

When the ovation subsided, Reverend Turner said, "That, ladies and gentlemen, is the result of God's work through our beloved Brother Williams. Praaaise Jesus."

The crowd chanted back, "Praaaise Jesus."

Reverend Turner took the mic from the podium and strutted back and forth across the stage as he launched into his sermon about God's Gift of Love and Forgiveness. He was like a symphony conductor, waving his hand in the air, his voice thundering over the loudspeakers while people in the audience shouted, "Praaaise Jesus. Preach, Brother." When he dropped his hand to his side and lowered his voice almost to a whisper, the crowd hushed, hanging on every word. Well into the sermon, the old reverend became winded, looking ready to collapse. He turned to the choir behind him, who filled the ballroom with gospel songs while he took a seat, wiping the sweat from his brow with a black hankie.

"You think he's going to make it?" Lee whispered to Brigid.

"Hush," she whispered back.

The choir finished with a stirring rendition of "Hallelujah." After the last verse, Reverend Turner rose and continued the sermon with renewed vigor.

As Reverend Turner came to the end of his service, he asked everyone to stand and hug one another. Alexus hugged Lee and Brigid, then went to Mitch, Jennie, and little Jasmine. Miss Bernie made her way to Lee and Brigid. The three of them embraced. "I can feel Clarence's love shining down on us. God bless you, both."

Reverend Turner said, "Do you feel it? That's the good Lord's love you're sharing." When the hugging was done, he asked everyone to continue standing. It grew silent. Brother Williams' rich baritone came over the loudspeakers, "Amazing grace. How sweet the sound..."

He stretched the words of the hymn into a heart-wrenching rendition. The crowd swayed, some with their hands in the air, many with tears streaking down their faces.

Lee looked down the row. Jasmine and Lettie swayed with Miss Bernie, who had a look of pure bliss. Brigid leaned her head on his shoulder. Alexus burrowed into Lee's side. He peered down at this little girl who adored him and had opened his heart. A warm glow rose into his chest. His throat tightened when she looked up at him.

Her dark brown eyes had a radiance that needed no words.

Chapter 60

Eight Months Later

Lee waited in Doctor Bennet's reception area at the VA while she counseled a new patient in her office. He had been spending a lot of time here the last four months. Sitting in the quiet with the murmur of voices from the other room, he was lost in thought about all that had happened since the Christmas Morning Massacre.

Brigid's contacts in the MPD and FBI who owed her for tipping them off kept her updated. Two girls the Milwaukee Disciples had been prostituting showed up at the Repairers of the Breach daytime shelter on that Christmas Day. They had nowhere to go. The house where they had been kept was burned down and the men in charge of them taken away. The police were able to get them to cooperate, which led them to more girls the gang had enslaved.

With the testimony of these girls along with the DVDs, CDs, and Manson's video, members of the Guardians, including the police chief and Detective Boyle, faced serious criminal charges. State Senator Decker was indicted on racketeering charges that included human trafficking and money laundering. Federal agents picked him up at O'Hare Airport attempting to flee the country. He was now in federal prison awaiting trial.

The news media had played up how inner-city gangs were implicated in the attacks on the Hells Disciples, but the new police chief would only say they were investigating all possibilities during his initial news conferences. They never were able to get enough evidence to connect the One-Niners or any of the other street gangs with the attacks on the Disciples. Not one witness came forward and no members of the Disciples could be located.

As news of the sex trafficking of young inner-city girls by the Hells Disciples came out—some of whom had been tortured and killed—there was little public pressure to go after the street gangs. The personal belongings of the young victims that were found in the cavern were returned to grief-stricken family members. Jerome Kaufman, the United States Senator from Wisconsin, pledged to ensure families of the victims would receive compensation from the confiscated assets of the crime ring.

Over the winter when there were few chores to do on the farm, Mitch had been coming to Milwaukee to help renovate Lee's house. They insulated and finished off the attic, converting it into four bedrooms. They knocked out the wall between the kitchen and front room to create a space large enough to fit the ten-foot plank-topped table Mitch had built—a table large enough to seat all of the children at one time. He had also built two ten-foot-long benches like the ones destroyed in the house fire.

Lee donated the house to Miss Bernie. He had no need for the three-story house. Brigid had told him—more like ordered him—to move in with her. They were too old to play around with that dating crap. She was still estranged from her daughter and needed Lee as much as he needed her.

Miss Bernie had found Shanice's mother, who wanted a second chance with her. She also found Tiffany's mother, who was in prison for murder. Social Services was more than happy to allow Miss Bernie to take Tiffany in; she was a deeply troubled girl. Jasmine and she became close, helping each other cope with their traumatic pasts.

They were seeing Dr. Bennet, who had broadened her research in PTSD to young women who had been forced into the sex trades.

Lettie was also seeing Dr. Bennet. She had stayed with Miss Bernie through the spring while going through the early stages of therapy and then moved to an apartment on the East Side. Miss Bernie had told Lee how much it hurt when Lettie moved out, but she was proud that her daughter was strong enough to go out on her own. Lettie stopped by Miss Bernie's house every day to help with the kids.

Brother Williams' Odyssey School was renamed the Williams Academy. The new building would be dedicated in two weeks, at the end of August, with Reverend Turner as the acting administrator. He had been a public school administrator before becoming a full-time reverend. Lettie would be the assistant administrator. When the reverend felt she was ready, he would step down and allow her to take over. Jasmine volunteered to be a student peer counselor at the school.

Lee took disability retirement four months ago. His back couldn't take the stress of any more firefights. Dr. Bennet was also concerned there were too many triggers on the job that could send Lee spiraling into a PTSD relapse. His disability pension covered his mother's long-term care and his joint living expenses with Brigid.

His crew had thrown him a surprise retirement party at the union hall. Lee was shocked by how many people showed up. There was no sign of the chief of the department, which was no surprise. During therapy, Dr. Bennet and Lee had worked on the seething anger he had carried against Chief Brian Peters. The toxic space Brian had occupied in Lee's head had been tempered. The memory of him causing the death of Lee's fiancé was still there, but no longer carried the emotional toll it once did. Brian Peters was nobody to him.

Kenny pointed out during his speech that no one at the retirement party liked the captain. They were all there to make sure he didn't pull his retirement papers and come back to make their lives miserable again. He finished by saying, "Congratulations, Captain. Love you, man—not!"

The union hall erupted in laughter and applause.

His crew lined up to shake his hand. Ralph was last in line. When it was Ralph's turn to shake, Lee reached his hand out. Ralph stared at it. "We both did what we had to do. You kept your word." He grasped Lee's hand. "Still don't like your ass."

Lee grinned. "Mutual."

The memory of the retirement party had Lee smiling to himself. His thoughts turned to news reports that had come out last week about the FBI rounding up members of the Chicago Disciples on racketeering charges. An unnamed source informed the Chicago Tribune that a confidential informant had supplied the FBI with the evidence they needed to indict them.

The door to Dr. Bennet's office creaked open. She asked Lee to step inside. A lanky man with tousled graying hair stood when Lee entered her office. Dr. Bennet said, "Lieutenant Gorski, meet Captain Garrison. Lieutenant Gorski is from the Greenfield Fire Department."

Gorski's mouth worked into a grim smile. Lee recognized the hollow look.

"I remember reading about the save you made of that little girl in the school fire," Gorski said. "Damn solid, Captain."

"Call me Lee."

"Lee is our peer counselor for firefighters," Dr. Bennet said. "He knows better than I do what you're dealing with. You two get to know each other. I have some calls to make. I'll be back later."

After spending the afternoon with Gorski, Lee stopped at Miss Bernie's house. He entered without knocking to the sound of chattering children and the comforting smell of roast beef and biscuits. The family was seated on the long benches at the ten-foot table laden with two platters of roast beef and vegetables, two baskets of biscuits, and two pitchers of grape Kool-Aid. They stopped eating, all eyes on him. Alexus jumped up from her seat and ran to him, wrapping her arms around his waist. He enfolded her in his arms just like she had taught him.

Miss Bernie said, "Got something for you." She went to the counter and got an envelope. "Found this in the mailbox." Captain was written on it. No address or postage. "You staying for supper?" she asked.

"No. Brigid's cooking tonight. That doesn't happen often. I better get home."

Alexus crossed her arms. "Aww."

"How about me and Brigid come by tomorrow night for supper?"

Miss Bernie said, "Yes. You bring your lady. The kids love her."

Lee stuffed the envelope into his pocket and headed home.

When he stepped inside the front door, Roscoe trotted up and licked his hand. Brigid followed with her fists on her hips. "Sure. Now you're the alpha. You males just gotta stick together, don't you? Damn pack animals."

Lee pulled her into his arms. "Talk nice or I'll have him attack. What's for supper?"

"I was going to make that dish from the fire department recipe book that's called Woof and Poof, but I nodded off this afternoon. Sorry. How about frozen waffles?"

"Make me a promise? Never make that foul dish. I hated it but knew better than to tell the cook at the firehouse because he would have made it every shift to get to me."

"So all I have to do to get to you is make that? Good to know."

Lee shook his head and let out a low chuckle. He took the envelope from his pocket. "This was left at Miss Bernie's house." He opened it and read the handwritten note.

I told you I would stop it if I could.
Give that little girl a hug for me. And get her a dog.
A fellow vet

The End

Acknowledgements

I have to thank my wife Paula for her unwavering support as I worked through the mood swings, imposter's syndrome, and the gripping self-doubt I struggled with on this second novel. I heard from other authors that the second book can be the most challenging. I don't know what the future holds for my next one, but I can attest I found this second book far more challenging than my debut novel *BENEATH THE FLAMES*. Without Paula's encouragement, I may never have finished it.

The stories I heard from first responders during book talks about my debut novel and how it triggered memories of tragic responses that never go away encouraged me to go deeper in this story about the effect these responses have. As the therapist in this story says to Captain Garrison, "The human brain is not designed to constantly be bombarded with the things you experience on a daily basis."

A first responder informed me about EMDR therapy that was helpful in treating his PTSD. When I mentioned this at my book talks, I heard from a number of first responders and military people that it had saved their lives. I realized I needed to include that important message in this book. I have to thank Mechele de Avila Evans, LCSW, a clinical therapist who works with EMDR, for her invaluable professional insight into the therapy scenes. If I got anything wrong, that is on me, not her.

Writing a follow-up story to *BENEATH THE FLAMES* was not on my radar. Countless readers said how much they loved the characters and pleaded with me to revisit them and Engine 15. One reader stated that she reads a book a week and *BENEATH THE FLAMES* was the first book she read where she went to bed praying for the characters. Thanks to her and these other readers, this story was born and I can't thank them enough.

Tim Storm's incredibly detailed developmental edit of an early draft of the manuscript saved me countless hours wasted on extraneous scenes that needed to be cut and flawed storylines that needed to be addressed. Laurie Scheer's fiction workshop through the Wisconsin Writer's Association was incredibly helpful in polishing the final manuscript. I have to thank her for her continued support as a friend and mentor.

Christine DeSmet is responsible for patiently mentoring this retired fire captain who thought he might like to write a novel. I had twenty-eight years of unimaginable experiences, worked with a cast of colorful characters, and worked in the unique setting of the inner-city of Milwaukee. I was lacking one thing; any knowledge of the craft of creating writing. Through creative writing courses, workshops, and critiques, Christine guided me from aspiring novice to multi-award-winning author.

A huge thanks goes to my publisher Kira Henschel of HenschelHAUS Publishing for her belief in me and this story.

And thanks to all who have played a part in my writing journey. You know who you are.

About the Author

Gregory Renz served the citizens of Milwaukee for twenty-eight years as a firefighter, retiring as a fire captain. He was involved in a dramatic rescue of two boys from their burning basement bedroom. For this rescue, he received a series of awards, including induction into the Wisconsin Fire and Police Hall of Fame in 2006. Gregory thought, maybe, he could craft a compelling novel if he could learn how to get these stories onto the page. After only ten years of conferences, workshops, and creative writing courses through the University of Wisconsin, Gregory typed *The End* to his highly acclaimed debut novel, *BENEATH THE FLAMES,* which has won the Gold Medal in The Readers' Favorite International Book Awards, the IAN Debut Novel of the Year, a Midwest Book Award, an American Book Fest International Award, and a Public Safety Writers Award. Gregory writes from Lake Mills, Wisconsin with the help of his wife Paula, his chief editor and business manager.

Please visit www.glrenz.com for additional information.

Thank you so much for investing your time and money in my story. If you enjoyed it and think it's an important story, I would be deeply grateful if you would leave a review on Amazon or Goodreads or both. Smaller publishing houses don't have the funds to promote their books like the major players. We rely on word-of-mouth and these reviews. Please consider leaving a review even if it's only a few lines or a few words.

Thank you,
Gregory Lee Renz

If you enjoyed *BEYOND THE FLAMES*, be sure to read my multi-award-winning debut novel, *BENEATH THE FLAMES*.

www.ingramcontent.com/pod-product-compliance
Lightning Source LLC
Chambersburg PA
CBHW070641310726
48982CB00001B/373

9781595989987